THE MARRIAGE
Of
SILENCE AND SIN

by
JACQUELINE M. LYON

THE MARRIAGE
Of
SILENCE AND SIN

THE MARRIAGE
Of
SILENCE AND SIN

Jacqueline M. Lyon

Literary Legends
Cincinnati, Ohio

The Marriage of Silence and Sin

Copyright © 2011 by Jacqueline M. Lyon

Literary Legends Press, Cincinnati, Ohio

Cover Illustration: Blake, William. *Visions of the Daughters of Albion* copy P, c. 1818 (Fitzwilliam Museum). Object 1 of 11 (Bentley 1, Erdman i, Keynes i). William Blake: author, inventor, delineator, etcher, printer, colorist. Origination: Catherine Blake: printer. Publisher: William Blake. Place of Publication: London. Note: The place of publication is not given in the book, but Blake lived in London during the writing, etching, and printing of this copy. Date: 1793. Composition Date: 1793. Print Date: 1818. Location: Fitzwilliam Museum Cambridge, United Kingdom. Date: by bequest in 1950. Printed with the express permission of the Fitzwilliam Museum, Cambridge, United Kingdom, 2010.

ISBN-10: 1453793534
EAN: 13-9781453793534
Library of Congress Card Catalog Number is: 2010916895.

Summary: Two young professionals, Gale Knightly and Dicey Carmichael, are faced with the alleged suicide of a close friend, Elle Pandion. The two friends discover themselves while revealing the true cause of Elle's death.

FOR MICHAEL, MY *RARE BOOK*, AND
GRACE AND MARGO, MY *ANGELS*

PROLOGUE:

A PRIVATE CONVERSATION BETWEEN BEST FRIENDS

She dwells with Beauty— Beauty that must die . . .

—John Keats, "Ode on Melancholy"

As an immutable law of nature, all women scrutinize their own sex's appearance, even that of their best friends.

"Now, I'm certain this is only a nightmare. Coral lipstick and beehived hair disappeared with white gloves and virgins," whispered Dicey.

Gale nudged her best friend to stop the commentary, but she received only a nudge in return. "And her dress— ivory chiffon with cotton candy sleeves. She looks like a damn cupcake."

"Is your snark really necessary today? Show a little restraint," Gale pleaded.

"Show restraint? I'm showing tremendous restraint. What I'd like to do is drag her ass right out of there and give her a little dignity. She looks like a cheap wedding cake decoration. Why would Dr. Pandion allow her to look so horrific?" Dicey's voice cracked with pain, and she wiped her nose with the edge of her sleeve.

"Here, take my tissue," Gale offered, handing over the Kleenex. "You can't be so critical. I'm sure some sweet, old lady dressed her and tried to coordinate her hair and makeup with the dress. Did you expect Dr. Pandion to say, 'Straighten my daughter's hair and apply a little rose lip gloss'?"

Dicey flashed irritable eyes at her friend. "Well, give me a comb, anyway. I'm going to, at least, fix her bangs."

"Her father is right there," Gale said, ignoring the request.

"He's not looking." Dicey rummaged through her purse and pulled out a brush. She quickly combed down Elle's curled bangs and continued, "You know it's true, Gale. This whole situation is strange. Dr. Pandion is weird. He reminds me of a mortician I once dated who creeped around like a spider. He had long, meticulous fingernails."

"Yuck. You never told me about him."

"A weak moment," Dicey admitted as she tucked the brush back in her purse. "But, he made my skin crawl just like Dr. Pandion. Look at him," she said, glancing in the direction of Elle's father, "even his fingernails sparkle."

"What does that matter?"

"Listen, this is no magic pumpkin taking her to Never Never Land," Dicey said as she touched the cold steel. "So, you tell me—why would a man, who is that meticulous, dress his twenty-three year old daughter in a meringue for her burial?"

"Please, watch your tongue. Someone may overhear you, and I don't want to offend her father, for God's sake."

Dicey pulled a pair of dice from her pocket and toyed with them between her fingers. Gale's piercing look said put them away. She disregarded the order and rattled the cubes so loudly that other mourners finally turned to identify the source of disruption. She stared back but quieted the cubes. Dicey's real name was Aster, but friends called her Dicey because she kept close a set of lucky dice that never rolled far from her pocket. Each cube was carved with pairs of alabaster and scarlet snake eyes. When Dicey faced a tough decision, she tossed the dice. It was curious how the red and white talisman seemed to always land on the right side of right. Whether or not Dicey followed their direction was a different issue.

"You need to get a hold of yourself, now!" snapped Gale under her breath.

"I'm sorry, honestly. It's my nerves. If I stop reacting and start thinking, I'm going to start crying. I only wish that I could have saved her. She's dead for Christ's sake!"

"I understand that, but you need to take a deep breath," Gale said as she touched the edge of the coffin. "You couldn't save her before. You can't save her now. If someone really wants to die, they're going to find a way to die. This isn't about blame today."

"But I should have paid more attention to the signs. I've seen them before, Gale. How could I blow it, again?"

"You didn't. You can't blame yourself nor can you castigate her father. That's wrong. He just lost his daughter."

"I'm sorry. I know that I'm a little out of hand." She squeezed her eyes tightly and took a deep breath. "Man, this is tough."

Gale picked at the edges of her purse strap as she stared at the young woman held in the satin folds of the casket. Elle's typically straight blonde hair was teased around her petite head. Her face was different, too. With so much plastic surgery, she had morphed into a set of bulbous lips and protruding cheek bones.

"I am sorry, too. I don't understand why she killed herself. She went through so much pain to perfect her body, and then she overdoses. I don't get it, but I never get why someone chooses to die when so many people are fighting to live." Gale pulled her hand from the edge of the coffin to wipe a tear from her eye.

Dicey's lips quivered in pain. "I just wish Dr. Pandion would bury her with more dignity. Forget the funky dress and hair. An open coffin with a suicide is macabre."

"I agree with you, but it's not fair to judge a parent when a child dies, especially like this."

Silence and sadness filled the space between the two women as they stood together with their friend for the last time, wondering what forces brought about her fate. While Gale clung to her rosary beads for understanding, Dicey toyed with her set of dice. Pairs of blood-red snake eyes scored in her palm more than once. Her stomach curdled. She turned from the coffin and went outside for some air.

Kneeling close to the casket, Gale made the Sign of the Cross and began to recite her prayers. *Hail Mary full of grace, Lord that is with thee, blessed art thou among women . . . .* The petition was interrupted by a soft tap on her shoulder.

"Am I bothering your meditation?" asked Ken Tereus as he knelt beside her. His feral breath skimmed her cheek.

"No, not at all," she said and stood up.

"How are you, Gale? It's been a long time," he said, looking up into her eyes.

"I'm fine, sad, but fine."

"Life will eventually ease up. The ebb and flow of pain maintains our sanity," he offered, rising next to her. "Traditional funeral ceremonies seem cultish to me, anyway. People prolong their own pain and suffering while the one who suffered most is pain free. A simple funeral pyre is my preference."

Gale's patience was waning. She wondered if it was the fear and awkwardness of death that made people say such awkward things. "Elle no longer looks like herself. The beauty is gone," she finally said.

"I find it interesting when mourners comment on whether or not someone looks like themselves at their funeral," Ken said. "The person is dead. Their spirit has been released. How could they possibly look like themselves? This isn't how I prefer to remember Elle, anyway."

"I suppose you've got a good point. When was the last time you saw her?"

"It has been almost a month. I've been out of the country."

"Asia?"

"Yes. I acquired a stunning Quianlong rose vase to add to my collection. I'd love for you to see it sometime."

"It sounds interesting, but if you'll excuse me, I have to be leaving soon and haven't spoken with Dr. Pandion."

Gale pushed her way through the band of mourners in search of Elle's father. She spotted the tall, slender man in a vestibule close to the mortuary. As she approached, Dr. Pandion's gaze floated above her head.

"Hello," he said quietly.

"Dr. Pandion, Gale Knightly. I don't know if you remember me, but I cared deeply for your daughter . . . I am sorry for your loss."

"Thank you." He turned and stared toward the casket and asked, "Doesn't Elizabeth look lovely today?"

"Lovely, Dr. Pandion . . . her dress is lovely."

"Her mother's wedding gown. Elizabeth adored wearing the dress for me."

Dicey found Gale in the restroom sitting in a chair with her head drooping between her knees.

"You look beat. And I am probably going to make your day even worse," Dicey said as she sat down next to her friend.

"Nothing gets much worse than a day like today, but tell me anyway," Gale said, raising her head.

"Guess who's here?"

"I already saw him."

"Don't tell me that you're going to go weak in the knees for him all over again."

"I never went weak in the knees for him in the first place, and I certainly don't have time for a man in my life right now?"

"I can't figure out what Ken Tereus does for women, including you."

"Beside the fact that he is gorgeous, rich and engaging, I'm really not sure what he does for women."

"He's pretty, not handsome," Dicey said, picking at her thumb nail.

"Whether he's pretty or handsome, I'm not interested. I'm sitting in this chair because my feet are swollen and my back is killing me, nothing more."

"The lady doth protests too much," Dicey mumbled under her breath.

"Very funny," Gale said irritably. "Forget your own musings for one second and listen to me. I spoke to Dr. Pandion while you were outside," she said, lowering her voice. "He is an odd man, a very odd man."

"He's more than odd. The guy's bizarre," Dicey whispered.

"He told me that Elle is wearing her mother's wedding gown."

"That's strange, but now we know why she looks like a giant cotton ball," Dicey said as she toyed with her cubes.

"Yeah, she wore the gown for him— often. He "adored" her in it."

"I've always told you that he was strange, something out of "The House of Usher.""

Gale raised an eyebrow with annoyance. "I don't remember ninth grade English."

"Edgar Allen Poe. And why are you being so testy with me? We're on the same side, remember?"

"Sorry, but like Poe or not, it still must be devastating to lose your child. I can't comprehend how people have the courage to take another breath of life after facing such a loss."

CHAPTER I

Tyger, Tyger, burning bright,
In the forests of the night;
What immortal hand or eye,
Could frame thy fearful symmetry?

—William Blake, "The Tyger"

Ken Tereus was immortalized among elite women approaching thirty and beyond. As a revered plastic surgeon, he molded perfectly firm, perfectly round buttocks to match perfectly pointed breasts. Women from Los Angeles to Milan made pilgrimages to his office to be transformed into goddesses.

Gale Knightly was a medical malpractice lawyer. She met Ken Tereus on a case involving the death of a young woman. Dr. Kerry, a seasoned ENT surgeon, penetrated brain tissue while performing a standard rhinoplasty, and the thirty-one year old patient, who was a mother of two, bled to death on the steel surgical table. Dr. Tereus was an expert witness prepared to testify that the woman

1

had an atypical facial structure and that this irregularity led to the puncture rather than negligence by Dr. Kerry.

Before hearing any testimony from Tereus, Gale caught wind of the guano, the night soil that doctors, lawyers and even plaintiffs use to mix and mutate facts to mold their case. Hank Daimon, Kerry's attorney, was trying to mix some magic crap to get Kerry off, but even Hank Daimon couldn't change these facts. Kerry blew the operation.

Dr. Kerry was a twenty-seven year veteran who had performed 8,126 nose jobs on people with distinct and distorted facial structures. White men, black women, teenagers, dwarfs, Amazons. You name it, he transformed them. In this case, however, the patient's face wasn't faulty; Dr. Kerry faulted. The guy simply stepped out of the moment. The surgery was all on video. Dr. Kerry was describing his Sunday parachute jump with a half-interested surgical staff when he cut through the paper thin barrier separating sinus tissue from brain tissue.

Gale wanted to ask Dr. Kerry if he ever worried about the flight technician who packed his parachute before Sunday jumps. Did the tech always check for sharp edges that could rip through the thin material, separating him from life and death? Just like his patient depended upon Dr. Kerry to stay in the moment, did he rely on someone else to stay in the moment as he drifted through the heavens, dangling from the silky thin mushroom?

It was nine-forty a.m. The deposition was scheduled for ten. Gale always made it a point to arrive first for meetings. Selecting her seat was important. If the conference table was long and rectangular, she sat in the center, facing the door. If the table was square or circular, she sat on the right side facing the door— always prepared for those who walked in or out of her life.

While Gale reviewed a yellow legal pad indexed with color-coded Post-it notes and measured script, Dr. Tereus arrived. The man didn't walk into the room. He moved into the room, quietly, deliberately. Gale watched him as if he was forcing her to acknowledge each muscle flexing beneath the pin-striped suit tailored to his body. His hair was a rich auburn with a few gray streaks. A thick piece of red fell onto his brow as he placed a mahogany briefcase on the conference table directly across from her. His body blocked the exit. She slowly stood and extended her hand.

"Gale Knightly." She looked into his eyes. Piercing gold irises glistened back.

"Dr. Tereus." He grasped her hand with a firm grip. Pulling away, Gale slowly sat down, fingering the pale notebook to steady her thoughts.

"Are you a misanthrope or a redeemer?" he questioned.

Gale was forced to look back into his eyes and said, "I beg your pardon?"

"A misanthrope, someone who hates all man kind or–," Dr. Tereus began, but Gale interrupted.

"I know the definition of misanthrope, doctor. I don't get your point."

"Are you plaintiff or defense?"

"It all depends," she said.

"You are a plaintiff's lawyer, then?"

"No, I'm not this time, but not always. Our firm is unusual. We do a few plaintiff cases a year but mostly defense litigation."

"Who do you represent?"

"Dr. Robins, the resident present in the surgical suite. She'll be released from the case before it goes to trial."

"A confident lawyer."

"I am confident, but this has nothing to do with my expertise. It's a no-brainer. Dr. Robins was only observing the surgery, not assisting. Jeff Moscowitz is the kind of lawyer who likes to sue everybody."

Gale's heart rate eased as the conversation continued. "I believe you've been an expert for Hank Daimon several times. Is that true?"

"Sure, I love him. He's a ringmaster in the courtroom. He knows how to put on a show for the jury like no other defense lawyer I've ever seen. He's the best."

Gale hated working on cases with Hank Daimon. He was unilateral. Right or wrong, Daimon defended doctors and only doctors. His attitude toward plaintiffs spilled out like bleach, blotting out any color of empathy for the plaintiff. Gale struggled over his myopic approach to malpractice. Doctors were a part of the human race, too, just like lawyers and hairdressers and teachers. Some were dedicated miracle workers, some were negligent, but some, though rarely, were undeniably deviant. In this case, Dr. Kerry was negligent.

Daimon arrived at exactly ten. He was attractive in a classic 1950's kind of way with broad shoulders and thick gray hair that swept back from his forehead. Gale was disgusted when skimpy court reporters oozed from their chairs as he walked into the courtroom. Glancing at Tereus, she blushed at her own reaction to the doctor.

"How are you, Gale? I'm surprised your doctor's still in the trenches on this one,"

Hank Daimon said and plunked down his double-wide briefcase.

"They'll release her soon. I don't think Dr. Robins is even a flicker on their greed meter. It's all Kerry. But Hank, when are you going to settle? That video is pretty incriminating."

"Gale," he drawled, "you know everyone has a right to be defended, even doctors. Now, as I've asked before, are we high paid mediators or are we high performing litigators?"

"But this one is on video tape, Hank. Dr. Kerry's cognitive process was jumping from a plane when he penetrated Darlene Johnson's brain, not focusing on reconstructing a nasal passage."

"Gale, listen, if every surgery was videotaped, we'd hear about golf strokes, football scores or some doc's latest piece of poontang. They listen to Bach as well as Bon Jovi. That's how surgeons operate. Just because the guy was telling a goddamn story about a parachute, it doesn't make him negligent. Now, I want to get this deposition going, unless your client wants to pay for the court reporter's time," he said snapping his files on the table.

Gale fumed as she listened to Daimon's questions drone on. Did he have to redress her in front of Dr. Tereus? She was a lawyer, too. He carried an extra fifteen or twenty years but respect was respect, and he had no right to embarrass her. But that was it, he had embarrassed her. Why was she bothered by his typically acrid behavior today? Daimon talks to everyone like that, and people learn to ignore it.

After the deposition, Gale quickly declined an invitation to lunch with Daimon and Tereus. She'd rather peel back her fingernails than eat a sandwich sitting across from Hank Daimon.

CHAPTER 2

O Goddess! Hear these tuneless numbers, wrung
By Sweet enforcement and remembrance dear,
And pardon thy secrets should be sung
Even into thine own soft conched-ear . . . .

—John Keats, "Ode to Psyche"

William G. Pandion, M.D. learned that he was different from other boys at an early age. He couldn't remember whether he was six or seven, but he was old enough to peer out his mother's bedroom window and watch other kids play stick ball in the street. He lived on a wide lane paved with grey cobble stones and lined with great oaks. When the trees turned golden and the acorns dropped, William collected the nuts with his mother to make holiday wreaths for their neighbors. Life was good along Hemingway Lane. Most fathers had returned from the war, and mothers were back in the kitchen baking apple pies in their new General Electric ovens.

It was early June, and William was gazing out his mother's bedroom window with his nose pressed against the screen. His buddy Franky Ammorini waved to him from the street and yelled, "Come on down, Willy. We need a catcher. Lugers got his tooth knocked out yesterday, and he won't play."

William yelled back through the screened window, "Can't right now. Gotta wait for my mom." He pulled down the window and threw himself onto the bed.

His mother came out of the bathroom with wet hair and dressed in a pink terry cloth robe. "Are you ready, my little Wills?" she asked in the same buttery tone that she used every morning. Elizabeth Pandion sat down in the rocker and patted her knees. "Come along Wills. It's time for Mommy."

Wills, so he was tagged by his mother, pushed himself up from the bed and walked over to the rocker. His mother drew him down onto her lap and hugged him. She parted her robe and pulled his head to her breast. His tongue instinctively pushed the hard nipple out of his mouth, but she forced it back between his lips with her thumb and index finger.

Droplets of water fell from her wet hair onto his forehead. The water rolled down the side of his head and settled in his ear. He pulled away to shake the moisture from his ear, but his mother forced his head back to her breast.

William was forced to suck until he heard a soft moan from his mother. Then, he was set free for the rest of the day. The ritual was always the same.

Godwin Pandion, William's father, was unaware of the attachment between his wife and son because he was rarely home to notice. He was the president of an electronics corporation profiting from post World War II reconstruction in Europe. He spent most of his time across the Atlantic Ocean negotiating export contracts for American toasters, refrigerators and stoves with France and Germany when Europeans still found status in American products.

Though he was indispensable to clients, Mr. Pandion always remembered to steal a moment and send a telegram on his son's birthday. Tucked away in his son's desk drawer were thirteen notes that read the same for each year. *William, Happy Birthday. Take care of Mother. Yours, Father.*

William did as he was told for as long as he could remember. He took care of his mother.

As William grew too tall to climb onto his mother's lap, cries from Elizabeth Pandion's bedroom summoned him to her like a siren's song. He peeled away his own blankets to quell his mother's sadness. He did as he was told. He took care of his mother. He slipped into her room to calm the pain and remained there until the dawn crept across the blankets. William continued to do as his father told him through his adolescent years. Patiently, William waited for his father to return home to take care of his mother, but he never returned.

It was a week before Halloween when Elizabeth received the telegram. Her peals of agony echoed down Hemingway Lane. Mr. Pandion died of a heart attack while traveling in Germany.

At nineteen, William stood before his father's grave with lips that curled like an autumn leaf drifting along the edges of life. He tossed a clod of dirt into the black hole. Mr. Pandion would not return in eight or twelve or sixteen months for a three day visit. There would be no more letters on his birthday directing him to take care of his mother. There was no more hope that his father would return from Europe to take care of him.

Dutifully, he would continue to take care of his mother.

William Pandion became a cardiovascular surgeon because he wanted to erase pain and eradicate diseases of the heart. He saved people by extracting waste that built up from too many years of living. He sucked out stress and guilt that clung to the artery walls of men caused from too many late nights not at home. He wiped away the sludge that clogged the arteries of women who filled up their emptiness with hidden vodka bottles and Camel cigarettes.

Dr. Pandion was successful at mending broken hearts, but the disease could never be truly eradicated. Life festered far too long for most of his patients. The heart was worn out from hate and an unwillingness to forgive. It was worn out from years of shunning personal responsibility and exacting blame on others. There was nothing he could do to save a muscle refusing to pump out its own self-made destruction, for William, himself, was not exempt from the living. A silent disease circulated through his conscience, corrupting his soul. William Pandion understood that he could not excise his own damage caused by missing a father too much, while caring for a mother much too much.

☜☞ ☜☞ ☜☞

On the day of William's fortieth birthday, a painful deliverance was finally bestowed upon his mother and himself. He sat close to the hospital bed, holding his mother's wilted fingers, when the oncologist walked into the room.

William stood to shake Ted Canton's hand. "Thanks for moving in on the case so quickly, Ted."

"The ER docs are trained to look for this kind of problem. When someone hits something or somebody with their car and isn't aware of it, we scan the brain. Last May, I had a fifty-two year old father of four hit a college student on a bike. He dragged the kid 200 yards. The man never knew it. We scanned the brain and found a ping-pong ball size tumor. I'm surprised that he was still walking and talking. People get spatial and visual neglect with brain tumors. Luckily, your mother didn't hurt herself or someone else. She only damaged a few cars."

Elizabeth Pandion opened her eyes and peered at Ted Canton. "So, what's my prognosis?" she asked with a weak voice.

Ted Canton pulled up a chair and sat next to her. "Mrs. Pandion, your tumor is located in the central part of the brain. It is a stage three pineoblastoma. It's my policy to be straight forward with my patients. I think that most accurate information received with a diagnosis helps people cope."

Elizabeth Pandion closed her eyes and whispered, "I'm ready to hear everything. I've had a good life." She opened her eyes and gazed at her son.

William squeezed his mother's hand and asked, "Is it aggressive, Ted?"

"Unfortunately, pineoblastoma is a highly aggressive malignancy. And because of the location and size, the tumor is inoperable. We will try radiation and chemotherapy to shrink the tumor."

☙☙ ☙☙ ☙☙

William brought his mother home from the hospital to care for her in the final months and days of her life. Each night he sat by her bedside, watching as the cancer burrowed through her brain like termites through rotting wood. One evening was especially difficult. His mother had been vomiting for several hours because both the chemotherapy and the tumor were causing violent waves of nausea.

As William picked out half-digested carrots from her hair, he finally relented. "I've dedicated my life to saving people, but providence's judgment proscribes me from saving you, Mother," he sighed with indignation.

Elizabeth looked up through the papery thin slits of her eyes. "Wills, you saved me for forty years. It's time I go," she whispered.

Throughout the night, William stayed close to his mother. He thought, at times, he could see her soul slipping out of her slight body. Relief and pain battled within him as she lay dying. The only certain part of her looming death was that he would no longer have to take care of her.

☙☙ ☙☙ ☙☙

After his hospital rounds, William repeated the midnight vigils over his mother's bed in the last weeks of her life. It was nearly two in the morning one evening when his mother began to spill out words in a rush of confusion. "Don't leave papa! I will be a good girl. Don't go. I won't say anything, papa." William grasped his mother's hand to reassure her. "Mother, it is Wills. I am here."

"Papa!" She gripped her son's fingers and rubbed them hard against the flesh of her deflated breast. "Papa, don't leave me?"

William's fingers trembled beneath the heat of his mother's hand. The bridled memories flashed through his brain. All at once, he could feel her sweltering body pressed against his, and he cried out.

"God, help me!"

He left his mother in delirium and ran to the bathroom. In the mirror, he saw a young boy wriggling under his mother's heavy breast. He could feel the thirteen-year old boy growing hard from his mother's touch. He felt the memories rise between his legs and vomited onto the mirror. Chunks of pain splashed back onto his face, and he vomited again.

William stumbled into the shower to scrub away the stains that penetrated his body. He dug deep into his flesh and droplets of blood splashed onto the tile. Cleansing was futile. The scourge that had festered for thirty years could not be erased. He fell to his knees and began to weep. He stopped crying only when his mother's own wails grew louder than his. He returned to her.

William's fingers now burned with repulsion. One thing was clear, though. He no longer had to do as his father told him.

CHAPTER 3

Little Fly
Thy summer's play
My thoughtless hand
Has Brush'd away.

—William Blake, "The Fly"

It was nine-thirty, and Gale was exhausted. Jamming the key into the front door, she heard the phone begin to ring. Only her mother or telemarketers called on her land line, and it was too late for a sales call.

"Mother, I'm too tired to talk!" she yelled back, but a daughter's guilt drew her to the phone.

"Hi, Mom," Gale sighed into the receiver.

"Not your mother, but hasn't she ever warned you about listing your number in the phone directory? Strange men search for such soft spots."

Gale was pleasantly startled by the voice.

"I listened to you for two hours today, and you probably are dangerous, Dr. Tereus, but only to the plaintiff's bar."

"You never know, Gale. But call me Ken."

"No, that's true, Ken, but why are you calling me at nine-thirty at night?"

"Because you weren't home at seven, seven-thirty, eight or eight-thirty, my dear."

"Was there something urgent?"

"There was."

"What?"

"I was hungry, and I hate sitting at restaurants alone."

Ken's amber eyes came to mind. She sat down on the couch and stretched out her legs.

"How may I cure your hunger, doctor?"

"Dinner, tomorrow night, seven o'clock at The Sake Bomb."

"Can we do eight, and I'll meet you there?" Gale never permitted a man to drive on the first date.

"I'll be there. You sound tired. Go to bed counselor," Ken commanded.

"Goodnight." Gale hung up the phone and smiled. A date, novel idea, she mused.

☯ ☯ ☯

Gale arrived for dinner at seven-forty. Ken Tereus was already at the bar. Drawing in a deep breath, she headed toward him. Sweat trickled from her armpits.

"It's just a date," she mumbled.

Ken stretched from the stool like a lion waking from a nap. He pulled her fingers into his grip when she approached.

"You look lovely," he said.

She glanced around the room to avoid his eyes. "Nice place."

He directed her to a stool.

"I ordered a bottle of wine and some sushi for dinner. I'm hungry," Ken said, tapping the breathing bottle.

"Great. I've always loved sushi, even before it replaced brie and Chablis at my mother's cocktail parties," Gale said with a nervous laugh.

"Who introduced you to sushi in the heart of the Midwest?"

"An older man. I was twenty; he was thirty-one. It was my first adult date with a guy who didn't freak over a fifty-dollar check. This guy loaded up a piece of sushi with a giant wad of wasabi and shoved it into my mouth."

"Whooh!" Ken said.

"Yeah, my brains blew out of my nose and my eye balls."

"I bet that was attractive."

"I'm convinced that the guy did it on purpose, but I couldn't figure out if he thought it was funny or if he was really trying to hurt me."

"Why would he want to hurt you?"

"I've given up trying to understand the male psyche."

"You have such cynicism at such a young age."

"No, I just don't like people who try to destroy my nasal passage and vision in one swallow."

"No, I agree. That's not cynical."

"Speaking of noses, you did a bang-up job at the deposition yesterday. Only Daimon could have a shot at winning this case, now. He amazes me," conceded Gale.

"He's the master."

"So, what have you mastered in your lifetime?"

"What do you mean?"

"Successful people are masters. Somehow they're able to master–," Gale began, but Ken interrupted.

"Few people master any part of their world. It takes an inexhaustible control over something or someone else to be a master at anything. Most people don't have that much drive."

"So, I guess you've thought about this before?" Gale asked.

"A surgeon must. To be a master, you have to first understand how your object of interest functions. You have to dissect it into minutiae. Identify its potential. Then, you learn how to manipulate it, alter outcomes. Then, you become the master. Not until this point, do you possess true power or control."

"Why did you choose surgery as a career? I could never slice into someone's body."

"It's a rush for me. People would be shocked to know how fine the line is between life and death. The power to bring someone to the very edge of existence, hanging between our world and eternity, is exhilarating. It's the ultimate high."

"Interesting, maybe guys like Jack the Ripper and Jeffrey Dauhmer felt the high, but in a twisted way," Gale said.

"This talk is too heavy for a first date," he said. "Aren't you supposed to ask how many brothers and sisters I have, or if I prefer cats over dogs, or, if I like The Beatles more than Sting? You know, the normal date questions."

Ken scooted his stool closer to Gale and took her hand in his. She looked down at their entwined fingers and smiled. "Do you mean the superficial questions that lead to the second date-killer questions?"

"Yeah, that's right. What are some of your date-killer questions?" he asked.

"I won't divulge my secrets."

"Go ahead, ask me one," he said, squeezing her fingers.

"No."

"C'mon, I want to see if we'll have a second date."

She hesitated then asked, "Okay, have you been married before?"

"Yes, briefly. No children," answered Ken.

"Are you married now?"

"No. What kind of question is that?"

"A date-killer question!" Gale laughed and took a sip of wine. She felt wonderful.

"So, does it bother you that I'm divorced?"

"No, it doesn't, not at your age. I'd be suspicious if you weren't married before."

"What do you mean at my age? I'm only forty-five."

"That's my point. A forty-five year old male living alone his entire adult life is a dangerous proposition to a woman. At some point, a man has to learn to give, and living with a woman and/or children is the true test."

"You're a wise woman, Gale Knightly."

When the sushi was served, Ken went to work preparing a piece for Gale. He topped the tuna roll with spicy mayonnaise and slowly slid the piece onto her tongue.

"So, did I explode an m-80 in your throat?"

"No, it was the perfect amount of heat. Sushi is the only thing that I know that can hurt so good," added Gale.

"I'm not so sure that's limited to sushi."

"How is that so?"

"I know some pretty physical things that can hurt so good," answered Ken.

Gale shifted on her stool. "Admit it, though, there is something sensual to this food."

"The most sensual." Ken leaned forward and touched her cheek with his fingers.

The evening was sumptuous. Ken moved in tandem with her body's every need. When she stood, he reached for her seat; when she sat, he placed the napkin on her lap. He sated her appetite for food, conversation and attention.

On their second date, Gale drew Ken's hand close to her face and breathed deeply. He owned an exotic scent, patchouli mingled with tangerine and oriental grass. He looked at her inquisitively.

"I'm memorizing your smell. It's remembered forever now." To Gale, a man's body scent was more important than his looks.

"Even if Michelangelo's *David* stood before me, I could never make love to him if his body odor was foul. Scent is primal. It signals warning or attraction. I don't ignore it," Gale explained.

"Is there anything else that I should know about your likes and dislikes?" Ken asked.

"Well, there is the hand thing."

"What hand thing?"

"I have big hands. A man has to have larger hands than mine." Gale pressed her palm against his; she was dwarfed inside his fingers. "I need masculine hands, too. Roughed- up around the edges. Soft, pretty fingers make my skin crawl."

"You like the Marlboro man?"

"Yes, the Marlboro man in a suit. I'm not into metro-sexual stuff. I like hair on a man. I stopped dating a guy because he spent more time than I did shaving and sifting through his closet before a date. Women should own the market on grooming and clothes. They're the few stocks that we've cornered."

"Feminists may think you're a little outdated."

"I'm feminine. That makes me a feminist along with my career and everything else about me. A man should be a man, and a woman should be a woman. That doesn't make women inferior, just different."

"Well, I'm sure that the male population will be pleased with your conviction to womanhood. Are there any other rules that I should know about?"

"I'll certainly let you know if I think of them."

CHAPTER 4

The Door of Death I open found
And the Worm Weaving in the Ground
Thou'rt my Mother from the Womb
Wife, Sister, Daughter to the Tomb
Weaving to Dreams the Sexual strife
And weeping over the Web of Life

—William Blake, "For the Sexes:
The Gates of Paradise"

*A*s Mrs. Pandion's condition quickly deteriorated, William brought in twenty-four hour nursing care to assist with the last days of his mother's life. The night shift nurse, Diana Goldberg, was a registered hospice nurse who came with excellent recommendations from the hospital. She was a slight woman just about Elizabeth Pandion's size with a heart-shaped face protected by thick blonde hair.

Diana looked like a woman who battled pain. The deep line that was chiseled between her eyebrows and the thin wrinkles that gathered above her upper lip exposed a suffering beyond her twenty-eight years.

On her first night of care, William watched as Diana combed his mother's hair and buffed her nails with a calfskin buffer.

"I've never thought to fix her hair. Is that horrible of me?" he asked the nurse.

"Of course it's not horrible, but even very sick women care about their appearance. It's important to maintain dignity, even in the worst of times," Diana said, looking at William with a gentle smile.

"So simple, but so true," he said

William liked the shape of her eyes. They were slate blue almonds. "I want to warn you ahead of time."

"Warn me about what?" Diana asked, tilting her head to the side.

He liked the way her hair curled around her chin. "I'm not sure if the nursing service told you or not, but Mother has a tough time coping with the pain. It's been hard, even for me, to manage."

Diana looked directly at William. "I can handle it. I learned a long time ago that pain is relative. It's a ubiquitous monster that is scary for most but much scarier for others. If you don't try to judge it or reason with it, the pain is easy to manage. 'Just accept it and respond' is my motto."

☙❧ ☙❧ ☙❧

The next evening William found himself rushing through his hospital rounds. At eight o'clock, he glanced at his watch and made a mental note to himself: Diana Goldberg's twelve hour shift just started. He hurried onto his next patient.

Two hours later he softly skipped up the steps to his mother's bedroom. When he walked into the room, Diana was bent over his mother, who was sound asleep.

"Good evening," he whispered.

Diana jumped with fright. "Dr. Pandion! I didn't hear you come in," she whispered back.

"I'm sorry, Diana. May I call you Diana?" he asked, checking himself.

"Certainly, you may, Dr. Pandion."

"Please call me Wills."

"Wills. Is that possessive or plural?" Diana teased, but then she blushed. "That was a really stupid thing to say, wasn't it?"

He nodded in agreement, but with a smile. "Call me William."

"I'm sorry." Diana's cheeks were burning.

"No worry," he said, approaching his mother's bed. "How's the patient?"

"She's had a rough day. We upped the morphine a bit to ease the pain."

William picked up a chair and set it down next to Diana. "You know a lot about pain for someone so young."

"I deal with it every day. Pain's a part of humanity, an unavoidable affliction embedded in existence. For some, the only escape is through death."

William grimaced. "That's a very morose thought."

"No. It's reality. You're a doctor— you know. People die everyday. And, at the Hospice Center, they actually do die every day. I've learned a lot about people and agony through my profession."

"Tell me how."

"Some patients who experience only intermittent tinges of pain can't seem to endure the monster. Others, who are drenched in agony, manage to weather the final storm with dignity."

"I thought you said that you don't judge other people's pain," William pointed out.

She gave him a dry smile. "I don't judge it. I observe it. And one thing is for sure, pain does not discriminate. All walks of life are invited to the show— rich, poor, black, white, Christians, Jews and Moslems. Pain's always playing on the wide screen. It has a way of suspending in time a person's past to foreshadow the future."

☙☙ ☙☙ ☙☙

It was on their fifth evening together when William learned just how accepting Diana was of others' torment. His mother was suffering from hallucinations that evening. She was crying out for her father.

"Papa, Papa! Hold me. Don't leave me, Papa!" she wailed.

William grasped her hand and whispered soothing words. "Mother, it's me, Wills. I'm here. Calm down."

"Papa, you're here!" At that moment, she took William's hand and pushed it between her legs. She moved it up and down with her bony fingers. "Papa!" she cried.

William yanked his arm away. He sprung from the chair and sent it crashing against the wall.

"I can't wait until you die. And you will rot in hell, buried right next to your father's rotten carcass," he yelled as he ran from the room.

Left alone with Mrs. Pandion, Diana silently picked up the overturned chair, collected scattered bandages and tissues and dropped them back into the waste basket.

She simply did her job; she collected the misery that gathered around the room and put it in some semblance of order.

But most importantly, she didn't judge.

☙☙ ☙☙ ☙☙

The next night William worked late. He went directly to his bedroom after arriving home. Two nights later he walked into his mother's room at nine-thirty. By this time, Elizabeth Pandion was fading in and out of consciousness.

"How is she?" William quietly asked.

"It won't be long. She may have a day."

William came close and sat down next to the nurse. He stared at the soft lines gathering around Diana's eyes. What kind of tragedy caused this premature aging, he wondered. His instinct was to reach out and smooth away the wrinkled skin, but he couldn't. He wouldn't. He would never touch another woman, as long as he lived.

Knotting his fingers together in his lap, William asked her, "How do you do this everyday?"

"Do what?"

"How do you deal with the death and dying and the pain. You're so deft at managing the insipidness of mortality," he said, scooting his chair closer to her.

"That's what I have done for most of my life."

"In what way?"

"My mom and dad died in a car crash when I was ten. That was the last time I was happy. That's also how I learned to understand other people's pain."

"What happened?" William asked, placing his arm on the back of her chair.

"Do you really want to hear it?" she asked, looking into his sharp eyes.

"You've witnessed the hidden torment in my war chest. I'd like to hear what caused these tiny lines around your eyes." William gently touched the corner of her eye with his index finger.

Diana pulled her head away and looked down.

"I'm sorry, Diana. I didn't mean anything by that," he said in a voice jumbled with embarrassment.

"It's okay." Diana looked up and smiled.

"Tell me what happened," he asked.

"It was a warm September evening. All the windows were rolled down in my dad's brand new 1960 Oldsmobile. I remember the details like they happened last night. My head was against the window frame, and my hair was whipping around my face. I was listening to Mom and Dad arguing about the Kennedy-Nixon debate. We were driving home from a friend's house where we had just watched it. We didn't have our own television set. Mom refused to buy one. She thought that the television waves would make me go blind."

William laughed. "No offense, but your mother's reasoning sounds like a democrat. I bet you were Kennedy supporters."

"Well, you're half right. Mom agreed with the majority of the 70 million American viewers who thought John Kennedy won the debate that night. She said that Richard Nixon's scruffy beard and pasty complexion made him look too old next to the sex appeal of John Kennedy."

"I guess your mom was right."

"Ultimately, yes, but Dad complained that appearances had nothing to do with substance. He agreed with the radio listeners who thought that Nixon won the debate based on his policies and ideology, not good looks. 'Thick brown hair and blue eyes, alone, can't fight the Communists,' he'd say.

"Just as I was casting my vote for John Kennedy from the backseat, a drunk driver crossed the double yellow line. The crash tossed the Olds on its roof. My parents were instantly killed, and I was trapped in a hospital bed for a couple of months. That's probably how I became interested in medicine."

William reached out and touched her hand. "Diana, I am so sorry."

"I've had many years to adjust. There was nothing easy about the loss, though. It was tough because I really didn't have any family."

"Were your parents both single children?" he asked.

Diana took a heavy breath and slowly released the air. "No. My mom's family lived in Des Moines, Iowa. Her parents refused to speak to her since she married a Jew whose family was in the whole-sale diamond business, no less. My father's parents lived within ten miles of our house, but I rarely saw them. Their son had married a poor Irish Catholic, daughter of immigrants."

"Sounds like a typical American family," he teased.

Diana laughed. "The problem for me, though, was that no one wanted a Jewish-Irish Catholic orphan. My mom's side was out of the question. And my Jewish aunts, Iris, Ruth, and Barbara, almost killed each other, trying to figure out what to do with me."

"How can adults be so cruel to children?" William asked.

"Who knows? I used to sit at the bottom of the steps at my Aunt Ruth's house and listen to the family argue about me. They thought that, by closing the swing-door between the kitchen and the dining room, I couldn't hear them."

It was true. Diana heard it all, straight from the kitchen, the heart of a happy home. The argument was always the same.

"You should take her, Iris. You're the only one who talked to Walter, anyway. I haven't seen nor heard from him in five years," Barbara snapped.

"No. Sarah and David are almost out of the house. I don't want another kid. Besides, Bob would never have it. Ruthie, your kids are young. You take her. Take all the money, too. You're the one who needs it."

"Needs what?" Ruth yelled.

"Are you even listening to what we're talking about? We're talk-ing about the cash. Isn't Rich still painting houses? Or, is he mow-ing lawns, now? Either way, with four kids, you need the money," Iris said with a smirk.

"It's not about the money, Iris. I've got four kids already. Barbara, it's your chance to be a mother. Why won't you take her?"

"If I wanted to be a mother, I would have had kids. Christ, I just put in white, shag carpeting throughout the house. And Iris is right, Ruth. You need the money, so stop being so damn proud about it. We all know that you're strapped for cash. Rich called Sam two weeks ago to ask for help with your house payment, for God's sake."

"Here we go again, here we go again. Somehow the conversation always gets back to Rich. He's a good father and a good husband. Can't you leave him alone?" Ruth asked with tears pooling in her eyes.

"Maybe, if he'd get a real job, you wouldn't have so much time on your hands to have more babies," Barbara said looking at Ruth's burgeoning stomach.

"Okay, okay. Everybody calm down," Iris interrupted. "Let's all agree that nobody wants the kid, but the fact is, we're all that she's got. I say we divide up the time, six months here and six months there. Besides, Ruth, she can help out when the baby comes."

⚚ ⚚ ⚚

So, Diana's fate was decided. She stumbled through her teen years carrying her pain from one aunt's house to the next. Every five or six months, she would pack up her grief and move between the three homes. With each rotation, Diana would carefully unpack her misery and fold it neatly at the foot of a new bed. After a month or so, her despondency would fall from the blankets and litter the bedroom floor. When gloom dirtied the entire house, she was instructed to box up her pain and move on to the next rotation of aunts.

No one ever stopped to ask how Diana was doing. She was almost twelve and living with Barbara when she started her period. Too frightened to confront her aunt about sanitary napkins, Diana, instead, cut up strips of hand towels and washcloths to stuff in her underwear. Eliza, the wash woman, was fired when the monogrammed towels went missing.

Diana moved between Iris, Ruth and Barbara for eight years, always alone, carrying her sadness with each stop. College was a haven for Diana, though. She finally had the freedom to dump out her pain and leave it on her apartment floor until she was ready to sort it out. Like piles of dirty laundry, she sifted through the colors of her life and separated out the times with her parents from the times with her aunts. She bagged up the past eight years and threw the miserable garbage to the curb. She cleansed the memories of her parents and stored them away for safekeeping.

Diana attended nursing school and graduated with a mission to help sort out the suffering and despair of others. So, when other's anguish splattered onto her white uniform, Diana refused to be revolted by the human condition.

It was on the last evening of Elizabeth Pandion's life when Diana told her tragedy to William.

As his mother's soul was leaving this life, William was discovering a different kind of passion. Before his mother passed on, however, she cried one last time. "Papa, hold me." William released her fingers from his palm and said goodbye to his mother forever.

Diana reached across to take his hand.

CHAPTER 5

What is it women do in men require
The lineaments of Gratified Desire

—William Blake, "Several Questions Answered"

*A*fter a handful of dates with Ken Tereus, Gale unlocked dusty emotions and allowed them to crawl out. Whenever she checked her text messages, she searched for his name first and was rarely disappointed. Ken empathized with her when she was sickened over a brain-damaged baby case and remembered to ask about a shaky deposition. He listened and responded.

Gale rolled over alone in bed one evening and listened to the noisy crickets who were clicking their legs together to attract a mate. She thought about Ken. He was the epitome of Sir Gawain by obliging her every need, except for her physical desire. Their dates numbered in the double digits, and the most aggressive sexual act that he had performed was a kiss on the lips. Nothing more. Why not? If he wasn't interested, why ask her out again? By this time, most men would have slipped a hand inside her blouse or at least tried to sneak under her skirt. Maybe he's gay or impotent. But these things didn't make sense either.

At dinner, his stories were increasingly sexual. That very evening he told her about Eva, a Swedish model whom he dated a few years ago. Eva liked to grip his hips in an almost painful vice with her long legs. He also told her about another woman who enjoyed being tied up with silken cords. It was mystifying. Why the erotic stories if he was only going to hold her hand? She wasn't longing for Calypso-style sex, but her body ached for at least a glimmer of passion.

She yanked the blankets closer to her body and a tear trickled down her cheek. So, what if I'm twenty-nine, unmarried and childless? I'm happy. I have an incredible career and great friends. She battled with the state of her life and with her blankets until the next morning. Finally at seven-thirty, she pushed away the covers and tears and tugged on her running shoes and sweat pants.

Before she could escape outside, the phone rang.

In the receiver, she heard, "Why aren't you at mass?"

"What time is it, Mom?"

"Eight o'clock. Don't you usually go to eight o'clock mass?"

"Why are you calling if I'm usually at mass?"

"Gale, you know your life would get better if you went to mass every now and then."

"Mom, my life is better. I love my life." Gale slumped against the kitchen cabinet.

"You need to go to church. Your life isn't perfect. No one can live without going to church."

"I pray when I run."

"That's not the same."

"Mom, I'm really not in the mood for one of your sermons," she said flicking a crumb across the counter.

"I'm not preaching, Gale. Did you go out last night?"

"Are you asking me if I had a date? No, you'll be the first to know," she lied.

"If you went to church, you might find a husband."

"Yeah, right Mom, that's like saying, 'If I go to church, I'm going to win the lottery.' God doesn't work that way."

"Do you want to go to the club tonight for your birthday? You could bring someone."

"Dicey and I are going out, but maybe we could join you." Gale stood up and stretched. There was silence on the other end of the phone. "Forget it. Why do you have to hate her so much?"

"Why can't you find other friends?"

"You've been saying that since I was in the fifth grade, Mother. Get over it!" Gale pushed a finger through a banana sitting on the counter.

"I just wish you'd expand your horizons and meet another circle of friends."

"Why, Mom? Why should I? Why don't you finally get it off your chest!"

"Get what off my chest? I don't know what you're talking about."

"The fact that you think Dicey is a lesbian. Just say it. You've danced around the topic for ten years," Gale said as she kicked the refrigerator.

"Well!"

"Well. What, Mother?"

"Everyone knows about that organization she tried to form in high school for queers. So, don't act like I'm just creating gossip."

Twitching with anger, Gale said, "You have absolutely no clue what you're talking about. Dicey has been my best friend for twenty years. That will never change, whether you like it or not."

"Then, why don't you marry Dicey, if she means so much to you!"

"There, you finally said it."

"What do you mean?"

"You've finally gotten it off your chest. You've always wanted to ask me if Dicey and I were lovers." Gale's lips curled in a tight grin. How was her mother going to claw out of this corner?

"Don't talk to me like that, Gale! I'm still your mother."

"What are you worried about, Mom? If Dicey and I show up at your country club, people might think that Mrs. Knightly's daughter is gay. Oh my God, how would that look?"

"Stop it, Gale, just stop it!"

"You stop it, Mother. You're late for church anyway."

Gale hung up the phone and walked out the back door. As her feet slapped against the pavement, her mother's hypocrisy stung her cheeks. Mrs. Knightly was sincerely dedicated to only two things in her life, the Church and the country club. Aside from the cross and the stained glass windows, both institutions were interchangeable and, in fact, were supported by the same benefactors. Her country club subjugators poured a lovely Cabernet for the priests who manipulated little boys. The same people poured a Johnny Walker Blue for the CEO's who manipulated profit margins for their own benefit. Yesterday's ice water was served to the staff who dragged out their trash on a daily basis.

CHAPTER 6

Remove away that blackning church
Remove away that marriage hearse
Remove away that--------of blood
Youll quite remove the ancient curse

—William Blake, "An ancient Proverb"

*O*ne broken soul can easily spot another broken soul, and sometimes these relationships are successful at rebuilding shattered lives. An unspoken circular covenant formed between Diana and William: We both are tainted. I'll embrace your scars, if you promise never to expose mine.

Within this realm, Diana and William came together emotionally, but their physical relationship teetered on the brink of disaster with his first attempt at intimacy.

One month into their relationship, Diana cooked a pot roast with red potatoes and green beans for dinner. William brought red wine. He sopped up the remaining gravy with a slice of bread while she chattered about her Aunt Ruthie.

"A beaten down woman, she was. Her husband, her sisters, her kids, they all tore her apart, piece by piece. Chewed her up and spit her out. She had nothing left to offer me, and not that I expected it, nor that she wanted to give it.

"But she taught me how to cook. Ruthie could make dirt taste like chocolate pudding."

William laughed and poured more wine. He raised his glass, "Cheers to your Aunt Ruthie. At least one thing good came from eight years of hell."

"That's about the only good thing." She stood and gathered the plates from the table. William made an attempt to help, but she insisted that he stay seated. "I have a surprise, and you can't peek."

He listened to her bustle around the kitchen. Glasses clattered and silverware jingled as coffee bubbled in the percolator. Diana was softly singing, "I feel pretty, oh so pretty. I feel pretty and witty and bright." William smiled. *West Side Story* was one of his favorite Broadway shows. How did she know that? He was happy; for the first time in his life, he was actually happy.

"Close your eyes," Diana yelled from the kitchen. He heard her walk into the dining room, accompanied by the aroma of coffee. Chattering china told him she had put a dessert before him.

"Open!"

He opened his eyes and looked down at a long, doughy dessert resting on his plate. He glanced across the table.

"Where's your plate?"

"Taste it. I made it special for you."

"What is it?" He poked at the pastry log with a fork, and raisins fell out of the center.

"Rugelach. It's a Jewish dessert. Ruthie taught me how to make it."

He dug into the pastry. It melted in his mouth. He was finished in five bites. "Masterful, simply masterful," he said.

34

William reached across the small table and took Diana's hand. "No one's ever done anything like this for me before. You care, you really care about people, don't you Diana?"

"I do care about people, but I especially care about you."

William stood up, pulled Diana to her feet, and embraced her. She bent her head back and stood on her tip-toes. "Kiss me," she whispered. It was a dry, closed mouth kiss. "No, really kiss me." Diana reached up with her hands and drew his head back down to hers. She touched her lips to his and gently pushed her tongue into his mouth. His body responded.

Diana guided him to her couch. He sat down, and she reclined across his lap. Gripping his neck, she tugged him close and began kissing again. William wrapped his arms around her, but like a tin soldier rather than a lover. She shifted in his hold to help him relax, but his arms grew more rigid.

Disentangling herself, she moved from his lap to his side. Diana began to play with the buttons on the front of his shirt. One by one, she undid the buttons to expose a taut chest. She ran her fingers through his chest hairs and worked her way down. He was erect. Diana loosened his belt. When she touched the top button of his trousers, William jumped from the couch, knocking Diana to the floor.

"I'm sorry, but I just can't do this," he said with agony glittering in his eyes. "I'm the wrong person for you. I'm a monster. You don't understand. And it is something that I could never tell you."

Diana lifted herself from the floor, sat down on the couch and stared up at William. "You're wrong. I do understand. I know what your mother did to you. I watched her die with a twisted conscience. You're not the monster. She was."

"I come from a long line of monsters, and I can't continue to perpetuate the destruction. I'm the last living male Pandion, and I will never bring children into this world to perpetuate a legacy of pain and agony."

"Please, listen to me. I love you. I want to be by your side forever. Together we can conquer the demons."

After weeks and months of patient coaxing and tender touches, William welcomed Diana's love and acceptance. Within a year, the couple married, and within eight months, she was pregnant.

Diana hated living in the house cherished by William's mother. The dark curtains and heavy furniture seemed to stand motionless in the large rooms, as if they were waiting for the parasites and bacteria to begin their ugly process. They sold the house and found an airy home composed of fieldstone and large bay windows. Diana painted the nursery in a dusty blue with strokes of wispy clouds.

William came home from the hospital late one evening and found his wife in the baby's room folding miniature undershirts and socks. Her belly, heavy with nine months of life, made him happy. And he believed for that moment that the monster had disappeared from the shadowy corners of his life.

Sadly, he was wrong, for tragedy was inescapably inherent in the Pandion ancestry. He was correct when he told Diana that his family came from a long line of monsters. Somewhere along the way, a great grandfather had sold his soul for money, power, sex or some other deadly sin. The prize, itself, didn't matter. It was the price to be paid that mattered. William Pandion was included in the generations of Pandions required to pay off the debt. Even a doctor who sets out to make restitution by correcting the imperfections in mankind can't escape his heritage.

Diana's water broke that night. She was in steady labor for twenty-four hours. Ten minutes into the twenty-fifth hour the baby monitor strapped around Diana's belly screamed in distress. The baby's heart rate was accelerating. Diana's blood pressure shot to 220/115. She was prepped for an emergency cesarean section, but it was too late. The undetected pericarp had rooted and raised its lethal head. Diana hemorrhaged to death from a ruptured placenta on the day that her daughter was born.

CHAPTER 7

My mother bore me in the southern wild,
And I am black, O! My soul is white
White as an angel is the English Child:
But I am black as if bereav'd of light.

—William Blake, "Little Black Boy"

Mrs. Knightly hated Dicey since the first day Gale brought her home from school. Over chocolate milk and Oreos, Mrs. Knightly discovered that Dicey's father was a derelict carpenter, she had no mother to speak of, and the pair was not from the east side; they weren't even from Crystal Springs, Ohio. Reaching for her fourth cookie, the eleven year old proudly told Mrs. Knightly,

"I've lived in six different towns, and I've gone to five different schools. St. Matthews is my last. All Catholic. Daddy says that I need to go to Catholic schools. My grandma said that it's real important. Before Grammy died, Daddy promised her two things.

He would take me to church every Sunday, and he would send me to Catholic schools."

"Your grandmother was correct. Going to church and attending parochial schools are very important for good girls," said Mrs. Knightly.

"Don't tell anybody, but we don't always make it to Sunday mass, Mrs. Knightly. If Daddy gets a little too tipsy on a Saturday night, I cook up some goetta and coffee in the morning. Then, I go down to the corner for a newspaper. I read it to Daddy while he eats and 'rejoins the living' as he likes to call it. It's about my most favorite time of the week."

"Young lady, I thought it was your father's duty to take you to church," Mrs. Knightly commented with distaste.

"Yeah, well. We take a walk after breakfast and do some praying. Daddy says that's just as good as going to church."

"I should say not."

"Why not, Mom?" interjected Gale. "I think that Dicey's dad is right. Gee, they're still talking to God, aren't they?"

"Quiet, Gale Marie. No, that is not right, and I'm the one talking to Dicey. Your father should take you to church. You must receive the Eucharist each week in order to go to heaven. How does he expect you to have any sense of decency? Morals don't grow on trees like apples," snapped the woman.

"He does teach me morals, ma'am. He reads me the catechism every night. My Grammy read it to me before she died. Now, Daddy does. You know the catechism. It's that little pink book. It has the name of a city. . . Baltimore."

"Yes, Dicey. I know *The Baltimore Catechism.*"

"Ever read it Mrs. Knightly? It's a pretty good book."

"Well, no. Gale has studied it, though."

"I memorized it, Mom, but I never knew what it was talking about," added Gale.

"Oh, come now, honey, of course you know," said her mother.

"No, I don't."

"Yes, you do, Gale."

"I don't, Mom."

"Gale, I'll tell you all about it. It tells you how to be a good Christian Catholic," offered Dicey. "My grandma said that to be a good Christian Catholic you have to love people and forgive people. That's what it's all about. Even when people do bad stuff, you gotta forgive, cause that helps them do better. She always loved my daddy and forgave my daddy. That sure helped him."

"How so, my dear?" asked Mrs. Knightly.

"Grandma loved him even when he got into a little trouble with the law."

"The law?" Harriett Knightly interrupted.

"Yes ma'am. He never told me what happened, but I think it had to do with selling stuff. That's what he called it— stuff, but I know what it was. It was bad stuff. I heard my grandma tell my Aunt Stella that she flushed a grocery bag of grass down the pooper one day. Daddy was burning angry, mad as a fire ant. So, I went out and cut up a bunch of grass and put it into a brown lunch bag for him. He said it wasn't the same. Mrs. Knightly, I'm not stupid anymore. It was a different kinda grass, if you know what I mean?"

"Ah, yes, Dicey, I do know what you mean, but we don't need to hear . . ."

"Grandma said it was that kind of grass that put my momma off the deep end. She supposed that Momma liked her vodka and grass a little more than she liked us. Cause she wandered off when I was about four trying to get some more. Daddy couldn't give it to her anymore. Daddy was spending a little time at the dormitory. Mrs. Knightly, you know what the dormitory is, don't ya?" Dicey slowed to grab two more Oreos.

"Yes, Dicey. I really think that it's time. . . . "

"What was the dormitory, Dicey?" asked Gale.

"Quiet, young lady!" said Mrs. Knightly.

"Mom, I can talk, too. Dicey is my friend," demanded Gale. "What is a dormitory?" she insisted.

"Gale, it was a jail. But I just let Daddy keep on thinking that I thought the dormitory was some kinda 'recreational facility' like he likes to call it. My Grammy died when I was seven. That was after Daddy came home from the dormitory."

"God, Dicey. I'm sorry. I've never known anyone who died. That's scary," said Gale.

"Gale Marie, we do not say God in this house!" scolded Mrs. Knightly.

"Sorry," Gale offered sheepishly. "But, was it hard, Dicey? I mean your grandma and all?"

"Yeah, it was. It was worse than when my mom left me. After that, me and Daddy moved around a lot looking for jobs. He made sure I went to a Catholic school, though. Grandma was a high school teacher. She always said, 'If you don't have an education, you don't have nothing . . . anything.' I'm going to be a teacher just like my grandma. She said I'm smart, really smart. That's because she taught me to read when I was four."

Harriet Knightly grabbed the bag of Oreo cookies from the little girl.

"Mrs. Knightly, you're looking at me like I'm crazy. It's the truth. Ask me anything. Do you know who Charles Dickens is?"

"Of course I know Dickens, dear."

"His mom and dad were put in jail because they were poor. And he was a great writer and wrote all about poor people."

"I've read Dickens, Dicey."

"Grandma talked about him a lot. *Tale of Two Cities* was her favorite book. When things got bad, she used to say, 'These are the best of times; these are the worst of times.' That's from his book. I'm going to be like Mr. Dickens." Dicey looked straight at Mrs. Knightly. "You're looking at me like you don't believe me, ma'am."

"Of course I do, dear," Mrs. Knightly said as the skin around her lips grew tighter.

"It's not angel food. My writer's name is going to be Dicey Dickens. How do you like that? My real name is Aster Rose Carmichael. But Aster Rose Carmichael isn't an interesting name. No sir. Dicey Dickens rolls right off the tongue. Don't ya think?"

Mrs. Knightly cleared her throat.

"Why do people call you Dicey," asked Gale. "I like Aster Rose better. Dicey sounds kinda like a boy's name," concluded Gale.

"It's from Daddy. He was down in Jamaica on a little trip. He was playing dominoes with an ancient medicine man. Daddy said the fella had a face like chocolate Easter egg, after you peeled off the foil. He was all wrinkly and friendly. Anyhow, my daddy beat him at dominoes. Daddy's prize was a pair of magic dice. They're red and white, here look, go ahead, touch them," Dicey said as she pulled the cubes from her pocket and rolled them across the kitchen table. Gale grabbed them.

"Wow, a real medicine man made these. Is it like voodoo?" asked Gale.

"Please, Gale. There is no such thing as voodoo," confirmed Mrs. Knightly.

"Mrs. Knightly, my dad said there was. He gave them to me before he went to the dormitory. Daddy said that the old man said that the cubes were carved from a magic tree. He told Daddy that if you listen to the voice that blows through the magic trees, you'll always roll on the right side of right. So, when I get real confused, I talk to the trees. I roll my dice, and there you go. Two whites is good. Two reds is bad. A red and a white means I need to do some more talking with the trees."

"Dicey, we don't have magic trees in Crystal Springs."

"How do you know, Mom?" asked Gale.

"I know because I know. And it's time for your piano lesson and time for Dicey to go home."

After a quart of milk and a dozen Oreos, Harriet Knightly forbade Gale to play with Dicey ever again. This would lead to a very early instance of Gale disobeying an outright order from her mother.

Mrs. Knightly's reasoning didn't make sense to her daughter. So, what if Dicey didn't have a mother? Dicey was a wonderful cook. She made the best tomato soup and grilled cheese Gale had ever tasted. She wore fresh creases in her uniform to school every-day, too. So, what if her father was a carpenter? He knew how to carve statues of the Blessed Mother Mary. Dicey kept one next to her bed, right along side the picture of her grandmother. So, what if she spent most of her time alone? Dicey always completed her homework, and she really was the smartest kid in her class at St. Matthews. She was even smarter than Gale.

Mrs. Knightly stuck her nose in the dirt whenever Dicey was involved in a "little incident" at school, which was frequently. Gale never uncovered the informant (although she suspected Sister Mary Edward); nonetheless, her mother was able to memorize the details of each incident before school was dismissed at two-thirty. Dicey's troubles were not typical smoking-in-the-bathroom-troubles. Rather, her troubles involved her unruly mouth.

Mrs. Knightly was especially peeved when Dicey informed Sister Mary Edward that "The pope isn't the only person who has God's right ear. My grandma said that little children have God's right ear, too, because they know how to listen to God. Grandma said that, by the time adults become adults, they are too busy making up their own rules to really listen to what God has to say, anyway."

Dicey's most severe altercation occurred the day that she told Sister Mary Edward that she thought everybody believed in the same God and went to the same heaven, including Jews, Baptists, Buddhists, Moslems, Native Americans and space aliens, for that matter. She told Sister Mary Edward that God just had to speak to people in different ways so they would listen to his message. Gale battled with her mother that night at the dinner table because Mrs. Knightly called Dicey "a fly-by-night Jane Fonda wannabe" who defended everything but the truth. For the first time, Gale told her mother to go to hell, but the taste of rebellion wasn't quite worth the penance. Mrs. Knightly drove Gale to early morning mass for an entire week after that fight.

Throughout high school, Dicey never ceased to voice her opinion or give words to those without a voice. And because of her perpetual near-perfect national test scores, the school hesitated in quelling Dicey too much in fear that she may transfer to another school and take her scholastic achievement test scores with her. The only time St. Matthews silenced Dicey occurred when she campaigned for a gay/lesbian club for the high school. On a Monday morning before school started, she marched in front of St. Matthews with a poster that read, "V*gin*'s deserve a voice!" It took Sister Mary Edwards about a minute to figure out that the asterisks were used in place of the letter A.

Though Aster Rose Carmichael graduated as the valedictorian of St. Matthews and was awarded scholarships to prestigious universities, Mrs. Knightly never considered the girl good enough for Gale. Because of Dicey's total acceptance of everyone from blacks to tree huggers, Mrs. Knightly was convinced that the girl would sway her daughter into becoming a "liberal haired lesbian who prayed to oak trees." Because Dicey's father was no better than a laborer who had "dealings with the law," Mrs. Knightly was convinced that Gale would become a social worker and, at best, waste her time with Dicey trying to save the homeless and drug runners.

Neither woman became a social worker. Dicey received her doctorate in English from the University of Iowa; she graduated first in her class. Gale graduated from the University of Chicago law school; she was ranked twelfth. Mrs. Knightly continued to attend daily mass and pray that Gale would find a husband.

CHAPTER 8

The modest Rose puts forth a thorn:
. . . . While the Lilly white, shall in Love Delight,
Nor a thorn nor a threat stain her beauty bright.

—William Blake, "The Lilly"

D r. Pandion named his daughter Diana Elizabeth. As soon as he saw her in the hospital bassinet squirming like a bruised worm, he regretted the decision to make her Diana's namesake. He hated everything about the child. She would be called Elizabeth, never Diana.

A series of nannies were hired to provide food, clothing and any other necessities required to maintain the child. In spite of her dispassionate life, the little girl managed to survive. Dr. Pandion worked with an international au pair organization providing services of young women for a twelve month contract, never longer. Elizabeth experienced ten nannies in ten years. Many of these young women came to America for reasons other than the children. On nights off, they gathered at January's, a steamy discotheque, learning to do The Hustle and blow lines in the bathroom stalls.

Each au pair left a lasting impression on Elizabeth. Antoinette, a nineteen year old from France, thought she was clever when she taught the three year old to say fuck in both Portugese and Dutch. The child rattled around the nursery babbling "Foda! Neuken! Foda!" Greta the German was conscientious as she tied the child to her bed before crawling onto the roof to smoke dope. Hillary from Sweden locked the six year old in the bathroom whenever Richard from Cleveland came over to foda.

Elizabeth liked her seventh nanny, Cecilia from Spain, the very best. She was an artist who gave the girl her first sketch pad and colored pencils. She watched Cecilia for hours as lines and colors joined together to form people born from just paper and pencil. She mimicked the artist with rudimentary shapes where circles became heads and triangles became necks and torsos. Rectangles formed stubby arms and legs. These anamorphous figures became the child's first friends. Elizabeth explored jungles, climbed mountains and created a land of talking elephants in her polygonal world. She created her first birthday party by drawing party hats on her five circle-headed friends and coloring seven candles on a birthday cake that was decorated with pink Crayola roses.

Because of Cecilia, Elizabeth began to live a tolerable existence with her pencils and paper. However, the seeds of destruction could not remain dormant forever. The pericarp that was silent for over eight years had seeded and was working its way toward the girl. On a chilly Sunday in November, the beast took hold and crawled up inside her. Elizabeth's spirit suffocated and died.

The tenth nanny, Ernestine from Ireland, who enjoyed copious amounts of whiskey, dozed on the couch while the child silently lost her soul. Whenever Ernestine passed-out, Elizabeth slipped inside her mother's bedroom to explore the woman whom she never was permitted to know. Since the day of

Diana's death, Dr. Pandion forbade anyone to enter the room but himself. When her father was at the hospital, however, the bedroom became Elizabeth's secret sanctuary. On restive nights, she crept into the dark, silky folds of Diana's closet and rubbed her face on the dresses searching for the scent of her mother. Sadly, the only scent she gathered was that of must and moth balls.

The only photographs of Diana were stored in the bedroom. From these pictures, Elizabeth began to draw portraits of her mother, and the pair became close allies. The child glowed as her mother planted daises and dahlias in her garden. She warned Diana about electric eels as they canoed down the Amazon in hollowed-out tree trunks. On this particular Sunday, Elizabeth was planning a dazzling tea party to introduce her mother to her circle-headed friends. She plunged into the back of Diana's closet and pulled out the gown she never dared to wear. The dress had a chiffon skirt with puffy sleeves and pearl buttons down the back. She pulled the dress over her scooter-skirt and shifted the tiny pearls above her belly so she could button up the gown.

Lost in the tea party, Elizabeth was unaware of her father's early return from his hospital rounds. As Dr. Pandion went upstairs to shower, he saw Diana's door ajar. He pushed the door open and found Elizabeth sitting at the vanity in her mother's wedding gown. She was just finishing the picture of her five friends and mother who were seated around a tea table.

For a split second, Diana appeared to be seated before the mirror. However, reality ruptured through Dr. Pandion's body, and his fist tightened in rage. Sweat balled-up on his forehead, and he lunged at his daughter. Elizabeth was knocked from the cushioned seat and reeled into the bedpost. The little girl crumbled to the floor, dazed and bleeding.

Dr. Pandion stared at the blood trickling down his daughter's face. She looked strange, like a china doll with a head too large for its body. Her arms and legs were rigid. Trembling, Dr. Pandion gathered up his daughter and lay her down on the bed. He stared at the outline of her body under the heavy dress for several seconds. The form blurred into the shape of Diana. He reached out and touched her lips. He moved his fingers down her neck, outlining the arteries that protruded with fright. Dr. Pandion closed his eyes and tried to smother the feelings that were surging through his body. He opened his eyes and looked down to find the vision of Diana.

Elizabeth was too frightened to glance up. His fingers slowly moved down her back as he pretended to ease away the pain. He stared at the petite child as if he had never seen her before. When he touched her undeveloped body, images of his mother flashed before his conscience. Tears and sweat pooled around his collar. He battled with desire and disgust. Rage and passion exploded through his loins. The debt had to be paid with yet another life. I won't give in. His shirt was drenched with sweat. I'll beat this, I can!

Droplets of sweat fell onto Elizabeth's forehead. I've won the battle for nine years. Just nine more! I will save her from the sins! The gown was becoming drenched from his perspiration. Don't touch me! He fingered the tiny buttons on the dress. Stop, Mother! Wool britches and brown buttons penetrated his mind. A soft, feminine hand slipped inside the scratchy pants. Stop, please stop! Was it too late? Never! Just nine more years, I can do it! He undid the first button of the gown, but it didn't matter, for the battle was lost many years before.

ᐯᐰ   ᐯᐰ   ᐯᐰ

Elizabeth was wedded to a new life with her father after that day. Ignorant of appropriate boundaries shared between a father and child, she never dared to protest against her father's demands. Dr. Pandion would visit Elizabeth's room late in the evening, when the lights in the carriage house were off for the night. Afterward, he sat outside on his bedroom's balcony. Sometimes he would weep. Other times he would toy with a scalpel between his fingers. He drew imaginary lines across his wrist. With just the slightest pressure, he could open the artery and every last drop of his toxic blood would drain from his body. As much as he hated his existence, he wouldn't do it. No Pandion had ever committed suicide, including his mother. It wasn't part of the price to be paid.

Dr. Pandion wanted to stop hurting Elizabeth. He loved his daughter. He really did, but it was the wrong kind of love, for it was the kind of love that conquers all. Dr. Pandion's love was the same kind of love that drives the alcoholic to cross the double yellow line. It was the same kind of love that rushes the heroin addict to kill for his next fix or the gambler to lose his home for the next royal flush. Dr. Pandion's love was the love of an addiction, not of his daughter.

☙ ☙ ☙

None of the nannies suspected the relationship between Dr. Pandion and his daughter, except for the thirteenth, Elsa from Britain, an astute academic who prided herself on proper grammar, especially regarding the use of the auspicious semi-colon. The Brit was an early riser who liked to have her washing and ironing completed well before noon. One morning while peeling the sheets from Elizabeth's bed, Elsa noticed a crusty white stain in the center of the girl's bed. She leaned across the mattress and sniffed around the marking.

Elsa stood up and grimaced. She was very familiar with the sour odor; it held the stench of bleach. In her former position, she was the nanny of four teenage boys. For six years, she washed bed sheets and boxer shorts crusted with the same noxious scent of pubescent desire.

"Damn," she whispered. "The girl's only thirteen. What kind of bloody bugger would be droppin' his drawers for that? If the doc gets wind o' this, it'll be back to Liverpool for Elsa."

She pulled the fitted sheet from the bed and bundled it with the rest of the laundry. The morning sunlight drew her to the window. The carriage house that stood directly across from Elizabeth's room was a haven for her. She would do almost anything to remain there. Liverpool was a sixteen hour day, six days a week slave driver to Elsa. She toiled as a nanny eight hours a day followed by eight hours of cleaning office buildings. If she wasn't wiping crap from some kid's bottom, she was wiping shit off a toilet seat left behind by some bloke at the insurance agency. She was through with wiping up other people's crap. She was determined to make something of herself and of her writing.

Elsa stared across the driveway and into the window of the carriage house. She spotted her teacup glistening in the sunlight. Next to the cup was *The Golden Notebook*, her favorite work of Doris Lessing. Elsa longed to have the courage of Anna Wulf, the struggling author in the story, who fought the constraints of society and finally found herself. If she was sent back to Liverpool, the only thing that she would find would be a one room, concrete flat and the same sixteen hour work day.

"I'll find the little twerp," she mumbled. Elsa turned around and stared across Elizabeth's room. She moved over to the bed and pushed it three feet to the right. She crawled to the center of the mattress and looked across the room and out the window. The tea cup was barely visible, but with a pair of binoculars, she would be able to count the hand-painted flowers that decorated the cup.

That evening, Elsa sat at the same table she saw from Elizabeth's room and sipped her tea. Periodically, she tested the view into Elizabeth's room with the binoculars that she found in the study. The moonlight slowly crawled across the sky and not until midnight did it shine into Elizabeth's room. Elsa spotted only the girl asleep in the bed.

She continued her surveillance for four more nights and found nothing. On the fifth night of her watch, Elsa was frustrated and tired. She fell into bed at one in the morning, but by three o'clock, the four cups of tea that she drank were pushing on her bladder, so she got up to pee. Heading back to bed, she grabbed the binoculars for one last peek. The waning moon shone directly into Elizabeth's room. Elsa spied two bodies entangled in the sheets.

"My God, the man's a monster," she breathed.

The next morning Elsa carefully set out Dr. Pandion's black coffee, oatmeal and prunes. She unfolded the newspaper as he liked with the *Wall Street Journal* resting on top of the *New York Times*. He entered the kitchen at 6:10, as usual.

"Good morning, Elsa," he offered.

"Sir," she returned with a nod.

Elsa pulled out the chair that sat across from Dr. Pandion. Before she could sit down, he glanced up and twitched his brow with irritation. Elsa pushed the chair back under the table but gripped its sides to steady herself. He turned back to the newspaper.

Elsa cleared her throat and said, "Sir, I know where you were last night at 3 a.m."

"Where might that be, Elsa?" Dr. Pandion asked, setting down the newspaper.

"In your daughter's bed!"

Dr. Pandion slowly raised his head and said, "No, you're quite wrong. I was in her room. Elizabeth was ill. I was caring for her."

"That's a lie. I saw you two tangled in a mess. And I have found stains on her sheets, stains left by you."

"Really, Elsa, I'm not sure what you are talking about. What's your point?"

"The point is that you've been shagging your daughter." Beads of sweat were forming on her upper lip.

"Shagging, interesting," he chuckled. "Don't try to hold me hostage with some cheap tale. If you do so, I'll have you tossed across the Atlantic as quick as you can say 'Simon Says,' and you'll never shag again."

Elsa's fingers curled around the back of the chair and her breathing grew shallow. "I can prove it," she whispered.

"Please, you're irritating me. You can prove nothing. What do you want, twenty thousand, fifty thousand? Just tell me what you want, so I can go back to reading the newspaper."

Elsa left quickly and silently that day as Dr. Pandion agreed to pay the au pair service for the entire year. Elsa rendered her own silence through a mutually agreeable yet unholy contract.

Without Elsa in the house, Dr. Pandion's addiction spun out of control. Elizabeth was tormented by his hands that pressed into every corner of her small reality. Each time her father's presence invaded her, Elizabeth crawled deeper into a dark, silent abyss. Her only medium of communication was through those people who spoke to her from pages of books or who reached out to her from the canvas. These people were familiar characters. They, too, were trapped in worlds crafted by someone else, a master to whom they were also indebted for their existence.

Elizabeth's circle-headed companions eventually grew into incongruous human forms with twisted images of little girls gripped in the jaws of half human monsters. As Elizabeth matured, the girls grew older. Young women peered down from distant windows or from unreachable parapets. The wind whipped golden hair away from their faces to expose exquisite beauty, except for a single deformity that each woman bore with grace. Where one expected a sensuous mouth, a gaping hole hung in horror with shredded tissue flapping in the wind. Elizabeth created her companions late at night, after Dr. Pandion had left his stain on her sanity.

Dr. Pandion discovered her sketch pads one evening when he entered her room earlier than usually. Proclaiming that he would not let her create monsters nor become one herself, he burned all of her materials. On that single evening, he destroyed her friends and allies but not her spirit, for that was already dead. It died years earlier, but her mind and body still lived and suffered. Without her pencil and paper, Elizabeth had nothing.

ᏬᏭ ᏬᏭ ᏬᏭ

Trapped in isolation, Elizabeth was responsible for the cooking, cleaning and anything else that her father demanded. She was setting the table one evening and pulled out a heavy table cloth from the sideboard. Fluttering to the floor was a black and white photograph of her father as a boy. Never before had she seen a picture of him or his family. He was about four years old and sitting on the lap of a petite woman with light hair. Their identical angular noses revealed that this was her grandmother. The child and mother both wore grins on their faces, as if they had just shared a secret.

She slipped the picture into her pocket and finished preparing dinner. In bed that night, she was irritated by the tinges of jealousy that kept her awake. Elizabeth wasn't jealous of her father's affection given to his mother; she was jealous because she never felt a mother's lap. She longed to have her mother back in her life, even if it was just through thick parchment and oil pastels. To quell his anger about the gruesome images and to earn back her art materials, Elizabeth began a pencil sketch for her father. She worked on the picture at night while he sat outside in the dark.

ᏬᏭ ᏬᏭ ᏬᏭ

It was an early April evening when Elizabeth was ready to unveil the drawing of her father and grandmother. She was satisfied with the detail and likeness of the picture. The marriage of the black and white hues caught the shadows and figures clinging to each other in the photograph. Even the position of the child's head resting on the mother's breast captured their intimacy.

Elizabeth promised her father a special treat for dessert that evening. When she returned to the dining room with the shrouded portrait, she was unprepared for Dr. Pandion's reaction. Elizabeth slowly slipped the sheet from the frame. When the material settled on the floor, a queer yelp spurted from her father's throat. Elizabeth shielded herself with the portrait.

"Elizabeth! How dare you?" he erupted.

She pulled the black and white photograph from her pocket and offered it to him with trembling fingers.

Dr. Pandion grabbed the photo and stormed into the kitchen. Drawers yanked open and slammed shut. Cooking utensils banged together like warning bells. A glass crashed to the floor. Then a long silence shivered across the house. Elizabeth stood still as Dr. Pandion walked back into the dining room wielding a long, thin knife. She hugged the picture closer to her chest as her father moved toward her. She tried to speak, but Dr. Pandion stopped her words as he brought the knife to the center of her chest where small breasts created a valley. With the precision of only a surgeon, he took the tip of the knife and sliced the picture down the center.

"She was a monster as I am a monster. Now you are destined to become a monster," he roared, turned around and stormed out of the room.

That night Elizabeth stiffened with a new level of fear of her father and vowed to escape her hell. She possessed only one mode of communication with the outside world; it, alone, would have to serve as her harbinger.

❦ ❦ ❦

At her high school graduation, Dr. Pandion did not clap for Elizabeth when her principal acknowledged that she was the recipient of full scholarships to four colleges including both the University of Chicago and New York University. He couldn't bare the loss. She was turning eighteen in two weeks and was free to leave his home. That evening he begged Elizabeth to accept the scholarship to Thrace University. The college, Dr. Pandion's alma mater, was just minutes from their home. He promised to never touch her again if she chose Thrace. Otherwise, he didn't know what he would do if she left him.

Elizabeth couldn't predict what her father would do if she went against his wishes, for she never had. As the silenced often do, she abandoned her dreams and did as she was told.

◕ ◕ ◕

Elizabeth had no friends on campus. The girls were put off by her muted aloofness and the boys were intimidated by her translucent beauty. Her thick, creamy hair and gray-violet eyes titillated the fraternity boys, but Elizabeth looked like the type that required too much effort. Elizabeth's only friends were loneliness and isolation, but that, too, was fine, for they had been her constant companions for eighteen years. She walked from class to class with the pair clinging tightly to her body.

Elizabeth's art history course offered her a new medium for expression. As if she was seven years old all over again and painting with Cecilia, Elizabeth found companions who accepted and understood her world. She discovered women who were captured inside frames and smothered in the rich oils of the Italian Renaissance, a time when sensuality mingled with the sacred and agony was hidden behind thin smiles.

Elizabeth talked to the women who exposed their pain through a shadow in their eye or a slight grimace in the cheek. Elizabeth told them that she understood the invasion and the destruction of their spirit. She understood the hidden scars that crippled their hearts and destroyed their desire for any other living being, scars that hurt the soul so deeply that breathing became unbearable. She understood the fear of touch, the fear of exposure and the fear of blame.

The first friend with whom Elizabeth shared her feelings was Lucretia Borgia, a young Italian girl forced into silent enslavement five hundred years earlier. Elizabeth promised Lucretia that she would discolor the guilty man who shackled her with shame for so many centuries. Elizabeth painted a gossamer haired woman entombed in a stone casket that was lined with amethyst satin. Standing over the casket was Pope Alexander VI, Lucretia's priest, father and lover, who resided over Lucretia's burial mass wearing dove grey vestments and a scarlet cap. Instead of wearing a ring engraved with his papal signet, Alexander VI's ring was adorned with the initials, *WGP.*

CHAPTER 9

Strengthen the female mind by enlarging it,
and there will be an end to blind obedience.

–Mary Wollstonecraft,
"A Vindication to the Rights of Woman"

A continuous flow of students moved in and out of Dicey's classes, but few were truly thirsty for the fluid language of the great poets and authors. Seldom did a student listen to the voice of Samuel Coleridge or William Wordsworth. She was in constant search for the student who was willing to risk a dialogue with these masters of language who challenged the heart and spirit.

When a teacher is granted that rare gift, a student who laughs out loud at Miss Elizabeth Bennett's wit or wipes away a tear when Michael Henchard requests in his Last Will and Testament that no one remembers him, including his daughter, she is profoundly gratified. Dicey received this gift one day as she read the beginning stanza of Keats' "Ode on a Grecian Urn":

What men or gods are these? What maidens loth?
What mad pursuit? What struggle to escape?

What pipes and timbrels? What ecstasy?

Dicey paused asking the class, "Someone tell me what's going on so far?" Blank stares answered back. She waited. With her palms firm against the podium, she finally pleaded, "Okay, guys, tell me what kind of struggle is going on here!" A brave soul raised his hand.

"Some guy's trying to pop the shot, ya know, close the deal." Everyone laughed.

"Yeah, you're right. But do the fair maidens want to seal the deal?"

"Sure, they all play games, act like they don't want it. It's part of the program," the young man said.

"Ladies, what do you think? Is it all part of your program, part of the chase?"

"It depends on who's doing the chasing!" a girl in the third row said. Again, the class laughed. Finally, a young woman, Elle Pandion, who sat in a stubborn silence throughout the semester, raised her hand. With hushed deliverance, she explained that the maidens were struggling to escape from an ecstasy that only pleased men, masters who were self-appointed gods. The women were muted, never permitted to express their own pain or pleasure. For eternity, the maidens were enslaved on the urn that held their ashes of desire, their ashes of love and their ashes of existence.

The girl appeared to be around twenty but the pain in her voice resonated from years of experience. Intrigued, Dicey continued, "Elle, what is your take on Keats's "Ode on Melancholy?" Dicey read aloud the last stanza of the poem to the class.

She dwells with Beauty— Beauty that must die . . .
Turning to poison while the bee-mouth sips:
Ay, in the very temple of Delight . . .

The girl's understanding of "Melancholy" was equally discon-certing and provocative. Elle suggested that Keats was exploring the bounds of pleasure and pain. One cannot grasp the blossom of life without experiencing the fields of death. One cannot taste tenderness in a kiss without first tasting blood from a bruised lip. If pain is guised in affection, the human soul can never again taste pleasure, she explained.

Dicey's arm pits felt moist. Other students shifted uncomfortably in their seats, and a few coughs cracked in the room. Dicey should have seen it coming. She went too far with the last question. The girl would regret it later. It was too much information and too much emotion. Dicey was relieved when the class ended. The young woman slipped out of the room as quietly as she slipped in.

After that day, Elle Pandion retreated back into her quietude. Not until her final paper on Mary Shelley's *Frankenstein* did she hint at the specters haunting her life. Elle portrayed the Monster as a child born into a world void of a mother and rejected by her father. The only attention bestowed on the monster-child was abusive rejection as the father reproached his child. Elle referred to the Monster as a "she" throughout the essay. Dicey wondered if the "she" was intentional; did the student purposely attempt to convey her own tragedy? If so, she wouldn't be Dicey's first student to reveal inner anguish through writing. Samantha Seine was a student in her first Feminist Themes in Literature course. Students were required to keep a journal. In her writing, Samantha fantasized about hanging herself. She envisioned tying a rope around her neck and leaping from a tree branch. Suspended in air, she would feel the freedom of death as she released her last breath of life.

Unfortunately, Dicey was too much a novice to recognize the cry for help. During exam week, Samantha hung herself in a closet with a man's belt. It was the same belt with which Samantha's father used to beat her. Samantha described the same black belt in her journal writing. Dicey promised herself never again to ignore such cries for help. She promised herself that she would never let someone like Elle Pandion end up with a suicidal sentence like Samantha Seine's.

During her following class, she requested a conference with Elle Pandion. The girl was guarded, but at least Dicey had the content of her essay from which to draw out discussion.

"Your images of a motherless child were compelling. You tapped raw emotion, emotion that I thought only a child without a mother could ever understand."

The student sat in silence. Dicey continued. "My mother left me when I was around three or four. I don't remember her. I only remember the vacancy left from not having a mother."

Elizabeth, or Elle as she preferred, explained that her mother died during child birth, her birth.

"What about your father?"

Dicey pulled out that Elle's father was a cardiovascular surgeon. Never home. She lived on campus. Art major. Grew up in Crystal Springs. She enjoyed the literature class. Her responses seemed to be nothing more than a murmur emanating from her lips. Dicey wanted to bite through steel. How can I help you if you won't share, Dicey wanted to scream.

"Your Dad's a doctor. Did he want you to be one, too?" she asked. The girl only shrugged her shoulders.

"Does he like your art?"

She shook her head with a no.

"My father wasn't too artful or too smart, but he was a good man. He stumbled in most nights at around four in the morning but always woke up to pour me a bowl of Lucky Charms before school," Dicey explained.

Elle laughed.

"He thought I studied too much, too. He would say, 'Dice, you don't want to get all them A's. Boys'll think you're too damned smart to be around.' I was bent on becoming a teacher, though, just like my grandmother. My daddy also told me to never stand around with my hands in my pocket. He said, 'People will think you're lazy or up to something you shouldn't be doing with them hands.' I really didn't get what he meant until I started teaching boys. They don't realize a teacher can see what they're doing underneath the desk with their hands stuck in their pockets, and it's not rearranging furniture!" Elle laughed, again. She seemed to be relaxing.

After their initial conference, Elle dropped by a few times a week. Dicey introduced her to artists from the Romantic period as another springboard for discussion. When Dicey offered to Elle *The Art of Henry Fuseli*, the girl was caught breathless by the illustrations. She watched closely as Elle flipped through the prints. The girl seemed transfixed by the images of sexual agony. She fingered the pictures as if anguish was actually bleeding from the pages, and she was there to quell the hemorrhaging.

Dicey wanted to break the trance that Elle seemed to have fallen under. "The pictures are riveting, aren't they? Fuseli explored a fantasia of the bizarre and sensual. He transformed art into a visionary metaphor for physical passion and physical pain, human frailty and human desire, temporal forgiveness and eternal damnation." Suddenly, she stopped. Dicey caught herself in the middle of a rambling discourse on torment, something that could easily feed into the girl's strange disposition.

She looked at Elle. Beads of perspiration were forming along the girl's hair line, but she continued to thumb through the pages. She paused at a picture of a young woman sitting on a darkened floor cradling herself. The monochromatic figure was draped in a transparent white dress with silvery white hair falling over her face. The picture's title was *Silence*. Dicey touched Elle's fingers.

"It's a powerful image. What do you think the woman was contemplating?" she asked.

The woman was trapped in a way that she'll never be able to escape.

"But how is she trapped? From where is she escaping?" Dicey nudged.

The picture wouldn't disclose the woman's anguish; the pain was hidden just below her skin's surface.

Elle's visits multiplied, and the women became friends. Dicey understood that she served as Elle's mentor but never her confidant. The girl defined a certain distance that Dicey chose to respect. As long as she wasn't strangling herself with a belt or cutting her arms with razor blades like some girls, Dicey was satisfied with the boundaries and intrigued by the friendship.

On an April afternoon, Elle stopped by Dicey's office with an invitation to her Senior Art Exhibit. Dicey accepted the invite and asked if she could bring a friend. Gale needed aesthetic exposure beyond legal briefs; the worker bee was running out of honey. Dicey also wanted to meet Dr. Pandion, Elle's father. Begrudgingly, Gale agreed to accompany Dicey to the exhibit. The friends chattered as they walked across campus, inhaling honeysuckle. Anything but blossoming life greeted Gale and Dicey at Elle's show.

"Happy thoughts," Gale mused. "I need Norman Rockwell, not Picasso's early dark period."

"You don't know Rockwell from Raphael. So, be quiet. I want you to meet Elle. I think she needs a few friends."

"I think she needs a little more help than our guns can offer, Dicey. This stuff is damn depressing. It's Friday night, not a funeral dirge."

"C'mon." Dicey dragged Gale over to Elle who was standing with an art professor. Her description was accurate. The young woman seemed translucent. Gale eyed her. If the wind blew too hard, a feather could drive a hole straight through Elle's stomach and reach her spine.

"Hi, I'm Gale Knightly," she said, sticking out her hand. Gale was met with a grip that vanished in her own strong fingers. She felt manly standing next to the waif and wasn't quite sure if she liked her or not.

Elle introduced the small group of guests to her most haunting painting that was entitled, *My Last Duchess*. It was painted at her father's desire and represented Dr. Pandion kneeling by the coffin of his dead wife. Dicey asked, "Elle, the title, how did you come up with that?" The woman hesitated, and then explained that Dr. Pandion referred to his wife as Duchess. Bull Duchess, Dicey wanted to say. "My Last Duchess" was the title of a Browning poem about a Duke who attempts to marry a fourteen year old after knocking off his first two wives. Dicey knew that Elle was aware of the poem because she taught it to her. She wanted to stay and study the picture, but Gale pulled her arm to follow the group of guests.

The next painting beheld a woman stretched across a huge boulder. The lighting was intriguing. As the sun set in the west, the woman stared at the moon hanging in the eastern sky, watching for the new dawn to break.

"Elle, this is so . . . peaceful . . . I like it," Gale said with surprise.

"Yeah," Dicey said, perturbed at Gale, whose attorney's eye appeared to miss detail that would never escape her if it was a piece of evidence. Didn't Gale notice the droplets of blood on the woman's thigh and a pink stain on the edge of her gown? The girl wore a signet ring on her left hand bearing an illegible letter. The same girl was featured in the next piece and was tethered to a looming sycamore with a scarlet cord. From the west, the moon shone a lurid glow upon the girl; from the east, the rising sun competed for attention. She was wearing the same ring.

"Elle, what are these pictures called?" asked Dicey. The two pictures were a set entitled *Hyperion Lights*. The woman was a muse; she was the sun and the moon and the dawn to her lover.

"Who is the muse and who is the lover?" asked Dicey.

Irritated by the question still dangling in the air, Gale whispered into Dicey's ear, "Not that I don't like the pictures, but I'd like a glass of wine and pizza to be my muse right about now. Up for it?"

Dicey responded by rolling her eyes. One of her motivations for showing up hadn't arrived. "Is your father coming tonight, Elle?" she finally asked to quell Gale's impatience. A shake of the head indicating no was the only answer provided from the artist.

As the two friends walked back across campus that evening, Gale was testy. "I'm not trying to be rude, but did we really have to waste a Friday night with a struggling artist who paints like she's the only person who understands pain and has to show the world about it?"

"That sure is a mouthful of nastiness," Dicey said with a snip.

Gale just shook her head and walked on. Elle was going to be another one of Dicey's needy projects who bolts as soon as she sucks dry the pools of generosity from her best friend.

👁👁 👁👁 👁👁

Blowing cool air on her mocha latte one evening, Dicey asked Gale, "Do you think Dr. Pandion killed his wife and Elle's hiding it."

Gale coughed as hot liquid burned her throat. "No, she died while delivering Elle. She's told us at least that much in the past few years. Remember, it was a failing placenta or something."

"I remember, but he probably punched her in the stomach while she was pregnant and ruptured her."

"My God, Dicey, you're sick. I think that your literary imagination needs a little reality check. OB/GYNS detect trauma. Think of a different angle?" Gale said, biting into her crumbly scone.

"We all have our own coping mechanisms to shut out pain. Elle's is through art. I think she paints about her life in her pictures."

Between bites of her pastry, Gale warned Dicey. "Be careful not to make her life the storyline for one of your books. If she gets wind of that, her flimsy trust in people may completely dissolve."

"I'm not going to make her a story line. We've been friends with her for two years, now, and every time the word "father" pops up, she still turns into a pasty mute. Whenever we're together, I always ask, 'So, how is your dad? Seen him lately?' And, there she goes, turns into wet bread dough. Not pretty."

"Elle's fine," Gale offered out of both frustration and boredom with trying to figure out their strange and obscure friend. As a diversion, she moved on and told Dicey about an invitation from Ken Tereus.

"Dr. Tereus, Ken, asked me to invite a few friends to a cocktail party. Will you go? Elle agreed to go."

"Gale," Dicey moaned, "you know how I hate that social-lite shit. Don't make me go."

"Please, I want your take on Ken. I may be interested in him."

"I trust your judgment. You don't need my opinion."

"Yes, I do," pressed Gale.

"Then, there must be something about the guy that's bugging you."

"Dicey, I just want you to meet him."

"Tell the truth, what is it?"

"Nothing."

"I won't go unless you tell me."

"It is nothing, really."

"Tell me."

"Okay . . . we've gone out a handful of times, and he's never done anything."

"What do you mean?"

"Physical. The only thing he's touched is my elbow, and the only thing he's given me is a peck on the lips," Gale said as she stirred her coffee.

"Hmm. It sounds like he is either gay or married."

"Divorced, and he talks about other women."

"He's gay. Window dressing is my guess."

"I don't think so."

"What's his house like?"

"I've never seen it."

"There you go, Gale. The guy's married. He can't take you home because wifey's there. He's lying."

"Dicey, the party is at his house. C'mon, you have to go," begged Gale.

Instead of agreeing to go to the party, Dicey asked about Dave Broadbeck, Gale's on-again-off-again boyfriend since law school.

"What about Chicago Dave, when was the last time you saw him?"

"It's been a few months."

"Why so long?"

"I don't know." Gale looked down at her plate. She picked a blueberry from her scone and squished it.

"Is that a straight 'I don't know'?" Dicey asked, nudging her friend's foot with her boot.

"Sure," Gale said reluctantly.

"Are you off-again?" Dicey asked. "It's hard to keep track of what's going with you two."

"Honestly, I don't know where the relationship is headed."

"Gale, you haven't known for six years where the relationship is headed," Dicey said a bit too caustically.

"Be nice. You're supposed to support me, not tear me apart."

"I'm not trying to hurt you; I'm trying to help. I'm finally going to be straight with you about Dave Broadbeck."

"Since when haven't you been straight with me about him? Isn't it you who said that we need to either 'shit or get off the pot'? That's pretty straightforward."

"Did I really say that?"

"Yes! Several times, and you know it."

"Well, then, I'll say it again. You two need to either shit or get off the pot. You've dated him since your first year in law school. For God's sake, that's six years."

"No, it's been seven years, eleven months and twenty days."

"You even count the days! Why are you wasting your time with Sonny-the-surgeon when you're still in love with Dave Broadbeck? Mick Jagger could ask you out and you still wouldn't be interested."

"Mick Jagger?"

"You know what I mean. Be honest with yourself. You're not going to give anyone a chance until you make a decision about Dave."

"What do you think I should do— dump a thriving law practice and move to Chicago based on a hope and a prayer?"

"I'm not saying that you need to move. Just figure out, once and for all, if you two have a shot at getting married. If not, move on with your life."

"Dice, you know what it is. If he would just say those three little words, I would consider turning my life up-side-down for him. I would have stayed in Chicago after law school if he told me that he loved me. But he never has."

"Have you ever told him that you love him?"

"I tried a few times, but he always found a way to change the subject. He won't talk about his feelings in the same way that he won't talk about his mother's death. I think I told you that she died when he was eleven."

"I don't know what to tell you. Maybe he is emotionally stunted. Losing a mother can really mess with your emotions. My mom might as well have been dead, but I had Grandma. If it weren't for Grammy in my life when I was a kid, I'd now be a psychiatrist's worst nightmare."

Gale laughed. "You're probably right. But at least you talk about it. I don't know how to get Dave to talk about his feelings, and I'm tired of guessing."

"Are you ready to move on?"

"That's the billion dollar question that I've been asking myself for four years. That's why I'm pushing myself to date other people. Maybe that will help me shit or, at least, find another pot!"

"I hope so. It's about time," Dicey said. Then, she narrowed her focus to the pastry on Gale's plate. "Are you going to eat that scone or destroy it? I'm still hungry."

Gale lifted her plate into midair. "You can have all that is left if you go to Ken Tereus' party with me."

"Sure. I'll be waiting on pins and needles, until the day arrives!" Dicey grabbed the scone and stuffed half the pastry into her mouth.

"You're very funny."

CHAPTER 10

Man's a strange animal, and makes strange use
Of his own nature, and the various arts,
And likes particularly to produce
Some new experiment to show his parts...

—George Gordon, Lord Byron,
Don Juan, Canto I.

Gale demanded Dicey and Elle to be on time for Ken's party.

"Honey, I'm not obsessive-compulsive like you, and I'm not going to be the first to arrive at a party that I don't want to go to. I'll be at your house around eight," argued Dicey.

"The party starts at eight. Dice, please. I don't want to drive by myself," said Gale.

"Elle and I will be at your house at seven-fifty, no earlier."

Even Dicey was a little surprised by Ken's home, a regal, three-story brick colonial overlooking the city. The interior was a collection of exquisite antiques from the Ming Dynasty to the

69

Federalist period. The home and its belongings contrasted with the energy that sprung from Ken Tereus. Dicey felt the electricity in the room change when he greeted them.

"Welcome to my home. Gale, you look spectacular."

Dicey watched his eyes wandering to Elle as he complimented Gale. Keep your eyes to your slimy self is what she wanted to say, as she toyed with the snake-eyed cubes in her pocket.

Ken greeted Elle and said, "Gale tells me you're Dr. Pandion's daughter. I've worked with him on a few trauma cases. Superior doctor."

She responded with a smile.

Turning to Dicey, "I understand you're a teacher at Thrace," Ken said.

He refuses to acknowledge that my title is doctor, the same as his, Dicey thought and said, "Yes, I'm a professor of anthropology. I study the mating patterns of the aboriginal pygmy population."

Ignoring her answer, Ken turned to Elle saying, "Gale also tells me you're quite the artist. I have a lovely collection of 18th century miniatures I would like to show you." Taking her elbow, Ken escorted Elle to a cherry curio cabinet across the room.

Gale dragged Dicey into the dining room.

"What are you doing? I told him that you're an English professor. Please don't get on one of your high horses tonight," pleaded Gale.

"Oh God, he won't remember diddley about me. I'm just having a little fun. Loosen up," said Dicey.

"Just be nice. Now, tell me, what do you think? Do you like him?"

"Gale, I just met the guy. Give me a chance," Dicey lied.

"C'mon, it takes you all of three seconds to size up a man."

"The statues of animal heads in the foyer are a little strange, but other than that, I like his house. Look at these tiny jars over here." As Dicey was reaching for one of the porcelain bottles, Ken walked back into the dining room with Elle.

"Don't touch!" he demanded.

Dicey jumped from his rebuke. "Sorry."

"I didn't mean to be so loud," he apologized. "But they're rare snuff bottles and are quite delicate. The one you picked-up was recently acquired for $43,000.00." He then added with a chuckle, "Maybe I should have a Do Not Touch sign on the buffet."

After he walked away, Gale again asked both of her friends what they thought about Ken. Elle just stood there with a strange blush that diffused over her cheeks.

Curbing her tongue, Dicey whispered, "Don't get your hopes up– the guy is gay."

"What are you talking about? He's been married, for God's sake."

"Yeah, and so have a lot of other gay men. Look at his house. How many guys collect tiny porcelain bottles displayed in fancy, shmancy curio cabinets?"

"Why do you have to be so cynical?" Before she received an answer, Gale spotted Hank Daimon. "Look who is here. It's Hank Daimon's. He's like sandpaper. Dicey, you'll love him. C'mon, I'll introduce you."

As Gale waved, Hank approached their circle. "Did I play matchmaker, Gale. Are you Ken's date tonight?" he asked.

"Not exactly, Hank. Please meet my friends, Dicey Carmichael and Elle Pandion."

"Are you related to Dr. Pandion?" asked Hank.

Elle nodded.

"Would you please tell him that Hank Daimon said hello. He has testified for me on several malpractice cases over the years. I'm a lawyer."

"And what do you do Miss Carmichael?" said Daimon turning toward Dicey.

"I'm an English professor at Thrace."

"Ah, 'We few, we happy few, we band of brothers, for he who lives and dies with me, is truly my brother,'" recited Daimon.

"The Bard, Mr. Daimon, *Henry V*, I believe," Dicey said, wondering why people felt compelled to quote literature when they learned her profession.

"William Shakespeare was the master of emotions, the master of deceit and disclosure. I often quote him in the court room. Juries love it."

"Maybe I should invite you to lecture for my students. Someone needs to impart the importance of literature and language in the real world."

"It would be a pleasure. Call me at the office," he said pulling out his wallet for one of his business cards.

"I think I might just do that."

The conversation with Hank was the highlight of Dicey's evening. For the first time, she met a man who had a reason to quote Shakespeare. After that, she watched as Tereus slithered around Elle. She knew that he wasn't gay and wondered what Gale saw in him. She never went for the pretty boys.

With every ounce of superficiality drained from her system, Dicey begged to leave at ten. Elle also had to meet her father for a late dinner after his rounds. When Ken offered to escort Gale home, Dicey was relieved.

CHAPTER II

My heart aches and a drowsy numbness pains
My senses, as though of hemlock I had drunk,
Or emptied some dull opiate to the drains . . .

—John Keats, "Ode to a Nightingale"

Gale begrudgingly woke as the sun prodded her eyes open. She peered around the room and was alert enough to recognize from the Irish linens and the four poster bed that she wasn't in her own bedroom. She was wearing her now crumpled cocktail dress from the night before. She focused in on the clock sitting on the dresser.

"My God, it can't be two o'clock in the afternoon!" Gale moaned. As she pulled herself from bed, a faint knock sounded from the door.

"Come in," she whispered.

"Hey sunshine, feeling better?" asked Ken politely.

"What happened last night?"

"I guess you had a few too many martinis," he offered, relaxing against the doorframe.

"I don't drink martinis," answered Gale. She remembered drinking only a few glasses of wine.

"Well, it hit you like a bulldozer, so I put you to bed."

"Did I embarrass myself?"

"I don't think so. No one would have known the difference."

Gale was too mortified to ask any more questions. She wanted to be anywhere but standing there with puffy eyes and bad breath.

When she sat down to pee, her body burned and her stomach flip-flopped. "God, how much poison did I pour into my system last night? I've got to get out of here." Steaming oatmeal and coffee were waiting for Gale when she went down to the kitchen. Dragging the spoon through her cereal, she apologized about her behavior.

In Ken's car on the way home, she again offered, "I rarely drink too much. It must have knocked me from here to church and back. I'm very sorry, Ken."

"Don't worry about it," he said glibly.

Pulling up to her apartment, Ken informed Gale that he was leaving for Thailand on Monday for an extended vacation.

"I must say that that comes as a bit of a surprise. You never mentioned a trip to Asia."

"I do it a few times a year. I'm sorry if I didn't mention it." He bent over and pecked Gale on the cheek as if to dismiss her.

Gale silently climbed out of the car and shuffled away. She wanted to yell, "You bastard! Just because I had little too much to drink you say, 'Adios'. Then, out of the clear blue sky, you gotta go to Asia— do it every year. Well, I've dated you for almost two months, and you've never mentioned Thailand. You're a weirdo, anyway. Something's wrong with a man who pecks a girl on the cheek instead of pecking her with his pecker. No wonder you're not married at forty-five. Who wants to marry an uptight surgeon who collects queer, flowered bottles, anyway? And on top of that, you yelled at my best friend, you pig. What a low-life loser. It's no wonder Dicey didn't like you. She read straight through your phony ass!" That is what Gale really wanted to shout, but she couldn't, because Mrs. McCafferty, who was weeding her flower beds, would hear, and Gale had had enough embarrassment for one life, let alone one day.

CHAPTER 12

I was angry with my friend:
I told my wrath, my wrath did end.
I was angry with my foe:
I told it not, my wrath did grow.

—William Blake, "The Poison Tree"

After Ken dropped her off, Gale walked in the front door, crawled into her bed and fell into a deep slumber. When she woke up, the clock on her night stand read seven-fifteen. She bolted upright and jumped from her covers. "Shit! I've got a deposition at eight." She ran to the bathroom, turned on the shower and tore off her clothes. The water was ice cold, and she cringed. She soaped down her body, rinsed and jumped out of the shower. "Just hurry!" She pulled her hair back in a pony tail, dusted blush on her cheeks and swiped on mascara. The clock read seven twenty-three. Two minutes later Gale was dressed in a grey flannel suit and black heels.

Her stomach grumbled. "I've got five minutes," she breathed. Gale darted to the kitchen, yanked milk from the refrigerator and Cheerios from the cabinet. Standing at the counter, she dumped both into the cereal bowl and began to munch. After, three or four bites, she took a deep breath and sighed, "I'll make it."

She flicked on the counter top television to grab a glimpse of what she missed yesterday. It was Mike Adams, *CNN*'s financial correspondent, analyzing heated comments from Alan Greenspan that were televised on *Meet the Press* earlier in the day. "What? This morning? What the hell?" Gale zeroed in on the time located in the lower left corner of the screen. Seven thirty-three p.m., Eastern Standard Time.

"Shit, it is still Sunday!" she screamed. "I can't do a damn thing right."

She grabbed her bowl of cereal and plunked down at the table for dinner, instead of breakfast. She watched Mike Adams blab on about Greenspan's loose credit policies and how the former Federal Reserve chairman destroyed U.S. financial markets for years to come. The screen blurred as tear drops slid down Gale's cheeks.

"So, Greenspan can screw up, too. At least he knows what day it is."

She reached for a towel from the counter and blew her nose into the rough terry cloth. When she opened her eyes, the picture taped onto the refrigerator was staring at her. The photo was of Dave and her taken at Chicago's Navy Pier. It was shot in August, the last time they were together. Tears welled up again. It seemed like piles of unspoken words stood between them during that weekend. She wondered what he couldn't tell her then or even now.

He hadn't called on Friday, the only time when he had forgotten to call on the anniversary of their first date, and his phone calls had dwindled to two or three times a month. Maybe that's why she drank the martinis last night.

Gale dragged the spoon through the soggy cereal. Dave liked his cereal almost dry, smothered with sugar and a sliced banana. He drank his coffee black. She loved his scent in the morning, a hint of cologne mixed with sleep and body heat. Delicious. Ken Tereus was so different from Dave. He was so refined, almost feminine. "What was I thinking," she said to herself. "Dicey is right. I've got to figure things out with Dave, once and for all."

She stood up and poured out the remains of her Cheerios into the sink. She picked up her cell phone, held it for a few seconds, and dropped it back onto the counter. The third time she dialed his number. He answered with Sunday night football blaring in the background.

"Hey, Dave, it's Gale.

"Hi, babe, how are you?"

"Great!" She yelled over the noise in the background. "Happy knowing you for eight years."

"Ah, man. I'm sorry for not calling. I just got back from a job in the Dominican Republic. I'm all screwed up with times and dates."

"It's okay. Listen . . . ."

"Hot damn!" he yelled into the receiver.

"What's going on?"

"The Bears are spanking the Giants. It is killer!"

"Great. Hey, do you want a visitor this weekend? I need to get out of here!" she yelled back into the receiver.

"I'm busy Saturday. Come up Thursday and Friday, instead."

"Okay," her voice fell slightly. "That works for me."

"Damn!" he yelled again.

"What?"

"The Giants are driving again."

"I'll see you Thursday around four o'clock. Should I come to your office or apartment?"

"Come to the office. Dad misses you."

"I'll be there. Call if anything changes."

As God's punishment for her bacchanal display at Ken Tereus's party, Gale had to trudge through a week of human waste.

"Thank God tomorrow's Thursday," she said to herself as she finished reading a wrenching deposition. The case concerned the death of a thirteen-year-old girl who died because an ER doc refused to listen to the mother.

William Osler, the great father of medicine, said, "Listen to the patient, you will get your diagnosis." That should be a part of the Hippocratic Oath, Gale thought, or at least, "listen to the child's mother." How many doctors destroyed lives by ignoring such a simple rule?

Julia Rheinhart suffered from Marfan's Syndrome, a rare but manageable vascular condition that can weaken the wall of the aorta. She entered the hospital with stomach, chest and jaw pain, classic symptoms of aortic dissection. Nonetheless, the doctor ignored the mother's demands that the pain was related to her Marfan's condition. The walking hubris-in-scrubs attributed Julia's discomfort to gastroenteritis or the stomach flu. Julia died six hours later from an aortic dissection, a death easily prevented by surgical intervention if the doctor had only listened to the mother. What jury would have a bone of sympathy for the doctor or the hospital? Dicey's little talisman would, no doubt, roll a double red on this one, she concluded closing the file.

Platinum letters displaying The Broadbeck Group welcomed Gale as the elevator doors opened. When Dave came from around the reception desk to greet her, she held him tighter than usual.

"God, you smell good," she breathed into his ear while standing on her tip toes. Dave was 6'2" with broad shoulders, thick black hair and a perpetual glow bug smile.

"What a welcome, babe!"

"I really needed to see you."

"My little G never needs any guy, including me," he gently teased. "Is everything okay?"

"Yeah, just some rough cases," she lied.

"C'mon. Dad wants to see you before he leaves. He's flying to New York in an hour."

As the pair headed toward his office, Tom Broadbeck rumbled down the hall, pulled Gale into his arms and lifted her off her feet.

"Where've you been, Galey? It's been too damn long, and you're too damn skinny. I can feel your ribs," Tom said as he squeezed her. "Dave's right. That uppity firm of yours is working you too hard. Come work for me, and I won't drive you to the bone."

"Then, I'd have to live up to the way you push yourself."

Gale loved Tom Broadbeck. He packed more common sense and hard work into an afternoon than most people did in a year. He created a multi-hundred million dollar company with a few bucks, a high school education and the ability to tie steel and run concrete. He possessed a keen insight into human motivation and desire. He managed crews and served his customers like a sheep dog nudging them right where he wanted. Dave inherited his father's happy disposition, but as a second generation rich kid, the fire under his feet hadn't quite ignited, and that worried Gale.

Tom released Gale from the hug but held tightly to her hand. "Seriously, why have you been away so long, my dear? You know I can't plan a wedding without a bride," he said teasingly as he led her into his office.

"Dad, cool it. You can't negotiate everything."

☙❧ ☙❧ ☙❧

Dave's apartment was just a few blocks from the office and Chicago's Gold Coast. An off-duty police officer stood at the entrance door instead of Ricardo the doorman, whom Gale had known for years. "What's up with the cop?"

"It's extra security."

"Why? Where's Ricardo? I thought he never had a day off. Just think of the secrets he must keep about people's lives."

"He had lips of steel."

"What do you mean had?"

"He took a bullet through the head for twenty bucks on a crisp September day. Not a cloud in the sky and boom, he's dead. He left a wife and a kid."

"My God, that's horrific."

"Tragic. The sad thing is that there's always some other nut ten steps behind. You can be eating a burger at McDonalds or falling asleep in a chemistry class and boom. Shot dead by an angry idiot who was beat up by his dad or bullied by some punk in the seventh grade. Hell, look what priests have done to screw up kids. Everybody's got their reason to be angry. Couples have to think twice about bringing kids into the world," Dave said as the elevator doors opened at his floor.

"Did they get the guy?"

"Yeah, he was ignorant enough to try to use Ricardo's ATM card. They caught him on camera. It doesn't matter, though. Ricardo's dead for a twenty."

"But it does matter. We've got to figure out a way to make this a better place so we can bring kids into this world," she said at Dave's back.

"Gale, sorry, but you sound like an old Coca-Cola commercial. You know the one about teaching people to sing in harmony, so the world can be a better place. Kids are singing about drugs and gangs and guns, not harmony. Real life isn't Crystal Springs, Ohio," Dave said while he unlocked his apartment door.

"Life and chaos exist in Crystal Springs, Dave. I deal with it everyday."

"I know you do, but Chicago is different. So, tell me about your week from hell," Dave said as he dropped her luggage on the floor.

"Let's not talk about death or pain or my week right now," Gale said as she folded into the curve of Dave's chest. "I am terribly sorry about Ricardo, but I've been dealing with a death case of a little girl, and I need a mental break from tragedy and mortality." Gale unknotted Dave's tie and worked her fingers inside his starched shirt. Pulling the tails from his trouser and unbuttoning his cuffs, she was free to remove his jacket and shirt in one sweeping movement. She wrapped her arms around his bare back and climbed up his chest. She sucked a nipple between her teeth and swirled her tongue around the firm tissue.

"Lord, that's nice," Dave said softly. He lifted her legs up round his waste and walked into the bedroom.

After they made love, Dave dozed off and Gale toyed with the hair that covered his chest. She called his upper body her playground, and she missed it like a kid misses July in the dead of February. As she lay next to him, Ken Tereus crossed her mind. The guy was yet another unsuccessful stab at moving on with her life, but she couldn't. He must have sensed her lack of sincerity. The man wasn't obtuse. She was the one who should give him the break. Why would a gorgeous and successful man beat the door down for sex when he could have any woman in the world? He had no need to play games. If truth be told, she never showed an overt interest in having sex with him, so how could she have expected him to pursue her. Honestly, he let her off the hook easier than others. "Ice princess" or "frigid as a fish" were words that she had heard more than once from men. The fact of the matter is that Gale had made love with only one man in her life and wanted to make love with only one man.

She nestled her head against Dave's chest and listened to his steady breathing. From the depths of her subconscious, "I love you" murmured from her lips. Gale's eyes shot open, and her breathing ceased. Blood pounded through her ears like war drums. Did Dave's own breathing change? Did his eyelids flicker? Did he hear the words that had always remained suppressed between them? Reckless, reckless, reckless roared inside her head. Eventually, Gale's heart rate slowed as Dave's breathing remained the same.

Certain that he was still asleep, she scooted to the edge of the bed, stood up and took a deep breath. She pulled open his closet door to grab Fred, a tattered flannel robe that always hung on the back of the door. The state of his closet stopped Gale dead in her tracks. His shoes were tidily tucked in new cubbies with wooden shoe horns. Ties hung from racks and were organized by color. Dave's suits were neatly divided between summer and winter wear, and there wasn't a single pair of dirty underwear piled on the floor.

"Interesting," Gale whispered as she padded to the kitchen. When she opened the refrigerator door, equal surprise shot back. His moldy collection of Styrofoam boxes with half eaten sandwiches was replaced with a row of apples and oranges and a plastic container labeled "tuna casserole" in a feminine script. Organic milk and two bottles of cranberry juice filled the top shelf.

"Somebody must have a urinary tract infection," mused Gale. She slapped the door closed and noticed, for the first time, what was hanging from the front of the refrigerator. It was a typed paper held by a magnetic clip and labeled with a pink sticky note that read, "David, could you proofread my essay over the weekend. It's due on Tuesday. See ya, BFF. ♡ Mimi."

"Very clever. 'See ya, BFF.' Unbelievable. BFF. I wonder if the little protégée is also the cook, maid, and lover," Gale whispered.

Dave's cell phone rang, and Gale jumped. She headed back down the hall but slowed when she heard his voice.

"Damn, Spike, I forgot! Yeah, I'll be there. Give me an hour," Dave said. He then added, "Gale's in town." There was a long pause. Dave finally said, "No, it will be fine."

From the bedroom door, Gale asked what would be fine. Spike was throwing a birthday bash for his girlfriend, Mandy. Dave assured Gale that Spike wanted to see her. The lie hung in the air between them. Spike had always referred to Gale as "Tick-tock" because she was so tightly wound. In turn, she called Spike "Gatsby", but he thought the name was a compliment.

Spike was the guy in the crowd who kept all of his college buddies from marrying for as long as possible, so he could maintain his entourage. When one of the boys would finally break free, Spike was the "best friend" who hired a stripper for the bachelor party. Consider it a wedding gift, he would say. Whenever Gale and Dave took a "hiatus" during law school, Spike always had his brood of women ready and willing to fill up Dave's empty time. Rational or not, Gale blamed Spike, in part, for Dave's inability to move off the double yellow line. He had to keep all lanes open and moving.

☙☙ ☙☙ ☙☙

Stale beer and deep fried onion rings smacked Gale in the face as they walked into Rancho Diablo. It had been seven or eight years since she was last there, but the rancid smell and black vinyl bar stools remained the same. Even back then, she couldn't handle the stench of a college bar. She hated when her shoes stuck to the floors caked with hot wing sauce and spilled beer. The cigarette smoke made her feel like a human ashtray.

Gale spotted Spike saddled up to the bar with a litter of blondes crowded around him. His head was thrown back with laughter, and his blue eyes glistened with too much alcohol. One of the blondes, whose markings were indistinguishable from the other girls, yelped when she saw Dave.

"Yo, Rodeo! Ready to ride? I'm twenty-one, now!"

"Must be talkin' to you, cowboy," Gale muttered under her breath.

"She's talking about the mechanical bull. That's Mandy, Spike's girlfriend," he said.

As they approached, Spike yelled, "Hey, Tick-Tock. It's been a long time." Mandy and her friends gave a knowing giggle.

"Too long, but it doesn't seem like I've missed too much, Spike." For a split second, a shadow crossed over his face.

Gale scanned the crowd. Flanked by college girls, she felt like a pair of clogs in a pile of pink stilettos. She slumped up against the bar and motioned to the server. No Chardonnay. There was only one type of white wine at $4.50 a glass. She ordered a club soda. After last weekend, she didn't need to drink, anyway. Ken's party was worlds away from the Rancho Diablo. She watched Dave as he gripped the reins of the mechanical bull and yelled, "Ride em', Cowboy!" to his groupies.

The party ended by ten-thirty because the next morning Mandy had a nine o'clock communications class, and there was going to be a quiz on a chapter that she hadn't read. Dave and Gale were back in his apartment by eleven, and he was sound a sleep fifteen minutes later. Gale rolled over on her side and squeezed the pillow. Maybe it's me. Maybe I've really lost that bling-bling. How can I compete with Spike's girls or BFF, whether I live in Crystal Springs or Chicago?

Dave's alarm clock went off at five-thirty. He pulled Gale close and kissed the back of her head. "I'm going to the gym. Do you want to come or sleep some more?" he whispered. She turned over and gently bit his bottom lip. "I'll go, but do you have a few minutes first?" He had more than a few minutes.

Dave cleared his entire schedule for the day to spend time with her. He stared down at his bagel and cream cheese when he told her about his plans to go to the Art Institute and then to the Claude Monét Café for lunch. They went to the same museum and diner on their very first date, eight years earlier. Gale reached across the breakfast table and grabbed his hand. She breathed into his palm and kissed it. "Dave, it sounds delightful."

"Gale, I appreciate what you did last night. I know that a deposition on tax evasion would have been more fun for you than hanging out with Spike and his gaggle. You could have been a jerk, but you weren't. It meant a lot to me."

"Dave, it was fine. I would have rather had you to myself, but my trip was short notice. I understand."

"Thank you. I mean it."

"Mandy is young but seems nice."

"She's great. Spike has fallen head over heals in love. She is young but smart and ambitious, too."

"And gorgeous."

"And gorgeous. She's an intern at WGN. The station has offered her a job after she graduates in June. Here's the real kicker, Gale. Spike told me last night that he bought an engagement ring. He's proposing at Christmas."

Gale's mouth fell open. "I am filled with nothing less than shock and awe. The Bastion of Bachelorhood is getting married? Honestly, I can't believe it."

"It's the God's honest truth. He's been talking to me about marrying her for the past six months. He wants to have time for an extended honeymoon before she starts her job at the station."

"Amazing," Gale said breathlessly.

Chicago's bitter winds swirled around Dave and Gale as they headed east on Michigan Avenue. She pulled her scarf high around her face and burrowed her head deep into her coat. The wind was too severe for the pair to talk as they walked toward the museum, and Gale was glad of that. She needed time to process Spike's pending engagement. Her heart hurt from disappointment. Maybe Spike wasn't the reason for Dave's reluctance to ever talk about a future.

Gale spotted the giant marble lions that guarded the Art Institute of Chicago. She raced toward the warmth and distraction of the museum. Dave checked their coats and laced his fingers through hers as they headed up the wide stairs to the Impressionism collection. Cassatt and Renoir were Gale's favorites, so he led her first to Cassat's *The Child's Bath*. She was drawn to the painting with a private sense of melancholy. The mother held the child with a firm arm while she gently bathed the feet with her free hand.

"You'll be like that mother," Dave said in her ear. Gale squeezed his hand but said nothing. How could she?

They worked their way toward the Miniature Room collection located in the basement of the museum. It was a fascinating peek into over fifty miniature rooms scaled from European and American homes from the thirteenth century in Europe to the early twentieth century in America.

As they strolled through the collection, Dave and Gale argued over their preference of interiors. Surprisingly, he preferred the ornate Renaissance decor while she preferred the sparsely furnished cottage kitchens with large hearths. He argued that the Renaissance rooms embodied a time of art, science, life and celebration. Gale argued that the kitchen, with its hearth, was the heartbeat of any home. Without the kitchen, the Renaissance would never have been ignited. They agreed to disagree and settled on the Claude Monét Café.

Gale's pulse raced as she crossed through door of the tiny café. Dave walked straight to the table where they first sat eight years earlier, the table where she first fell in love with him. Gale stood up on her tip-toes and kissed him.

"This is nice," she said quietly.

They sat down, and Dave ordered a bottle of wine. The place was weathered but hadn't really changed. The cheesy charm was still there with the fake Monet oils decorating the walls. Dave asked why she seemed subdued.

"I'm not. Maybe it's my case with Julia Rheinhart. That's always hanging over my head." Gale lied. "Give me a glass of wine, and I'll snap out of it."

Dave poured the wine and raised his glass. "Here is a toast to your random trips to Chicago and that one day you may consider staying longer than just a few days." Gale smiled and asked what he meant.

"Gale, have you ever thought about moving back to Chicago?"

"No," she said. "What would be my motivation? I like my job, and my friends and family are back at home."

"How about you and me," Dave said looking into his glass.

"What do you mean?"

"If you moved here, we could hang out longer than two or three days."

"I've got a lot of vacation stock piled. I just need to be a better planner. Why don't we fly down to the Bahamas between Christmas and New Year's?"

"I mean longer than a week or two or a trip to an island. Maybe we should finally see if we could make it stick."

"Dave, I couldn't quit my job and move just to see if we could date."

"Gale, I'm not talking about dating. I'm talking about getting married."

"Wow, honey. This is a shock, to say the least. Give me a moment, here." Gale picked up her glass and swirled the wine in circles. "Dave, can I ask how long you have been thinking about this. Your phone calls have been a little sparse lately, and we haven't seen or touched each other in two or three months."

1JACQUELINE M. LYON

"Does it matter how long I've thought about it? We've been together for eight years. And Dad would be elated. This is what he has always wanted."

"What about you? What have you always wanted, Dave? I love your dad, but this is about us, not about making him happy. Have you forgotten that I am leaving in the morning because you have a date tomorrow night? I just need to understand."

"Gale, you gave me three days notice, and yes I do have plans, but it's not like that."

"Are you telling me that you don't date other women?"

"Of course, I'm not saying that. I date anybody and everybody but really no one."

"Then, who is Mimi and why is your house so damn clean?"

"Mimi is Ricardo's daughter. She's taken a liking to me since her dad was shot. I try to give her a little direction when I can. Maria, Mimi's mom, cleans apartments in the building. She's also a live-in nurse for Mrs. Grimaldi on the fifteenth floor. She cooks and cleans for me now, too. The building has come together to help the two out. I'm taking Maria to Mimi's school play on Saturday."

Gale stared at the circles swirling in her wine glass. "How sweet and cozy," she wanted to say.

"Are you dating Maria?" she asked, suppressing other nasty thoughts.

"No. She works her ass off, and I'm just trying to relieve some of her stress."

"I'm sorry for asking," Gale said stiffly.

"Listen, we've been messing with long distances for a long time. Why don't we see if we can make it work?"

"What does that mean, though? I move to Chicago, we date, maybe get engaged and then maybe get married? I can't change my life on a few maybes."

"I'm not talking about maybes."

90

"So, you want to get engaged and get married? Make it clear for me."

"Yeah, that's it."

"Do you love me? We have known each other for a long time, and you have never said I love you. Do you love me, Dave?"

The question hung in the air for several seconds. Dave finally said, "Of course, I care for you. Why would I essentially ask you to marry me if I didn't care for you?"

"Then say it. Just say, 'Gale, I love you.' Say the three simple words that I have been waiting to hear since the first time that we sat at this table."

"I would if I could. I just can't say it. Trust me."

"How can I trust you if you won't tell me that you love me? Why would you want to marry a woman to whom you can't speak those words?"

"Please, Gale, just trust me."

"Dave, are you suggesting this because of Spike, because you are afraid of being without a buddy to hang with."

"No. That's not it. You know this has been on both of our minds ever since you bolted out of Chicago."

"I didn't bolt. You couldn't tell me that you loved me then, either. Dave, I simply can't come back to Chicago for a man who doesn't love me. Can't you understand that? Let me ask you a question. When an ambulance siren blares in the distance, have you ever thought, God, don't let that be Gale? I used to think that all the time about you, and it freaked me out to think that I may never be able to touch or taste you again. That's why I had to bolt from Chicago. When you have those types of feelings for me and can say those three little words, then I'll think about moving to Chicago. Can you do that for me, Dave?"

Tears began to roll down Gale's face as Dave sat in silence.

CHAPTER 13

To her father white,
Came the maiden bright:
But his loving look
Like the holy book,
All her tender limbs with terror shook.

—William Blake, "A Little GIRL Lost"

When Elle was barely six and burying herself beneath the folds of her mother's clothes and fragrances, she fantasized about being her daddy's wife. Her lonely six-year-old mind contrived that her daddy would finally hug and kiss her and love her, if she was just like her mommy. This was when Elle began to study her mother's pictures. Elle memorized her mother's style, how she wore her lipstick or tilted her head. She began to copy her mother so her daddy would love her, too.

On one exploration into her mother's room, Elle discovered a picture of her parents hidden in the drawers of the bureau. In an intimate embrace, her mother was nestled on her father's lap cradled by his arms. Even though she was only six years old, Elle understood that she never felt that kind of tender hug.

Longing for the same family and affection that she saw in the picture, her father became Elle's object of desire. She would steal into her mother's room and make believe that her father loved and protected her, too. One day, she took the photograph of her parents and carefully cut out the image of her mother. She then colored her own portrait and carefully glued it on the photograph. She was finally embraced by her father.

Because of her desire to be loved and welcomed into the folds of her father's arms as a child, Elle was guilt-ridden as an adult. She imagined that these infantile fantasies translated into conjugal sex with her father. Elle never played house with other little girls who also pretended to marry their father. So, how could she understand that her imaginary games were a normal part of growing up, not a consent to her father for his deviant transgressions? How could she understand that childhood dreams and desires were natural and not provocation for someone else's destructive actions, especially those of a parent? Without a clear grip on reality, Elle served as a most desirable host for guilt. It crawled up inside her to feed on the dis-torted concepts of truth that were lodged in her mind. Guilt was a relentless predator that threatened and bullied Elle into bearing the responsibility for her father's behavior.

Also tangled in the twisted reality of guilt was an unbearable fear of loneliness. Elle spent the first nine years of her life void of parental touch and attention. If she completely denied her father, she feared a return to utter isolation. Was her father's destructive love better than the complete loss of love?

This unanswered question chained Elle to the bounds of a relationship with her father. Not until she met other women like Lucretia Borgia, Pope Alexander VI's illegitimate daughter and lover, did she begin to understand her plight. The canvas became

Elle's medium to tell her story and to unravel her distorted sense of reality. Art became an honest and willful listener.

⚭ ⚭ ⚭

Throughout her four years in college, Elle was noted for her period art work echoing masters from the Renaissance to the Romantic period. Once she graduated from Thrace, she landed a steady job illustrating covers for romance novels with titles like *Love's Passionate Fury* and *Pleasures, Pain and Desire*. Elle mused over the irony. Nevertheless, the steady pay afforded her the opportunity to rent an apartment by herself and continue with her personal painting.

Guilt and agony continued to serve as a propitious subject, though. In her *Allegory of Reproach*, Elle created a woman pounding spikes into her dead lover's palms as he lay prostrate on a mountain top. The scene was washed in the blood red of dusk while the head of the spike was inscribed with a barely visible P.

Through her conversations with the canvas, Elle began to ease some of the pain and to eradicate her demons. Her art assumed a lighter hue by replacing the violent red in her pictures with a sorrowful but softer tone of pink and pale blues. With this positive change in style and voice, her public following increased.

Nonetheless, she could always count on two loyal patrons in Dicey and Gale. It had been two years since she graduated from Thrace. She relished the friendship that she had formed with the women in the past couple of years. It was the first time in her life when she truly had girlfriends.

.

CHAPTER 14

I want to seize fate by the throat.

−Ludwig von Beethoven, Letter to Franz Wegler,
16 November 1801

More than a month had passed since Gale spent quality time with Dicey. She was locked in a trial for three weeks following her Chicago trip. At the same time, Dicey had a looming deadline to meet for a research article; she was impossible to be around just before her papers were to be submitted. This article compared the private insecurities of Mary Godwin Shelley and of Samuel Taylor Coleridge and, then, discussed how Shelley subconsciously manifested their similar issues in *Frankenstein*. Gale was always diverted by the fact that literary scholars, including Dicey, had so much to say about stuff that so few people really cared about. Who cared if Shelley or Coleridge was insecure? Back then, writers would just take a spot of opium and be on their way to imaginary land.

Dicey was more distracted than usual, and it hurt Gale. Between her psychotic Romantic writers and course exams, Dicey could have found time to talk. For six weeks, Gale had bottled up disappointment and resentment over Dave. If he could never admit to loving her, she could no longer hang on to his dangling strings of hope. It was time for both of them to move on.

Furthermore, Thanksgiving only added more angst to Gale's life. Still pouting over the birthday feud involving Dicey and accusations of lesbianism, Harriett Knightly barely spoke to her daughter throughout the holiday.

It was mid December and Elle was holding a holiday exhibit. Gale wanted to give her mother a peace offering for Christmas and thought one of Elle's landscapes would be appropriate. "Somber distance meets somber distance," she chuckled as she drove to pick-up Dicey for the show.

"Do I know you?" Gale asked when Dicey climbed into the car. "Did we go to high school together, or something?"

"You're very funny. Don't give me a hard time, Gale. I submitted the paper yesterday. It's over and done with."

"Great. Now I have my best friend back."

Gale was shocked and Dicey was confused by Elle's almost joyful, fluid landscapes. Her *Allegory of Dawn* glowed with a lemony sunrise and a placid morning lake. At the far eastern corner of the scene, a bird interrupted the serenity, spreading rippling ringlets through the water.

"Elle, this is almost happy! What's come over you," asked Dicey.

Elle's canvas was speaking with a different voice, a voice that was filled with color and light and space. The dialogue of images flowed with exhilaration but also left a sense of peace in its wake. Gale bought the *Allegory of Dawn* and hoped that Mrs. Knightly would see her daughter in a new light, as well.

Dicey was drawn to a diminutive pastoral scene where grassy fields held a single lamb. After settling on the picture, she invited Gale and Elle home to help hang the lamb and to toast the artist's new found liberation.

Every now and then, their girls' night out included a bottle of wine and Truth or Tale. It was a game that Dicey's father taught her when she was little. He made up the round-about game to help him tell his daughter "awkward" news that he really didn't want to share. Harvey would start with a long, tall tale and Dicey would have to guess which part of the story was true. The first time Dicey played the game was when her father went to the reformatory. Dicey taught Gale the game in fifth grade. It was a way for Dicey to tell about her life without boldfaced embarrassment.

Dicey pulled out her lucky cubes to play Truth or Tale; whoever rolled double scarlet, went first. Elle had always been the passive listener but finally agreed to participate that night.

Gale rolled red snake eyes. She took a gulp of her wine and stared into the fire for a minute. "We're waiting," Dicey prompted her.

"Give me a second. I'm thinking," Gale said. She paused for another moment and then began, "Well, you both know about my trip to Chicago to see Dave last month. But, what I didn't tell you is this part. We were in bed, just after we had—"

"Okay, that's enough detail," interrupted Dicey.

"Be quiet, let me continue. Just after we made love, or had sex, rather, Dave asked me to marry him. That's right, he asked me to marry him. Not because he loved me. He couldn't even say the L word. Instead, he said that he wanted to marry me because it would make his father happy. He said he really cared about me. I was his 'buddy'. He said that he still got an erection when he thought about me. Can you believe it? After eight years, he can still manage a horse size erection. What a compliment, Mr. Big. That's it. That's all I have to say," Gale said with her eyes glistening. "Well girls . . . what do you think, 'truth or tale,' what's true, what isn't?"

Dicey stared at Gale and suddenly felt horrible. She hadn't given her best friend the time of day in almost two months. She even neglected to return a few of Gale's glum messages. She got up from her seat and moved next to Gale on the couch. Dicey pulled her close and saw a tear drop slip down Gale's cheek.

"Gale, I am so sorry. I've really screwed up. Why didn't you just beat me over the head with a baseball bat and tell me? It's all true, isn't it?" Gale shook her head no. "Dave asked you to marry him, but you're not happy. The only guy you've ever loved proposed and there's no ring. I know it's true," said Dicey.

Gale shook her head no. "It's not all true. I made up the part about his penis," she finally said through tears and a half laugh.

"What a shithead friend I've been. I am so sorry, Gale. Where is he now?"

"He is nowhere. I've got to move on. I can't marry a guy who doesn't hear the sirens for me, who can't even say 'I love you.' That's not asking too much. I've been festooned to hope for years. It's time to give another relationship a chance. I've sabotaged them all, including Ken Tereus."

"Gale, you're right, but only you could have figured it out. I've thought this for a long time," said Dicey.

"God, I'm a fool."

"No, you're not. Anyone who doesn't take a chance on love is a fool," said Dicey.

"Can we move on? I don't want to dwell on it tonight." She liked Elle, but she really didn't want to delve into a deep discussion with her there.

Dicey and Elle rolled the dice: a red and white for Dicey and a double red for Elle.

"Dicey, I think you fixed those cubes somehow. Why do they always roll your way?" asked Gale, trying to be playful.

"Be quiet. It's Elle's turn."

She told her tale with hesitance.

"Come on, Elle, get it going!" prompted Gale. "We need some laughs."

Elle began with confessing that Dr. Tereus– Ken had visited her studio a couple of weeks ago. He bought her *Irony of Passion*. He then asked her out for dinner. With much debate, Elle accepted the invite. The two had met twice since the purchase.

"Hell, no, I don't believe you! Sisters never buy the same dress a sister's already bought. I don't think your story is a bit funny. It's like wearing the same underwear I wore yesterday. Elle, think of something else," slurred Gale. After one glass of wine and her story, Gale now seemed drunk.

Dicey wanted to believe that Elle had more sense than to date a man who dumped Gale, but she knew better.

"I think Elle's tale is true, the whole story. You know, I could tell at his party you two weren't a match made in heaven. You really weren't his type. C'mon, Elle is a little more reserved than you. She's more his style. You would have been bored in a nano-second."

Dicey watched Gale sink deeper and deeper into the couch. "Oh please, Gale, I'm not going to let you get upset about a guy whom you never diddled nor liked that much!"

Gale looked like she was about to cry.

"Stop it, Galey, you're ruining my turn. I haven't seen you this upset since senior year when I got an A in calculus from Mr. Ulrich, and you got a B," teased Dicey.

Finally, Gale smiled and threw another pillow at Dicey. "I'm not jealous. Give me a break. I'm emotional! Can't I just be emotional for once?"

"Sure, but may I tell my story now?" begged Dicey, for she didn't want Gale to sink back into tears.

"Proceed! We're all ears, aren't we Elle?" said Gale trying to hide her discomfort. Elle remained silent.

"Y'all remember when Hank Daimon offered to lecture in my Studies in Fiction class? Well, I took him up on the offer. And sisters, let me tell you, was he the man! He walked in looking all bad-ass with a spanking white shirt and cuff links, solid gold lions with itty-bitty ruby eyes. He popped open a fresh copy of *Jane Eyre* and read the passage about lunatic Bertha setting fire to her husband, Mr. Rochester, as he attempted to marry Jane. Then, he compared the incident to Mary Nettles, a woman whom he defended in a murder case. Mary's wife-beaten-cheaten husband came home one night and plopped his nasty ass on the front porch. Mary popped the old man a cold one, but instead of Budweiser, the can was filled with Drano. After Mr. Nettles took a long gulp and belched, he rolled off the porch in pain as little razor blades sliced up his throat. Mary sat down in his spot and poured herself a tall, cold beer to watch Mr. Nettles roll and wriggle around on the front lawn, until life just wriggled right out of his body. After Mary sucked down the last beer she'd ever enjoy, she called the police to haul her ass to jail.

"The students went wild. Once the kids were panting for more, Mr. Daimon stands up tall and says, 'Ladies and gentlemen, you can't separate life from literature; they are intrinsically inter-twined. I submit this question for discussion: Do you think that Mr. Rochester and Mr. Nettles were subjected to brutal torture because of their wives' lunacy, or did each man contribute to their own demise through their own deviant behavior— in other words, did the men deserve it?'

"The class erupted in debate with the guys pitted against the gals. Mr. Daimon, Hank, left the class in chaos but called two hours later to see if I'd share a bottle of wine instead of a bottle of beer with him. I'm not sure when I fell in love with him, though. Maybe it was when he was describing the old man rolling around in the dandelions. Or, maybe it was later that evening when I was weaving my fingers through his curly chest hairs— right before we made love!"

If Gale wasn't shell-shocked before, she was galvanized now. "Aster Rose Carmichael, where in the hell did you get such a long, tall tale, honey. I barely believe Hank came to your class. That old, crotchety guy couldn't entertain a dust bunny if his life depended on it!"

Elle disagreed. She always believed that Dicey was a closet romantic beneath all her vinegar. She simply hadn't found her match.

"Elle, you think that because you have an extra sparkle in your eye tonight," insisted Gale. "Tell us, Dicey, truth or tale."

"Everything's true up until the chest hairs part. Don't get me wrong, I wanted to play with those little black hairs peeking through his shirt, but I thought the man might be put off by my advances. I waited until our second date to say 'howdy' to those sexy curls waving at me. The love-making part isn't true at all, though I sure wish it was," she admitted with an uncharacteristic blush.

"So, my Dicey Rose is infatuated . . . maybe even in love. I can't believe it. So, it wasn't just your research and exams that were tying you up the past few weeks. It was Daimon. Why didn't you tell me?"

"Gale, don't make me feel guiltier than I already feel. I think that I was embarrassed and scared. I didn't want to tell anyone in case he wasn't interested in me."

"My god, what's Harriet going to say to my father about this one. 'Mr. Knightly, it's outrageous. You must talk to Gale. Her lesbian friend found a boyfriend before she did.' Then, she'll start her novena to St. Jude all over again so he'll find a husband for me! She sneaks holy cards in my mail box every Monday morning. You have to love (and hate) the woman!"

Exhibiting an uncommon display of affection, Elle hugged Dicey. She then reached out and touched Gale's hand apologizing for her own insensitivity about Ken Tereus.

"Elle, go for it. Face it, we weren't a match. My ego can take a few puncture wounds here and there. But be careful. Don't fall in love like our Dicey. I don't think Dr. Tereus would commit to a favorite flavor of ice cream, let alone a favorite woman."

"What does old Dr. Pandion think about your relationship with him? I got the impression he was pretty protective over his baby," Dicey asked refilling her wine glass.

Elle's face paled at the mention of Dr. Pandion. Her father wasn't aware of her interest in Dr. Tereus. The men were colleagues, and she thought it best to remain quiet on the issue.

Dicey wanted to say, "You remain quiet on all issues when it comes to your father," but they were having too much fun to alter the mood.

CHAPTER 15

— A simple Child.
That lightly draws its breath,
And feels its life in every limb,
What should it know of death?

— William Wordsworth, "We are Seven"

When Gale awoke the morning after her Truth or Tale date, she was nauseous and exhausted. She swore off alcohol for life and pulled the covers back over her head. By Monday morning, Gale felt worse. Reluctantly, she scheduled an appointment with Dr. Leighton, a kind old man with chubby cheeks and a balding head.

"So, how is Gale Knightly, the arch-enemy of ambulance chasers?" asked Dr. Leighton, the Knightly family physician for more than thirty-five years

"I'm not so hot, Doc. I've been tired and nauseated for the past couple of weeks. I feel like I just can't kick the flu or something."

"Well let's have a look." As Dr. Leighton examined Gale, he asked about her parents and sister, Amy.

"Your sister drags her boys in for check-ups. They roll straight through the front door like bowling balls, knocking everything in their path. Amy seems as happy as can be. Your mom sure brags about those boys."

"Mom comes from the era that values country clubs, husbands and grandkids. I offer none of these."

"There's plenty of time, Gale. Your chest sounds fine. Your glands are normal. Let's feel around your belly," he said probing with his fingers. "Do you have pain above or below the navel?"

"It's all-over nausea."

Pushing around on her lower abdomen, he asked the date of her last pap smear.

"It's been about six or seven months, last summer."

Dr. Leighton pulled Gale up to a sitting position and explained, "We're going to take a little blood to check your thyroid– make sure its not working too slow or too fast. That can make you pretty tired. I don't think you're anemic, but we'll test for that and mono. You gave us a urine sample, so I'll have Betty check for a bladder infection or pregnancy, you know the works. Why don't you get dressed, I'll be back in a few minutes," said Dr. Leighton.

"Don't waste your money on a pregnancy test, Doc. I don't even have a boyfriend," Gale lamented as she slid off the table and thought about Dave. She hadn't spoken to him in a month.

Gale dressed quickly in the frigid examining room. She thumbed through an old copy of *Good Housekeeping*. The articles included, "Beyond Witches and Demons: The New Halloween Costumes for your Trick or Treater," "How to Outwit the Ornery Eater," and "Sleep vs. Sex: A Mother's Dilemma."

"Wow, cutting-edge information!" Gale mumbled. "How does Amy do it every day?"

After shivering for fifteen minutes, there was a knock at the door, and Dr. Leighton re-entered. He fumbled at the sink for several seconds. Gale knew there was something he didn't want to tell her. Blood washed from her own face.

"Doc, what is it? C'mon, why are you shuffling around, something's up? I know you. I can take it, whatever it is."

"Gale, honey, it's not bad news. It's just surprising news, but it will probably make your mother happy."

Gale sat still for a very long minute. "No, Doc, it can't be . . . I'm not pregnant. Are you certain?" She tried to breathe without hyperventilating.

"Absolutely certain," he assured her. "My best guess is about six or eight weeks, but I want you to schedule an appointment with your OB/Gyn. He'll want to see you as soon as possible, if you are that far along . . . are you okay, Gale?"

"Sure." Gale couldn't move.

"I'm going to write you a script for a pre-natal vitamin. Remember, no alcohol and try to avoid cigarette smoke."

"Thanks, Doc." He gave her a quick pat on the back and moved on to the next examining room.

Gale wandered out to the parking lot and found her car. She crawled behind the steering wheel and counted back eight weeks. "Chicago . . . with Dave. We used a condom. He always called it his goddamn Clydesdale," she cried. "I'm pregnant with a man who doesn't love me." Tears washed down her face as she pressed her head against the cold window of the door. The icy glass stung her cheek. Her arms were too heavy to turn on the ignition. She slumped against the steering wheel.

A piercing tap on the roof of her car startled Gale. She opened her eyes to a woman staring at her through the glass and mouthing, "Are you okay?" Gale cracked her window answering, "I'm fine, thank you."

She grabbed her cell phone and dialed 411. A foreign voice came on the line and asked for city and state. "Crystal Springs, Ohio," she answered.

"No, not Creestal Sings," Gale snapped. "Crystal like glass and spring like the season," she added. Eventually, she was connected to her gynecologist's office.

Dr. Anthony was a no-nonsense physician. "You're about two months along, Miss Knightly. I see from your chart that your last period was October 10th, give or take a few days. Your due date will be around the first of August. We'll schedule you for an ultrasound to firm up the dates."

Gale felt like an idiot. How could a thirty-year-old woman not know she was pregnant? Dr. Anthony promised that it wasn't unusual, especially with patients who have irregular periods. She was sure that there was a touch of sarcasm in his voice with his reassurance.

"Miss Knightly, I sense that you're not too thrilled about the pregnancy. There are options. I don't perform them," he added distastefully, "but time is running out for that decision."

"No doctor, everything is fine. I'm just a little jolted. I'll be fine," Gale lied.

"Okay, talk to Jenny on your way out. I'd like to schedule an ultrasound to establish a more accurate due date, since you have an irregular cycle." The receptionist congratulated her with a jolly smile while Gale wanted to puke in her face.

👀 👀 👀

Gale waited to get home to call Dicey, instead of calling from her car.

"Dice, are you busy?" Her hands were shaking as she spoke.

"Hank's coming over later on, why?"

"I need to . . . the doctor . . .," and Gale broke down in sobs.

"Where are you? Are you okay?"

Gale couldn't answer.

"Tell me what's wrong!" Dicey yelled into the receiver.

"I'm, I'm . . . ."

"Gale, where are you?" Dicey demanded.

"Home," she cried.

"I'll be right there."

Dicey repeated the Hail Mary as she sped through stop signs. "God, don't let anything happen to her, please dear God!" she prayed.

When Dicey saw Gale leaning in the doorway, her heart froze. "Just tell me!" she cried. "It's cancer! Just tell me!"

"No, Dicey, It's not cancer," whispered Gale.

"What is it?"

"I'm pregnant," cried Gale.

"What! You had me drive ninety miles an hour to come two miles to tell me that you are pregnant. My God, Gale," Dicey breathed, grabbing her chest. Once she caught her breath, Dicey said, "You're not pregnant. You don't have sex. You have to have sex to get pregnant, remember health class?"

"Remember Chicago?"

"Okay, I understand. You've had sex one time in the past six months. That doesn't make you pregnant?"

"I've been to two doctors today."

"What did they say?"

"That I'm pregnant, about two months."

"With a baby? You are really going to have a baby?" Dicey grabbed Gale and hugged her tightly.

Gale pulled away and walked into the living room. She sat down on the couch and put her hands between her legs. "Dicey, I don't have to have a baby. There are options."

"What? What are you talking about?" Dicey asked moving into the room. "It's not a baby, Gale. It's your baby and Dave's baby. I don't know what options you are talking about."

"I'm not going to spell it out. Listen. I'm pregnant with a man's baby who looks at me like one of his buddies. That's nice, but it certainly won't hold up when life gets rough in a marriage. And look at my career; it's just starting to take off."

"Have you talked to Dave, Gale?"

"Why?"

"He's the father. He's not just some guy all of a sudden. You've known him forever. He has a right to know."

"Not if there is no baby, Dice."

"What are you talking about?"

"I'm not going to spell it out?"

"Well, if you are contemplating an abortion, you sure as hell should be able to spell the goddamn word."

Dicey walked to the couch and sat down. She put her hands over her ears to muffle what Gale was trying to say.

"Please talk to me. I don't know what I'm thinking. I just found out. That's why I called you."

"Just tell me that you really aren't contemplating an abortion?"

"I don't know," Gale said, squeezing the back of her neck.

Dicey and Gale talked for hours. This was the first time that dissension had ever penetrated their relationship. Dicey toyed with her red and white talisman as Gale spoke. She wondered how her best friend could see such a blessing so differently?

After hours of arguing, tears and talking, Dicey finally said, "I've known you most of my life. I know what you're about, and I don't think that this is the right decision for you. I'm not casting stones at this point in my own chaotic world. A woman's choice is a woman's choice. Other women can handle it emotionally, but at this stage in your life, I don't think that abortion is the right choice for you. As your best friend with your best interest in mind, this is what I believe."

Gale was worthless in the office on Monday. She read through the same paragraph six times and had no idea what it said. Impulsively, she grabbed the phone and dialed Dave's office. The receptionist forwarded her to Dave's secretary whom Gale had known for many years.

"Merry Christmas! How are you, Gale?"

"Great, Sara. Merry Christmas to you, too. Is Dave around?"

"No. Mr. B and he just left for a skiing trip in Austria. Sounds like fun, doesn't it?" she said.

"A ton of fun," Gale said flatly.

"They'll be back in January. Dave should be calling in for messages. Would you like to leave one?"

"Nah, that's okay. I think that it can wait two weeks. I hope you have a great holiday." She hung up the phone and rested her head on the desk for several minutes. Finally, she lifted her head and dialed telephone information. She was searching for the number to the Women to Women Center?

At six o'clock Gale grabbed her purse and headed home for a long run. She needed to feel the pavement under her feet. The only thing that had crystallized during the six miles of road, though, was that she was ill-prepared for motherhood. She was headed for partnership, working eighty hours a week. The legal and medical communities were beginning to applaud her skill in the court room. Diaper bags never did and never would accommodate legal files. She wanted children but not this way, alone and without a man in her life. She wanted to provide a normal home for her kids with a mom and a dad and dinner on the table at six o'clock.

Later that night, Gale talked to Dicey on the phone. "I'm just not there. I don't want to bring a child into my world and screw it up. I want kids when my career and a man are in place. Kids, the dog and a husband are great, but not in that order. I don't want to be one of those mutations that call themselves a family now days."

"What do you mean by 'mutation'?"

"You know the single moms, the single dads, aunts and uncles, gay and lesbian couples all trying to raise kids in a world that's already screwed up."

"All of a sudden, I don't think I know you. The last time I looked, the perfect Knightly family portrait wasn't under *Webster's* definition of family. Dad and Grandma dished out more love to me than your parents could cook up in a life time. Grandma's love wasn't limited to pretty little girls in fancy dresses. Furthermore, you've always agreed that Rhonda and Debra are great parents to little Ethan. Were you lying to be politically correct? A family is more than what looks good at the country club. I thought you really believed that. Now, I'm wondering if I'm even a part of your family."

"You don't understand. It's different for you. People expect different things."

"Yeah, they expect me to cavort around town because my father was in jail and my grandmother was high yellow. They expect me to get knocked-up because poor people don't have any morals. If they had morals, they'd be rich like you, Gale, wouldn't, they? I'm hanging up now, and I'm telling you, so you can't accuse me of hanging up on you.

"In forty-eight hours, you've transformed from a woman in control of her life to a massive train wreck," said Dicey, before Gale had time to slam down the phone.

ଓଡ଼   ଓଡ଼   ଓଡ଼

Gale needed no directions to the Women for Women Center. In high school, she and Dicey organized Right to Life protests one weekend a month on the sidewalks bordering the facility. As women walked through the doors, the girls would yell, "Abortion Kills! Save your unborn child!"

There was only one time when they chose not to scream and, instead, hid behind their large posters. A yellow Toyota pulled up to the curb and out stepped Maria Fairbanks, a superstar volleyball player from school. The car pulled away, and Maria stood by herself, alone with red, swollen eyes.

"What do we do?" whispered Gale.

"I don't know. Let me think for a minute," said Dicey.

"Think fast. She's walking toward the front door."

For the first time in their pro-life campaign, Gale and Dicey were caught in the snare of reality. They didn't want to embarrass Maria by approaching her, but if they just stood their and did nothing, in their mind, a baby would die.

"Come on. We've got to stop her." Both girls ran after Maria, carrying their bulky signs by their sides.

"Maria, wait a minute," Dicey yelled.

Maria turned around, her face went white, and she covered her eyes. "Please, leave me alone," she cried.

"There are other options. Just think about it. That's all we're asking," said Gale gently, as she stuck the sign of the mutilated baby behind her back

Maria uncovered her eyes. "You don't understand. I can't disgrace my family. I'm their star."

"But it's a baby," said Dicey.

"Please leave me alone. And please, please don't tell anybody. I'm begging you." With that, Maria turned around and hurried into the abortion clinic.

Three years later, Maria went to the Olympics. Her team won a gold medal in Women's volleyball.

Fourteen years later, here was Gale, walking into the same clinic. She looked at the posters of mangled babies carried by the protesters. Even at seven-thirty in the morning, they rallied for the cause. She could neither avoid the agony of their taunts nor the agony of walking through the abortion clinic doors.

When she signed in, the receptionist handed Gale a stack of forms to complete. Gale provided all requisite health information and signed the informed consents. As she waited to be called into the examining room, Gale eyed the receptionist, wondering if she had had one. The young girl was pleasant and perky. If she had had one, the procedure didn't seem to have ruined her life.

Eventually, Gale was guided into a surgical/examining suite and sat down on one of two metal chairs. A violent wave of nausea hit her for the second time that day. She took a deep breath and put her head between her legs. The doctor walked in while Gale was dangling toward the floor.

"Rough morning?" she asked in a soft voice.

Gale raised her head with tears in her eyes. "In more ways than one."

"It's never easy, Miss Knightly, easier for some, but never easy."

"No, I guess not." Gale whispered.

"The file indicates that you're approximately nine weeks pregnant," the doctor commented, flipping through the chart.

"That's right."

"You won't want to wait too much longer. Let me examine you, then we can discuss a time for the procedure."

As the doctor performed the examination, Gale was surprised by her kindness and patience. She always envisioned wicked witches wielding sharp knives behind the brick walls of the clinic; she never imagined an empathetic woman with gentle fingers.

"Everything seems fine, Miss Knightly." She held out her hand and helped Gale to a sitting position. "Why don't you get dressed, and I'll check the surgical schedule. You'll feel some discomfort for a day or so. Arrange to have someone available to drive you home, too. Is there any time this week that won't work for you?"

"No. The sooner the better, I guess."

"Since your health is not at risk, it's our policy to wait twenty-four hours between the exam and the procedure. The time is important. Women need to feel comfortable with their decision." The doctor patted Gale's hand and went to check the schedule.

As Gale tugged on her slacks, she noticed that buttoning the waistband was difficult; her stomach was already beginning to expand. She wondered how big it was at nine or ten weeks. The doctor tapped on the door and entered with the procedure schedule.

"Miss Knightly, you're scheduled for Wednesday morning at nine. The nurse at the desk will go over the details with you. Do you have any other questions for me?"

"No thank you, doctor. Everything seems under control."

"Good, we'll see you on Wednesday."

Gale sat at her kitchen table eating tomato soup and crackers. Her stomach felt bloated, and her breasts felt like water balloons. After this week, though, her chest would shrink back down to size, her uterus would soften, and her life would return to normal.

It was the first time in twenty years that Gale hadn't talked to Dicey for an entire week. The last time that they did speak, Dicey had offered to adopt the child. Now Gale was trying to figure out a way to tell Dicey that she had gone ahead and scheduled the procedure.

The fact that the doctor never used the term abortion bothered her. Instead, she referred to it as a "procedure". Did she call it a "procedure" to help women feel better? Could she feel better by calling it a procedure? Probably not, but if she didn't have the procedure, the thing called a fetus today would soon be called a baby. She was resolved to move forward with the procedure.

Pictures of mangled babies greeted Gale on the day of the appointment. There was also an elderly man handing out rosaries for a small donation to "Help Save Unborn Children," as his sign read. The door to the clinic was much heavier on this trip. She dragged it open with both hands. The same pleasant girl was seated behind the reception window with the same perky smile. Gale would be called for the procedure in just a few minutes.

115

As the minutes ticked by, Gale pulled out her planner to check her schedule for the following week.

The ER doctor who took care of Julia Rheinhart on the night that she died would be deposed by the plaintiff's lawyer on Friday. She dreaded it. The doctor had ignored the mother's correct diagnosis of an aortic dissection due to complications from Marfan's syndrome, and now the girl was dead. How could this be defended? Gale thought of Julia and her mother. Mrs. Rheinhart would die for just another minute with her daughter, just a minute to kiss and hold and caress her daughter's face.

Gale thought about the many women who would embrace an expanding waistline and morning sickness as a sign of new life, the women who couldn't conceive. A baby was growing inside her. This child did not request to be born into this world, nor did this child request banishment. Whether Gale was ready or not for motherhood was irrelevant. Wasn't it? She wasn't a teenager; she wasn't broke— she could afford a nanny. Women more isolated than she accepted pregnancy as their option.

Why couldn't she? Because, she just couldn't.

A nurse called her name, and Gale was guided toward a changing room. Before she went in for the procedure, Gale made arrangements with the receptionist to have a cab called for her when she was ready to go home. She was given a hospital gown, brown sure-grip footies and a locker key for her personal items. As Gale undressed, she carefully folded her slacks and shirt and placed them on the top shelf of the locker. She climbed on the hospital bed and waited for the nurse to return and start the I.V.

As the minutes passed, Julia Rheinhart's mother hung heavy on Gale's mind. The nurse came into the room prepared to start the I.V. As the needle pricked Gale's arm, her reality ripped through her heart, and she embraced it.

Another woman would be comfortable choosing abortion, but for Gale, it was not the right decision, not at this time in her life.

She quietly canceled the procedure. She unfolded her clothes and dressed. She walked out of the center and into the sunshine.

It was the day before Christmas Eve.

❧❧ ❧❧ ❧❧

Gale rushed into Kmart for a last minute shopping stop before her Christmas luncheon with Dicey and Elle that was planned on the night of Truth or Tale. It never crossed Gale's mind to cancel the date, and she was relieved that she hadn't.

When Gale arrived at the restaurant, Dicey was stiff and aloof. Their conversation was a series of stilted detours to avoid any direct discussion of the baby. Sensing the tension, Elle pulled out Christmas gifts for her friends.

For Gale, she painted a lamb similar to Dicey's, but this picture was decorated with daisies and daffodils, instead of lilies and violets.

"Oh look, a baby sheep," Dicey said.

Gale responded with a phony glare.

The other gift was a rendition of a photograph that Elle had seen in Dicey's home. It was a picture of Dicey as a toddler, seated on her grandmother's lap.

"Elle, this is the most beautiful and thoughtful gift that I have ever received," Dicey said. "My father will love this, as well." Dicey reached over and gave her a huge hug.

"Dicey, I'm afraid that my gift is not as extravagant," Gale said handing over a small package.

Dicey unwrapped the present and pulled out a book and read the title, *The Official Lamaze Guide: Giving Birth with Confidence.*

"I don't understand. What is this for?"

"You're going to be my birthing coach, aren't you? If not, I'm going to have to pick a new godmother for this baby," Gale said as she rubbed her belly.

CHAPTER 16

My mother groand! My father wept.
Into the dangerous world I lept"
Helpless naked piping loud:
Like a fiend hid in a cloud.

—William Blake, "Infant Sorrow"

*C*hristmas Eve dinner was marked with tradition at the Knightly house. Gale's mother set an elegant table of prime rib and crystal, and she always permitted Maria, the housekeeper, to go home before dessert was served. Amy and her husband, Cortland, entertained with their sons, Benjamin and Christopher. Cortland was a mirror reflection of Mr. Knightly, both pleasant men who surrendered the check book and domestic duties to their wives in exchange for freedom. Everyone was happy; neither man ever explained his actions and neither woman was ever in want of worldly possessions. Mr. and Mrs. Knightly were pleased with Elle's landscape, though Amy's Irish bread maker seemed to be a bigger hit with her mother. Amy's mini-men of destruction tore

119

open their gifts from Gale and pulled out miniature tool boxes. The boys promptly attacked Mrs. Knightly's coffee table, and the tools were confiscated. Gale handed the last gift under the tree to her father. He ripped at the paper and found a white photo album adorned with pink and blue giraffes. Confused, he handed the gift over to Amy,

"Sorry, Amy, I opened your present from Gale."

Amy opened the album and read aloud,

"Dear Mom and Dad, please welcome into the world my child with the same love and devotion that was provided to me. Merry Christmas! Love, Gale."

"Oh, sweetheart," said her mother. "What a silly gift. Of course we'll love your children, just like we love Amy's. But please, dear, don't bring tool boxes to my house when you have little boys."

"How does August sound, Mom?"

"August, for what, a boy's name? Too trendy," Mrs. Knightly said, crumbling gift wrap into a garbage bag.

"No, not a name, a month for a baby to be born," Gale offered.

"Amy's due in February, not August," her mother slowly responded.

"No, Mom. Not Amy's baby, my baby."

Mrs. Knightly held tightly to her bag of garbage.

"What do you mean?" her mother asked as the room hushed; even Ben and Chris quieted down.

"I'm pregnant, Mom. Your dream come true."

"I don't know what you are talking about, Gale. What kind of dream?"

"You've always bugged me about babies."

"But you're not married, Gale. Is that not obvious, or have I missed an event in the past few months?"

Gale was silent as her mother stuffed wrapping paper deeper and deeper into her bag of trash. She was mentally prepared for her mother's storm.

"Are you going to answer me, Gale Marie?"

"Mother, please!" interrupted Amy.

"Quiet!" responded Mrs. Knightly. "And who is the father, may I ask since you never date?"

"I am the mother, does it matter beyond that?"

"You've been with so many different men that you don't know the father of your own child, Gale?" Mrs. Knightly asked. "George, are you just going to sit there and say nothing?"

Mr. Knightly answered by standing up and pouring himself another scotch.

"Well, there are options. You profess to be so smart; you'll figure something," snipped her mother.

Gale's lips trembled. "What do you mean options?"

"Go to Canada for a few months. No one will know the difference . . . or just get rid of it, Gale. You're the one who heralds women's rights!"

"Are you implying abortion, Mother?"

"Isn't that the easiest solution?"

"The last time I checked, your faith was opposed to abortion. Has it changed?"

"Oh please, Gale, do I look like the Vatican? You're pregnant and not married. How does that look? Stop antagonizing me by playing the Virgin Mary. You're the one who's pregnant with an illegitimate child!"

"So, it's okay for you to cherry pick, now. Isn't that what you accuse me of— cherry-picking? Follow only those rules of the Church which work for me? Well, I'm keeping my baby. I guess the Church will approve of me for a while. And, I'm profoundly sorry that you possess such a vile reaction to my good news. Merry Christmas, Mother. Wish baby Jesus a happy birthday for me at Midnight Mass! Thank heaven Mary didn't have the same reaction to her untimely birth; otherwise, your sins may never be forgiven, Mother!"

"Gale Marie!"

"Goodbye, Mother."

No one grabbed her arm to stay. No one said congratulations. No one said go to hell.

Gale reached over the hood of her car to scrape away the snow from her windshield. Tear drops fell into the slush and disappeared. She climbed in behind the steering wheel and headed for the only warmth she knew.

Gale banged on Dicey's front door as snow fell on her nose. Dicey's father, Harvey, pulled open the door and roared, "Damn girl! What is the ruckus about? I thought it was Santa Claus stuck in the chimney."

"Thanks, Harvey," Gale laughed. She wiped her nose with her scarf. "I can always count on you to be happy to see me."

Dicey walked out of the kitchen with Hank Daimon following her, carrying a tray of food and drinks. They were shocked to see Gale standing at the door, a snow-covered specter.

"Gale, what's going on? Where are Harriett and George tonight?" asked Dicey.

"Don't ask." Tears crested in her eyes.

"Dad, can you grab her coat."

Gale handed Harvey her coat and plopped down on the couch. Hank offered her a cup of steaming eggnog that he was holding. Gale reached out for the cup but then asked, "Is it spiked, Hank?"

"You might taste a few drops of rum. It's my specialty. Go ahead. You look like you need it."

"I'll pass, but thanks," said Gale as she glanced at Dicey.

"You can't be on-the-wagon during Christmas. Go ahead."

"No, really, that's not it."

"Ah, come on. It's a party," he pushed.

"I can't drink, Hank. Really, no thanks."

"Nah, won't take no for answer."

"Do you want some hot tea?" Dicey interrupted.

"My eggnog will warm your soul."

"I'm pregnant, Hank. Can't drink!" she finally blurted out.

"Really, so am I!" Hank teased, "And I'm still drinking."

"Please, Hank, stop. She is pregnant. No joke."

"No joke," Gale repeated and started to cry.

"Ah, I'm so sorry," Hank said softly.

"Everybody seems to be so sorry about this baby," she wept.

Dicey sat down next to Gale and hugged her. "You told your parents, didn't you?"

Gale nodded yes and took a deep breath. "Mom basically threw me out of the house, and Dad just sat there sipping his scotch." Gale began to sob.

"Was it that bad?"

"Yes, that bad. She said that I should start planning other 'options'."

"What did Amy say?"

"Not much. She just herded Ben and Christopher out of the room before the yelling got too graphic."

Dicey's father sat down on the other side of Gale and grabbed her hand.

"So, Harvey, who in the hell would think that I'd be the first to get pregnant?"

"Gale, you'll be a great mama." He leaned closer and whispered, "Man or no man in your life."

"Thanks, Harvey," she said and kissed his cheek.

"So, that mama of yours is takin' it hard?" he asked.

"Can you believe that she, the woman who lives her life at the foot of the cross, suggested 'options'? This is her grandchild."

Harvey put his arm around her shoulder and pulled her close. "I'm sure she's not serious. The wiring between your mama's mouth and her brain has always been a little screwed up. She'll cool off in a day and come to her senses."

"I don't know."

"Give it time. Don't be so hard, she's—," Harvey was saying, but Dicey interrupted.

"Dad, what are you talking about? She told Gale to get an abortion and then practically threw her out of the house on Christmas Eve. We're not talking about criticizing a new tattoo, here."

"Gale, your mother's never been full of a whole lot a surprises. She's always been the same way," Harvey started to explain, but Dicey interrupted again.

"Yeah, if it doesn't fit in between her tee time and bridge game, she doesn't get it. Gale could have said that she's marrying a garbage man from Gallipolis, and Harriett would have reacted the same way."

"Not if the guy owned the dump," offered Gale. "Maybe she's secretly relieved. This confirms that Dicey and I aren't lovers. I wonder which is worse to the country club scene: a lesbian daughter or a knocked-up daughter."

"Wait a minute," interrupted Hank. "Have I missed something here?"

"Don't worry, Hank. My mom is a lunatic. I'm too tired to even try to explain right now."

"Well, Gale, honestly, congratulations. I sincerely mean it. Kids are great. I've got three," he said. "I never really thought about kids before I had them, and all of a sudden they became my life, my joy."

Dicey looked up at Hank when he said this but then quickly turned away.

"Well, we'll have to see how the judge and jury react. I'm not sure whose reaction will be worse, my mother's or my partners'."

"Ah, screw them all. If anyone can ignore ignorance, it's you. Dig in your heels like you do in the courtroom, and you'll be fine. Let me know if anybody messes with you, and I'll mess with them," he said protectively.

Gale was surprised by his kindness and candor. "I really appreciate it, Hank, but that doesn't mean I want you to go easy on me."

"I go easy on no one, do I Dice?"

Dicey stood up and wrapped her arms around Hank's waist. "No one but me," she said with a wide smile.

Gale was happy to see this unusual display of affection flowing from Dicey. Though they had been best friends for most of her life, Gale had never witnessed Dicey falling in love. She always worried that Dicey had seen too much as a child to ever trust herself in a relationship.

"Hank, maybe I should give you my mom's number. Nobody else seems to be able to deal with the wrath of Harriett."

"Listen, here," Harvey interrupted, "your mama never liked me or Dice. But she's your mama, and you got to take the good with the bad. The woman loves you."

"Dad, please!" Dicey said. "The woman doesn't accept her baby. So, why should Gale accept her?"

"Dicey, give me a chance, here. That scratchy woman has been the same way for the twenty-some years I known her. She's isn't going to change now. But you always know where you stand with her. Now, Gale, do you go to the pickle jar to get a chocolate chip cookie, honey?"

"No sir."

"So, don't go to your mother expecting chocolate chip cookies, and you won't be disappointed. Your mother is a pickle jar, and pickle jars hold pickles. As soon as you stop going to her looking for cookies, you'll stop being disappointed. Once you get that into your head, you'll be okay with her. Pickles ain't too bad ever now and then, anyway."

"You're a wise man, Harvey," said Gale.

"It took me two turns in the penitentiary and nine years and two hundred and fifty-six days of sobriety to get this smart."

CHAPTER 17

Conviction is worthless until it converts itself to Conduct.

—Thomas Carlyle, "Sartor Resartus:
The Life and Opinions of Herr Teufelsdrockn"

A s Gale became visibly pregnant, she learned to stomach the awkward stares from coworkers and clients. She assured her partners that the pregnancy wouldn't interfere with her professional life.

She bought a three-bedroom ranch in Pleasant Park with shady sidewalks and stay-at-home moms. It was safe. The smallest bedroom was transformed into a fully equipped office while the adjacent room was made into a nursery. On a wintery Sunday in March, Hank and Dicey christened her new home with a crib and matching rocker. Dicey and Gale sat on the nursery floor pouring over paint colors while Hank cussed at the crib directions.

Gale pushed for pale yellow, but Dicey stone-walled the color. "There's nothing soothing about yellow, Gale. It's like blowing peppermint in a kid's face and then saying sleep. Lavender is the only option for my little Lucy."

"This isn't going to be some kind of newfangled feng shui room with funky lighting and energy sources, but I think I can handle purple."

"That was an easy win. Since I'm on a roll, how about the subject you hate most right now?"

"Don't start, Dice. We're having fun," Gale said handing Hank a screw driver.

"He's the father; he has the right to know. Don't you agree, Hank?"

"Nope! Don't ask. I'm not wading in on this topic."

"Go ahead, Hank. I won't bite your butt off," said Gale.

"No, I'm not crazy. I refuse to get involved."

"You're already involved. You're putting together the crib, for God's sake! You owe me that much."

"Okay, but you may not like what I have to say."

"I'm game."

"Okay. Gale, I think the man has a right to know that he has a child on the way. Love or no love between you two, he is still the father. Your child has a right to know his father, too. I'm sorry, but I don't think this is a unilateral decision. My ex-wife and I had a terrible relationship. I was a mean man for fifteen years because of it, but I always had my kids. Men get a bad rap. People just assume we shun the responsibility of kids. I have to admit, when I got married, I couldn't have cared less if I ever had a child, but once I held Sally, my oldest, life changed forever. My children became my life. They still are. I don't know what kind of man Dave is, but he's been close to you for a long time. I trust your judgment in people. I can't climb inside his head, but I do believe that he has the right to know he's going to be a father."

Gale scooted closer to Hank and hugged him. "You're a good man. I'm glad Dicey gave you a chance. I can't promise to call Dave, but I will think more seriously about it."

After the happy couple left, Gale picked through different shades of purple. Dave would hate purple. When they first met, just after he had graduated from Notre Dame, Dave told her that there were really only two colors on the entire color spectrum, Notre Dame blue and gold. "They symbolize truth and light," he said. "What more do you need to win?" She rolled her eyes at the time, but now tears blurred her vision.

Gale threw the color swatches across the nursery and went to her own room and crawled into bed. She rolled over and stared outside as raindrops pelted the window. She was envious of the droplets as she watched them join together to form narrow pathways down the glass. Why couldn't life be that easy? Just follow the path of least resistance. Gale's stomach fluttered, and she wondered if it was the baby moving. She rubbed her belly, and a sad smile spread across her face.

👁️ 👁️ 👁️

Gale arrived at the office late on Tuesday morning because of a prenatal visit. The receptionist greeted her with a stack of mail and a few phone messages. "Busy morning already, Gale," the receptionist commented.

Shuffling through the stack, she saw a message from Dave. Her heart skipped a beat, but then she recognized the local number. It was Dave Clemmens, another lawyer in town.

"God, I have to call him," she said out loud.

"Do you have a question about something?" the receptionist asked.

"No. It's just a lawyer I've been avoiding," Gale answered and turned toward her office.

Gale hung her suit jacket on the back of her door, dropped her briefcase on her desk and began to unload it. She removed each file, placing them on her desk in the order of priority. The Rheinhart case was on top of the stack. Gale sat down at her desk, pulled out the top drawer, organized the paper clips and rubber bands in their proper compartments and sharpened two pencils. She grabbed her time records and jotted down one quarter of an hour for a phone call that she made while waiting for the obstetrician. She flipped through her messages one more time. It was definitely Dave Clemmens' number.

I've got to do it, she thought, and reached for the phone. Instead of punching in Dave Clemmens' number, she took a deep breath and punched in the number for The Broadbeck Group and asked for Dave.

"Please tell him that Gale Knightly is calling," she asked.

Gale waited for two or three minutes before the receptionist came back on the line.

"Mr. Broadbeck is with someone but asked if you could hold on one more minute, Miss Knightly."

Three minutes and forty-seven seconds later she heard his voice. Hello was all that he said.

"Dave, it's me, Gale."

"How are you?"

"I'm doing okay. How are you?"

"Fine."

"And your dad, is he okay?"

"Fine. Dad's fine."

"How was your trip to Austria?"

"Dad broke his ankle."

"Is he alright?"

"Sure. He liked the attention better than skiing, anyway."

"Sounds like him. How's work?"

"Busy."

"You sound busy."

"I am."

"Well, I guess I'll let you go. Tell your dad hello for me."

"I'll do that, Gale. Take care," Dave said and hung up the phone.

Gale sat stunned with the phone glued to her ear. That's it, "Take care." He can't do that to me. I'm pregnant with his child. Damn him. I'm not going to let him get off that easily. He's the one who could never say "I love you." She hit redial and asked for Dave again. This time he came on the phone immediately.

"Dave, it's me again."

"Hello, Gale."

"I was wondering if I could drive up to Chicago this weekend. There's some stuff that I want to talk to you about."

"It's not a good time. I'm busy."

"Is it something you can cancel?"

"No, it's nothing that I can cancel."

"Is it something with Mimi and her mom?"

"No, Gale."

"Is it a date?"

"Listen, this conversation is really inappropriate," Dave charged.

"Why? We've always been honest with each other."

"Gale, you're exactly right. You are one of the most honest persons whom I know. You never say anything that you don't mean. Some pretty awful words fell between us in November. I listened to what you said. You told me that it was time for both of us to finally move on with our lives. Your word is as good as gold, Gale, so I listened."

"Does that mean that you have moved on? You've completely moved on from us?" Gale was shocked.

"Gale, that's what you wanted."

"I see . . . is there someone else?" She felt like a wad of clay was caught in her throat, and it hurt.

"To be honest, yes, I am seeing someone."

The wad in her throat was expanding, but she controlled her tears. "Is it serious, Dave?"

"I'm not sure."

"You've never said that before. So, it must be serious." Gale waited for him to deny her statement, but there was only silence.

"I understand, Dave. I won't bother you anymore. If you ever want to talk, give me a call," Gale said and hung up the phone. She stood up from her chair and walked to the window. The sky was dark gray and heavy raindrops pelted the window. Gale cradled her stomach as tears rolled down her face. She felt like she couldn't breathe.

Her phone buzzed several times, but she couldn't answer it. Finally, her secretary cracked open the door to remind her about the Rheinhart deposition that was beginning in five minutes. Mrs. Rheinhart was waiting in the conference room. She pulled herself together and grabbed the file. She read Julia's name and headed out the door.

CHAPTER 18

O Rose thou art sick.
The invisible worm,
That flies in the night
in the howling storm:
Has found out thy bed
Of crimson joy:
And his dark secret love
Does life destroy.

—William Blake, "The SICK ROSE"

*E*lle winced the first time Ken touched her body. He drew circles around her breasts with his finger. "You're beautiful, but I can make you perfect, Elle. Would you like to be perfect for me?" he asked.

She nodded.

"Would you like perfect breasts? I can do that for you. I can make perfect lips, perfect eyes, and a perfect body."

Elle agreed. She wanted to be perfect. She wanted to be loved.

❀❀   ❀❀   ❀❀

It was early May, and Dicey and Gale hadn't seen Elle for several weeks. The last time the three were together was in January, and she was more distant than her usually estranged self. When Dicey called to invite Elle for pizza and a beer, she declined. Dicey was determined, though. She had to witness Gale's "skinny ass" growing bigger with each day. After several pleas, Elle relented and agreed to go. Dicey was pointing out the benefits of breast feeding with Gale when she spotted Elle walk into Dominic's.

"Holy hell!" Dicey said.

"What's wrong?"

"What in the hell did she do to herself, Gale?"

Gale turned and saw Elle. "My God! They are bigger than mine." Gale waved to draw Elle's attention. "Well, hello . . . Wilma and Betty!" Gale said under her breath.

"Shush," Dicey said as she stood up to give Elle a hug. "The Ethereal Elle, where have you been hiding, honey? We've missed you."

Elle sat down, and Dicey poured her a drink from the pitcher of beer.

"So, what do you think about Gale? A little larger than life, wouldn't you say?" asked Dicey.

"Be quiet," said Gale as she rubbed her stomach. "I'm proud of this. I think it's beautiful. You're just jealous, Dice."

"There's probably a lot of truth in what you say, my dear," Dicey said raising her glass.

Shifting uncomfortably on her stool, Elle agreed that Gale was glowing.

Gale thanked her and said, "Didn't you know? The glow is a part of the whole procreation package, a gift from God. If pregnant women didn't have the glow, they'd jump off a cliff– head first. Who could survive nine months of exhaustion and bloating without the glow? I toast to the glow!" she said raising her root beer.

The girls dinged their glasses together, and Dicey refilled her beer. After several minutes of chatter, she finally said,

"Okay, Elle. There's an elephant in the room, and you've known me for long enough to know that I can't ignore an elephant sitting at my table. You're looking mighty beautiful and a bit bigger yourself."

Elle dropped her eyes.

"Well, let's put it this way," Dicey continued, "It's like a pimple on the tip on your nose on prom night, but in a good way."

"Ignore her. You look fabulous," said Gale. "May I ask why, though?"

Ken liked perfect breasts. He wanted her to have them. He performed the surgery.

"Get serious, Elle. You got new boobs for Ken Tereus?" Dicey asked. "You've dated him for three or four months, and you got breast implants for the man? What were you thinking? I'm not saying you don't look great, but for a guy?"

"Dicey, give her a break. Why do most women get bigger breasts? For themselves? For other women? I don't think so. It's always for the guy," said Gale.

"Wait a minute! This is surgery we're talking about, not a new hair color. How does your father feel about them? This must have raised an eyebrow or two," said Dicey.

Elle hadn't seen her father in quite a while.

That was almost as surprising as the new breasts. "How will he react to the fact that Tereus performed the surgery, considering your dating him? Aren't there ethical complications with that?" asked Gale.

Dr. Pandion didn't know that Elle was dating Ken Tereus.

"Really, Elle, how can you trust a man who wants you to change your appearance because it's something that he likes?" asked Gale.

Elle wanted the implants, too.

"But Ken wanted you to get them," said Dicey. "What's the true story, here?

Elle was mute. She stood up from the table and vanished from the restaurant. Dicey rose to go after her, but Gale grabbed her arm. "Sit down. She wants to be left alone."

"Let go of me. Maybe we were too hard on her."

"Dicey, she doesn't want us around right now. You practically forced her to come out tonight. Just leave her alone for now."

"Gale, she looks ridiculous, and she is dating a guy whom we both hate. I've got to do something," Dicey said, settling back into her seat.

"I don't hate Ken Tereus. I was at fault in that deal. I'm woman enough to admit that."

"I stand corrected. I'm the one who hates Ken Tereus, but I can't just stand by and do nothing to help. Her father's a creeper, and now she's dating Dr. Frankenstein."

"Face it, Dicey. She's an enigma. I don't know if there is anything that we can do."

☙❧ ☙❧ ☙❧

Elle went home that night and dragged out a fresh canvas. She squirted blood red paint on her palette. Black was slathered next to midnight blue and grey. Her brush strokes were short and feverish, like a dog pawing at a locked cage. An ashen woman quickly took form. She was naked with pale hair swirling above her head. Her own protruding breasts got in the way as she painted a scarlet bosom with deep purple nipples. She stroked in a thin, grey arm with delicate fingers that were attempting to cover one of the burgeoning breasts, while the other arm was reaching above her head into dead space. The background of the picture flowed with midnight colors. Elle panted as she dabbed in tiny bubbles escaping from the woman's lips. She then stepped back to study her progress. Would Ken approve of this painting? In a few strokes, Elle cast a heavy shadow across the woman's eyes.

When Elle first started dating Ken, shame continued to haunt her world. He noted the pain embedded in her pictures and celebrated the expression. That frightened Elle for she feared that he would uncover the scars left behind by her father, the ones just below the surface of her skin that burned as a daily reminder of her sin. She feared that Ken would somehow smell the stench left behind, the stubborn stench that she had been trying to scrub away for years. This fear of discovery was relentless.

Ken was perceptive and sensed Elle's resistance when they first began their relationship. He was a patient man; he rushed nothing, everything in time. To Ken, Elle was perfect; Elle was broken. Ken loved broken women. He accumulated wealth from broken women, women who looked in the mirror and hated what they saw. He studied body parts and rearranged them to make the most perfect species in the world. Women were indebted to him for their flawless existence. If they cracked or crumbled, women returned to Dr. Tereus to be, once again, transformed into perfection.

With shame and fear prodding her, Elle succumbed to Ken's attention. He tempted her with the same hypnotic that almost trapped Gale. Elle, unable to distinguish good from bad or love from sex, was easy prey for Ken Tereus.

She was determined to block out the inner voice that warned about her father's reaction to a relationship with another man. Now, she was pushing away her friends and their caution about a man whom they accused of altering her body for his own measure. Gale and Dicey were wrong. Ken was eradicating her flaws and sins; he was making her perfect.

Elle was adding a deep hue to the lips of the ashen woman when she heard a step outside her apartment door. Her fingers twitched, and too much color smeared across the mouth of her subject. She stood up and placed the palette on her workbench. She reached for a can of paint thinner but pulled back as a sharp pain darted through her chest muscles. The muscles still had not healed from the surgery. Squeezing her arms together to calm the spasm, Elle heard a second step outside the door.

She glanced at the deadbolt but already knew that it was unlocked. In the many years that she had lived there, Elle never invited a single person into the apartment. It was her sanctuary. Four elderly women and a business man, who was rarely home, also lived in her building. There was a security lock at the front entrance, so Elle had little concern for her safety. She now stared at the unlocked deadbolt and cursed herself as she watched the door slowly open and in step her father. Elle moved behind her easel and stood silently.

William Pandion walked into the studio and looked at his distorted daughter. "You broke your promise, Elizabeth. I didn't break mine," he said with bulging eyes. "And look what you've allowed him to do to you. You've turned into a hideous monster.

"Because of your bad decisions, things have changed," her father said as he moved toward her.

☙☙ ☙☙ ☙☙

Elle toyed with exquisitely carved chopsticks as Ken explained that the centerpiece, a pear shaped porcelain vase holding daffodils, was from the early period of the Ch'ing dynasty. His table was set on the patio with exquisite china from Asia. As he talked on about his antiquities, Elle was mesmerized by the folk music that floated through the garden with a blend of the flute, harp and Chinese fiddle.

"I'm boring you with my talk about antiques. I'll stop, Elle. Your body looks lovely tonight."

He stood up and reached for her hand. Elle followed him into his bedroom where he began to slowly undress her. Ken saved her blouse for last. As he undid each button, he kissed her skin. He pulled the silk away from her body and drew his fingers around her breasts.

"They're perfect, nothing like the hard knots of your friend, Gale," he whispered. Elle's lips trembled. "Didn't you know?" he cooed.

She shook her head no. Ken rolled Elle onto her stomach and began to caress her spine. He pushed her hair away from the nape of her neck, his favorite part of a woman's body because it was the most vulnerable. When he moved her hair aside, Ken hesitated. Her own body stiffened. When they made love, it was different. Was it her imagination or his preoccupation?

A soon as she got home that night, Elle went to the bathroom and pulled her hair into a high ponytail. She grabbed a mirror from the vanity drawer and held it behind her head. She looked at its reflection in the wall mirror and spotted an unmistakable bite mark where her hair formed a V at the base of her neck. The scars left by her father were no longer just beneath the surface of her skin.

ॐ ॐ ॐ

As he leaned against the trunk of the tree, evening air fell against Ken's face. He swatted a mosquito that buzzed around his ears and felt a sense of accomplishment when he flattened the pest in the hair and sweat that covered his arms. He stared at the dull light in the window of Elle's apartment and was suddenly agitated by the fact that she had never invited him in her building. "I'll be with you tonight," Ken said aloud as he flattened another mosquito on his arm. He then glanced down at the remains of the bug and the fluid mixed in his hair.

Long after the dusky swirls in the sky disappeared, a cab pulled up along the sidewalk outside of Elle's building. Ken stepped out of the shadows as he watched an elderly woman struggle out of the backseat of the car. She fumbled with her purse and two grocery bags as she made her way up the front walk.

Ken stepped up softly and offered, "May I give you a hand? I was just going in to visit Miss Pandion."

"Thank you, young man. That would be nice. I was out to the movie show with a few lady friends, you know. I stopped for a quart of milk for me and my cat, Milly. Now, here I am stumbling around in the dark," she rambled.

Ken offered a warm smile. "Let me hold your bags while you find your keys." She handed over the two sacks of groceries. Ken took her bags as she unlocked the entrance door. Her apartment was the first door on the left. He handed her back the groceries and said goodnight.

"Thanks, again," she said and closed her door.

Ken walked up the steps to the next landing and found Elle's apartment. He turned the unlocked knob. He cracked open the door and peered in. It was a large studio with a dinette and sitting area. Most of the space was filled with paint supplies and several easels. Ken stepped into the apartment and saw another door ajar. A dim light and faint sound emanated from the room. He moved to the door and looked in. He saw Elle on her bed under the weight of a heavy figure. Ken pushed the door open. The man on the bed jerked his head toward the sound of the door. Ken glared at the man, then turned and walked out of the apartment.

On the following day, Ken went to Dr. Pandion's office. The nurse assistant at the front desk told Ken that Dr. Pandion was booked solid for the entire day, but she would gladly leave a message or make an appointment for him for another day. Ken gave the young girl his name and informed her that he was certain that Dr. Pandion would see him. Within a few minutes, Ken was escorted into Dr. Pandion's private office. The doctor stood behind a cherry desk, elevated a step from the floor. A Tiffany lamp illuminated the room casting a soft glow on a portrait that hung on the wall behind the desk.

"Lovely picture," said Ken.

"It is my wife, Diana, Elizabeth's mother."

"If I didn't know Elle so well, one might mistake the portrait for your daughter."

"Yes."

"Dr. Pandion, we both know why I'm here, yes?"

"Presumably, we do."

"If you want to keep your filthy secret safe, end it."

"Of course," Dr. Pandion conceded almost too quickly.

"Be careful, doctor. You will be destroyed if you go near her," Ken warned.

"I won't go near her. I know the damage that I've caused. I'm sorry. So sorry . . . but it's like a dr–."

"Hold your breath. I'm not your confessor," said Ken.

"Just promise me that you'll be kind to her," pleaded Dr. Pandion.

"Kind! What kind of fucking word is kind? You're a fucking coward! Don't tell me to be kind!" Ken snapped. "Men who torture their children and then blame the kids for the sewage that they leave behind are cowards, and you're a fucking coward. Don't tell me to be kind," Ken said and walked out of the office.

❦ ❦ ❦

After his meeting with Dr. Pandion, Ken ceased making love to Elle, shrouding the relationship in sterility. Elle was tortured by the loss. Instead of the role as a lover, Ken now played the surgeon who was strictly focused on perfecting his patient's existence.

Elle, however, no longer wanted perfect breasts or plump lips. She simply wanted Ken's fingers to touch her body, to revive the senses that were dormant for so long before she met him. She longed for his tongue that teased and tasted her inner self. She would fall

141

into bed at night and run her fingers over her naked body. Feeling the curls of her pubic hair made her stomach churn. Her nipples grew flat with disgust when her fingers touched the firm, pink mounds.

If she was so revolted by her own body, why would Ken want to pollute himself with her filth? It was now clear to her that Ken Tereus would never again touch her intimately, unless her stains were erased. If she wanted him in her life, she would have to accept what he was willing to offer. She would allow him to alter her body in anyway that he demanded. She would allow him to perfect his masterpiece.

Elle had ample vacation time banked, allowing her to hide in her apartment while she recovered from the swelling and bruises caused by the adjustments that Ken was achieving with her face and body. A cheek implant gave her face more definition while liposuction and a buttocks lift balanced her pear shaped figure. She would be lovely, but while she was becoming a vision of perfection, Elle was drowning in isolation. Void of any human engagement, she turned back to her only constant friend for companionship and to tell her story.

CHAPTER 19

Adversity is the first path to truth.

—Lord Byron, Don Juan, 12.50.

Brain-damaged-baby cases rarely bothered Gale, before she was pregnant. True, they were catastrophic, but she was able to disconnect from the emotional component of the files. Pregnant, however, she scoured depositions and medical records searching for symptoms and signs that might relate to her own baby.

Gale was reading the transcript of a deposition to be used at a trial in six weeks; by then, she would be eight months pregnant. The case involved a blind and profoundly brain-damaged baby who was exposed to the herpes virus while traveling through his mother's vaginal canal. The mom had no prior documented history of herpes but tested positive for the virus following the delivery. The mother was suing her obstetrician for neglecting to detect a barely visible vaginal lesion at the time of birth.

It had been a difficult deposition. Trouble started when Gale asked the woman's husband the following question:

143

"Did you have intercourse in June, two months before your child was delivered?

"Yes," he answered.

"Are you sure, Mr. Riley, that it was the month of June."

"Yes, I am sure."

"How do you remember that, Mr. Riley?"

"The kids were still in school. The Reds were beating the Dodgers fourteen to seven. The radio was on in the bedroom. It was an afternoon game. You don't forget what you're doing when you listen to a game like that."

"I see, Mr. Riley. Did you have intercourse in the month of July?"

"Yes," he answered.

"Your wife testified in her deposition yesterday that the two of you did not have intercourse during the months of May or June because your relationship was strained, Mr. Riley. Your wife's employment records indicate that she did not miss work any day in the month of June, Mr. Riley. Was your wife lying to her employer?"

Ultimately, Gale uncovered an extramarital affair between Mr. Riley and his daughter's ballet teacher. Mr. Riley had inadvertently infected his wife with the herpes virus just prior to the delivery of their third child. Regardless of the facts, both the mother and father were convinced that Dr. Larson should have detected the lesion. The couple refused to understand that it was not the doctor's negligence that injured their newborn son; it was the father's silence that caused the brain damage.

Gale shifted in her desk chair. She tried to massage the foot that was sticking in her rib cage.

Could Dave have herpes, she wondered. Maybe she was infected with the virus. She knew little about Dave's own medical history. Just his name made her shiver with pain and with guilt. She refused to tell him about the baby. It was the best thing, for he had moved on with his life, something she told him to do. Besides, she had asked him to call if he ever wanted to talk. He never called.

◕◔ ◕◔ ◕◔

Father Larry Chandler's office was in a crowded, dank room stuffed behind the altar of Our Lady of Loretto Church. It was decorated with pictures of rainbow crosses and motley angels drawn by the Sunday school children from the neighborhood. The space was filled with Father Larry's humble energy and his Aramis cologne. He was a stocky man with ruddy cheeks and hair the color of Elvis Presley's. Gale met Father Larry when she moved into her first apartment. Her building sat on the fringes of a tired neighborhood worn down from years of flooding and a backwash of poverty. Gale was touched by the deference with which Father Larry served his Appalachian family as well as his wealthy parishioners whose magnificent homes overlooked the valley of the poor.

Father Larry had not seen Gale for several months and welcomed her with obvious surprise.

"Gale, I clearly have missed you! I've wondered where you've been lately. I see busy," he said smiling at her stomach.

"Father Larry, this is why I'm here," Gale responded caressing her bulge, "I need to ask for your forgiveness and for your counsel."

"Sit down. How about a brownie?" he offered, grabbing one for himself. "I shouldn't eat them. I blame the ladies in the neighborhood for my few extra pounds," he laughed.

Father Larry settled in at the squeaky card table to listen to her problems. For thirty minutes, Gale rambled in overdrive about the pregnancy. She was honest in telling Father Larry about the abortion clinic visit along with her mother's reaction. He smiled, nodded and frowned at the appropriate times but never seemed to cast a shadow of judgment over Gale. Then, she began to trip and fall over a tangle of words.

"Gale, you can trust me."

"Father Larry, I need to confess something that I'm sorry about, but I can't, or really, I refuse to change."

"Tell me," he said patting her hands.

"The father doesn't know about the baby. He's moved on with his life, and I'm the one who told him to. The guilt is eating me up inside. I feel guilty for pushing him away. I feel guilty for not telling him for so long. He's a good guy. If I tell him that I'm pregnant, he'll do the responsible thing. But really, I don't want him to feel obligated to me or to the baby." As tear drops plopped onto Gale's belly, she watched Father Larry look away.

"Father, I'm sorry about the tears. I just can't help it right now," Gale said.

"It's okay," he said and patted her hand again and again.

Gale pulled her hand away and said, "Father, I'm in a mess, and I know it. You have to help me."

"This is a tough one. I usually come up with a parable about myself to guide people from their darkness, but this one's a little hard to relate to from your perspective."

"No kidding, Father, but please, I need your help, now!"

"Okay, Gale, I'll try. Maybe I can from the father's viewpoint. When God called me to be a priest, I wasn't ready. A rusty Harley Davidson lived in my garage. I tinkered with it day and night. My cycle, girls and my mother's fried chicken were all I really cared about and in about that order. But then, I met a Jesuit priest who introduced me to this incredible world of spirituality. I resisted it, fought it and even got angry at the priest for showing me this side of holy existence. Eventually, the calling became more powerful than my Harley or my hankering for girls. I was awakened to a different life."

"Father, I'm not talking about fried chicken and motorcycles. I'm talking about a baby and its father," interrupted Gale.

"I know. Just give me a chance. Whether I was ready for it or not, I became the father of a spiritual family. It's a different type of calling, but maybe Dave is ready for fatherhood, and he just isn't aware of it."

"Father, that's very sweet, and I like your story, but we've never even said, 'I love you' to each other," cried Gale. "Actually, I told him that I loved him, but he didn't say it back. He told me that he could never say those words to me.

"And on top of that, I'm sure that he's going to marry some woman! He's never been serious with anyone but me, and he's serious with her. Even if I go to hell, I can't tell him right now," Gale said frantically.

"My dear," Father said patting her hand, "you're not going to hell, but I do want you to pray for strength and direction."

"Father, forget strength right now. It's not going to happen. I can pray, but that is all I can do right now."

"That's enough. Prayer has gotten people pretty far in life, but I really think that you can and want to do more. You came here knowing pretty well what I would recommend you to do. Isn't that true?"

Gale slowly nodded her head yes and then said, "Can I ask you a serious question, Father?"

"I'm not sure we can get much more serious tonight."

"Please," she said with a slight smile.

"Go right ahead."

"Will you baptize my baby if I'm not married and don't have his or her dad standing at the altar?"

"Don't be silly, with all blessings that the little guy deserves."

After meeting with Father Larry, Gale went home for a snack and to call Dicey. As Gale chomped into an apple, Dicey scrutinized her meeting with Father Larry.

"He was telling you to give Dave a chance at being a father. You can't prejudge his reaction to fatherhood without informing him. It's wrong."

"Dicey, you don't have to get mean. I'm trying my hardest to make the right decisions. Maybe you're wrongly judging me."

"Somebody needs to be honest with you. You're walking around all proud and pregnant while Dave is completely in the dark."

"Excuse me? That was a bit harsh. I'm all proud and pregnant? My whole world has imploded. My mother won't talk to me. My partners look at me with disdain, and the ladies in the neighborhood snub me. Let me celebrate the fact that Father Larry didn't act like I was the dirt under his fingernails. Beyond Hank and you, those were the only kind words I've heard in eight months. And now you're turning on me— again! You can't Dicey. Hank and you are going to be godparents very soon."

"I'm not turning on you, and please don't rush to include Hank in the godparent equation."

"It's settled. What do you mean by that? Of course, I want him in the equation," said Gale.

"It's not you that I'm worried about."

"Why, what's wrong, a fight?"

"It wasn't a fight. It's nothing."

"What is it, Dice? Tell me."

"He doesn't want children."

"Ah, honey, sure he does. He just wants to do it the right way. Marriage first. You know, like I should have done," Gale said as she pulled cheese from the refrigerator and then kicked the door closed with her foot.

"No, that's not it. He said that he already raised his children. He doesn't want to be fifty-three with a two year old. I love Hank. He's my soul-mate, but I want children, too. Look at you, I want that."

"Dicey, you don't want what I have right now. Trust me. Maybe he'll change his mind after you get married," she said and crunched on a pretzel.

"Stop eating for one minute! I'm not banking on that. There's a woman at school who married an older man. They fought over having kids. He conceded to one child but said it wasn't his responsibility. The guy stuck to his guns, and now she and the child essentially lead lives separate from the dad."

"Hank's different. He's a very caring man. Give him a chance."

"Why should I give him a chance when you won't even give Dave a chance?"

"Okay . . . you win. I'll drop it, but the odds are that you two are going to be stuck together like peanut butter and jelly— forever!"

"Would you stop thinking about food," asked Dicey. "I've been meaning to tell you something."

"What?"

"I called your mother."

"You called my mother? Why in the hell would you do that?"

"Because all this fighting needs to end. You both need to forgive and move on, Gale."

"For God's sake, Dicey, she thought I should have an abortion."

"No, she didn't. That was just your mother doing her normal yapping. You've got to get over it. It was just a knee-jerk reaction. I'm not trying to start a fight, but you had the same knee jerk for one split second . . . you know that that's not what your mother really wanted."

"Since when do you defend my mother?"

"Since she offered to have your baby shower at the country club, and she's paying," laughed Dicey. "She wants to invite all the cousins and aunts and neighbors. Let her. My godchild needs accessories beyond the paper clips and computer ink stacked in her closet."

CHAPTER 20

True dignity abides with him alone
Who, in the silent hour of inward thought,
Can still suspect, and still revere himself,
In lowliness of heart.

—William Wordsworth ,

"Lines left upon a Seat in Yew-tree," 1798.

E lle's life plunged into deeper agony and isolation. The more she struggled for a glimpse of reality, the faster sanity slipped through her fingers. Dr. Pandion discontinued all communication. Ken never spoke about that night or about her father. He was behaving with a strained aloofness that frightened Elle. On one hand, he repelled her emotionally, but on the other, he had become obsessive and controlling about her external transformation.

When he was physically close to her, Ken moved with deliberate restraint. His chest heaved in a deep, controlled rhythm. When Elle pulled back from further changes to her body, the pressure heightened. She had already lost her spirit to her father, now she was losing her body, but if she were to stop the makeover, Ken would completely disappear, too.

She was given a reprieve from the tension, however, in early July. Ken was leaving for a brief trip to Asia. A rare vase from the T'ang dynasty had surfaced on the market, and he wanted to see it before making such a substantial purchase.

👁️👁️ 👁️👁️ 👁️👁️

Elle couldn't avoid Gale's baby shower without arousing further concern from her friends. Over six weeks had passed since her facial surgery, and the lesions from the cheek implants had disappeared. She was beginning to look less bruised, but this did not diminish the shock that Gale and Dicey felt when Elle arrived at the country club.

Dicey couldn't control her emotions when she saw her. "My God, Elle, what has he done to you? Your face, your sweet face. . . ."

Tears welled up in Elle's eyes, and Dicey begged, "Oh God. Please don't cry, honey. I'm sorry." She pulled Elle over to a seat and sat her down. Dicey's heart sank as she watched her curl into the corner of the couch.

"Listen, calm down. I'll go and get you a drink and find Gale. You can congratulate her. Don't worry, Elle. She's changed a lot more than you," said Dicey. Elle tried to smile, and Dicey went to grab Gale from a crowd of women.

"Now, don't act shocked because she'll cry, and we don't need a scene today."

"Dice, what are you talking about?" asked Gale.

"It's Elle. You won't believe what Tereus did to her face. She has giant jaw breakers in her cheeks now. She started to cry when I asked what he did to her. So, just act like everything is normal."

"Okay, but how can I possibly act like that?"

"God, I don't know. Say something about your own basketball!"

Gale looked toward the couch where Elle was sitting but only saw the back of her head.

"Please go over there while I get her a drink."

Gale moved Elle from the couch to a large circle of chairs formed to play baby shower games. A tray was passed around the group with twenty baby items on it that ranged from a thermometer to a nose plunger. Once the tray was taken away, the women raced to write down all the items that they could remember. Two women with infants won the game by remembering eighteen of the twenty items.

Dicey was sitting next to Gale and whispered, "They cheated. Your mother held the tray in front of them longer than she did for me."

"They're cousins. Mom's favorites," Gale laughed.

"You know your sister's going to win the next game."

"Of course, she will."

Dicey was right. Amy won the word scramble by making thirty-one words out of "Gale's Baby Shower" in two minutes.

"Is it time to open the gifts, yet?" asked Dicey.

"This party was your idea. So, don't complain."

Gale received one highchair, two strollers, a plastic tub filled with baby soap and shampoo. Mrs. Knightly gave her a silver baby cup and spoon that was Gale's grandmother. Elle painted a picture for the baby's nursery featuring a delightful violet bird with golden eyes. It was perched in a gilded cage. Its tiny neck was arched and beak wide open as if captured in song. Gale thought that the picture was lovely, but Dicey disagreed.

When Elle went to get a glass of punch, Dicey said, "I think that bird looks like its choking. You can't hang that in the baby's room."

"The picture is fine. In her state, I would never hurt her feelings by not hanging it. The purple bird matches the bedroom— the color that you picked."

Dicey sensed a frantic desperation in the painting and in Elle. She chastised herself for not keeping in closer contact with her over the past few months. Dicey had been too caught up in her own life to detect Elle's spiraling physical and emotional regression.

Listening to Gale field questions about the father of her baby distracted Dicey from her concern for Elle. Mrs. Knightly revealed to the guests that Gale had a history of fibroid tumors and emphasized that she wanted children before she was "as barren as a damn desert!" Then she said, "Don't ask her, but I think the sperm bank was stocked with Harvard grads. The whole process was very avant garde."

As Gale stood with her mouth hanging open, Dicey grabbed her stomach in laughter. It was one time in her life when she loved Mrs. Knightly! Gale turned to Dicey for help, but her friend only offered shakes of laughter in return.

⚬⚬ ⚬⚬ ⚬⚬

Later that evening, while Dicey helped Gale arrange the nursery with new baby clothes and gifts, Gale fiddled with the feet of a pair of footed pajamas.

"Dice," she began, "just think about it. I can count down my days to delivery on the fingers and toes of this little guy who is pushing and poking inside me. I'll be a mother in less than three weeks, and I'm terrified. It's a lot scarier than standing in the courtroom before a jury and a judge. I'll be responsible for my own child's life, not some client that did or didn't do something wrong."

"It's a huge responsibility," Dicey agreed as she held up bunny pajamas. "These are too cute."

"I'm serious. I'm really frightened. What if I fail? Mothers can do a lot of damage to a child. Not even knowing it, we can dump our own baggage on our kids and really hurt them. And look at me already, my child won't even have a normal family— not even a father— and please don't start."

"I wasn't going to say a word."

"Honestly, I want to do everything exactly right. Whatever I have strived for, I've gotten. I've always been in control of my own destiny, but somehow, I know I'm not exactly in control anymore. I want to be perfect at being a mother, but I'm afraid of making a mistake and ending up with a kid who is a drug addict or a mental case. It's crazy. I'm just so scared about making a mistake."

"You'll be lucky if you make only one mistake an hour as a mother. And sure, you could end up with a teenager who survives by selling grilled cheese sandwiches at rock concerts. One of my students did that for a while. Somehow, I just don't think that it's going to happen that way. The kid will want to know who his father is, but that's a different issue. That has nothing to do with you failing as a mother."

"Who knows? Whoever thought that I would be having a bastard as a child? I don't think that I really know anything right now. I just wish that I could bring my child into this world with a normal family."

"Honey, there's nothing normal about families, and there are no perfect mothers in this world. Not even June Cleaver," said Dicey.

"Who in the hell is June Cleaver?" asked Gale.

"You know, the "Beave's" mom from *Leave it to Beaver*, that old TV show from the sixties. Grandma and I used to watch the reruns together. I always wanted my mom and dad to be perfect, like on *Leave it to Beaver*. Mrs. Cleaver was always so patient with the Beave. She gave him enough rope to hang himself but always guided him down the right road in the end. When I played house, I was always June Cleaver. I told my grandma that I was going to be a perfect mother, just like Mrs. Cleaver. Then, she'd start in on me."

"What do you mean? From what you tell me, your grandmother was damn close to perfection."

"No, Gale, not really, but she was smart as hell. She taught me that a woman shouldn't strive to be perfect. Instead, she should strive to be excellent. Be happy with excellence. But remember, it takes a lot of mistakes before you get excellent at anything."

"Thank heaven one of us had an excellent mama. Now, tell me, how is Hank?"

"Gale, I love the man. He is a good and decent person, but I don't think that he'll ever budge on the baby business."

"How are his kids?" asked Gale, "Are they still pretty nice?"

"They were cordial in the beginning, but now the fire's dwindled. The relationship was okay at first, when it wasn't serious, but now . . . maybe they feel a little threatened. They're a lot nicer than I would be, though. I remember one time when Daddy brought home some tramp named Peggy. Her hair was teased into a giant puff ball, and her eyes were lined like Cleopatra's cat."

"Was it *Rocky Horror Picture Show* material?"

"No worse. This trash bag passed out as wide and bald as an American eagle on his mattress. They were both too drunk to even close the door. I was pissed. That night, I made a poster in red crayon that said, "Go Home." The next day, I had to call her nasty ass and apologize. I hated Harvey more than anything for months after that."

"Maybe his children have something to do with Hank not wanting kids?"

"I don't know. I doubt he's even talked to them about it."

"Yeah, but maybe they talked to him. It would be natural for them to feel jealous. Dicey, he's a great man and, I'm certain, a great father. He's got to be concerned about them. Talk to him."

"I've tried. There's a fine line between nudging gently and pushing a topic right off the cliff. . . . Now, don't get mad, but what have you decided about Dave?"

"Here we go again!"

"I'm not giving up."

"Dicey, I don't think you really understand how much this is tormenting me. Not only do I want to be a perfect mom, but I want to do what's right with Dave. Time hasn't told me what to do yet."

"What do you mean?"

"Things work out with time; I'm waiting for an answer."

"My God, that is such crap, Gale. You've got to make this happen. Dave isn't going to call up one day singing, 'Havin' My Baby?' . . . I'm giving you one week to call him."

"Okay, Okay. I'll call him tomorrow at work."

"You can't call a guy at work and say, 'Hey, guess what? You're going to be a daddy.' Call him at home, now. It's a Sunday night. He's got to be home." Dicey picked up her cell phone and handed it to Gale.

"All right, I will. There you go, Dice, you win. After nine months, you've worn me down. I can't fight with you or myself any longer. You win," Gale sadly said.

"Thank the Lord and my grandma, too. See, I knew you'd do the right thing. I rolled a double white for you this morning!" she said rattling the cubes in Gale's face.

Gale's hand shook as she dialed his number. The phone rang several times before his machine finally picked up. Gale listened intently to his message. "Hi, it's Dave. I'll be out of the country for a few weeks. Call my office if you need me. Chao!"

She swallowed hard and said, "Hi, Dave. It's Gale. Give me a call when you're back in town. I need to talk to you. It's very important."

Gale hung up and a tear trickled down her cheek. "He's out of the goddamn country. If he got married without even telling me, I'll hate him forever. How could he keep that from me?"

Dicey hung her head. Dave and Gale were too much alike, too proud to ever know how much they really loved each other.

☙☙ ☙☙ ☙☙

That night Gale lurched in bed. With less than three weeks from her due date, she was too big to find comfort. Her ribs felt like a batting cage as tiny elbows and feet poked and kicked. Gale stuck a pillow between her legs for some relief. Just as her body and the baby calmed, the phone rang. She stretched for the receiver,

"Hello."

"Gale, it's me."

"Dave?" Gale propped herself up in bed.

"Yeah, you called."

"I thought you were out of the country."

"I'm back for a week. We're still on a job in the Dominican Republic. I'm going back in a few days."

"What time is it?" Gale asked squinting at the clock.

"I don't know— ten, eleven your time."

"How's life?"

"Great."

"How's your dad?"

"He's well."

"Dave, I've got to cut through the small talk."

"What is it, Gale?" Dave asked with a shift in his tone.

"It's nothing that I can talk about over the phone."

"Gale, this is a busy time for me. The project in the Dominican Republic is already running three weeks behind schedule."

"Dave, please. I know this is my fault and that I should have made the call before, but I really must see you."

"Gale, are you in some kind of trouble?"

"No."

"Are you sick?"

"No, just trust me, Dave. I need to see you."

"Gale, it's over between us. It's been over for eight months. What could you possibly need to talk to me about in person? If you're getting married or something, I bid you best wishes, but there's nothing for us to discuss any longer."

"Dave, I'm begging you. Please, just trust me that it is important."

Dave agreed to see her. "I'll trust you, Gale. I'll take the company plane into Crystal Springs tomorrow and catch a flight to the Dominican from there. It will be in the late afternoon. I'll call when I get in."

"Thanks, Dave," Gale said, but wanted to say I love you.

After hanging up the phone, Gale plopped back down in bed and groaned, "I'm massive. What is he going to say?" She grabbed the phone and dialed again.

"Dice?"

"Gale, are you okay? It's midnight."

"I'm going to see him tomorrow."

Dicey rolled away from Hank. "He called back?"

"He's coming in the afternoon."

"That's a good thing."

❦ ❦ ❦

The next day, Gale left work early to prepare. She squeezed into her fifth outfit and again looked into the full length mirror. She started to cry and called Dicey.

"I can't go through with this. Everything I put on makes me look like a Volkswagen bus."

"You're just overly sensitive. Your hormones are in overdrive."

"You would be sensitive, too, if you had a day like mine."

"Why, what happened?"

"You promise not to laugh?"

"Yes."

"I was standing at the elevator with a client and two partners, and just out of nowhere, I farted. It wasn't a little fart. It was a loud squeaky, fart." Dicey laughed.

"Stop laughing."

"Gale, people don't just involuntarily fart."

"I did, and these three men just stood there and stared at me. No sympathy, no ice-breakers. They just stared until the elevator doors opened. Stop laughing, Dicey. You're no help. I'll call you later."

Gale hung up the phone and decided on black clingy slacks with a deeply cut pewter shirt.

"At least he'll like these," she said and cupped her breasts.

Dave called from the plane. They agreed to meet at The Pump Room at five o'clock. She arrived one half hour early. This was one time in her life that her seating really was important. She selected a spot with a high bar table and stools; she could watch the door as Dave approached but also hide her swollen belly.

She spotted him first. Her stomach contracted. He was a beautiful man. Even nine months pregnant, her body responded. His broad smile began to change, though, as he approached.

"Gale," he breathed hard. She stood up and came around the table reaching to hug him. He pulled away.

"What's going on with you?" he demanded.

"I'm pregnant."

"No shit, Gale. What in the hell is this about?"

"Would you please lower your voice!"

"I'm not going to lower my voice. You're ready to deliver a baby, and you tell me to lower my fucking voice."

"Please, Dave."

"Don't 'please Dave' me. This didn't just happen. What is going on with you?"

"Sit down and let's have a drink or something."

"You sit down. You're the one who's pregnant. What in the hell is this? What has been going on for the last nine months? A phone call would have been nice."

"You don't just pick up the phone and tell someone you're pregnant."

"Why wouldn't you? You wouldn't only if there was something to hide."

"I have called you."

"Well, you sure didn't say much."

"But you did. You told me that you were practically engaged."

"No, I didn't. I told you that I moved on with my life. You told me to. What in the hell does that have to do with you getting knocked-up?"

"I didn't get knocked-up."

"So, you're married. What else are you hiding?"

"Nothing! I'm not married. You're being cruel."

"Cruel? At least I was honest with you. We've been together for eight years, and you pull this shit on me."

"Dave, stop. You're the one who's with someone else."

"Obviously, you were too!"

"Stop! Stop! Stop!" She began to cry.

"Don't lay tears on me. You waddle into a restaurant after nine months and expect me to be nice. Did you ever stop to think about me? If I remember correctly, the last time we were together, I asked you to marry me. I rush my ass down here in the middle of the biggest project of my life because I think that something tragic has happened, and I get this!"

"Dave, you asked me to marry you like it was a business proposition between your dad and you."

"Listen, I'm sorry that I'm not as articulate as the Miss Gale Knightly, but at least I'm honest."

"I tried to tell you. I called you when I found out about the baby. First, you were in Austria. The second time I called you had already moved on. Remember, you said that you were finally in a 'serious' relationship. How could I tell you then?"

"What does any of this have to do with you getting pregnant, for God's sake?"

"I never knew you could be so mean."

"I never knew that you could hurt me so much."

"I was trying to think of your feelings. I didn't want to lay this responsibility on you if you were in love with someone else."

"What are you saying? What responsibility? This isn't my responsibility. I'm not pregnant."

"Dave, what responsibility do you think I'm talking about?"

"Oh no, Gale, don't think about laying that shit on me. You're not trying to suggest that I'm the father, are you?"

"What else would I be saying?"

"We've had sex one time in a year, and you want to suggest that I'm the baby's father. You're fucking nuts."

"I'm not fucking nuts. You are the only man that I have ever had sex with, ever!"

"Gale, I think you've really lost it. Do you really want me to believe I'm the father? I know you. You're too up front to hide something so important. Why are you doing this?"

"I'm doing this because I thought I had a duty to tell you that you're going to be a father. I'm not asking you for a goddamn dime, and I'm not asking for your help. It's only information. Take it or leave."

"Is that it? Take it or leave it? You tell me I'm going to be a father after nine months of hiding it, and then you say you don't want anything from me. Don't reduce a baby to money, Gale. That's disgusting. And it's not like you're destitute and living out of the back of a Toyota . . . unless that's changed, too. Did the high and mighty Smith, Kennedy & Clark fire you?"

"No, they didn't fire me, Dave, and you don't have to believe a word I say. I wasn't going to tell you anyway. I've obviously made a huge mistake."

"It's obvious that this isn't the only mistake that you've made. You're crazy. I don't know what's happened to you, but you've really lost it."

"You know what, Dave, just leave and get the hell out of my life. You've hurt me enough."

"This pain isn't all about you, Gale. Think about what you are telling me. If I was really the father, you wouldn't have waited nine months to tell me. I know that much. So, you know what, I will get the hell out of your life."

And Dave walked straight out the door.

ᖇᖇ ᖇᖇ ᖇᖇ

Gale sat in the rocker moving steadily back and forth, back and forth. She stared at the songbird Elle had painted for the nursery. The golden eyes of the bird returned her stare, as if the creature had a secret to share. Gale began to weep. Not only was she alone and pregnant, but she managed to alienate the only man whom she had ever loved. As her sobs grew more intense, an unbearable contraction ripped through her body. Her water burst.

CHAPTER 21

And the deaf tyranny of Fate,
The ruling principle of Hate,
Which for its pleasure doth create
The things it may annihilate,
Refused thee even the boon to die:
The wretched gift eternity
Was thine— and thou hast borne it well.

—George Gordon, Lord Byron, "Prometheus"

The chaotic drive for perfection dominated Ken Tereus's childhood with the same intensity that perfection dominated his adult world. He was born with a head of scarlet hair that quickly deepened into a rich auburn crown. His speckled brown eyes defused into golden amber by six months of age. Dr. Tereus, Sr., and his wife doted on their infant son with direction and guidance. At an early age, Dr. Tereus destined his son to be a magnificent surgeon, a physician to whom mankind would be indebted for wiping out the imperfections of nature.

The education of their only son began when the child was just an infant. Baby talk or nursery rhymes sung by his mother were prohibited. When the boy took his first teetering steps, wobbly falls were met with a swift swat. As the child took bigger steps in life, missteps and falls were met with a harsher hand. The infliction of pain was essential in the formation of an omnipotent adult. Pain molded Walter Tereus into a great man, and it promised to do the same for his son. His son would learn perseverance from the searing agony of frostbite. His son would learn endurance from hours of kneeling or standing in a single position. His son would learn resolution from days without food. His son would learn to be a man because of pain, not in spite of pain.

Dr. Walter Tereus' education began on November 30, 1950 when his battalion of the 2nd Infantry Division was captured by the Chinese, just south of Kunu-ri, North Korea. It was around midnight when the battalion was stopped by a road block. Soldiers were commanded to abandon the caravan and take concealment in the hills, while the wounded were left behind. As Walter Tereus headed for cover, he listened to sounds of gunshots bouncing off the icy hillsides. That night swarms of Chinese military slaughtered the wounded Americans and captured those who could still march, including Walter. The corralled soldiers began a three week frigid trek to "Death Valley", a make-shift prison camp where forty percent of the inmates died within three months of stay.

Death Valley taught men everything that they needed to know about the power of pain. Along with twenty other inmates, Walter crammed into an eight feet by eight feet, lice infested shack to avoid the sub zero nights. When the stench of bodies infected with dysentery grew too strong, he huddled against the shack's outside walls for warmth. He learned how to make a handful of soybeans or cracked corn last for a week. Years later, his knees still swelled up from many thirty hour stints of standing in icy rain. Because of these lessons in pain, lessons that he would teach his son, Walter Tereus became a great man, a great doctor.

Ken, like his father, was an outstanding athlete. He was the star pitcher for his little league baseball team the year that they won the Little League World Series at Atlanta. It was 1974, and Ken pitched 31 games that season. During the three hour bus ride back to Cincinnati, Ken led the team singing "Takin' Care of Business," and he was the first to climb off the bus carrying the thirty-six inch trophy.

Dr. Tereus was there to congratulate his son. "You won that game— those pussies on your team couldn't hold your jockstrap." Ken remembered this as the first and last compliment that he would ever receive from his father.

Dr. Tereus also coached Ken's basketball team the same year that he went to the World Series. The basketball team had a 21-0 season and was ranked in first place before the citywide tournaments began. Dr. Tereus met his match in the last game of Ken's fifth grade tournament. The opposing coach scouted out Tereus's strategy and knew that double teaming the star player would mean victory. By the end of the third quarter, Ken scored only a single basket. Dr. Tereus lost the tournament with a forty-one to forty score.

On the ride home, Dr. Tereus did not speak to his son. When they pulled into the driveway, Ken was sent to the basement without dinner. After he ate, Dr. Tereus went downstairs to teach his son his lesson.

"You're a pussy. You'll never embarrass me like you did tonight."

"Sir, I got tired. You never rotated me out."

"Shut up! You don't know tired. Get down on your knees." For the next three hours, Ken kneeled on the cement floor while his father lectured him on the power of pain. A single tear welled in Ken's eye as he listened to his mother move about in the kitchen.

Dr. Tereus' expectations of perfection infiltrated Ken's academic life, too. Through the eighth grade, Ken's lowest grade was an A-, but in the ninth grade, algebra tested his mettle. Even with tutoring, he couldn't earn above a B on tests.

It was a Wednesday night when Ken returned home from basketball practice. He walked in the front door and spotted the tub of ice. At that moment, Ken knew he hadn't received an A in algebra. His father stormed out of the kitchen with Ken's report card strangled in his fist. Mrs. Tereus cowered in the corner with her eyes staring toward the floor. Dr. Tereus directed his son to carry the tub down to the basement, and for the next few hours, Ken sat with his feet plunged into the sub zero tub of ice, while his father lectured him on the power of pain.

Despite the vicious struggle for his father's approval at home, Ken never battled for attention at school. He was courteous to adults, smart, athletic and had strikingly good looks. Even the mothers, who hadn't quite escaped the high school mentality, flirted with him. At school, Ken could do no wrong. Even when his behavior was extreme, it was passed-off as a "boy being a boy."

During high school, the football field served as an arena of misplaced anger. He delighted in hurting his opponent. After a tackle, he continued to pummel his man hidden under the mass of arms and legs.

Ken's discreet brutality and craving for control seeped into his relationships with females. He first tasted this sense of sexual power when he was a junior in high school. Ken was at a party where the parents were out of town and the pot and alcohol were flowing freely. An attractive sophomore named Stephanie offered him a drag off her joint. Both sky high, Ken invited Stephanie to his car. He drove to a wooded spot a few blocks from the party. He got out of the car and told Stephanie to get in the backseat. She did what he told her to do. He pulled off her shirt and grabbed her breasts.

"Suck me," he said. She bent her head and within seconds he was hard. Then, Ken pulled up her skirt and ripped off her panties. In a few quick thrusts he tore her skin and came.

The beautiful girls never talked about their experiences with Ken Tereus. Ken was smart. He was able to sense the girls who were already muffled by something else in their life.

❦ ❦ ❦

Ken was successful at controlling his outside world throughout college and medical school, but he never stopped yearning for his father's approval. His eyes scanned the audience, searching for his father. It was the most important moment of his professional career, and his father was a no-show. He had won the prestigious E. L. Swarts Medal, a national award given annually to the outstanding student in plastic surgery by the American Board of Plastic Surgeons. He stood at the podium before three hundred admiring people and hated his father more than any other time in his life. He was achieving everything that his father wanted. He was becoming the creator of perfection where mankind would be indebted to him for their rebirth. He possessed fantastical powers as a plastic surgeon. He could bring people to the very brink of death and then bring them back to life as a new creation, but it still wasn't good enough.

Ken became a masterful surgeon. His body pulsated with excitement as he sliced along a patient's hairline. He would carefully peel back the dermis and trim twelve years off a person's eyes, forehead and neck. When Ken operated on beautiful women, an erection would grow between his legs as his goddess was transformed on the steel surgical table, immobilized by him. Late in the evening or in the early hours of the morning, Ken visited his patients. The closer he brought these women to the edge of life, the more deeply aroused he became.

CHAPTER 22

Cruelty has a Human Heart
And Jealousy a Human Face
Terror, the Human Form Divine
And Secrecy, the Human Dress

—William Blake, "A Divine Image"

*T*he salty Bangkok air revived Ken after his tedious flight from the States. From the patio of his seaside bungalow, he watched the young Thai girls roll down their bathing suit tops and massage oil on their small breasts. His own hut mutt was no more than sixteen years old with long black hair that touched the top of her ass. As she handed Ken a glass of wine, he thought about touching her nipples. Sex was an unspoken amenity in Bangkok, anything for an extra charge. But he didn't want the distraction just yet. He was still waiting for Talat's call. He left a message with his new cell number over an hour ago and was growing impatient for a response. His phone vibrated as the mutt set down a second glass of wine.

"Ah, Talat, where have you been?" asked Ken.

"I am a busy man, Dr. Tereus," Talat responded in near perfect English.

"How is the green beauty, Talat?"

"Lovely as I promised."

"When will I see her?"

"Tomorrow, for tea. I am staying at the Oriental Bangkok. Meet me in the Author's Lounge at one-thirty. Then, I will bring you to her. You must decide soon. I have other interested parties."

"Yes, I understand. What about the porcelain snuff bottle?" Ken asked.

"That is easy. See you later," said Talat, and he hung up the phone.

Ken first met Talat Ashram at a Sotheby's auction in London about nine years before. A Qianlong rose hexagonal vase had just sold for over two million dollars. A cinnamon skinned gentleman sitting next to Ken leaned close and whispered in his ear, "Outrageous. I can get the same vase for one half of the price." He slipped Ken his card and then got up and left the auction house.

Ken looked at the card and read Talat Ashram, In the Business of Fine Rarities and Antiquities. Later that night, Ken called the international cell number and spoke to Mr. Ashram.

"Ah, Dr. Tereus, I was hoping that you would call."

"How did you know my name, Mr. Ashram?"

"That is my job to know who collects rare and beautiful art, Dr. Tereus. You have excellent taste in Asian objects."

"Thank you, Mr. Ashram, but you should know that I don't work with private dealers."

"I am not a dealer, Dr. Tereus. I am a collector. Let us talk. I would like to share my collection with you. Where are your accommodations?"

"I'm staying at Claridge's in Mayfair," answered Ken.

"Wonderful. I'm at The Ritz. Shall we meet tomorrow, say three-thirty. The Palm Court has a lovely tea, a delightful experience."

"Excellent, Mr. Ashram."

"Please, Dr. Tereus, call me Talat."

Ken met with Mr. Ashram and learned that he, in fact, was a collector. He collected very expensive clients and traded in beautiful and rare objects.

"Dr. Tereus, I must compliment you on your purchase of the bronze rabbit head last year in Cambodia. That was a daring proposition with no provenance to verify its authenticity."

"I had a gut feeling about the work, and its lack of provenance or possible provenance is what intrigued me, Mr. Ashram. Would you like more tea?" Ken asked.

"Please." He pushed his saucer toward Ken and asked, "Who knows? The piece could have been stolen by the Russian Empire before the Revolution."

"Or, the Anglo-French troops in 1860. One never knows what one cannot verify, Mr. Ashram."

"I've seen other similar pieces. One may suggest that your rabbit head is part of the twelve animals of the zodiac stolen from the Summer Palace in China. I believe only seven of the fountainheads still exist today," said Talat.

"I understand that." Ken paused, "Do you know anything else about the zodiac work?"

"Yes. Would you like to add more pieces to your collection of fountainheads, Dr. Tereus?"

"I only have a rabbit bronze. These types of statues are impossible to find, Talat. The Chinese government and UNESCO are tightening their grip on certain antiquities."

"Ah, you Americans are so smart, yet so naive."

Instead of responding to Talat, Ken looked around the lavish dining room. Elegant ladies with smart hats sipped tea and picked at raspberry scones. His eyes fell on one female in particular. She was the type of woman whom people referred to as a beauty in her younger days. Now, the soft folds of her face were being pushed forward by the weight of her hat, and her body seemed squeezed into the petite chair.

Ken turned back to Talat and said, "You appear to know a lot about me and my transactions, Mr. Ashram. Why is that?"

"That is part of my job, Dr. Tereus."

"In what way?"

"I only select clients who deal in exquisite items and have much to lose," answered Talat.

"Much to lose? What do you mean?"

"Men with too much to lose are discreet. I can trust them. You don't jeopardize me, and I don't jeopardize you— quid pro quo. Do you understand?" Talat asked.

"I think, but what is your exact line of business?"

"I told you, anything rare and beautiful, jewelry, antiquities, women. They're all the same. Anything can be bought and sold for a price, Dr. Tereus. You want the ox head to add to your zodiac collection, I can find it and have it hand delivered by a beautiful Chinese girl."

"How can I trust you, Mr. Ashram?"

"You can because we both have too much to lose," said Talat.

"I understand that the ox head is buried somewhere in the storage rooms of the Waibamiao Museum never to be seen by a capitalistic Westerner again."

"You forget what I just said, Dr. Tereus. Everyone and everything has a negotiable price— even in the People's Republic. There is a museum annex located in Chengde, a pleasant town in the northeastern part of the country. Your bronze bovine may be sleeping there."

"Maybe we should talk about awakening the bull," said Ken.

Talat Ashram was a clever business man. He discovered the chink in each of his client's drive for pleasure and intertwined it with his antiquities trade. He made more money from smuggling artifacts, but the interconnection with physical pleasure created a demand within his clientele that couldn't be repressed. He restricted his lines of business to illicit antiquities and human smuggling. He refused to dabble in the drug trade because the clients and the smugglers were of a lower class of people with very little to lose.

He identified his clients by the type of sex they desired and the type of art that they collected. Most were international political or social figures. One of his clients, a British Lord referred to as the Noble, had an odd penchant for plump, older women. He also maintained a fine figurine collection of fat ladies that were extremely rare and noted for their graceful modeling. The first piece that Talat procured for the Brit was a rare figure of a court lady from the Tang dynasty. The majestic piece of pottery stood with her full body swaying forward to display full breasts under the bodice. Her delicate upturned face tempted with ebony eyes and scarlet lips. The Noble was driven by the soft, fleshy folds of skin hidden beneath the sweeping robe. The figurine was delivered by a chubby, older woman dressed in a similar Mandarin gown.

Another client of Talat's was a Greek shipping mogul who loved boys. The most distinguished artifact that Talat procured for him was a jade figure depicting a young herder mounted on the back of a prostrate buffalo dating from 200 B.C. The Greek, however, preferred artwork that depicted multiple boys. His favorite piece was an ovoid vase finely painted with three naked boys playing in a sultry garden. Talat had the vase delivered by two nineteen year old boys.

Talat had difficulty in pinpointing Ken's pleasure spot as his taste in artifacts varied. Though he collected bestial statues and figurines, Ken also had an eye for rare Chinese vases. He was thrilled when Talat procured an extremely rare copper-red pear shaped vessel from the Ming Dynasty. The vase had a generously rounded body surmounted by a classic neck line and a delicate lip. Ken seemed equally pleased when he delivered a slender, pear shaped vessel wearing a well-rounded body with a tapering waist and elegant neck from the Yuan Dynasty. During this meeting, Talat discovered Ken's passion.

"Dr. Tereus, I see that you like this delicate vessel. Are there no other desires that I may fulfill for you?" Talat asked.

"I don't understand. To what are you referring?"

"My business is not limited to antiquities, as you know. There are other forms of lovely vessels available."

"Talat, Bangkok is overflowing with lovely vessels. I don't need you for that."

"But I can find one for you to purchase. Many families need money."

"What would I do with her once I bought her, Talat? I have no need for her in the States. How would I dispose of her?"

"That is not my business. That is no one's business in Bangkok."

Through this meeting with Talat, Ken discovered an arena where he could finally explore his desire to test the narrow boundary between life and death. Alone in bed that night, his body trembled with the ultimate power and control that was finally at his fingertips.

It was on this trip that Ken also began his obsession with Chinese snuff bottles. His first piece was a tiny spherical bottle painted with a garden scene of exotic lilies, asters and a crested long-tailed bird. Talat promised that the artifact was from the 18th century Beijing Palace workshop. The imperial enameled metal bottle was hand-delivered by an eighteen year old Mandarin girl whose parents had nine more children at home. No one was concerned when the ebony haired girl disappeared. All that remained was a locket of her hair held in the 18th century snuff bottle.

From that trip forward, Talat Ashram owned Ken Tereus. Six months after his first encounter with the young girl, Ken contacted Talat requesting a 15th century vase. Talat located a rose vessel with an elegant swollen body surmounted by a short tapering neck. It was delivered by a fifteen year old girl who also brought with her a spectacular soapstone and spinach jade snuff bottle.

When the fecund vessel walked into Ken's bungalow, his body pulsated. He was hardened by the beautiful perfection that stood before him. Ken carefully wrapped his legs around the pear shaped torso and slowly slid into the parted lips. Before his release, Ken extended his fingers around the delicate neck pulling all life from the girl, not until then was he freed to release himself.

Ken was satisfied. She was perfection tainted by an ugly world, and he had delivered her into an eternity of flawless beauty. The jade snuff bottle held the only remains of her contaminated life, a locket of her hair.

❦ ❦ ❦

The bright skylights and a cool breeze of jasmine struck Ken as he walked into the Author's Lounge to meet Talat. The elegant restaurant was resplendent with history as authors like Joseph Conrad and Graham Greene made it a favorite haunt. There was a small book shelf at the entrance that touted this history. While Ken waited to be seated, he read through some of the titles of these famous writers— *Heart of Darkness, Lord Jim, The End of the Affair.*

He was escorted to the table by an ebony haired hostess wearing a silk robe that fluttered between her legs as she moved through the room. Talat was already seated and waiting for him, relaxed in a bright white rattan chair.

"So good to see you, Ken," Talat said as he stood. "I promise to make this trip worth your while."

"You've never disappointed me, Talat."

Nibbling on crumpets and scones, Talat told him about a rare 'Xing' white glazed vessel with perfect ovoid proportions from the 13th century that had surfaced in the past few days. The vase had a satiny finish with a long neck and a rolled pink lip. The Qianlong-era jade vase was still available, but Talat explained that the Xing artifact was far more valuable.

"I will take the Xing vase, Talat. I do not have anything like it in my collection from the 13th century."

"I know. Very good decision," said Talat

After the selection was made, the two men continued with their tea and talked about the problems in the Middle East. Talat complained that the fighting was hampering his business. The next evening, a thirteen year old girl delivered the Xing vase along with a fine Suzhou jade snuff bottle that was hand-painted with cherry blossoms.

CHAPTER 23

Ah woe is me! Winter is come and gone,
But grief returns with the revolving year . . .

–Percy Shelley, "Adonais"

He stood in the center of a childhood bedroom pressing one of Elle's old nightgowns to his face. Her father breathed into the folds of the flannel and could still smell her powdery scent. Disgusted by his rising desire, he threw the gown against the wall and fell to his knees.

By agreeing to stay away from his daughter, William Pandion did not handover the rights of her body to Ken Tereus for his experimentation. He was aware that Tereus was playing Dr. Frankenstein with Elizabeth and was tortured by her transmutation.

He stood up and sat down on the edge of her bed. A picture of Diana rested on the night stand. He studied the photograph. Elizabeth no longer wore the delicate bow lips and soft cheek bones of her mother. She was transformed into an exotic creature with tumescent lips and chiseled cheek bones. One thing that remained the same, though, was her silky blonde hair. She still had Diana's hair.

He fought back his tears. Though he was determined to stay away from Elizabeth's body, he was also determined to stop Tereus's destructive game. He was aware that Ken Tereus was out of the country for two weeks.

☙❧ ☙❧ ☙❧

William Pandion walked around to the side of the apartment building and grabbed a handful of rocks from the path. Elizabeth's bedroom window was just twelve feet above his head. One by one, he pelted her window with tiny pebbles. Her light flicked on after fifteen taps. He stopped the barrage and waited several seconds, but then the light flicked off.

Dr. Pandion resumed his attack with greater intensity. A light went on in the apartment below Elizabeth's. An elderly woman came to the window and peered out. Dr. Pandion moved into the shadows.

"Goddamn it," he whispered.

The next evening Dr. Pandion drove past Elizabeth's apartment at six o'clock. He parked four houses away from her building and waited for her car. At seven-thirty, he spotted Elizabeth pulling into the drive. He jumped out of his car and headed for the entrance. He was waiting at the door for her as she came around the side of the building, carrying a shopping bag. She almost bumped into her father.

"Elizabeth, please let me talk to you."

She backed up two steps, but Dr. Pandion moved closer. "I'm not here to hurt you anymore, Elizabeth. I know what I've done to you. I know that I've destroyed your life, but now I just want to help you. Please let me speak to you."

Mrs. Longbottom came out of the building and asked Elizabeth if she was okay. Elizabeth nodded yes.

"Well, be careful, my dear. I heard my window rattling last night. Almost called the police," said Mrs. Longbottom.

"I'm Elizabeth's father, ma'am. Everything is fine."

"I'm not snooping. I'm just trying to look out for your daughter," said Mrs. Longbottom, and she turned to go back into the house.

"Please, Elizabeth. Let me into your apartment. Invite me in, or meet me in a public place."

Elizabeth conceded and unlocked the entrance to the building. Dr. Pandion followed her into the apartment and closed the door behind them.

CHAPTER 24

As the deer wounded Ellen flew over
The pathless plain; as the arrows that fly
by night; destruction flies, and strikes in darkness,
She fled from fear, till at her house arriv'd.

—William Blake, "Fair Elenor."

K en's breath grew deep and rhythmic as he stared from the plane's window into the icy waters of the Pacific Ocean. In that sunless world below lived the aquatic coconspirators who assisted him in disposing of the remains of his secrets. In the past six years, the pelagic animals had never betrayed him by revealing tooth or tissue. He reached into his pocket and fingered the hard surface of the snuff bottle that held strands of ebony hair. The girl, the box, the boat took no more than a couple of hours of his time. The other small box was safely stored in his suitcase.

"Excuse me sir, I asked if you would like something to drink," interrupted the stewardess. She was a blonde with bright green eyes stretched across her face. He watched her lips move in slight waves as she asked again, "A Coke or Sprite, sir?"

"Club soda, please," he answered.

The stewardess handed him the drink. Her breasts were a bit small, but he could take care of that. She could be a titillating challenge, Ken thought, as he took the glass from her.

👁 👁 👁

It was three weeks to the day from his last evening with Elle.

Ken leaned against his car and toyed with a small box. He watched as the same elderly lady whom he had helped with groceries now strolled down the street. The evening was warm and the sun was still lingering in the sky. There was no rush. He could see the light on in Elle's room.

Mrs. Longbottom fumbled with her keys and dropped them twice before managing to open the security door. After the woman was safely in her apartment, Ken moved toward the building, pulling out the set of keys Elle had given to him. He slipped in the front door and up the short flight of steps to her apartment.

He turned the knob. She still neglects to lock the door, he thought. As he pressed on the door, Ken heard a man's voice coming from inside the room. He paused.

"I'm pleading with you, Elizabeth. Stop this lethal odyssey."

Ken couldn't understand the muffled response.

"What more can you do to yourself? I've already done enough to destroy your life. I can't standby and ignore this destruction, too. Look at you. Look in the mirror. Where has my Elizabeth gone?"

Ken still couldn't make out Elle's words through her tears.

"Please, Elizabeth. I can't take it anymore. I'm not the one trying to hurt you. Don't you understand?"

Ken recognized the voice. He pushed the door open and saw William Pandion hovered over Elizabeth who was sitting on her cramped love seat. The pair turned a grizzly gray when they saw

184

Ken standing in the doorway. Dr. Pandion stood up and moved toward Ken.

"Stop," demanded Ken. "Don't even think about it! Why did you have to reduce Elle back to this hell?"

"You don't know what you're talking about, Ken. Leave her alone. Leave us alone. She doesn't want you in her life. You've destroyed Elizabeth more than I ever did. I, at least, love her."

"Get the fuck out of here, Pandion. You're a sick man."

"Elizabeth, tell him! Tell him that you want him out of your life!" demanded her father.

A stream of silent tears was her only response.

"Please, Elizabeth, I'm trying to save you. Tell him how you really feel!" her father begged.

"Get out before I call the police. Your options are gone. I will destroy you physically and professionally if you don't leave."

"I haven't touched her. I'll never touch her again. Please, tell the man, Elizabeth! I'm your father. I'm not going to hurt you anymore. I'm trying to save you from this monster."

Ken moved toward Dr. Pandion.

Dr. Pandion put his hands up in front of his chest. "Stop, I won't fight you." He stared down at his daughter for several seconds. She refused to look up. Finally, he walked out the door.

Ken went to the sink and poured a glass of water form the tap. He carried it over to Elle and set it on the coffee table in front of her.

"Here, hold out your hand. Take these. They'll calm you." Ken dropped two tablets in her hand. She did as he demanded. Elle tossed the pills in her mouth and took a gulp of water.

Ken sat down and took her hands in his. "Elle, I'm here to protect you. I'm going to save you— immortalize you, forever. You'll never have to experience pain like this again. I promise." Ken took her face in his hand. "I brought you a present from Thailand. Will you open it?"

Elle slowly nodded her head.

He pulled the small box from his coat pocket and handed it to her.

Elle took the package and tore apart the silver paper. Tucked in a velvet box was a small bottle that fit perfectly in the palm of her hand. The miniature vessel was made from flawless jade, with an inlaid carving of an artist painting lilies.

CHAPTER 25

Everything that lives is holy, life delights in life.

—William Blake, "America: A Prophecy"

G ale welcomed her child's life with a storm of screams. Dicey gripped her fists, coaching her to inhale and exhale.

"Come on, Gale, you can do it. Breathe! You can do it!"

"Would you shut the hell up! You breathe deeper. Why did I ever listen to you?" Gale panted.

"What do you mean?"

"GIVE ME DRUGS!! Damn it! I hate this! I don't want this natural crap anymore. Where's my mother? She'll get me drugs. She never suffers!"

"Your mother's on the way. Nobody expected this tonight. Amy's coming, too, and Hank."

"Hank?" Gale asked incredulously.

"Yes, he's out in the hall. Can he come in?" Dicey was thrilled.

"Hell, no! He's not going to see my legs spread from here to Texas!"

"I heard that!" Hank yelled sticking his head into the delivery suite. "Do you mind if I come in? I promise not to look."

"Come on in. The doc's not even here yet. My OB's out of town, and I get stuck with Ricky, the rookie resident."

"Shhh, even the residents are potential clients," teased Hank.

"Yeah, but I don't want to be the guinea pig who has to sue your client's ass."

He laughed and, moving closer to the bed, grabbed her hand that was gripped around the bars of the bed.

"You'll be fine. This isn't rocket science," Dicey said as she wiped Gale's forehead with a cool washcloth.

"You're not the one in pain."

"Dicey is right. Try to slow your breathing."

"Shit! Can you believe this? Hank Daimon, masked crusader for sued doctors, is my birthing coach!"

"Yeah, who would have thought it? Hanging out with Dicey has gotten me into some pretty tight places."

"Really?" Gale squeaked as another contraction came on. "I'm going to kill Dicey!"

"In all seriousness, being here with you is an honor."

"No sappy shit right now. I'm in pain," Gale panted.

"Honestly, this is one of the most important days of your life. Seeing your child for the very first time is a miracle. Thank you for allowing me to share this with you," Hank said holding her hand.

A tear welled in Dicey's eye. She tucked her head and gripped the bed rail. An uncomfortable silence was pushed away by another painful contraction.

As Gale was groaning, Mrs. Knightly and Amy strode into the obstetrical suite with a resident on their heels.

The nurse was accurate; Gale was ten centimeters dilated and the baby was crowning. Her coach took position urging her onward.

"Push, push!" cried Dicey. "Push, she's coming, honey. The baby's coming! Now, push down hard!"

Amy moved closer to her sister to calm the mounting hysteria. She whispered, "Don't forget to breathe."

Gale started to cry.

"What if I can't push hard enough to get the baby out?"

"Gale, every woman feels that way. Come on, push."

"Come on, you can do it . . . . Push, push! Bring my little Lucy into this world!" yelled Dicey.

As the doctor maneuvered the shoulders through the birth canal, she urged Gale to push harder. With a final thrust, the doctor pulled up a squirming baby girl.

After the cord was cut, Gale asked to hold her daughter. She coddled the child close to her breast. Instinctively, the tiny lips latched on, suckling her mother for the first time.

"Oh, my little Lucy," cried Dicey. "God, she's beautiful. She's perfect!"

"No, Dice, she's excellent!" whispered Gale. "And her name isn't Lucy."

"Then, what is it?"

"Julia Aster."

Dicey gasped. She had always loved her middle name. She believed that Aster was the only element of elegance in her life, other than her friendship with Gale. But she protested, "You can't hitch an awful name like Aster to that pretty little thing."

"Aster *is* an unusual name," Gale's mother said, raising her eyebrows.

Gale ignored the comment. "Of course Aster is for you, Dice. And Julia is the name of a little girl involving one of my cases who taught me a very big lesson in life," explained Gale.

After Gale was sewn back together and Julia was scrutinized by the doctors, the party reunited in a private room.

Hank fumbled around the bed for a minute, pulled a small box from his suit jacket, and handed it to Gale. "You let me be a part of your daughter's birth. I think all mothers should be celebrated when they bring a baby into the world."

Unwrapping the box, Gale found a golden Basha baby booty charm hanging from a delicate chain. She put on her first piece of "mommy" jewelry with pride, but she also watched as her best friend struggled with both pain and happiness.

That evening when she was left alone for the first time with Julia, Gale recounted her fingers and toes. She stared into the baby's face searching for her own features and those of Dave's. The baby wore a tuft of rich brown hair, had strong cheek bones and a delicate pug nose. Her tiny brown eyes were closed.

❧ ❧ ❧

Gale was right about Dicey. She went home with a shade of sorrow in her heart; she was elated for her best friend but saddened by Hank. How could he be so attentive to Gale's situation but insensitive to her own maternal desires? Simple, there was no duty or responsibility tagged to Gale.

Dicey called Elle several times to tell her about Julia, but the phone tolled an unanswered knell. By that evening, there was still no answer. *Maybe she's with her freaky father.* The doorbell sounded and she jumped.

"Who is it?" she grumbled. Peeking out of the sidelight, Dicey spied Hank standing at her door. Her heart skipped, but it always did when she saw him.

"I can't handle this tonight," she whispered.

Dicey dragged the door open. "What's up? I'm not dressed."

"That's okay. I've seen you in your pajamas before," Hank said. "It seemed like you were upset when I left the hospital. I kind of assumed that we would be together tonight. Can I come in?"

"Sure."

190

Hank bent down and kissed her on the cheek. "What a day, Dicey. I brought a special bottle of wine to help us celebrate. Do you mind if I open it?" he asked raising a bottle of Far Niente.

"A little extravagant for Saturday night in pajamas, don't you think."

"We're celebrating."

"We celebrated today, and I'm tired."

"You're irritated," he paused, "Tell me what it is?"

"I'm fine. It's been a long day."

"Should I leave, then?"

Dicey didn't answer. Part of her wanted him to leave, but she wanted him to stay, too. He knew exactly what was bothering her. So, why was he being so damn cavalier about the whole thing?

"Dice, do you want me to go?"

"Hank, what do you think!" Why couldn't he understand that she was only thirty years old and wanted kids, too?

"Then, I'll leave."

"That's not it."

"Then, what is it?"

"Why are you so insensitive?"

"What do you mean by insensitive?"

"Hank, if I have to spell it out, it's not worth saying." Dicey slumped on the couch and hugged a pillow to her lap.

"I don't get you," she blurted out. "You're all over Gale with that mommy crap, but you can't understand how that might make me feel?"

"Are you jealous? . . . My god! The woman is all by herself with this baby."

"You know I'm not jealous, Hank. For god's sake, she's my best friend. Honestly, answer me. Why do you think I am upset?"

"I guess it's somewhere between the baby and the gift I gave Gale."

Dicey squeezed the pillow to push back the tears.

"But I have a present for you, too!" he said pulling out a square box.

"You know I'm not talking about a gift. You know that's not what I want."

Hank sat down next to her on the couch and held her hand. "You look beautiful in your pajamas, Dice."

"Would you stop," she answered, pulling her hand away.

"Please, just open my gift," Hank asked as he placed the package in her lap.

Dicey stared at the present for several minutes trying to hold back tears, but their force was stronger than her might. She felt ridiculous and selfish for crying. Today was about Gale and Julia, not her.

"Please, open it," Hank quietly urged.

Dicey unwrapped the present. This wasn't what she wanted, a velvet box, just like Gale's. She opened up the lid. Inside a diamond baby booty glistened, one that was similar to Gale's. She snapped the lid closed.

"Hank, it's cute, but godmothers don't get diamonds. I think this is a tad ridic—"

Hank reached out putting his finger over her lips. "Aster Rose Carmichael, I love you. I'm asking you to marry me. I'm asking you to have a baby with me. I do understand how important it is for you to be a mother. It has taken me some time to come to grips with starting over with children, but I have."

"Are you sure about this?" she choked.

"Of course, I am," he said, drawing her hands into his.

"But I don't want to ever feel like I pressured you into marriage or kids, Hank. This commitment is forever. I don't want you to jump on the band wagon of excitement because of Julia. For me, this is life long."

"At my point in life, I'm not going to do anything I don't want to do, Dice. I want to be with you forever and that includes children."

"Maybe we should wait for the euphoria of Julia's birth to dissipate before we candidly agree on marriage and kids."

"Dice, I love you. I have been thinking about it for quite awhile." He pulled her close. "I don't want a whole brood of kids. One or two would be great, and having a child with you would be amazing."

Dicey took Hank by the shoulders and whispered, "I love you! I so truly love you!" Then, she hugged him with all her might.

He pulled away. "Damn! I almost forgot. I have another gift for you." From his pant pocket he pulled out another box and handed it to her.

The velvet case was indistinguishable from the other she had just received. Dicey caressed the box before pulling open the lid. Inside was a two carat yellow diamond engagement ring.

"Oh, Hank!" Tears crested and streamed down her face.

"So, is that a yes or a no?"

She grabbed him again and held tightly.

Hank cradled her in his arms, picked her up, and walked to the bedroom. Resting her on the bed, he slipped away the flannel pajamas. She gazed up inviting him to explore her body. He kneeled down and ran his finger over her lips, teasing her tongue. Moving down her body, he tasted and teased with his touch. Dicey rolled over on top of his chest pulling his love deep within her.

❧ ❧ ❧

Dicey strolled into Gale's hospital room the next day to gather her two bundles of joy. She didn't want to steal attention from baby Julia, but Dicey couldn't contain her happiness.

"We finally rolled a double white!"

"I know. She's spectacular?" Gale agreed with exhaustion.

"No, yes, I mean, Julia is spectacular, but I mean Hank and I rolled a double white, too!"

"What?"

"He proposed!" Dicey said proudly displaying her necklace.

"What's that?" laughed Gale.

"It's my engagement booty. Hank gave it to me to say that he wants to be the father of my children." She then held out her left hand, glistening was the yellow diamond.

"I never lost hope in him. Hank is a good and decent man."

Dicey picked up Julia and placed her into Gale's arms and wheeled mother and baby from the hospital room.

CHAPTER 26

The voice of Nature loudly cries,

And many a message from the skies,

That Something in us never dies.

—Robert Burns, "Quotations"

Dicey dialed Elle's number several times on Sunday to tell her about Julia's birth, but she never received an answer. By Monday morning, she was concerned and called her publishing company. Elle had not called in. Dicey asked for her immediate boss, Susan Miller. Elle had missed a copy meeting with a client. Worry was churning into a heightened state of panic. Reluctantly, Dicey headed toward her apartment.

Toying with her lucky cubes, she rolled a double scarlet twice and threw the dice into the cup holder. Frustration and anxiety tugged at her as she pulled up to the apartment building. Dicey had never been invited inside Elle's apartment, another part of her world sealed from view.

She buzzed the doorbell repeatedly but received no answer. She walked to the back of the building and spotted Elle's Honda in the carport. She saw a man pulling a duffle bag from his trunk. She approached him and asked,

"Do you know Elle Pandion, a blonde in apartment three?"

"Don't know her but know who she is."

"Have you seen her around the past few days?"

"Nope, I'm not around much."

"How can I find the manager?" Dicey asked.

"He lives in the second building over, on the first floor."

"Thanks for your help," Elle said and headed toward the building.

She knocked on the door posted management written with permanent marker. A surly man with a dingy t-shirt that barely covered his navel came to the door.

He wouldn't permit Dicey into Elle's apartment. He was required to call the police if anything "squirrelly" was going on in one of his units.

Dicey sat on the stoop outside Elle's building with the manager, waiting for the police to arrive. His greasy cigarette odor made her nauseous.

When the police cruiser rolled up, management took control. He told the officers that if anything illegal was going on in that apartment, he wanted to be the first to know about it. He escorted the police to apartment three. Dicey followed at their heels.

As the manager opened the door to the small unit, a wretched stench smacked everyone in the face. The taller officer stepped in front of Dicey and said,

"Ma'am, if you please, you'll have to stay out here." He recognized the rank odor.

Dicey began to cry while the officer called for assistance.

Elle's bloated body was found in her bed and was fully clothed. There appeared to be no forced entry and the two rooms had not been ransacked. An empty bottle of Vicadin stood next to a glass of water on the night stand. The computer in the corner of her room was humming. One of the detectives walked over to it. He pulled on gloves and tapped the mouse. The screen lit up with a white document.

"Look at this, Bob. It looks like a suicide note." The detective read the few words out loud. 'Father, I'm sorry. I can't live like this any longer. Goodbye, Elle.'"

"Short and to the point," said his partner.

"Well, let's find out which lucky guy is going to have to deal with this kind of guilt for the rest of his life."

"Yeah, because the little girl just couldn't live like this any longer," said Bob.

"Ever thought that we've been doing this job too long?"

"Don't go soft on me now, John."

While Dicey sat outside waiting for answers from the detectives, Mrs. Longbottom came out of apartment two.

"My dear, how did this happen to Elle," Mrs. Longbottom asked.

"I don't know. I just don't know," Dicey said tearfully.

"She was never a talkative girl, not even a bit friendly. She was a little too uppity for this neighborhood. Anyhow, I watched out for her."

"That was nice of you, ma'am. Elle was just quiet, not uppity. A lot of people took her the wrong way," said Dicey.

"Well, she sure seemed upset when her father was here the other night."

"What do you mean?"

"He was waiting for her when she came home. I watch everything that happens on this street from right there," Mrs. Longbottom said and pointed to the front window of her apartment.

"How did you know that the man was Elle's father?"

"I saw her from the window. She was getting upset, so I came out to offer a little help. Not being nosey or anything. I don't like to get involved with family disputes or anything. I asked the young lady if anything was wrong. The man said that nothing was wrong."

"How do you know that it was Elle's dad?"

"Cause I heard him say, 'I'm your father. You have to listen to me,'" said Mrs. Longbottom.

"Did you tell the police about her father's visit?"

"Sure, I will. I'm the only person in this building who pays attention to anything. Mildred in apartment one can't see or hear, and she's senile. And those people upstairs, they don't know anything, either. None of em' go to church, including that friend of yours."

"Well, I'm certain that you will be a wealth of information to the detectives," said Dicey.

Hank and Dr. Pandion arrived at Elle's apartment almost simultaneously. The police escorted Dr. Pandion into the building to identify her body.

"My God, why didn't I see this coming?" Dicey cried as Hank pulled her close to his chest.

"Don't start blaming yourself. When someone really wants to kill themselves, they just do it."

"I don't buy that shit. I know that I could have done something."

Dicey trembled as the paramedics carried Elle's body out in a black body bag. Dr. Pandion followed behind. Hank approached him as the body was placed in the back of the ambulance.

"Dr. Pandion, remember me, Hank Daimon? I defended you on the Beckman case. I'm so sorry. If I can do anything to help, I will."

"What are you doing here, Hank?" Dr. Pandion asked "I don't need a lawyer." "Yeah, I know that. Dicey and Elle were good friends," Hank said glancing toward Dicey. "She called me. She's my fiancé, Dr. Pandion."

"Okay. Goodbye, then. I'm headed to the coroner's office with Elizabeth."

"He's a strange man." Dicey added as she and Hank watched Dr. Pandion climb into his black Mercedes.

"Dice, his daughter just committed suicide."

"I'm sorry. I didn't mean to be so harsh. You're right. It's just that there has always been something ugly about the guy."

"Come on, let's go home."

CHAPTER 27

Mourn rather for the Holy Spirit,

Sweet as the spring, as ocean deep;

For Her who, ere her summer faded,

Has sunk into a breathless sleep.

—William Wordsworth,
"Extempore Effusion upon
the Death of James Hogg"

"**G**ale, I think that we must have been her only two friends in the world."

"Why do you say that? The funeral home is packed."

"Yeah, but look around at these people. Besides us, no one's under sixty years old, except for Hank and Ken and they're both pushing fifty," said Dicey.

"I can see why, though. Being Elle's friend was hard. It took a lot of patience. Now days, people don't have the time or take the time to find out what makes a person tick, especially someone like Elle who locked herself up in silence."

"I've been her friend for a few years, now, and I never understood her goddamn ticking, Gale. The alarms were blaring, and I didn't hear them."

"We've been through her death umpteen times. You can't feel guilty for not saving her. Hank is right. If she really wanted to die, my God, she was going to find a way. Maybe she's finally at peace with herself."

"That's bullshit," said Dicey. "Remember what her neighbor said. The last time anybody saw her, she was fighting with her father. Don't you think he has something to do with this?"

"Dicey, you must stop! This isn't the time for your surmising. The man is visibly upset. I've been watching him. Look, he's near the casket with Ken Tereus. His forehead is dripping with sweat."

"Maybe Dr. Frankenstein is giving Dr. Pandion some heat because his lab subject died."

"You're being cruel. This is her funeral, for God's sake," Gale snapped, irritated with Dicey's callousness.

"I'm not being cruel; I'm angry. She looks like a cartoon character in that casket, and I saw none of this coming."

"You are making Elle's death about you and your inability to save her from herself. You couldn't." Gale glanced over Dicey's shoulder. "Ken Tereus is coming toward us. Please watch what you say."

When he approached the women, Ken placed his hand in the small of Gale's back. "I'm sorry," he offered. This is a terrible loss for all of us."

"It's been very difficult," Dicey said as tears pooled in her eyes.

"I understand that there is some good news, though. I spoke with Hank. Congratulations on your engagement. When is the big day?"

"In June, during my summer break from classes," Dicey said. "How is Dr. Pandion? I saw you speaking with him."

"He'll get through it. Doctors are more resilient to death than most people. It comes with the territory." Then, Ken turned his attention toward Gale. "Something seems different about you, Gale. . . . You're rosier."

"Rosier is a nice way of saying it. Do you mean to say that I've put on a few pounds?"

"No. You just look healthier."

"Gale's a mother now, Ken. I thought Elle would have told you," said Dicey.

"You're a mother! As of when?" he asked, unable to suppress his shock.

"As of a week ago, a little girl," Gale offered.

"Lovely. . . I didn't know you had married in the past year," he said, with more control.

"I'm not, yet." A red flush started to spread across her cheeks.

"Well, congratulations to you, too, then," he offered graciously.

"It's been a long week. We'll be seeing you," Gale said. She grabbed Dicey's arm and headed toward the door.

"Please don't say a word, Dice. He caught me off guard. It's the first time anyone has asked me directly about a husband."

Dicey wrapped her arm around Gale trying to calm her. "I'm not going to bug you. I feel half responsible for the situation with Dave. Do you think he'll ever call?"

"Don't be crazy, never, ever. He doesn't believe me, and I'm sure as hell not going to beg him to."

"Why are you both so stubborn, Gale?"

"Dicey, please don't think about lecturing me. Haven't we all been through enough in the past seven days?"

CHAPTER 28

To live in the hearts we leave / Is not to die.

—Thomas Campbell, "Hallowed Grounds"

*I*t was four weeks to the day since Dicey had discovered
Elle's body. She was at home preparing her course syllabus
when the door bell rang. Peering out the window, she saw an
attractive man dressed in a navy suit and pale-blue tie. He had two
large packages resting against his thigh. Dicey cracked the door and
asked what he wanted.

"Is Dr. Aster Carmichael in?"

"I am she. May I help you?"

"I have a delivery for you from the estate of Elizabeth Diana
Pandion."

"Who are you?"

"Mark Johnson, Dr. Carmichael. Miss Pandion employed me
as her attorney. She bequeathed these paintings to you in her will."

Gale opened the door a little wider. "Why to me? Have you
spoken to her father or the police, Mr. Johnson?"

"Yes ma'am. I'm aware of the circumstances of her death."

Dicey allowed the man to enter with his packages. She stood staring at him. He cleared his throat.

"I'm sorry, Mr. Johnson. Please sit down. Would you like some coffee or something?"

"No thanks. Call me Mark."

"I must seem dazed, Mark. I'm just a little shocked. Why would Elle put me in her will? Why did she even have a will? The girl was twenty-three years old," asked Dicey.

"I don't know, Dr. Carmichael, but Elle was hard-pressed to draw up the will. She came to me back in April. She sat in my office for three or four hours, watching me type the entire document. She was going to have some kind of surgery. Maybe that was the rush."

"Maybe, but can I ask you a question?"

"Sure."

"Did Elle seem suicidal to you?" asked Dicey.

"I really didn't know her too well. We had a class together at Thrace. I was surprised that she remembered me."

Dicey stood up. "Thank you, Mark. I appreciate your time."

"No problem, ma'am. She wanted these pictures hand-delivered."

After the young man left, Dicey tore the paper from one of the paintings. The first was entitled the *Monstrous Heresy: Pope Alexander VI*. The composition was Elle-esque, strange and sorrowful. The jeweled colors were mesmerizing. Enshrouded in amethyst satin, a young girl rested peacefully in her crypt as Pope Alexander resided over her final mass. This must have been painted in Elle's darkest period as the girl in the picture resembled her dead friend, even the shroud resembled the wedding dress that Elle was dressed in at her own funeral. But why would Elle paint the pope? The Church wasn't a part of her life.

Dicey carefully peeled the paper from the second package. A wave of pain rushed through her. It was a rendition of Henry Fuseli's *Nightmare*; Fuseli, himself, had painted several versions of the picture. Dicey was familiar with the work as she incorporated the art into her course on British literature. Elle was enthralled with Fuseli's art. Her interpretation of the piece exposed a woman sprawled across a bed with her arms and head hanging from the side. Sitting a top her chest was a small, devilish fiend grinning at the extinguished beauty. In the background, a startled horse thrusts his head through a garnet bed curtain and, with bulging eyes, gazes in horror at the muted woman and her diabolic friend. Both pictures were imposing, but why hadn't Elle displayed them in the past? Her art was the only element in her life that Elle proudly exhibited.

CHAPTER 29

Late, late yestreen I saw the new Moon,

With the old Moon in her arms;

And I fear, I fear, my Master dear!

We shall have a deadly storm.

Thomas Percy — "Sir Patrick Spence"

Gale swayed back and forth on the porch swing while Julia suckled at her breast. She was entranced in the exquisiteness of motherhood, something she never quite grasped when Amy shuffled pictures of the boys in her face or when her college friends rattled on about their newborns' bowel movements and umbilical cords. Now, she understood. At times her emotions ran so strong that they acted like visceral clamps, squeezing the air right out of her lungs. She could move mountains for Julia, even kill for her.

There was little time and little room left for anyone else, including a man. Sharp twitches of guilt jabbed at her stomach as she stared into Julia's light-chocolate eyes.

"I'm sorry you don't have a daddy in your life, angel. I know that I've created a pretty big mess for everybody. But I'll never force anybody to love me or you."

@@ @@ @@

Dicey didn't have the distraction of a baby to keep her mind from Elle's death. She settled back into the thick of teaching her British literature course, and with each day of preparation, she was reminded of how much Elle loved Henry Fuseli and the Romantic artists of the time.

Her students were reading a strange novella by Mary Shelley entitled *Mathilda*. The story was about a young girl who was separated from her father for several years. When the two were reunited, the father fell in love with Mathilda. The story ends in the tragic death of the father and the girl. Incest was an underlying theme in many Romantic period novels, but it never ceased to revolt Dicey. She cringed when her beloved Jane Austen was included in the company of writers who dealt with incestuous themes. She attacked the argument with her own critical analysis entitled, "Too Sensitive and Sensible for Incest."

Hank was trudging through depositions one evening as Dicey sifted through stacks of reference material for her next class lecture. One name popped up a few times in her quest of incestuous themes in literature, Pope Alexander VI. Why did that name sound familiar?

She went to the kitchen to make a pot of tea. Sitting back down, she flipped through some indexes to find out more about the pope. It was alleged that Pope Alexander VI forced his illegitimate daughter, Lucretia Borgia, into an intimate relationship with him. Lucretia ultimately bore the responsibility for the deviant imposition and was possibly punished by death.

"My God, that's it! *The Monstrous Heresy: Pope Alexander VI*, Elle's picture!" Dicey said. She jumped up from her work, ran to her bedroom, and a minute later returned to Hank with the painting.

"Hank, look at this. I never delved into Elle's study of history and literature and how it influenced her work. Don't you think that the young woman in the crypt almost resembles Elle? The pope even resembles Dr. Pandion."

"Yeah, I guess so." Hank said and returned to his reading.

"Hank, look up, you're ignoring me! Give me the benefit of your lawyer's mind."

"Dice, I agreed with you. What do you want me to say? Elle's pictures are all weird."

"Don't you see it?"

"See what?"

"Look at the resemblance between Elle and her dad and the people in the picture," Dicey asked pointing to the woman in the crypt.

"I said that I did."

"Why would she paint herself in this picture?"

"She painted pitiful blondes in all of her pitiful pictures."

"How would you know that?"

"I know because, I have seen her paintings. If there was pain to be found, Elle put herself right smack in the middle of it."

"Hank, that was mean."

"Dicey, sit down and listen. It wasn't mean; it's the truth. The girl was over the edge with drama."

Dicey remained standing and asked, "How can you say that? She never spoke."

"That's just it. She acted like a mute half the time. I don't know if she was trying to be mysterious or what. Nevertheless, the act didn't work. She was just irritating."

Dicey glared down at Hank. "Why are you being so severe? She was my friend, and now she's dead."

"Dice, I'm not trying to hurt you. I'm just being honest about the girl. She acted like something out of a bad B movie. You asked for my lawyer's mind. That's what I see."

"Well, maybe she had reason to behave so grimly."

"Dice, she's gone. You're not going to figure out why she committed suicide."

"Maybe it wasn't suicide, Hank."

"Stop, you're not going to start playing Sir Conan Doyle."

"Well, then tell me why she painted herself in that picture."

"Well, maybe because she was psychotic."

"Well, maybe it was because Dr. Pandion killed her, and she had a premonition that it was going to happen."

Hank tossed the deposition on the coffee table and looked straight at Dicey. "Be careful," he demanded. "You are throwing around accusations of murder. That is a dangerous and a defamatory proposition. I've known Dr. Pandion for several years. The man is arrogant and aloof, but he is a great doctor and a fine man. His daughter was a mental case who committed suicide. That's it. End of story." Hank stood up and walked into the kitchen, but Dicey followed him.

"Then, tell me why she willed these pictures to me?"

"You were her only friend. And who else would want these pictures?" he offered over his shoulder.

"Turn around! Why are you being so cruel?"

Hank slowly turned around and narrowed his eyes. "I'm not being cruel. I'm being realistic. Maybe I'm angry with her. People who commit suicide are selfish people. They don't think about the pain that they leave in their wake."

"I don't believe her death was a suicide, and now I can prove that it wasn't. She revealed the cause of her death in the picture with Pope Alexander VI. The research I found explains that Lucretia Borgia was the daughter of Pope Alexander VI. It is widely believed that he had an incestuous relationship with her, and she was the one who was ultimately put to death because of it. That's why Elle painted that picture. She was trying to tell me about her detestable relationship with her father. Everything makes sense, now. She never spoke about Dr. Pandion because she was frightened to death of him. Maybe she knew she was going to die."

"Of course she knew that she was going to die. She planned it. She committed suicide. Listen, you need to get a hold of yourself. You have not only accused Dr. Pandion of murder, now you are accusing him of incest. Dicey, this is wrong, and you must stop. The girl is dead, and you need to get over it." The skin on Hank's face was taut with anger. He walked out of the kitchen and back into the living room, with Dicey close behind.

"I don't believe she killed herself," Dicey said with equal indignation. "Look at the picture. You agreed that the girl resembles Elle. She's even in a white gown, like the wedding dress that Elle was buried in. And don't you think that Dr. Pandion is in the image of the pope?"

"I don't know. It doesn't matter, though. A resemblance doesn't mean a murder was committed nor incest."

"Look at that guy! He looks just like Dr. Pandion."

"No, not really, Dicey. You're searching for a resemblance."

"Why are you doing this?" she shouted.

"Doing what?"

"You're blowing me off. You think that I'm crazy."

"No, I don't think you're crazy. I think that you are taking too much responsibility for her death. You can't save someone who has decided to die," Hank answered quietly.

"I'm not trying to bring her back to life. She was buried in her mother's goddamn wedding gown. That's weird, Hank. Stop trying to defend your sacred doctor!"

Dicey sat down on the couch silently, just staring at *The Monstrous Heresy*. Hank sat across from her and finally said, "Don't you think that this is all a little too contrived. The girl never spoke about anything. Why would she tell you this after her death? This theory is too convenient. You're making things up to appease your own guilt. You have nothing to feel guilty about. The girl wanted to die, so she killed herself. That is all there is to her death. Please, just let it go."

"Hank, life is contrived! I know that she never talked about anything. She was an artist, not an orator. I'm a writer. When I'm upset about something, I write in my journal. Why is it so contrived that she would paint about something that was causing her so much pain? If she willed me her journal, you wouldn't question that, would you? Remember my student, Samantha Seine? She wrote about death in her journal, and I didn't see her suicide coming."

"Dice, you don't have to find an answer for Elle's death. You're trying to clear your own conscience for not saving her. How can I convince you that it wasn't your fault? Look at the date on the picture. She painted that piece five years ago, probably when you first met her. She had plenty of time between then and now to give you a chance to save her, but she didn't. Elle wanted to die, no matter who would have tried to help."

☙ ☙ ☙

Hank went home that night without the couple making love. After he left, Dicey continued to study the picture. What was Elle trying to tell her with the picture? It was three in the morning, and she was still looking at the painting.

"What are you telling me?" she pleaded in the darkness. She was determined to study every last detail of the painting one more time, certain that an answer was there.

Dicey was bleary-eyed when she came to the pope's signet ring. She couldn't make out the letters. She went to her desk drawer for a magnifying glass then returned to the painting. She held the glass over the pope's ring. *WGP* .

"P for Pandion. But what's the guy's first name?" she whispered to Lucretia, who was eternally asleep in the painting. Dicey returned to her desk to grab the yellow pages of the phone book. She flipped to cardiovascular surgeons. She ran her finger down the alphabet and found Pandion. William G. Pandion, M.D.

Her hands started to shake. "It is him," she whispered. "That is what she's been trying to tell me. Her father's the pope in the picture." Dicey jumped up from her desk chair and ran back to the picture.

She glared at the man adorned in the holy vestments. "You were in love with Elle, just like the pope was in love with his own daughter. Your daughter died an early death, as did the pope's daughter. Do you have blood on your hands, as did the pope?" Dicey asked the man in purple vestments who was glaring back at her.

If he didn't kill her with his own hands, Dicey was certain that Dr. Pandion drove Elle to the brink of death with his perversion. She was trying to expose her secrets. Dicey looked at her watch. It was almost four o'clock. She picked up her phone to call Hank. Her hands were shaking too much to punch in the numbers. She sat down on the couch and took a deep breath. She closed her eyes and whispered, "Dear God, help me." She then dialed Hank's number.

"Honey," she whispered. "It's me. I found it. It's in the picture."

"You found what in what picture, Dicey?" Hank said in a grouchy voice.

"*The Monstrous Heresy*, the pope picture!"

"Oh, really, what's in it?" he asked with sarcasm.

"I found the answer."

"What answer?"

"The answer to Elle's death."

"Dicey this is getting out of hand."

"Just hear me out." Dicey was irritated.

"What time is it?"

"Four o'clock."

"It's four in the morning? What are you doing awake?" he grumbled.

"I knew the answer was in the painting, Hank. Now, I can prove that Dr. Pandion had a hand in Elle's death. Will you come over?"

"Dicey, I have to honest with you. Your sleuthing has stretched beyond my patience. This isn't some Nancy Drew mystery. You are messing with a man's life, a man who just lost his only daughter. It's crazy."

Dicey gripped the phone to remain calm. "I understand where you're coming from. I would never do anything to hurt Dr. Pandion, unjustly. This is for my own peace of mind, so I can finally sleep at night."

"Me, too," he said before agreeing to come to her house. "Okay. I'll stop by on my way to work, just to talk. Just to calm you down. That's it."

Over the next few hours, Dicey searched the internet to find out more information on Pope Alexander VI. She also dragged out Elle's rendition of Fuseli's *The Nightmare*. She looked at the fiend foaming at the mouth over the dead girl. "That must be Dr. Pandion."

When Hank arrived, she poured him a cup of coffee and proceeded to point out the *WGP* on the pope's signet ring. She also pulled out *The Life and Art of Henry Fuseli*, Peter Tomoroy's bible on the artist, and laid it open across the kitchen table. "Listen to this. I think Dr. Pandion was jealous and went nuts. Elle painted *The Nightmare* a few months ago, while she was dating Ken Tereus. It's a rendition of Henry Fuseli's *The Nightmare*. He painted it out of an obsessive and unrequited love for a woman. He says it right her," Dicey said, pointing to the text. "Elle had a copy of this same book. I know, because I gave it to her. She's always had a strange obsession with Fuseli. She was trying to tell me something."

"Calm down," Hank cautioned her.

"Elle was trying to tell me that Dr. Pandion was going to kill her, I know it."

"Dicey, you can't go to the police without more evidence than a few pictures. Dr. Pandion is a respected physician. No one will take an accusation like this lightly. He has the guns to crush you."

"You think I've cracked, don't you?" She turned scarlet with anger. Hank pulled her close, but she pushed him away with the palms of hands. "I'm not nuts. Hank, you're just trying to protect him because he was your client. It's not fair!"

"Wait a minute, now you're not being fair. I know how things operate, Dicey. I defend people. You can't saunter into the police station and make these accusations because of a few pictures. They'll laugh in your face. In addition, it could be considered defamation. Let's think about it for a day or so."

"Okay. It's getting late, and I've got to get ready for class, anyway." Her face and neck were burning red.

During her drive to school, Dicey called Gale to tell her about what she had discovered in the pictures. Gale's reaction was similar to Hank's, but she did agree to stop by that evening to talk more about the paintings. By seven o'clock, Gale was exhausted and didn't feel like loading Julia in the car. Furthermore, she was becoming frustrated with Dicey's obsession over Elle's death. She called Dicey and told her that she was too tired to stop by.

"Please, Gale," pleaded Dicey.

She sounded almost hysterical. Gale agreed to listen. By the time she arrived with Julia, Dicey seemed frenzied. She dragged Gale and the baby into the kitchen to see the paintings that were propped up against the cabinets.

"It's here, Gale. Don't you agree? Dr. Pandion did it. He raped Elle. We've known for years that the guy was creepy. This is it!"

Gale sat down at the kitchen table and fiddled with the salt shaker while Dicey bounced around the room with Julia. Dicey was slipping off the edge of reality with this stuff. How could she suggest that Dr. Pandion raped and killed his daughter?

"Listen honey, you've got to let it go."

"Don't start, Gale. You have to listen."

"Dicey, Dr. Pandion may have crossed some boundaries with Elle, but you can't prove that with a couple of pictures— maybe a diary or some letters but not these pictures." Julia reacted to the tension in their voices and began to whimper. Gale stood up and took the child from Dicey.

"You sound just like Hank. Why all this lawyer lingo? The guy did it. He should be thrown in jail."

"The police looked into her death."

"No, Gale there was a cover-up. I know it."

"Don't let your imagination run away with you, please. We both feel a smear of blood on our hands about her death. However, accusing Dr. Pandion of murder won't bring her back or make us feel any less guilty. Pervert or not, she's gone. It doesn't matter anymore. Let go of the guilt and move on."

"Guilt has nothing to do with this. Elle was trying to tell me something."

Gale scooted her chair closer to Dicey. "Let's assume Dr. Pandion did rape Elle. That doesn't mean he murdered her. She's dead, Dice. What's the point now? If she wanted you to know what her father did to her, she probably would have confided in you long ago. Not now."

"I don't buy it, Gale. Things changed. Don't you remember how horrible she looked at the baby shower? I'm sure that's when she painted *Nightmare*. Maybe Dr. Pandion was jealous over Ken."

"She looked horrible because she just had surgery, and I don't think that Dr. Pandion was jealous of Ken Tereus. They are friends. You saw them at the funeral. I saw no animosity between them. Dicey, really, you're a little out of hand."

"No, you're a lot in denial. I'm going to figure this out. Maybe I should make an appointment with Dr. Pandion."

Julia began to cry harder. Gale sat down at the table again and tried to nurse her.

"Please don't. What are you going to say, 'Hey doc, did you rape your daughter?' Now come on, just let this thing die."

"I already stood by and watched Elle die. She's finally telling me her story. I'm not going to let it die!"

"Dice, you can listen to her story. I'm not suggesting that you shouldn't. Chronicle it. Write about it, but don't destroy anymore lives with it. This is not your responsibility. If Elle wanted to destroy her father posthumously, she would have done that in the suicide note, not through a labyrinth of pictures."

Dicey sat down at the table and put her hands in her head. "Maybe you're right. Hank's angry at me. You're angry. Maybe I am going nuts." She grabbed a stack of mail on the table and sifted through it several times.

Gale watched Dicey lose a little steam. "Is there anything interesting in your mail? You've gone through it about ten times," she asked for diversion.

"There's an invitation for Ken Tereus' famous holiday party, if you think that is interesting. Do you want to go with Hank and me?"

"Is it the same party that I had to drag you to last year? Why in the world would you want to go to that?" asked Gale.

"Hank wants to go. Remember, that's where we met."

"I forgot about that." Gale was glad Dicey was calming down, so she continued with the diversion. "Oh, so much has changed in one short year. I was actually toying around with Ken Tereus a year ago."

"Yeah, remember how he bitched at me for touching his stupid little jars?"

"How could I forget?" Gale laughed.

"So, do you want to go?"

Gale repositioned Julia in her arms. "I really don't think I feel like going. It may not be worth the hassle. I've never left her at night."

"What about Harriet? Wouldn't she love to babysit her grand-daughter?"

"Do you really believe that?"

"No, but what are the other options?"

CHAPTER 30

When you find out a man's ruling passion, beware of crossing it.

–William Hazlitt, "Characteristics of Manner of
Rochefoucault's Maxims," 116

Dicey ignored Hank and Gale's warning about
Dr. Pandion. She called his office and scheduled an
appointment for the following Monday under the name
of Rose Carmichael. The nurse took her physical history before
Dr. Pandion came into the examining room. Dicey complained of
heart palpitations and blurred vision. The nurse took her temperature and blood pressure. After Dicey sat for several minutes in the
frigid room, Dr. Pandion entered. He didn't remember her. After
he poked around and asked a few questions, Dicey reintroduced
herself.

"Dr. Pandion, I believe you don't remember me. My name is
Aster Rose Carmichael. I am Elle's close friend from Thrace. I was
her professor . . . and friend."

"Yes, Miss Carmichael, I do remember you, now."

"Doctor, I'm not here because I have a headache." Dicey slid off the examining table and stood. "I'm here because I wanted to ask you about your daughter. You see, she willed me two paintings that you may be interested in seeing."

"I have plenty of Elizabeth's paintings, Miss Carmichael." He put his hand on the door knob.

"Yes, but these are curious paintings. I think they're pictures of you, Dr. Pandion, and your daughter together. There is a strong likeness." Dicey noticed that the doctor's upper lip twitched a bit.

"Why don't you dress and come into my office, Miss Carmichael. It's at the end of the hall."

Dicey threw on her clothes and headed for his office. She knocked gently and pushed the door open. Seated behind an elevated desk, Dr. Pandion waved her toward him but did not offer her a seat.

"Did Elle paint that picture, Dr. Pandion?" Dicey asked pointing to the work above his desk.

"Yes. It's her deceased mother."

Dicey recognized the puffy dress in the picture. "That dress looks like the one Elle wore at the funeral."

"It's her mother's wedding gown. I believe I told you that, at least I felt like I told everyone that, at the funeral. Elizabeth used to play in it."

Dicey noticed the use of Elle's formal name. "Elle bears a strong resemblance to her mother."

"Yes, Miss Carmichael, I know," he said curtly. "I am a very busy physician. Is there something else that you wanted to discuss?"

"As a matter of fact there is, sir," Dicey said and walked closer to his desk. "Elle bequeathed two pictures to me. They were delivered to me by her lawyer a few weeks ago. Maybe you're familiar with them."

"Elizabeth painted hundreds of pictures, Miss Carmichael."

"One, in particular, was of Pope Alexander VI. Are you familiar with the man, Dr. Pandion?"

"Miss Carmichael, if you came to discuss obscure pictures and popes, I'm afraid that I'm going to have to ask you to leave."

"Dr. Pandion, please be patient with me, for Elle's sake. May I sit down?"

"No."

She ignored his response and sat on the edge of his desk. "Did you know that Pope Alexander had a daughter? I assume that you didn't know that small detail; maybe only history buffs like me would know such obscurities. Did you know that Pope Alexander forced a sexual relationship on his daughter, Dr. Pandion?"

"Get out of my office!"

"I won't leave until I have answers! Did you know that his daughter was punished by death because of the incestuous relationship, Dr. Pandion?" Leaning closer to him, Dicey whispered, "I know what you did, doctor. Elle told her story to me!" Dicey really had no idea how close she was to the truth, but she stood her ground.

"Get out! Or I'll have you removed," he demanded. He stormed out the door, but Dicey ran after him whispering, "You'll pay for this Dr. Pandion, I promise."

☙❧ ☙❧ ☙❧

"My God, Dicey, what were you thinking? He could have had you arrested," Hank said a half-hour later, when he found Dicey banging on his office door. "Furthermore, if the guy's really dangerous, he could harm you. Why didn't you tell me about this scheme?"

"Please, Hank, don't criticize me right now. I didn't know what else to do. Neither Gale nor you would listen. Now, you know I'm right."

"I'm not convinced of anything, Dice. You went to a man's office in the middle of the day and accused him of being a pervert. I think that I would have behaved exactly the same way as Dr. Pandion, except I would have had you arrested. You don't understand. This man has been my client for fifteen years. My God, what were you thinking?"

"I'm thinking that everybody thinks that I'm crazy right now. You didn't see how he reacted, Hank," Dicey said angrily. She grabbed him by the coat lapels and pleaded,

"I'm begging you to just look into it, nothing more. I just want to give his daughter the voice that she deserves."

Hank wrapped his arms around Dicey and pulled her close. "I'll think about it," he conceded. "But we're going to have to move cautiously and think things out carefully," he said. "Don't you have anything else other than paintings? Do you have any of her old papers, a poem or two?"

"No, I've trashed my school office and house searching for clues."

"Honey, let me talk to a few people, discreetly, but promise to leave it alone for now."

"Do you promise to make a few calls?"

"I do."

◠ ◠ ◠

While Julia was sleeping, Gale typed feverishly on her laptop. Her partners were disenchanted with her absence. She took off the "optional" extra four weeks for maternity leave, something no one in her firm had ever attempted.

"What the hell, I've got more billable hours than any other associate, and I'm a single mom. No wonder they don't have any female partners. I'd like to see one of them do what I've done for the past three months!" she confided in her computer screen.

The clicking of her laptop keys was interrupted by the door bell. She darted for the sound before it rang again and woke Julia.

Dicey was standing at the door draped in a pasty hue. Before Gale said hello, Dicey plunged onto the couch and related her encounter with Dr. Pandion.

"Dice, I can't believe you did that. He could have done something. He's not the type of guy you take for granted," Gale said with disgust.

"What's he going to do? Kill me? I don't think so. I'll be fine."

"Really, what are you doing? If you're not careful, he could sue you for slander and defamation. You're out of control?"

"Forget it. I'm fine."

"I'm not going to forget it. You are worrying me."

"Don't start lecturing me again. Okay. Let's discuss something else, something fun. That's a novel idea, isn't it? What did you decide about Ken's party on Saturday?"

"Don't change the subject," Gale chided. She sat down on the couch and grabbed Dicey's hand. "What in the hell were you thinking?"

"Don't redress me, Gale. Hank already slammed me with shame. So, stop. I'm not discussing it any longer."

"Fine. That's what we all want. Never discuss it again!" Gale said indignantly. "Well, at least you'll be glad to hear that Harriet agreed to watch Julia."

"Excellent."

"She acted like I asked her to clean my toilets, though. She dotes on Amy's kids but rarely makes an effort see Julia. She's her only granddaughter, for God's sake!"

"Until you have realistic expectations of that woman, you're going to struggle. Trust me, I own four corners on shit mothers . . . just see her and use her for what she is, a phony with a conscience who wants to look good in other people's eyes," said Dicey.

☺☻ ☺☻ ☺☻

On Wednesday, Dicey's cell phone rang during class. It was Hank. He never interrupted her teaching schedule. She excused herself into the hall.

"Hank," she whispered, "I'm in class, honey. What's wrong?"

"Dice, have you listened to the news?"

"No, why?"

"I'm on my way to your office."

"Tell me what's wrong," Dicey said frantically.

"I can't. I'll be there in ten minutes. I'm already on my way."

Dicey returned to her class and excused the students for the day.

Hank was in her office within minutes. She shook when he arrived.

"Dicey, it's Dr. Pandion. He was found dead in his home this morning. The press isn't releasing any more information, but I contacted one of my buddies at District 1. Apparently, it was an overdose on morphine. He left an oblique note about not being able to live with the loss of his daughter."

"My God! It is all my fault! I should have listened to you. Instead of turning on me, he turned on himself." Dicey cried.

"No, it's not your fault. Even some of the most deviant seek repentance in a sick way."

☙❧ ☙❧ ☙❧

Colleagues from across the country filled the Athenaeum to offer their respect to a man who made significant contributions to the field of cardiovascular surgery. Hank and Dicey sat in the third row of the auditorium, listening to the memorial service. One by one, physicians filed to the podium to celebrate the career of William G. Pandion.

"He innately understood the conditions of the heart and the causes of the muscle's corruption," a doctor from Seattle said, wiping a tear from his eye.

"Dr. Pandion taught me everything I know about bedside manner. He was both tender and firm with his patients. He accepted the elderly and the poor without judgment or reservation," noted the Chief of Staff of Thrace Hospital.

"I've been Dr. Pandion's nurse for over three decades, and I've seen him suffer through the years. Bit by bit, piece by piece, the pain and agony destroyed him. He was a quiet man, didn't share much, but I could tell. When his mother died, a sliver of Dr. Pandion died right along with her. When his wife died, pieces of his spirit were buried, too. But when his daughter, Elizabeth, passed on, everything in Dr. Pandion's world shriveled up and died. It was a slow and wrenching death.

"Today, as his nurse and his friend, I ask you to celebrate the fact that Dr. Pandion is now reunited with his mother, his daughter and his dear wife. He is finally at peace with his life. . . Amen." The woman dotted the corners of her eyes with a tissue, made the sign of the cross, and then returned to her seat.

Most everyone in the audience was drenched in tears. Dicey's face was impassive. She struggled with her own conscience while she listened to the celebration of a man who contributed to the death of his daughter, directly or indirectly.

CHAPTER 31

How we clutch at shadows as if they were substances;

and sleep deepest while fancying ourselves most awake?

—Thomas Carlyle,
"Sartor Resartus: The Life and
Opinions of Herr Teufelsdrockn"

Gale finally returned to the office and was slapped with a week of chaos. Monday started the havoc. Thinking that the lenses were already in her eyes, she threw her last set of eye contacts down the drain, along with the saline solution. And the baby sitter was thirty-five minutes late.

On Tuesday, milk dripped through her blouse during a meeting with the partner in charge of her department.

By Wednesday, she had to find a new sitter, and Dave hadn't called after nearly three months.

On Thursday, an associate popped in on her while she was hooked up to the breast pump.

Friday morning some asshole taped a picture of a milk cow on her door. She had no right to think about Dave.

That night, Gale was finally reunited with her daughter in their evening routine. She sat in Julia's room nursing and singing, "Hush little baby, don't say a word, Momma's gonna buy you a mocking bird, and if that mocking bird won't sing. . . ."

As she sang, Gale stared at the picture that Elle painted and wondered what type of bird was singing. She stood up while Julia continued to nurse and walked closer to the picture. She never noticed the tiny inscription on the bird's cage, *The NightinGale's Song.* "It's a nightingale– no kidding. She named the little bird after me. That's so sweet."

She sat back down and continued to look at the picture. The purple bird with rich golden eyes stared back.

On Saturday morning, Gale went down to the office with Julia. It was a mistake as soon as she carried the baby off the elevator. There weren't any secretaries there to goggle over Julia, and it was beneath the female lawyers to acknowledge a cute baby. She stole to her office and closed the door. Sitting on her desk was a package from the mail room attendant with a quick note that read, "Miss Knightly, This package arrived for you a couple of weeks ago. It got lost in the shuffle while I was on vacation. Kiss Baby J for me. Bobby."

At least the mail room clerk was nice enough to acknowledge Julia. Taped to the package was a letter from Elle's lawyer, Mark Johnson, which explained the gift.

Gale unwrapped a painting that was entitled *Philomela.* It was a typical angry Elle picture. With sharp, contrasting colors, a sycamore stood in the eastern sky dressed in full autumn hue. Perched on a low branch sat the same violet nightingale painted for the picture in Julia's nursery. Shaded by the sycamore was a lone easel with a canvas resting against its frame. A single swallow sat on an empty artist's stool gazing at an unfinished painting.

"Obviously she painted this for you, Julia," Gale said to her daughter. "But I don't think this picture's going in the nursery. The pathetic thing must have been painted during one of Auntie Elle's bleak weeks."

"Look at the itty-bitty picture, though. It looks like a tiger with a bird in its mouth. And look here, there's another bird up in the tree staring at the easel. Man, she painted some weird stuff. Why would she ever think that I would want this, especially for a nursery?"

Leaving her stack of work behind, Gale gathered up the painting and Julia and headed home.

"Let's go you lucky thing. You get to spend an evening with old Grammy Knightly. Mommy's going out on the town."

Gale's stomach fluttered while she brushed on mascara. Life had changed immensely since Ken's last party. She had starred in her own tragic comedy with a mixture of death, sorrow and pleasure. Without Julia, though, there would have been no pleasure.

She looked in the mirror with approval. Gale glistened in a sapphire evening dress with a plunging neckline that was borrowed from Amy. "I might as well flaunt one of the perks of nursing."

By the time Dicey and Hank arrived for Gale, she was flooded with nausea. Fielding questions about Julia made her sick.

"Gale, you'll be fine. Dicey and I won't leave you stranded for a minute," Hank assured her.

"I know I'll be fine, but I also know that I'm open season for every petty woman in Crystal Springs."

"If you can handle your mother and sister, you certainly can handle these women. They're all colored from the same bottle of peroxide," added Hank.

"Sharpened claws! I like that," Gale said. "I knew you before Dicey, Hank. Why weren't we so lucky to fall in love?"

"Sandra Day O'Connor and Antonin Scalia in the same house would be a disaster. You both need me to shake up the bench every once in a while," Dicey laughed. "Gale, just promise me one thing about tonight, though."

"What?"

"Don't get your folders in a fluster over Ken, again. I've rolled a double red on him twice. Three times would be a disaster."

"Of course not, Dice. Do you think I'm really that desperate?"

"Yes."

Gale and her escorts couldn't find the host when they first arrived at the party. As Hank walked away for drinks, Dicey picked off crusted baby slobber from Gale's shoulder.

"You need a full length mirror and a little perfume. Sour milk is not the most attractive smell," recommended Dicey.

"No, what I need is a drink. I pumped six extra times this week so Harriet would have her own milk for Julia tonight."

Hank returned from the bar with Ken.

"You remember Dicey, Ken," said Hank.

"Of course, you're working miracles with this guy. He actually looks happy for a change."

"Thanks. Once again, your party is lovely."

"Gale, you look incredible, too," Ken offered.

"Thank you. It has been a challenging year."

"You're certainly rising to the occasion. How is Smith, Kennedy & Clark treating you?"

"As long as I'm churning out billable hours, they're happy."

"I can't imagine Bill Smith and Rich Kennedy not being pleased with an intelligent and gorgeous woman whom clients find stunning," said Ken as he moved closer to Gale.

Dicey suppressed her eyes from rolling and bit her tongue, but she was certain that Gale didn't have the same reaction to the man.

Gale, instead, said, "You're very kind, Ken. But the firm hasn't quite moved into the twenty-first century. I think that they're still adjusting to my baby's schedule."

"I'm sure that some men find this softer side of you very appealing, Gale."

"I don't know about that, but I'm sorry. I must excuse myself," she said and darted away.

"Where's she going?" asked Dicey who had been trying to avoid Tereus by talking with one of Hank's partners.

"I'm not sure," Ken answered.

Dicey headed for the restroom and tapped on the door. "Gale, are you in there?"

"Yes, it's me."

"Open the door. What's wrong?"

"Nothing."

"Just open the door."

When Gale opened the door, Dicey saw two symmetric wet spots the size of lemons on the front of her dress. "What did you do, spill wine all over yourself?" Dicey tried unsuccessfully to suppress a laugh.

"Don't you think about laughing right now," Gale demanded. "Look at me. While I was talking to Ken, my milk came in."

"What in the hell is wrong with you? The guy walks up for one minute, and he does this to you. It's been one year and a baby since you've dated him," said Dicey.

Tears crested on Gale's lashes. "I'm not worried about that right now, Dice. If I ruin this dress, Amy's going to kill me," Gale cried, as she stuffed toilet paper in her bra. "Just give me a minute to pull myself together, and I'll be right out."

"Here, wrap my shawl around your shoulders until you dry," Dicey said and left the bathroom.

Gale tied the shawl around her shoulders and looked in the mirror. "This looks ridiculous," she groaned. "Why in the hell do I care? It's not like any of these men want a babe with a newborn."

As she slipped from the bathroom, Ken was close by.

"Is everything okay? Can I help?" he questioned.

"No. I just leaked a little milk on my gown."

"You're right. I can't help with that," Ken said and excused himself.

Damn! Why am I even here, Gale thought? She found Hank and Dicey who were saddled next to the buffet table with fresh drinks. A long night ahead stood between Gale and her bed.

"Gale, excuse me for saying this, but when you first saw Ken, you looked like Hester Prynne when she first saw Arthur Dimmesdale," Dicey teased.

"I'm not in the mood for your literary bullshit," Gale retorted with all seriousness.

"C'mon, can't you take a little comic relief."

"No. I guess my sense of humor flushed out with my placenta."

"Would you please relax? Forget about Ken and have some fun."

"Dicey is right, Gale. Ken is harmless," added Hank. "By the way, remember he'll be at Dr. Berlan's deposition on Tuesday."

"Great, I'll have one more opportunity to make an ass of myself."

Gale wandered around the dining room, staring blankly at the Asian vases displayed on the sideboard. She toyed with Ken's collection of Chinese snuff bottles, the same jars that he admonished Dicey for touching last year. A few of the vessels had tiny cork stoppers. She picked up a light green bottle and tried to pull out the cork. A piece crumbled off. Looking around to see if anyone saw her, she flicked the piece of cork on the floor and quickly replaced the bottle. In her mood, she would have preferred to drop the tiny vessel onto the floor and crush it under her heel.

❧ ❧ ❧

Julia escaped Harriet's watch with only minor gas. "She wouldn't take a bit of rice," Mrs. Knightly complained, "and she cried half the time while you were gone. Gale, are you starving that child?"

"Mother, she's still nursing. She won't be on solids for another few months. That's why I gave you the breast milk."

"This breast feeding stuff isn't right, Gale. That child needs food or at least some formula. I know you won't listen to me, but at least talk to your sister. She never nursed those boys, and they're as healthy as hedgehogs."

"Okay, Mom, it's late. Hank's in the car waiting for us."

As Dicey grabbed the diaper bag, Mrs. Knightly mounted forces against her daughter. "You talk some sense into her, Dicey. She reads all those damn parenting books, and now she thinks that she's an expert on infants. I never had a book to tell me how to raise a child, and look at my girls."

"The jury is still out on Amy and me, Mother. Thanks for watching Julia."

Pulling into her driveway, Gale asked Hank and Dicey to help her in the house with the baby. She also wanted them to see Elle's painting that she had found at her office earlier in the day.

Hank's reaction to the picture was immediate. "Ladies, I know Elle was a friend, but she painted some whacked-out work, and I'm really very tired of it all."

Dicey wasn't so quick to react. The title lingered in her mind.

☙❧ ☙❧ ☙❧

Gale's second week back at work started as wretchedly as the first. She missed an important filing deadline with the court and managed to doze off during a departmental meeting. To make life more miserable, her breasts felt like water balloons stretched to their bursting point. The female office manager suggested that "it was time to turn off her faucet while on the job," so she was no longer pumping at the office. Gale rested her head on the desk and closed her eyes. Exhaustion and humiliation washed over her, and it was only Monday.

That evening she clung to Julia for comfort. Her tiny fingers pulled on strands of Gale's hair, and her delicious caramel eyes giggled out loud. Gale drew imaginary hearts on her cheeks and forehead. The tension trickled from Gale's body but only for a short while. She had to face the office and Ken in twelve hours.

In the old days, Gale would have been the first to arrive at the deposition and would have been seated at the center of the conference table, facing the door. Today, she walked in at seven fifty-nine and was panting. She slipped into the only open chair, which was next to Ken. From her brief case, she pulled out her yellow legal pad. It was still detailed with Post-It notes.

When she glanced up to acknowledge Hank who was at the far end of the conference table, her eyes met Ken's stare, instead. Gale sucked in air and smiled. She shifted in her seat, knocking a coffee cup onto her note pad. She watched as the blue ink blurred, and her words on the paper ran together. Ken grabbed napkins from the coffee tray and began mopping up the mess.

☙ ☙ ☙

Gale pulled into the parking lot of the Little Red School House Daycare Center at six-thirteen. Maria was glaring out the front door. Gale jumped out of the car and bolted into the building. She started to apologize for being late, but Maria interrupted and said, "Remember, five dollars for every minute past six." Gale glanced at the clock on the wall that read six twenty-one. Her own watch read six-fifteen.

"I'm sorry, Maria. My boss walked in my office with a deadline, just as I was leaving."

"Miss Knightly, my daughter's parent-teacher conference starts in twenty-five minutes," she said flatly. "Remember the rules. If you're late more than three times in a month, you'll have to find a new daycare. This is your second time in two weeks."

Gale gathered Julia from the crib and threw the diaper bag over her shoulder. "Goodnight, Maria. Please forgive me. I hope your teacher's conference goes well," she said and hurried out the door.

By the time she pulled in the driveway and unloaded the car, Julia was wailing from hunger. Gale kicked off her shoes, sat down on the couch and unbuttoned her blouse. The baby rooted in with relief, and in a minute or two, Gale was snoring.

An hour later, the telephone startled Gale out of her sleep. She fumbled for the phone and said hello.

"Did your note pad survive the spill, counselor?" asked the caller.

"Excuse me?"

"It's Ken Tereus. Remember this morning? Your notepad and the coffee spill?"

"Oh, geez, Ken, it's you. I was half asleep on the couch with Julia. My notepad was okay. Only the surface was smeared."

"I was surprised you were late this morning. That's unlike you."

"I wasn't late. I just wasn't early."

"That is late for you. I was disappointed. I arrived early to see you."

"Sorry to have disappointed you, but my morning priorities are a little different now." Gale sat back down on the couch and tightened her hold on Julia.

"Does your schedule ever allow for dinner?"

"Rarely, but thanks for asking."

"Then, lunch counselor."

"Thank you, Ken, but I work through lunch, so I don't get heat for leaving at five-thirty."

"Bill me for the time. How can your partners argue with that?"

Gale chuckled but declined.

A dozen yellow roses arrived at her office the next day with an invitation to lunch. Gale again declined. Two dozen white roses arrived the following day with an invitation to lunch.

"Isn't he supposed to be operating on an actress or seeing patients or something?" she grumbled to herself. Gale pulled her cell phone from her purse and scanned the numbers for incoming calls. She found Ken's number from his call the day before and dialed the number. His voice mail answered, and she replied, "Ken, this is Gale. I appreciate your persistency. However, I'm not interested in lunches or anything else at this point in my life. A professional relationship works best for me. I don't mean to be terse. I simply have to do what's best for Julia and me. I'll see you at the Calloway deposition in a week." Gale hung up the phone. She received no more roses or invitations to lunch. She was relieved.

☙ ☙ ☙

One week later Gale was awakened at five a.m. by piercing cries. She threw off her blankets, jumped toward the bedroom door, and promptly rammed her hip into the door frame. "Damn!" she grunted and headed into the nursery. The soft glow of the nightlight was distorted by Julia's screaming that had reached a newfound pitch.

"I didn't know that your tiny vocal cords could make such an awful noise, honey," whispered Gale. She reached for the child and felt the heat of her skin through the pajamas.

"Not a fever, I've got a deposition in three hours," she sighed with exhaustion. Gale laid Julia on the changing table and pulled out the thermometer. She placed it in her ear and listened to the "beep, beep, beep" as the temperature gauge continued to rise. Finally, there was a long "beeeep" indicating that the reading was complete. Gale looked at the digital numbers, one hundred and two degrees. The nasty virus that was snacking its way through the daycare had obviously discovered Julia. "What now?" Gale moaned. The daycare wouldn't accept kids with temperatures above ninety-nine degrees, and she had no back up.

Gale waited until six-thirty to call her mother. She dreaded dialing the number, but there was no other option. Harriett, groggy with sleep, answered the phone.

"Mom, it's me, Gale."

"What time is it?"

"It's six-thirty. I need to ask a huge favor. Julia has a fever, and I have to be at a meeting in an hour and a half. Do you think that you could watch her for a couple of hours?" There was a long pause on the other end of the line. Julia was asleep in her bumper seat that was set on the kitchen counter. Not thinking, Gale rocked it with a few quick jerks. Julia woke and let out a cry.

Finally, her mother answered, "Gale, I couldn't possibly handle her today. I've got a tennis game at ten and a lunch with the ladies at noon."

Gale slumped over the kitchen counter and caressed Julia's eyelids and lips. "Mom, the deposition might be over by ten."

"Sorry, dear. If you would have called me last night, maybe I could have changed my plans."

"Thanks anyway," Gale said and hung up the phone. A teardrop rolled down her cheek. "If either of Amy's boys was sick, you'd be there in a nanosecond," she told her mother's voice that was still hanging in the crowded space of her mind. She stood up from the counter and looked at Julia.

"I guess you're going to your first deposition."

Gale didn't bother showering. She washed her face, dragged her hair back in a ponytail, swiped on a little makeup, and slipped into a comfortable pant suit and low heels. She nursed Julia one last time and gave her a dose of Tylenol. "God, please let her sleep through this," Gale pleaded as she headed out the front door with the baby carrier, diaper bag, and briefcase in tow.

The deposition was taking place at Dan O'Neill's office. He was a decent Irish-Catholic man with five kids. He grew up on the west side and went to St. Theresa's. Maybe he would be okay with a baby at a deposition, or maybe not. Gale swallowed hard as she drove into the garage and parked the car. She unbuckled the baby carrier and lifted Julia out of the backseat. With her free hand, she popped open the trunk, grabbed the diaper bag and briefcase, and closed the trunk with her elbow. She steadied the weight in each arm and teetered into the building.

She spotted the bank of elevators. Everybody and their brother were waiting for a ride. The first elevator to appear was already stuffed with passengers. Gale waited for the second door to open and moved in with a wave of people. She shimmied herself toward the back of the elevator. "Can someone hit floor forty-eight, please," she called out. The red button was pressed.

A woman to her left muttered, "Sick kid?" The lady may as well have asked if she had swine flu for everyone in the elevator turned toward Gale and stared. She only nodded yes. She was afraid that if she spoke, tears would burst forth instead of words. Determinedly, Gale stared at the red buttons on the wall. Only fourteen more floors. Thank heaven Julia was still asleep.

When the elevator stopped at the fortieth floor, a man who was trying to text and walk at the same time banged into Gale. Her diaper bag strap got caught on his satchel, and the strap buckle snapped off. She watched in slow motion as breast milk, baby wipes, Tylenol, diapers and tampons crashed to the floor. The five men and a single female who remained on the elevator scrambled to pick up the mess. One kind gentleman drew the strap back through the buckle of the bag and knotted it.

"Good as new," he promised. "Make it a better day, anyway."

Gale smiled. "Thanks. I will. I still believe in guardian angels."

Her armpits were dripping wet when Gale finally got off the elevator. She gripped her bundles, walked to reception desk and asked for Dan O'Neill. The receptionist, who wore a deep tan and bright blue eyeliner, offered her a seat. She declined. Gale was afraid that if she set anything down then something bad would happen. Three or four minutes later, Dan sprung from behind the front desk. He was a wisp of a man with premature gray-white hair and a tomato red face. His head jolted back in surprise when he spotted Gale with her load.

"My, my, what a pot of gold we have here?" he asked.

"Dan, I'm sorry. She's got a fever, and I'm out of options. It's either this or we reschedule the deposition. It's up to you. Tereus is your expert, so I won't need to ask many questions."

"Is your doctor showing up, Gale?"

"No, thank heaven."

"Then, we'll give it a try," Dan said and grabbed her briefcase. "Follow me and let's get rolling."

"Has Tereus arrived?" Gale asked, chasing him down the hall.

"Yeah, we've been preparing for over an hour. That man is a genius."

Gale didn't respond. Instead, she took a deep breath and followed Dan into the conference room. Ken was pouring a cup of coffee for himself when they walked in. His brow knotted up when he saw the baby carrier.

"Good morning, Gale," he said with a chill. "This must be your daughter."

"No, not mine. Found her on a deserted corner as I was driving in," she said lightly, but no one laughed.

Three other lawyers, the defendant doctor, the plaintiff and the stenographer all arrived within minutes of each other. Julia slept for the first hour of the deposition. She woke only after the plaintiff, Mrs. Calloway, screamed at Ken Tereus. She was alleging that her nipples were completely numb following Dr. Brandt's breast augmentation and that her left breast sat two inches higher than her right breast. Ken disputed the allegation that her implants were asymmetrical by pointing to a giant exhibit of the woman's breasts.

That was when Mrs. Calloway screeched, "They're horrible! Would you like to live with boobs that look like this, Dr. Tereus?" and she grabbed her breasts.

Julia let out her own squeal that matched Mrs. Calloway's screech. Gale rushed to the baby carrier to quiet her. She picked her up and bounced her around the room, but her crying continued.

"Can't you shut her up," yelled Mrs. Calloway. "What's a god-damn baby doing in here, anyway?"

Eight pair of eyes turned on Gale. She grabbed a bottle from the diaper bag and bolted into the hallway. "Oh, man," she breathed. "Honey, you've got to quiet down."

Gale walked up and down the hall, teasing Julia's tongue with the bottle. The baby finally began to suck down the milk. Gale looked into her eyes. They were no longer glassy with fever.

"Thanks for getting me out of that room. I wanted to scream in there, too. That woman is a monster," she whispered.

Just as Julia was lapping down the last drops of her bottle, the deposition ended and Mrs. Calloway stormed down the hallway, leaving an odor in her tracks.

"That's one nasty broad," Gale said under her breath.

"I heard that," Ken said from behind her back.

Gale turned around to face him. "Sorry. It's been a long day."

"It's only ten o'clock."

"Yeah, I know."

"So, this is Julia?"

Gale pulled the blanket away from the baby's face, and Ken peered down. Ken stared into her face without saying a word. After a minute, Gale said, "You are supposed to say what a cutie-pie, or something. That's the polite thing."

"I'm struck, Gale. She's beautiful," Ken finally said. "You'll have to excuse me. I've got to answer a page from the hospital."

Gale's eyes followed Ken as he rushed down the hall.

🦋 🦋 🦋

"What in God's name are you doing?" the voice at the other end of the receiver blared.

"What are you talking about?"

"Hank told me he saw you having a cuddle lunch with Ken Tereus today, and Julia was with you!"

"I was having lunch, not a cuddle lunch, Dice. And yes Julia was with me along with Dan O'Neill, another lawyer."

"Are you out of your mind, Gale?"

"Why are you so upset?" Gale asked defensively.

"Really, do I have to spell it out? The guy dumped you. Then, he dumped Elle. Now, you're having lunch with him. Have you ever heard of karma?"

"Calm down. What's wrong with you? Julia was sick. I had to take her to a deposition. Then, Ken and Dan wanted to go to lunch to discuss strategy. The case goes to trial in a few weeks."

"I'm just worried about you. I don't trust Ken Tereus. Look what he did to Elle. You'll have pig lips in a week."

"Cool it. This is all work related. I've had a shit day, and I don't need you to yell at me."

"I'm sorry. It's just . . ."

"Just what?"

"I had a dream last night about Ken and you. It was one of those dreams that you have when you wake up and it still seems real three hours later. It's bugged me all day long. Then, Hank tells me that he spotted you having lunch with Ken."

"Did he really say "spotted"? I didn't see him. Why didn't he walk up and say hello?"

"He was with a client."

"Then, get off my back. Why was this dream so god-awful anyway?"

"Gale, it was so weird. It was your wedding, with Ken. You and I were in the back of the church, waiting to walk up the aisle. You were resting on the last pew and wouldn't get up. You were dressed in that ridiculous dress that Elle was buried in, and your hair was in a puff ball. I kept tugging on your arm. I pulled harder and harder until your arm finally snapped off. You were dead! It was horrible. The stupid dream haunted me all day long. Then, Hank calls and tells me that he saw you with Ken. So, why wouldn't I freak out?"

"Your imagination is becoming as strange as Elle's, Dice. Calm down. You don't have anything to worry about. I'm not going to date him. He has asked me out a couple of times, but I told him that I wasn't interested, Nada, nothing."

"Are you sure?"

"Yes. There's a part of me that's flattered by the fact that he even bothered to ask me out again, but that's it. I'm not interested, but I am lonely. You have Hank and wedding plans and everything else. I have dirty diapers and depositions."

There was a long pause over the phone line before Dicey answered. "I'm sorry for over-reacting. The guy just freaks me out, and you're vulnerable right now."

"No. I'm exhausted and lonely."

"Listen, Gale. There's a new guy in the English department. He's an expert on Virginia Woolf. He's never been married and is adorable. I've been waiting to introduce you two, until I thought you were ready for a man. He's perfect."

"You want me to date a Virginia Woolf expert?" Gale asked, shifting the phone between her chin and shoulder.

"Of course, his name is Brendan. You'll love him. He's smart, witty, and cute in a boyish kind of way."

"How much fun is a guy who idolizes a nut case? Didn't Virginia Woolf fill her pockets with rocks and walk into the middle of a lake? How much fun can that be?"

"Brendan isn't only about Virginia Woolf. He recycles. He rides his scooter to work. And he loves camping."

"Wow, that's cool. We could recycle and compost on the weekends. Sounds like a blast."

"Don't be so cynical. Brendan is a very nice guy."

"I'm sure Brendan is a very nice guy, but I don't think so."

"I'm not trying to push you into anything. I'm just worried about Julia and you," Dicey said gently.

"It's hard, Dice. I crave a little male attention. I crave Dave, but he's never going to call me, and I can't call him. Maybe I should go out with Ken, at least he calls."

"Never! Go out with Brendan or Hank or a priest, not that weirdo!"

"Would you please stop? Maybe we've both been wrong about him. Maybe Hank's right. Maybe he's harmless."

"He's as harmless as Hades, Gale. Don't be so naive. Ken Tereus is only worried about Ken Tereus."

"Listen, Dicey. I'm not looking for a soul mate. I just want a little companionship."

☙☙ ☙☙ ☙☙

At nine o'clock the next morning, a dozen pink roses arrived at Gale's office, along with an invitation to lunch from Ken Tereus.

Three hours later the receptionist buzzed her office. "Gale, your carry-out order has arrived," she said with a giggle.

"It must be a mistake. I didn't order anything," Gale said, and then it struck her. When she walked down the hall and into the reception area, she spotted Ken Tereus. He was holding two white carry-out bags from China Chow-Chow.

"You're very persistent," Gale said.

She led him back down the hall and into her office with a slight smile on her face. Gale and Ken lingered over lunch. She remembered his smell. It reinvigorated her desire for a man.

☙☙ ☙☙ ☙☙

"You promised me," Dicey blared into the phone, for the second time in a week.

"Promised you what?" asked Gale.

"You promised never to date Ken Tereus."

"I'm not!" Gale said flatly.

"That's not the word on the street," Dicey fumed.

"What word on what street?" Gale felt a sharp pain shoot through her neck. She massaged it with her free hand.

"Hank heard that you're hanging out with Ken. One of your partners told him that Ken brings you catered lunches and roses everyday."

"He's done that only twice," she lied.

"Damn it, Gale. Why didn't you tell me?" Dicey's voice went up three octaves.

The change in Gale's tone matched Dicey's in octave and irritation. "Why are you making such a big deal out of this?"

"There is something wrong with that guy."

"I've had lunch with him— that's all."

"Then, why didn't you tell me that? Why were you hiding it?"

"I wasn't hiding it." A drop of perspiration slipped down Gale's forehead. She brushed it off and said, "You're starting to make me mad with these accusations!"

"I've talked to you ten times this week, and you've never once mentioned his name," Dicey insisted.

"I didn't mean to hide anything from you. It was only lunch, nothing more. That's probably why I didn't think of telling you. I will say this, though. It was nice to be with a man who could carry on a conversation without hyperventilating because I have a child. Cut me some slack and trust my judgment."

"I'm sorry," Dicey clipped. "You just know how he makes my skin crawl."

"Just agree to trust me."

"Okay," Dicey conceded. "Listen, Hank and I will stop by with pizza and a bottle of wine around six. I think you need a few laughs."

After three slices of piece and a couple of glasses of wine, Gale asked Hank his opinion of Ken Tereus.

"I think that Dicey gives him a bad wrap. Just because he reconstructed Elle's face, it doesn't make him a demon. That's his job. Women from Saudi Arabia fly their personal jets into Cincinnati, just to have Ken transform their beauty in Crystal Springs. He is legendary, trust me. Nurses love him. Court reporters melt when he walks into the courtroom. When he's an expert witness, I want all women on the jury. Dicey's the only woman on earth who doesn't adore the man.

"I don't adore him," Gale protested.

"Hank, you don't get it, do you? Why would anyone give some guy with red hair and golden eyes a chance," argued Dicey.

"This is the first time that I've known you to be superficial. I'm quite surprised," Hank said, only half amused.

Gale stood up from the kitchen table and started to gather the plates. "Well, no matter how any of us feel about Ken Tereus, I'm not going to date the guy," she said.

"Dicey is correct on one topic, and that's Dave Broadbeck. Until I get him out of my blood, I'll never give any guy a chance."

Dicey stood up, came around the table and gave her a hug. "Honesty isn't always fun, is it?" she said to Gale.

"No, not at all, but let's not dwell on it. Hank, why don't you help me clean up, and Dicey can check on Julia."

While Hank and Gale cleaned the dishes, Dicey found *Philomela* sitting in the hall, next to Julia's room. The picture was Elle in her true form. A violet nightingale was perched on a low branch. Sitting under the tree was an easel with a canvas resting against its frame. A swallow sat on a stool gazing at an unfinished painting. It looked like a tiger with a bird in its mouth. "Why would she paint this for Julia's nursery?" Dicey whispered. "Both birds have wicked eyes. Her conversation with the picture was interrupted by Julia's cries. The odor emanating from the room confirmed a dirty diaper.

"Something smells awfully fishy in Denmark. Let's try to clean up this mess," she told Julia.

☾ ☾ ☾

The next day Dicey began her quest to reveal *Philomela's* secret. She pulled out her ragged *Benet's Reader's Encyclopedia*. It was like the *Physician's Desk Reference*, but for English teachers. It contained most every literary reference worth noting. Nothing was listed under the P's for Philomela. The index of Henry Fuseli's biography was also blank with references to Philomela. Why would she paint the same nightingale twice, especially a bird that looks like it is choking? Unconsciously, Dicey whispered, "Thou was not born for death, immortal Bird!"

"Her voice is immortal, too, but what is she trying to say?" Then it hit her. The nightingale was Philomela.

As she yanked her mythology dictionary from the shelf, Dicey's heart pounded.

"Elle, you knew I would find it," she whispered.

Dicey found the entry on Philomela. A powerful Greek soldier married the daughter of the king of Athens. The soldier fell in love with his wife's sister, Philomela, and raped her. He cut her tongue out so she could never reveal the crime to his wife. Philomela wove the story of the rape into a tapestry for her sister. The two sisters ran away and sought refuge from the gods. The gods offered protection to the sisters by changing the wife into a swallow and Philomela into a song bird.

Elle was silenced just like Philomela. She was telling her story in the paintings. But what did Gale have to do with this? The wife and sister both had sex with the soldier.

"Did Gale have sex with this asshole, and she never told me," Dicey said aloud. "No, that's not it. Gale would have told me. And whether she wants to admit to me, I know that Dave is the only man whom she has ever loved or made love to."

Dicey ran to her bedroom and dragged out *The Nightmare*. There had to be some point to this picture, but before she could begin her new quest, the door bell rang. Hank had arrived with egg rolls and sweet and sour pork.

When she opened the door, all that Dicey could say was, "I can't eat. I'm sick to my stomach."

"Why? Two hours ago you were craving Shanghai Mama's," Hank asked as he walked into living room.

"I know . . . but I think that I'm unraveling something."

"Unraveling what?"

"My best friend is being courted by a pervert who also dated my other friend who now happens to be dead. And you expect me to eat?"

Hank dropped the food on the coffee table with a thud. "Dicey, the fact that Ken has asked Gale to dinner is nothing new. When are you going to let go of Elle Pandion? I'm going to be honest with you. I'm tired of this shit."

"Please, just listen for a moment." Dicey went on to describe the research that she had uncovered about Philomela.

Taking her hand in his, Hank started, "Dice, I think the only thing that Elle was trying to say is that she was a off her rocker. You can't assume that, because someone painted a crazed picture, she was actually telling you anything other than that she was nuts."

Dicey pulled her hand away and asked, "Do you think Gale had sex with Ken, and maybe she just didn't want to admit it?"

"Wouldn't you lie about it if some guy dumped you ten minutes after you had sex with him?"

"Not to Gale. She's been my best friend since the fifth grade. She would never lie to me. It must be something else that has to do with Ken Tereus."

"I've known the guy for a long time. He's never shown any deviant behavior," said Hank.

"Men are different around women. He gives me the heeby-geebies. Maybe he forced sex on Gale, and now she's too embar-rassed to tell me."

"Dicey, you're getting out of hand. You are accusing someone of rape, again. You can't just go around accusing every man con-nected to Elle of rape. Gale was drunk the night of his first party. If she had sex with him and doesn't remember or doesn't want to remember, that doesn't mean he raped her. And I have no idea what this whole Philoman thing is about."

"It's Philomela. She sewed her secret tragedy in a tapestry. Elle sewed her soul in paintings."

"Dicey, this is real life, not some fantasy out of your mytho-logical dictionary."

CHAPTER 32

To defy Power, which seems omnipotent;
To love, and bear; to hope till Hope creates
From its own wreck the thing it contemplates.

—Percy Bysshe Shelley, "Prometheus Unbound"

Nine in the morning was a safe time to call Gale. Julia would be awake.

"Gale, it's me. Can I come over?"

"Do you mean now?" She was trying to complete time records and nurse at the same time. "I'm overwhelmed this morning. Can we meet tonight or maybe tomorrow?"

"It can't wait. I need to talk to you."

"What's wrong?"

"Nothing . . . I just want to talk. I'll bring a blueberry crumb cake."

Gale knew that Dicey was going to come over, whether or not she was invited. "Okay, only if it's is low fat. And, Dice, I know your 'nothings'. They're never just nothing."

As Dicey sliced through the blueberries and cinnamon, she began her subtle interrogation.

"Gale, do you think that you would ever date Ken, even in your weakest moment?"

"Is that what you're here for, to talk about Ken?"

"Why? Would it bother you?" she asked, nibbling on the pastry.

"At nine o'clock on a Sunday morning it would!"

"What do you see in the guy?" Dicey asked blowing on her coffee.

"I've told you that I'm not interested, but honestly, if I did see anything, it would just be male company. I already told you that."

"You splatter like rain drops whenever he's around. That's not like you. . . . Tell me, did anything ever happen between you two last year?"

"Like what?"

"You know, like diddling?"

"Hell, no! He never diddled as much as his big toe with me. Don't you remember? He dumped me before he barely kissed me," Gale said wiping crumbs from her mouth.

"Are you sure about that?"

"Dicey, it's too early in the morning to play mental games with me. What are you getting at? I have never slept with Ken Tereus. Fortunately or unfortunately, Dave is the only one. You know that."

"Well, this has something to do with Elle's picture."

"Dice, No way! You are not going there, again. The mystery stopped with her father. Leave it alone, once and for all."

"I've done research. You have to listen."

"What does research have to do with Ken Tereus? Dicey, your literary research deals with fiction, not with reality."

"Don't you understand, yet? Elle's paintings were her reality. I'm not sure what it was, but I know that she was trying to tell you something– like with her picture of the pope. Just listen for a minute."

Gale smashed a piece of cake with her thumb but agreed to listen. Dicey pulled her mythology dictionary from her purse and read the passage describing Philomela. She glanced up for a reaction from Gale. Her face remained in the same scrunched position.

"I guess I'm a little too literal, Dice. You're going to have to explain it."

"Elle is like Philomela. She's telling her story in her paintings like Philomela did with her weaving."

"But, what does that have to do with me?"

"Can't you see?"

"No."

"You're the song bird. You're Philomela's sister. You both had sex with the same man."

Gale jumped from the table with Julia in her arms. "That's bullshit! What in the hell are you talking about? Who's the guy?"

"What do you mean who's the guy? Ken Tereus."

"I never had sex with him. The guy barely touched me."

"Gale, please be straight up with me. Did you have sex with Tereus?"

"No, no, and no, damn it!"

"Then, why are you always so nervous around him?"

"I don't know. I'm not!"

"Gale, you spent the night at his house."

"That's because I was trashed, not because I had sex."

"Are you sure?"

"Listen to me! I never had sex with Ken Tereus, and you're pissing me off!"

"Then, why would Elle paint Philomela and send it to you?"

"Elle Pandion never walked a straight line a day in her life."

"She was coherent enough to paint the pope and Dr. Pandion."

Gale dragged her chair close to Dicey and sat down. She rested her free arm across Dicey's shoulder and pulled her close. "It's time to let her go. It's time to let go of your student who hung herself. You didn't snuff out her life. She made that choice. Both women did."

"Gale, you can't ignore the pictures, though."

"Elle teetered on the edge of sanity while she was alive, so I'm not surprised that her pictures take the leap after her death."

"I'm not sure about that. Just promise to be careful."

"Don't worry about Ken. He's gone off on another jaunt to Asia. He was telling Dan O'Neill about his trip at a meeting. I agree with you, honey; the guy is strange. No wonder he and Elle hit it off so well."

"It relieves me to her you say that."

"The only thing that has happened with him showing a little interest is that I miss Dave that much more."

"Do you miss Dave or miss the idea of Dave?"

"I think both . . . but I've tried to do something about it."

"Like? Let me guess. You called him for a date," she said with too much sarcasm. "I'm sorry. I shouldn't tease you about this?"

"But you are close."

"Seriously, what are you talking about?"

"I left a voice mail message for him last night."

"Honestly? The stubborn Wall of China has a little chink?"

"Yes, but don't get too excited, he never called back."

👀 👀 👀

Gale fought with her blankets that night and ended up with sheets tied around her ankles. The last time that she had spoken to Dave, he had told her that she was "fucking nuts." Maybe I was fucking nuts. Who wouldn't be nuts at nine months pregnant, single and scared. Maybe I'm still fucking nuts, she pondered.

Dave didn't call the next day, nor the next. On Friday afternoon at three-thirty, Gale was sitting in her office reading through a legal brief. As much as she fought it, her eyes kept drooping closed, and her head kept bobbing up and down with sleep. She stood up, kicked off her heels and did ten jumping jacks behind the desk. On the tenth jump, her phone rang. She hit the speaker button and said hello.

"Hey, Gale, it's me" a low voice came over the speaker. She grabbed the receiver.

"Dave," she said, and her stomach flip-flopped.

"Hello."

"Hi," Gale struggled. "How are you?"

"I'm okay, and you?"

"Fine, as well."

"How's your father?" Gale politely asked.

"Dad's great, and you?"

"I'm fine," Gale repeated. Her body couldn't move.

"How's your family?"

"We're all fine." She grabbed the edge of the desk to steady herself.

"And your mother?"

"Fine, too."

"You called?" Dave asked.

"I did. I wanted to see how you are."

"I'm okay, Gale."

"Well then," she said and sat down.

"Yeah, well, then. . . ."

"Well then, goodbye," Gale said and hung up the phone.

She picked up the receiver and slammed it down again. She jumped up from her desk and began to pace the room. She tripped over a box of medical records, turned and kicked the stack of papers into the air. Her tirade stopped only when she pressed her forehead against the icy window that looked out to the street, nineteen stories below. Tears crested in her eyes, and she wept. The phone rang, but she didn't move.

"What have I done to him . . . to Julia . . . to me?" she cried. Her cell phone began its own ringing. "Leave me be!" she yelled back. But Julia's image came to mind, and she went for the phone.

"Hello."

"Gale, it's me again."

Gale heard his voice and melted back into her chair.

"Thank you for calling back. I am so sorry, Dave. I just didn't know what to say."

"No, Gale. I'm sorry. Really, how are you?"

"Honestly, it depends on the day," she said, without disguising her exhaustion.

"Gale?"

"Yes?"

"How is she? Julia?"

"She's incredible." Gale sat up. "How did you know her name?"

"I've known it for two and a half months."

"But how did you know?"

"Your receptionist told me. She weighed seven pounds, five ounces and was eighteen inches long when she was born. And her name is Julia Aster."

"You really knew . . . but why . . . why haven't you called?"

"Ego, fear, I don't know."

"I finally did, though."

"I'm glad. I would have . . . I've been in a headlock since I last saw you. I did call; I just didn't call you. Gale, I said so many awful things to you that day. I thought you'd never forgive me and that you'd never let me see her."

"You're ridiculous." Gale laughed nervously. "She's beautiful, Dave. It is true what everybody says. Once you have a baby, it's impossible to describe the love that rushes through you, filling up all the empty spaces. Everything you do, every decision you make is colored in a new light."

"It's nice to hear you talk like that. I always knew that you'd be a great mom."

"Thank you. She's amazing. She has chocolate brown hair and big almond eyes. She's rolling over now. She giggles and gurgles all day long. She has a lot to say about life."

"Don't we all, Gale?"

"I guess so." She paused and finally asked, "Do you think that you would ever want to meet her?"

"Yes," he said, and his voice cracked.

"When would be good for you?"

"Today, tonight, tomorrow, I'll leave Chicago right now."

"She'll be sound asleep by the time you get in tonight. Tomorrow would be wonderful," Gale said but then asked, "Dave?"

"Yes?"

"Does your father know about her?"

"Are you kidding? I couldn't tell him. If he knew about Julia—Gale, you know what he would do. He would have driven my ass straight to your door with a priest and marriage license. I never wanted to force you into a marriage orchestrated by Dad. I'd never force you into anything."

"Dave, I am happy to hear your voice. We'll both be waiting at twelve o'clock tomorrow. Be safe, no accidents, not now."

She hung up the phone and whispered, "Jesus, Mary and Joseph . . . help me."

As Julia gurgled at her breast that evening, Gale told her how she met her father.

"I was studying in the law library for semester finals when this bozo sits down at my table. He dumped out his book bag. Crumbled papers and broken erasers spilled into my space. I glared at him. He grinned. Then, he had the nerve to bug me for a pen. I gave him one. Then he bugged me for a piece of paper. A few minutes later, he slipped the folded sheet back across the table. I opened it. Do you know what it said? 'I think you're cute. Will you go out with me? Check yes or no.' I fell in love with him that day. But he was too rich, too handsome and too funny for someone like me. Too much of a risk."

Julia passed gas as Gale finished the story.

Saturday morning Gale woke early to feed and bathe Julia. After she dressed her, Julia rolled around on the floor in pink corduroy overalls. She watched her mother throw clothes at the mirror. Two pair of jeans, black stretch pants, a skirt and plaid trousers were tossed across the room before Gale was dressed. She looked in the mirror and was finally satisfied with the black boots, jeans and a black sweater that hugged her swollen breasts.

She had one hour to clean up her trail of insecurities strewn about the room, but the door bell rang before the sweep began. She peeked out the sidelight of the door. A gigantic stuffed bunny peeked back. She spied him through the fur. He was beautiful. She pulled the door open wide. Neither said a word.

Finally, Dave stepped inside the door and pulled Gale close to his chest. Squeezing back tears, she whispered hello.

"Where is she?" he asked breathlessly.

"Stay here, I'll get her." When Gale returned to the living room with Julia, Dave's face quivered.

"I've missed so much, seventy-eight days. What an idiot I've been. She's beautiful. Dave moved close and touched Julia's hand. "She's so small. Is everything okay?"

"She's not even three months, not quite a linebacker. You can hold her," Gale said and pushed Julia toward him.

He grabbed her under the arms. Julia's legs dangled down, and her head flopped forward.

"Ooo, watch her neck," Gale warned. He tried to hand her back to Gale.

"No, you can do it. Just cradle her in your arms."

With Gale's help, he changed positions, bent his own head close to her face and said, "Hey, girly, it is daddy." Julia let out a cry.

"What did I do?" Dave was alarmed and handed her back to Gale.

Gale laughed and pushed Julia back to him. "Calm down. She knows that you're tense. Sit down and talk to her while I finish getting ready."

As Gale walked into her bedroom, Dave sat down on the couch with Julia who was crooked back in his arm. He touched her nose with his index finger and then drew a circle around her lips. He picked up her foot and measured it against his fingers. It was shorter than his pinky. She pulled back her foot and began squirming and straining in his arms.

"What's wrong with her?" he yelled toward the bedroom. He tried to rock her by rapidly shaking his arm. Her face went crimson, and Dave grew nervous. "Her face is scrunched up and turning red. Can she breathe?" he yelled again.

Gale stuck her head around the corner from her room and said, "Check her diaper. She probably had a bowel movement."

"How do I do that?"

"Stick your finger in or smell her bottom."

Dave lifted Julia in the air to eye level, stuck his nose in the seat of her overalls, and took a big sniff. He confirmed that she was, in fact, dirty. Gale directed him into the nursery where he received his first lesson on changing messy diapers.

ᴓ ᴓ ᴓ

Dave changed four dirty diapers that day and memorized the words to "Hush Little Baby." The most intriguing moment arrived with feeding time. Dave was mesmerized when milk sprayed from Gale's nipple, and Julia suckled in delight. Gale was embarrassed when Dave asked, "How do you turn it on and off?"

After Julia went down for the night, Gale stood alone in the nursery. The entire day had been filled with affection for Julia. Other than the initial hug, there was no intimacy shared between Dave and her. Gale was nervous. Was he there just as a Julia's father? Was he repulsed by her altered body? He had every right to divorce himself from her life.

When she finally mustered the courage to go into the living room, Dave was watching Ohio State play Michigan. There were two minutes left in the game. The Buckeyes were down by three. Gale sat down in the chair across from him. Dave shut off the game.

Gale was shocked. She looked at the television and then looked at Dave. "Wait a minute. I've never seen you turn off a football game."

"Do you really think that football is that important to me?" he asked.

"Oh, please!" Gale laughed. "Do you want a straight answer or a nice answer?"

He laughed, too. "No football tonight. Daddy wants you over here," he said, patting the couch. Gale moved next to him.

"Are we allowed to do this now?" he asked.

"What do you mean?"

"Touch. I didn't want to do anything in front of Julia."

Gale laughed again, nervously. "She's a baby."

"I know, but I don't want to screw up."

"You've been perfect all day," she said, reaching for his knee. "So, what's it like seeing me as a mom? Nursing, cleaning stinky bottoms, I guess it's not very sexy, is it?"

"No, Gale, it's not very sexy at all. It's down right incredible."

"I'll accept incredible."

"Your tenderness, your laughter, your messy house, it's an entirely new dimension of you."

"I'm a little shaky on my feet right now. So, please be kind."

Dave took her hand in his. Gale looked down at their entwined fingers and noticed her chipped nail polish. She tugged her hand away and curled her fingers into her palm.

"What's wrong, Gale? I am being honest with you. I've never been more honest in my entire life?"

"Look at me. My nails are a chipped, goo is stuck in my hair, and I smell like sour milk. I'm not the Gale you used to know."

"No, you're not that girl anymore. You are a mother and a woman, someone who is that much more amazing. I don't want a buddy or some chick." Dave paused and looked down at the ground. He then looked up at her and said, "I didn't want a buddy last year. I just didn't know how to tell you what I wanted. I'm sorry."

"Dave, what did you want?"

"I wanted you. I've always wanted you. I just couldn't say it. I was afraid that if I said it, you would go away, like my mother. I told her that I loved her, and she died. I've been a pain in the ass. I've been a 'run from reality' kind of guy. When I lost you, I slammed into a steel wall of reality, though. Then, I tried to recover with 'run from reality' women. I've stopped running. I'm hearing sirens, again."

"What do you mean by again?"

"I knew what you meant when you asked me about the sirens. When you were in Chicago, you asked me if I ever thought about you when I heard emergency sirens. Did I wonder if you were okay? Of course I knew what you were talking about. I just didn't want to admit it. The last time I heard sirens for someone I really loved was when the paramedics came to save my mother's life, but she was already dead. I never wanted to hear those sirens again."

"Why didn't you just tell me?"

"I couldn't. I thought that if I never said that I loved you, then you would never go away. The last words that I said to my mother were 'I love you.' I thought that you could just trust me, but then, you got all tangled up in the words. You said some pretty awful things to me last November. I know that I was stupid and childish, but what you said hurt, really hurt."

"I'm sorry. Dave, I did try to call you in January, but you were tied up with 'someone.'"

"I was angry at you. Maybe I was hoping to get over you or was trying to hurt you."

"That was the day when I called to tell you that I was pregnant."

"God, I'm sorry." He grabbed her hand and brought it to his lips.

"No, Dave. I should have told you, but my pride stopped me."

"I missed her birth. I don't want to miss the rest of her life. We need to be together."

"But, Dave, are you saying this just because you want to be a father? You can be her father— married or not."

"No, I'm saying that because I loved you before Julia, and I love you that much more as her mother."

As Dave was pulling out of her driveway to head back to Chicago, Gale was dialing Dicey's number.

"Hey Dice, how are you?" she asked casually. The phone was crooked in her ear as she rocked Julia around the kitchen.

"Great, now tell me."

"Tell you what?"

"Don't play games. My cell phone has been glued to my hip for the entire weekend. Hank wouldn't let me call you. Was he okay?"

"Okay in what sense of the word?"

"It went great, didn't it?"

"Oh, Dicey! I can't tell you how happy I am. He wants to get married. He really loves me . . . and Julia."

"Of course he does, you ding-dong. He's loved you since the day he met you. So when are you getting married?"

"We're getting married as soon as you and I can plan the ceremony."

"Damn!"

"What's wrong?"

"It's not fair! I wanted to get married first!"

CHAPTER 33

Tyrants are at all times mad with the lust [for] power.

—William Hazlitt, "Common Places"

Ken returned from Bangkok pleased to have added a fifteenth century snuff bottle and locket of hair to his collection; it was his youngest procurement to date. It was time to call Gale.

The hard-edged woman had changed so much, and the process was just beginning.

When Gale flitted into the office on Tuesday morning, the phone was already barking at her. "Somebody's desperate," she said grabbing for the receiver.

"Hello, Gale Knightly."

"Hi, Gale, it's good to hear your voice."

"Ken, hello, how was your trip to Bangkok?" Gale slowly asked.

"It was exhilarating, as always. I was wondering if you had time for lunch today."

"Listen, I'm a swimming in mud right now. Lunch is impossible."

"Can you give me some time this afternoon? I've got an hour break before I start my rounds at the hospital?"

"Is it something urgent? Julia has a doctor's appointment this afternoon."

"It's the Hanson case. I got some information on Dr. Chibabi that I think you should know about. A nurse came to me in confidence. She's alleging inappropriate behavior on Chibabi's part. I don't want to discuss the details over the phone."

Gale grabbed her calendar. "Can you meet tomorrow at four o'clock?"

"I'm at the hospital tomorrow night, too, but I'll swing by before I go in."

That evening Julia toyed with a rattle in her bumper seat while Gale and Dicey sorted through dinner menus and table centerpiece options. The wedding ceremony and reception were going to take place in a small room at the Knightly's country club, on the weekend following Thanksgiving.

"What is your guest count so far?" asked Dicey.

"If it were up to Dave's dad, we would rent out the entire club, but one hundred is tops. Now, he wants to have another party in Chicago on New Year's Eve. The city is invited. So, put that on your calendar."

Julia was irritable, and Dicey offered to change her into her pajamas. She carried her into the nursery and rested her on the changing table. "You've got your mama's rich head of hair, little girl." Dicey peeled away the dirty diaper, powdered her bottom, and taped together a fresh diaper.

"Let me look at those eyes. I'm not sure whose they are. They look like honey to me." Julia started to whimper, and Dicey picked her up to calm her. "Shh, shh," she cooed into her ear. "Let your mommy have a little break. She's a tired puppy." Dicey walked over to the nursery wall. "Look at your pictures from the ethereal Elle. You'll never know her, Julia, but she was a rare person."

Out of respect for Elle, Gale hung *Philomela* next to the other picture that she had purchased from the girl. Dicey pointed out objects in the painting to the baby. She pointed to the bird and said, "Bird, say bird. . . . Tiger, say tiger." Dicey paused and caught her breath. "Look at that tiny bird and tiger. They both have honey eyes, just like yours." She swallowed hard.

Later that night, Dicey went home and dragged *The Nightmare* from her office closet. It was Elle's last untold story. Dicey shivered as she looked at the painting. It was there, the answer she didn't want to see. Sitting on top of the dead woman was a wild fiend with a rich auburn coat and golden eyes.

"Please, Elle, please be telling me something else." Dicey went to her bookshelf and grabbed Tomoroy's biography on Fuseli, the same book that she had given to Elle as a gift. "Come on Elle, give me divine intervention. "It must be here." Shuffling through the index, she found *The Nightmare* listed and flipped back to its page. Dicey became nauseous as she read Fuseli's own words explaining why he painted the picture. He painted the violent image to purge his jealousy over a woman with whom he was obsessed.

"Last night, I had her . . . in my bed . . . my hot, grasping hands wound around her - Her body and soul melted into mine. . . . Anyone who touches her now commits adultery and incest. She is mine . . . ."

Fuseli purged his jealousy through his imagination. How did Tereus purge his jealousy, through death? He snuffed the essence of existence from Elle. Ken Tereus killed her emotionally and mangled her physically. Dr. Pandion stood by in silent omission. Dicey fought to repress her final question.

The next morning she carried *The Nightmare* into Hank's office. "Now, I want you to look at this. The fiend in this picture has golden eyes. In Gale's picture *Philomela*, the tiger and the tiny bird that's caught in the cat's mouth have golden eyes. Why is that, tell me why do they all have yellow eyes?"

"Because your strange friend, who never seems to die, liked yellow eyes. Dice, are you really back to this again?" Hank said irritably.

"Yes, I am, and I'm going to tell you why. I think this all adds up to the fact that that son-of-a-bitch raped Gale, and she doesn't even know it. I'm sure he drugged her."

"Goddamn it, Dicey! What in the hell are you talking about, now? I'm getting sick and tired of all this shit," Hank blasted.

"Stop screaming at me!" she pleaded. "There's something else here that's even worse than rape, Hank." Trembling, she dropped into a chair and cradled herself. When she finally looked up, agony drenched her eyes. "Don't you understand?" she asked with a softer voice. ". . . I don't think that Julia is Dave's child. She is Ken Tereus' baby."

Hank had never seen Dicey react like this before. Her body shook in an eerie silence. He came around his desk and knelt down beside her. "Honey, I am so sorry, but you're not thinking rationally anymore. None of this makes sense." He took her hands in his and looked deep into her eyes, searching for some reason. "Dice, again, you are accusing a man of rape, a felony. This isn't just any man. You've got to get a hold of yourself," he begged, squeezing her hands as if he was trying to squeeze some sense into her. "Gale is getting married in a couple of weeks— to Dave. Stop with this insanity, please!"

Dicey yanked her hands away and said, "I'm not crazy. Why in the hell is it so strange that an artist would paint a real life tragedy in her pictures? You'd believe photographs but not pictures painted on a canvas. I don't understand you, Hank. I keep trying to tell you that those pictures were Elle's reality. Don't you get that? It was her truth, and her truth scares the hell out of me."

"Dicey, I told you before. The police aren't going to buy your evidence. Didn't you say that this picture," he said glancing at *The Nightmare*, "is a copy of somebody else's work?"

"Why do you have to be so literal? Artists don't live in the literal."

"Dicey, the police live in the literal, for God's sake. Can't you understand that?" asked Hank who was drained of all patience.

"When was the last time you saw Julia?" asked Dicey.

"I don't know. I think a few weeks ago, the night of Tereus' party."

"Well, you know how a baby's eyes change color?"

"Yes, of course."

"Last night when I was with Julia, I realized her eyes were almost amber. Tell me who else in this city has yellow eyes?"

"I don't know. Who pays attention to eye color?"

"When they are yellow, people pay attention, Hank. Ken Tereus has yellow eyes. Genes don't lie! They are just like the fiend's eyes in this picture," she said pointing to *The Nightmare*.

"Dice, you must be mistaken. Gale would have noticed."

"She sees her everyday. Quite easily, she may not have noticed subtle changes. With the wedding and her work, and everything else, I'm not surprised that it hasn't crossed her mind."

"Dice, if it was Ken's baby, then Gale would know it. Women know these kinds of things. If it is true, then it means that she's lying to her family, friends, and Dave, for that matter. Gale would never lie like that."

"Don't you understand, Hank? I'm certain Ken raped her the night of his party, a year ago. She was supposedly too trashed to drive home. I've known Gale for twenty years. I've never seen her trashed. She refused to follow in her father's footsteps. I'm sure that asshole drugged her and then raped her."

"Honey, I love and respect you, but you have to listen to yourself. Ken Tereus isn't some junky hanging out in bars. He is a filthy rich, world-renowned surgeon who could screw almost any woman whom he wanted, including an oil-rich princess. He's not going to use some date-rape scheme to have sex with Gale Knightly. This is all absolutely ridiculous."

Dicey looked Hank straight in the eye and said, "I'm begging you, Hank. I know that you think that I'm off my rocker and that this is bullshit, but please help me. Don't you have a few favors to call in from some detective or somebody?"

"And ask them what?"

"Ask them to do a little digging into his life. Please. Give them the scenario. See if they'll investigate. Please, I've got to do something. I'm afraid."

Hank shook his head in frustration but agreed to call a few people. "Don't hold out any hope. Tereus is a powerful man. He gives substantial donations to both political parties."

"This is about rape, about someone's life. I don't give a shit about politics."

"Give me a few days to make some contacts," Hank said unconvincingly.

CHAPTER 34

Without Contraries is no progression. Attraction
and Repulsion, Reason and Energy, Love and
Hate, are necessary to Human Existence.

–William Blake, "The Marriage of Heaven and Hell"

Gale awoke Thursday morning like any other single mom trying to get to work on time. She flew through a shower, dabbed on makeup, jumped in a suit, then, pulled Julia from her blankets, changed her diaper, dressed and nursed her. It was a morning just like every other morning, except for one thing. In a few weeks, her life would be different. She wouldn't be doing it alone any longer. Dave and she planned to commute for a while, but eventually, she would move to Chicago.

Gale arrived at the office by eight and worked through lunch so she could leave no later than five. She had a wedding dress fitting at six and had wedding calls to make. At four o'clock, the receptionist interrupted her.

"Ms. Knightly,"

"Yes," Gale answered, stuffing a file into her briefcase.

"There is a gentlemen waiting to see you."

"Could you ask him his name?" Gale had forgotten about her appointment with Ken.

"It's Dr. Tereus, Ms. Knightly. I sent him back to see you."

Gale slammed down the phone. "Damn, I forgot. I really don't have time for Dr. Chibabi's antics today, and why does she think it is okay just to send the man back to see me?"

There was a soft knock on the door. Ken Tereus turned the knob and walked in before Gale could reach the door.

"Ken, come on in and have a seat," she said, motioning to a small conference table cramped in the corner of the room.

"How are you, Gale? Ken asked as he took a seat next to her. "You've seemed out of sorts lately."

"Being a single mom will make any woman out of sorts. Now, tell me, what kind of quagmire has Chibabi created for himself?" Gale said, suppressing a yawn.

"I understand that you're engaged to be married."

"How did you find out?"

"News travels fast in this town."

"At least it is good news," added Gale with a wide grin.

"How is your beautiful daughter?"

"Julia's wonderful. Listen, let's talk shop. Neither of us has a lot of time. What are these allegations against Chibabi?"

"So, you plan to marry a man from Chicago?"

"Yes, he's Julia's father. We've dated off and on for almost nine years. I only have fifteen minutes to spare. Let's talk Chibabi."

"Gale, there are no allegations against Chibabi. I just needed to talk to you about something. I couldn't get your time any other way."

"What is it, then?" Gale said slapping closed Chibabi's file.

"You need to know something about Julia?"

"What are you talking about?" she asked, narrowing her eyes.

"I'm surprised that you haven't pieced it together, as smart as you are."

She pushed her chair away from him. "I don't know if that was intended to be a compliment or an insult."

"Neither. I'm just a tad bit surprised about something."

"Surprised at what, Ken? Lay it on the table. What is it?"

"Look into your daughter's eyes tonight. Then, tell me who she is," he said, piercing her eyes with his golden stare.

Gale grabbed the file from the table and clutched it to her chest. "I know my daughter, Ken. Cut the games. What's your point?" she said, glaring back at him.

Ken's eyes cut through her glare. "My point is this. You know only half of her." He paused before continuing but finally said, "She has amber eyes. Think what that means."

Gale's brow knitted together in horrific confusion. She was trying to make sense of what he was saying, but couldn't. Her head was pounding too hard to think clearly. "I don't understand," she whispered.

"I am her other half," Ken said.

Gale shook her head, trying to find clarity. Her head was spinning. She had to stop it. "What in the hell are you talking about 'her other half'? I don't know what you mean," she cried.

"I'm Julia's father," Ken calmly said.

She jumped up from the table, knocking over her chair. "You're fucking crazy! You're not her father. Dave Broadbeck is her father. I've never touched a hair on your bloody body," Gale screamed.

"Quiet down," he demanded. "We don't' want the entire firm storming in here, now do we?" he warned. "You don't remember having sex with me last year at my party, do you?" he asked, not pausing for a response. "You wouldn't because you were too drunk to remember anything. Maybe I took advantage of a bad situation, but you certainly got what you asked for. That's your problem, not mine, but the fact of the matter is simple. Julia's my child, not David Broadbeck's."

"You're a sick man." She grabbed the edge of her desk as her head began to spin faster.

"I'm not a sick man. I'm just telling you the truth. I realized that she was my daughter at the Calloway deposition. When I saw her honey colored eyes, I knew it immediately. I was stunned. Julia's my child. Her eyes will continue to lighten until they glisten like gold." Ken stood up and moved toward Gale.

She backed away from him. "She is not your child. She is Dave's child. I never slept with you."

"Not that you remember."

"That's called rape, and you're a lying piece of shit."

"Gale, Julia is my child. I'm not suggesting that you marry me, but Julia is my daughter. She is my flesh and blood, and I intend to be part of her life. She is a Tereus."

"You're a psychopath. Now, get out of here!" she screamed.

"Lower your voice and calm down. I'm not a psychopath. And I'm not here to destroy your life. We need to map out Julia's future. She is my child. You or anyone else can't deny the fact that she has my eyes."

Gale glared at him. "What do you want, Ken, money?"

"Please, I don't need your money. I'm facing reality. Other than Julia, there is only one other person living in Crystal Springs who has amber eyes. That's me. It won't take long for people to put two and two together. The sooner we acknowledge it, the better off everyone will be. "

"She's not yours," Gale said clinging to her desk for strength.

"Gale, you're smarter than this. Don't fight it. A simple paternity test will verify what I'm telling you is true, but that's unnecessary."

"Then, you raped me. I never want you near her," Gale whispered, almost hyperventilating.

"I didn't rape you. Furthermore, it's not only your choice anymore."

"Are you threatening me?"

"I don't need to threaten you. Fathers have rights, too, and what would you tell people? 'Dr. Tereus got me drunk and raped me.' Who would buy that story? You're an intelligent woman, not some silly fifteen year old virgin. I've never needed to rape someone to get laid."

All the blood had drained from Gale's face minutes before. She stood motionless in the room, staring at his lurid yellow eyes.

"You can make this easy on yourself or hard on yourself. It's your choice. Why don't we meet tomorrow to map out some details for our future? This office isn't the place. We'll meet at your house, around noon?"

She couldn't think. His lips were moving, but she had no idea what Ken was saying. He reached out to touch her cheek, but she flinched with repulsion.

"I'll be at your house at noon," he said and turned and walked out of the office. She slid to the floor as her world crashed around her. She sat on the ground for several minutes, until the phone jolted her back into reality. She pulled herself from floor and slumped in her chair, still ignoring the phone.

"My baby," she whispered. "Dave is her father. I know it. I know it." But Julia's caramel eyes flashed through her mind.

Gale rested her head against the desk. Reality burned through her brain. The horror grew in its immensity as the minutes slipped by, and her lovely life vanished. Who in the hell would believe that a thirty year old woman was raped and didn't know it? After everything that she had put Dave through, how could he ever believe her? Most importantly, how was she going to protect Julia?

She gathered herself, grabbed her car keys and purse and ran out of the office. Stepping off the elevator and into the parking garage, Gale spotted Ken leaning against her car. She walked directly toward him.

"Get the hell off my car," she said.

Ken ignored her command. "I thought you might be upset, Gale. Are you okay to drive?"

"I said get the hell out of my way!"

"Don't make this difficult."

"Fuck you," she said.

She walked past him and unlocked the car door. She climbed in and pulled out of the parking spot and drove straight to Julia's daycare.

When she walked into the Little Red Schoolhouse, Gale looked pasty and damp. Brenda, the facility director, asked if everything was all right.

"I'm not feeling well. I thought Julia and I could spend a little extra time together."

The woman went to wake Julia from her afternoon nap and returned with the baby and a stuffed panda bear. Gale asked where the toy came from. Brenda explained that she had met Julia's father earlier that morning, when he delivered the bear. Brenda handed over Julia and the panda.

"You let someone into this facility to see Julia without my permission?" Gale growled

"No, Miss Knightly!" Brenda assured her. "He just came to the front desk to drop off the gift. Nothing more, I promise you. That would be against our safety policies."

Gale leaned close to the woman. "Never, and I mean never let anyone get near her who has not been authorized by me. Do you understand?" Gale demanded.

"Of course, I understand," Brenda said indignantly. She watched as Gale walked toward the door and dumped the stuffed animal into the trash can that was standing near the entrance.

Gale secured Julia's car seat into its frame and then climbed into the car. She hesitated and considered driving directly to the police station. What would she tell the police? Ken Tereus wanted to give his child his name? That he wanted his full paternal rights? That he was rich and successful as hell and just wanted to have a relationship with his daughter? That she was a smart, accomplished lawyer who didn't know that she had been raped a year ago? Who in hell was going to believe whom?

Gale pulled into the driveway. She climbed out of the car, unbuckled the car seat and carried Julia to the front door. She held the baby carrier in the crook of her arm while unlocking the door with her free hand. The contents in her stomach began rising up through her esophagus. She unbolted the door, dropped Julia at the entrance and ran to the kitchen sink. Gale vomited into the drain until specks of blood spattered the white porcelain.

She wiped the vomit from her mouth and drank a glass of cold water. Julia started to whimper. She released the baby carrier straps, pulled the little girl up, and stared into her eyes. Deep amber glistened back. Gale sat down on the couch and flicked on the reading light. She drew Julia close to her face. Specks of gold were forming in the amber irises. The color was undeniable. The color change had never once crossed her mind.

Resting her head on the cushion, Gale tried to think back to Ken's party, the year before. She remembered Ken snapping at Dicey for playing with his stupid-ass mini bottles. She remembered him dragging Elle around the house to show off his epicene antiques. The last thing that she remembered about the night was Dicey and Elle leaving to go home. Everything else was a blur. She didn't remember a thing until the next day when she woke in Ken's guestroom, still dressed in her crumpled cocktail dress. He told her some idiotic story about drinking one-too-many martinis. What? Was there a lampshade involved, too? The whole story was a crock of shit. Gale never touched a martini in her entire life.

The next day he had pushed a bowl of nasty oatmeal on her and then drove her home in silence. He pulled up to the curb of her house, pecked her on the cheek, and said that he was off to Asia for a month. That was the last time she saw Julia's father, until Elle's funeral.

What in God's name was she going to do? Go to the police? It would be her word against his. How could she possibly prove that he raped her after the passage of one year? Smart, savvy Gale Knightly was raped and didn't even know it. Yeah, right! He's the multimillionaire legend, so why would he lie?

The life she knew just one hour ago, a life filled with wedding dress fittings, menu selections, and a perfect husband had been annihilated. Her world was blown apart, and she had no choice but to tell Dave and deal with the fallout. No matter what, though, Tereus would never be a part of Julia's life. Rape never yielded paternal rights. Whether anyone would believe her or not, she would battle every last deviant bone in his body.

She closed her eyes and thought about the next day. A deposition was scheduled for nine. Maybe she could teleconference it from home. At noon, she would listen to what Tereus had to say and then drive to Chicago. She had to tell Dave as soon as possible, and it had to be in person.

Gale dug her cell phone from her pocket. She paused and stared at the numbers. "Just do it," she willed herself. She punched in the numbers, and Dave answered on the first ring.

"It's me, honey," her voice quivered. "Can Julia and I drive up to see you tomorrow?"

"What's wrong? You sound terrible," said Dave.

"I am just stressed. I need to see you . . . for support."

"Honey, I'd drive down tonight to see you two, but I've got a few meetings tomorrow that I can't miss."

"That's okay. The drive will help clear my mind."

"Are you sure you're okay?"

"No, but we'll talk." Her voice was weak and wispy.

"Is everything okay between you and me?"

"Dave, I've never loved you more in my life. It is work and everything else. I just need to see you."

"Sure, Babe, Dad can finally meet Julia. He'll be elated."

☙☙ ☙☙ ☙☙

"Dice, I wanted to catch you before you went into class," said Hank, calling from his car.

"What is it? I was just leaving for class," asked Dicey dropping her briefcase.

"I talked to Roger Becker, a detective from District One. The guy can't investigate a crime without a victim, and Gale isn't claiming any of this."

"Hank, that's because she was drugged. How could she know?"

"Listen to me. This is a convoluted theory based on a few pictures. The police aren't going to do anything with it, unless Gale steps up. And to be honest, once I started telling Roger the story, I was embarrassed by suggesting the whole matter."

"Fine, Hank," Dicey snapped. "I've got to run. I'll call you later."

"Listen, Dice, even if Julia is Tereus's kid, he can claim that it was consensual sex. Then, what's Dave going to say? The whole thing will blow up in Gale's face. For her sake, just leave it alone! I'm begging you," pleaded Hank.

"I said fine. I'm late. I call you." Dicey grabbed her briefcase and headed to class. The day was cold with a sharp wind that whipped between the buildings. Dicey waved to a few students who braved the weather for a quick drag on their cigarettes. We're all going to die one way or another, she thought. She passed the smokers and headed into the lecture hall.

Her class was a disaster. Dicey spent thirty-five minutes lecturing on the African-American experience explored in twentieth century literature. She explained that the *Invisible Man* written by H.G. Wells best demonstrated man's struggle for personal identity in a world tainted by racism and repression. Not until she noted that Wells had won the National Book Award for his masterpiece did one of her students interrupt.

"Professor Carmichael, are you sure that you're not talking about Ralph Ellison?" The only response that Dicey could summon was, "It must be early Alzheimer's," but no one chuckled to make her feel better about the error. She closed her lecture notes and walked out of the hall. A cold rain drizzled on her head. She turned her face toward the sky and whispered, "I'm not demented. I know I'm right on this."

Sitting at her small kitchen table, Dicey dipped her spoon into a cup of yogurt, nibbled on a few slices of apple, and stared at the *Nightmare*. No one believed her theory about Elle's *Monstrous Heresy*. Now, everyone was ignoring her about *The Nightmare* and *Philomela*. Admittedly, Elle's perception of reality was skewed, but there was truth, even in her distorted mind. As she ate her dinner, the golden-eyed fiend glared at her from the frame, taunting her with his secret.

"I'll force you to talk— just like I forced Dr. Pandion. I'll find the truth you bastard!" she yelled at the animal.

The clock on her mantle read four fifty-five. Dicey picked-up her phone and dialed information. The operator connected her directly to Dr. Tereus's office. The receptionist explained that Dr. Tereus was unavailable and would be on-call at the hospital the entire evening. If the situation was emergent, she would be willing to page Dr. Tereus. Dicey said that that wouldn't be necessary and hung up the phone.

She waited an hour and arrived on the surgical floor of the hospital at six thirty-five. Dicey walked up and down the u-shaped hallway, carrying a vase of flowers. After forty-five minutes of avoiding the nurses' stares and ducking out of their view, Dicey spotted Ken Tereus standing at the physicians' desk. He was dictating notes into the hospital's online dictation service. Dicey slowly walked toward him, waiting for him to complete his dictation.

"Ken, how are you?"

He looked up with confusion.

"Dicey Carmichael, I'm Hank Daimon's fiancé."

"Oh, Dicey, of course, what are you doing at the hospital?"

"I came to visit a friend who had breast implants today. I didn't realize that the surgery was same-day surgery."

"Yeah, from an A to D in just one hour," Ken said and smiled.

"Have you seen Gale lately?" Dicey asked studying his face.

"No, I've been out of the country."

"Now, I remember. You like exotic destinations."

"I like to get lost in the anonymity of the East."

"I see. Do you have time for a cup of coffee? I'd like to hear about your trip. I'm trying to plan a honeymoon. Anyway, you look like you could use the break."

"Give me five minutes. I was just heading to the cafeteria for some dinner."

Dicey ordered a bowl of tomato soup and cup of green tea. Ken had a turkey sandwich and a black coffee. The hospital cafeteria was populated with only three other people. They were all dressed in scrubs and were scattered about the dimly lit room. Dicey set her tray down at an isolated table. Ken sat across from her.

"It's going to be a cold night. South Asia sounds great right now," Dicey said with a shiver.

"I was in Thailand to be exact. Exoticism is always in the air there. The wind doesn't blow through the trees in Bangkok; it undulates. Some nights it comes quietly and rubs you all over, massaging the full length of your body. Other nights the wind comes on with hard thrusts."

Dicey gripped her hands together in her lap to stop from reaching out and slapping Ken's face with his own obnoxious sexual innuendoes. She had never been impressed with his shellac and never would be. Gathering together her anger, she asked, "Have you ever taken a woman to Thailand?"

"I told you– I go there for anonymity, not love-making."

"Interesting," said Dicey. "Ken, when was the last time you saw Julia, Gale's daughter?"

"That's an odd question. I've met her just once. It was at a deposition. She was sick or something." He stuffed the first bite of turkey into his mouth.

"I was with her last night. She's beautiful."

"Yeah," he said and glanced down at his plate.

"Ken, look up." He paused but then slowly tilted his head toward her. Dicey continued, "You know that her eyes are honey, almost as light as yours. Strange, don't you think?"

"Why?" Ken asked calmly.

"I would imagine that honey colored eyes are a rarity."

"I imagine so," he said scrutinizing her. "There was no friend with a breast augmentation, was there?"

"No, Ken, there wasn't. I came here to talk to you. I want to know how Julia got your eye color."

"How do you think, Dicey?"

"Gale told me that she never slept with you."

"She's lying, and she's lying about the identity of Julia's father."

"I've known Gale for twenty years. She has never lied to me."

"I know nothing about what she has done for the past twenty years, but I do know that she is lying and that Julia is my child. Our eyes and DNA can easily substantiate that fact."

"Maybe Gale has a reason to lie."

"I'm not going to run around your pithy circular arguments, Dicey. What's your point?" he asked.

"Maybe she's scared of you, or maybe she really doesn't know that she had sex with you."

"Stop screwing with me. Why would she be scared of me?" Ken asked as he moved his head closer to hers.

"Maybe because you got her drunk or you drugged her to the point that she lost consciousness, and then you raped her."

"This isn't one of your silly little stories that you teach to your brain-dead students. This is reality, grownup talk. It's not a fucking fairytale. You believe what your little friend wants you to believe, but it's a lie. Gale wanted me that night, and she got me. Julia is my child, and I am and will always be her father, with or without Gale's acknowledgment."

Dicey leaned in closer to Ken's head and narrowed her stare. "I'm on to your game, buddy, just like I was on to Dr. Pandion's game. Look what happened to him. I know all about the jealous love triangle between you and Elle and her father." Though she was only testing the waters, Dicey had no idea that she was dangerously close to the actual truth and continued, "I know about your games with Elle, and she didn't overdose, did she?" Dicey ventured.

"Shut up, you little cunt."

"I won't shut up until you leave Gale and Julia alone. Stop your egocentric head trip about being Julia's father, and I will leave you alone. You don't love Julia. What do you want with her?"

"You surprise me, Dicey. I thought that you were much smarter than a mentality defined by love. This isn't about love. I don't love anyone or anything. I master people, and I master things. Julia is mine to master, to mold, to shape into what I want her to be. Her body and mind will become perfection for eternity under my mastery. She is my child, and I have the right to do as I please."

"You're a sick son-of-a-bitch, and I *will* stop you."

"Oh, please, don't threaten me. You are a nothing in my world of operation, a nothing."

"Don't be so certain," Gale whispered from deep within her gut. "I have evidence. The same evidence that I used to expose Elle's father will cut your life line, as well," she warned.

"You are a very clever little fiction reader, aren't you? Gather up your pencils and papers and literary research and convict me," Ken chuckled. "If I need anyone to read a bedtime story to my daughter, I know whom to call." Ken laughed and stood up to go.

"If you don't stop, I won't stop until every deviant piece of your fucking ass is exposed," Gale hissed.

"Nice language from an English professor. Have a delightful evening," Ken said with a grin and walked away.

Dicey's scalp burned, and she needed air. She took two wrong turns driving home and ended up in sketchy neighborhood. She pulled into a convenient store to fill up her tank. Glancing up, she saw herself on the security camera. "Man, Elle, why didn't you leave me a goddamn video."

The Nightmare was there waiting for her when she got home. Dicey changed into her pajamas and made a pot of tea. She sat down on the couch and glared at the little monster.

"If that asshole is not going to tell me the truth, I'm going to get it from you," Dicey told the fiend. "Ken Tereus is a lying piece of shit. Either Gale's too scared to tell me the truth or he really did rape her. One way or the other, he wants to destroy her life, just like he destroyed Elle's."

Dicey stood up from the couch and sat down cross legged in front of the picture. She studied the image of Elle who was tossed across the bed. The monster was sitting back on his hind legs, perched on her belly. His hairy paws were balled into fists, pressed against her chest. He was holding a narrow silver object that had a needle point edge.

"Why haven't I ever noticed that before?" she asked the monster. He just grinned back in her face.

"What are you holding, you little fucker?" she pleaded. Was it a fountain pen? Was Elle trying to write a letter, and Ken destroyed it. Dicey closed her eyes and murmured, "A needle point edge, a needle, a needle . . . a hypodermic needle."

Elle's arm was hanging from the bed in the picture. Dicey leaned closer to the picture and spotted tiny flecks of blood on her arm.

"He drugged her, just like he drugged Gale. It's there. I don't need a goddamn video. You horrible fiend, I'm dragging you to Gale's office tomorrow. We're all going to finally face the truth," Dicey told the monster. The shrill cry of the phone interrupted her confrontation with the demon.

"Where have you been? I've been calling your cell phone all night!" Gale demanded frantically.

"I'm so sorry," Dicey said breathlessly. "I've been out of sorts all day. I left my damn cell phone in my office. Is everything okay? What a stupid question. Nothing is okay." Dicey ran her fingers through her hair, yanking on a few strands.

"I've got the most horrible news." Gale began to cry.

"You don't need to say it, honey. I already know," Dicey said pulling her legs close to her chest.

"No, you don't know, Dice," Gale sobbed.

"Yes, I do. Gale, I know about everything."

"No, you don't," she screamed. "Dave isn't Julia's father!"

"I know. I know about Tereus," Dicey tried to stay calm. "I figured it out from Elle's pictures and . . . Julia's eyes."

Gale cried harder. Dicey could hear Julia wailing in the background.

"Gale, calm down. You're making Julia upset."

"He raped me," she screamed. "He raped me!"

"I know he did, honey," Dicey said softly. "Calm down. I know he did."

"Do, do you believe me?" she begged. "I knew nothing about it!"

"Of course, I believe you." Tears began to stream from Dicey's eyes, as well.

"How is Dave ever going to believe me? How will anyone believe me? Look what I've done to Julia's life. I've destroyed it with that monster," Gale yelled.

"Get a hold of yourself!" Dicey demanded. "You've got to for Julia. The man drugged you. It's in *The Nightmare*. Elle knew it and painted it in her picture. I believe you. Everyone will believe you," Dicey said, though a shiver of doubt ran up her spine.

"He's coming here tomorrow to talk about his rights. What do I say? I don't know what in the hell to do, Dicey."

"Listen to me, Gale. The guy is evil. Elle was trying to tell you that in *Philomela*. The tiger and the little bird both have yellow eyes. She was warning you."

"Dicey, I know that Elle was your friend, but why didn't the goddamn freak just tell me all of this? Why did she have to paint it in some goddamn animal picture?"

"Gale, her reality was something that neither of us could ever comprehend. Some women will do anything just to feel loved. But that's not the issue right now. Ken Tereus is. I have to tell you something important."

"What?" she demanded.

"I went to the hospital tonight and confronted him. As you can guess, his position is that you're lying, but he knows that I'm onto his game. Gale, I have to tell you something else, as well. I'm certain that he had a hand in Elle's death. She must have had some premonition about him or he directly threatened her. Why else would she have pushed so hard to write a will and then bequeath these pictures to us?"

"Oh my God, Dicey, now, what do I do?"

"Everything's under control," Dicey lied, but went on. "Hank is giving lecture tonight that ends in an hour. We will map out a strategy and be at your house tomorrow before Tereus arrives. We'll work through this, Gale, I promise," Dicey said with little confidence in herself or what she was saying.

"Lord, what is Dave going to say?" Gale cried. Her chest heaved with sobs.

"Do you want me to come over and stay with you through the night?"

"No," Gale breathed. "I'll calm down."

"Call me at any hour if you want me to come over. I'll be there in a heartbeat."

☙☙ ☙☙ ☙☙

Gale survived the night by watching the liquid-red numbers on her digital clock shift, minute by minute. She stayed in bed until six-thirty, Julia's normal wake-up time. Maintain normalcy, just act normal, she told herself.

She showered then woke and fed Julia. At eight o'clock, she phoned Earl Burnett. He was scheduled to depose one of her clients in an hour.

"Earl, Gale Knightly. I've got a sick infant. We can reschedule the deposition, or I can teleconference it from home. What works for you?" she asked.

Unless she was willing to pay the stenographer's cancellation fee, he wanted to go ahead and teleconference the deposition. Gale was patched into the deposition at nine. For an hour, she carried Julia around the living room while she listened to Earl drill Dr. Santos about proper protocols for early detection of melanoma.

Earl's client had a mole on his lower back that had changed in size, color and shape in the past several months. The man waited ten months before he ever made an appointment with Dr. Santos, his dermatologist. Gale wanted to strangle Burnett. She wasted an hour listening to frivolous allegations, when she could have been protecting her daughter and reorganizing her life.

After hanging up the phone, Gale flew from drawer to drawer, stuffing clothes in her luggage. She dragged the suitcases to the front door and headed back to the nursery to gather Julia's diaper bag and a few chewy toys for the ride. When she returned to the living room, Gale spied Ken's black Mercedes sitting in the driveway.

"Damn! You're way too early," she cried. The door bell rang, and she saw Ken's yellow eyes peering at her through the front door's sidelight. She dropped the bag, gritted her teeth, and glared back at him.

"You bastard!" she mumbled.

Ken rang the doorbell a second time. He tapped on the glass and mouthed, "Open up."

She walked toward him, unlocked the deadbolt and cracked the door.

"May I come in?" Ken asked through the crack in the door.

"No, you're early. I've got some business to tie up. Come back in an hour."

He glanced down at the luggage that was resting against the door. "I have to be in surgery in an hour. Let's talk now."

"No. I've got to take care of a client. See you in an hour or some other time," Gale said and started to push the door closed.

Before she could snap the deadbolt in place, Ken slammed against the door, throwing Gale onto her heels. She stumbled backward and fell into the entry table. Gale and an oriental vase went crashing to the tile floor.

Julia's screams from the nursery galvanized her mother. Gale tried to scramble to her knees, but he grabbed her one hundred and ten pound ball of rage and threw her onto her stomach. He stepped on her back, grinding his shoe into her spine. He pulled a syringe and vial from his pocket. As Gale squirmed in the broken glass, Ken tried to punch the needle through the rubber seal of the bottle.

"Hold still and shut the fuck up!" he demanded.

"Fuck you!" Gale shouted. "If I go down, you're going down, too. You'll never get her!"

Ken plunged the needle into the rubber and sucked out the deadly cocktail. He crouched down with his right heel still pressed firmly into her back. Gale thrashed under his weight, but Ken took hold of her backside and jabbed the needle into her flesh. With one last thrust, Gale pitched against his force. The needle snapped from the plastic syringe tube.

"You bitch!" he shouted, raising the tube to his eyes. Only a quarter of the fluid remained. He paused but smiled. "You'll die. . . It might be a slower death, but you'll die," Ken said as Gale's thrashing subsided.

Julia's cries brought him back to his task. He found her in the nursery squealing like a pig ripe for slaughter. He picked her up and grabbed a duffle bag that was sitting on the changing table. He returned to the living room and spotted the diaper bag that Gale had dropped at the front door. He set Julia on the carpet and rifled through the bags. She had done a nice job packing. Ken unzipped an insulated bag and found small plastic baggies of frozen breast milk buried in ice. He jumped up and ran to the freezer. He grabbed a few more bags and stuffed them into the cooler. Ken then carried Julia and the bags to his car. He set Julia on the floor of the front passenger seat and threw everything else into the back. He glanced down at his watch. It was only ten-fifteen, plenty of time.

☙ ☙ ☙

Ken pulled into the dilapidated strip mall and saw a few battered cars parked near the Payday Quick Cash. The remaining cars were crowded in front of Mama's Pancake House. He drove around to the back of the mall and parked behind a rusty dumpster. He jumped out of the car and popped open the trunk. He yanked out an overstuffed paper bag and tossed it toward the mouth of the garbage bin. A few tendrils of hair fluttered to the ground as the bag flew through the air.

He grabbed Julia's bags from the backseat and combined all of her belongings into the duffle back. He pulled a backpack from the trunk and tossed the empty bags into the dumpster. He lifted Julia from the floor. She was asleep. Her breathing was a little shallow. He felt her pulse. It was steady and strong. He unzipped the duffle bag and rested her on top of the clothes and diapers.

Ken's feet crunched under broken glass as he hurried around the side of the building. He spotted the cab waiting in front of the pancake house.

When he approached the car, he knocked on the cabby's window. "Hey, sorry I kept ya' waitin. I was takin' a leak out back. Mama's plumbing sucks." Ken opened the back door and gently pushed the duffle bag across the seat. He shoved his backpack onto the floor and climbed in.

"I'm headed to the airport. About how much is that fare?"

"Thirty-five dollar, for you," the deep-skinned driver said and pulled away from Mama's.

Ken watched as the man looked at him from the rearview mirror. He pulled on his sunglasses that were hanging from a rubber neck cord and tugged down the bill of his baseball cap.

"So, how about dose Bengal tigers, you know? Can't vin a fuut-ball' game, can da?" the driver asked.

"I'm a Cleveland Brown's fan. The Cincinnati Bengals suck."

"I vatch soccer, myself, you know. Dose people in L.A., Da crazy. Da pay Daveed Beckham all dat money, you know. For vat? For heem to retire. Dat's all, you know."

"I guess they got the money in L.A. It's not like Ohio."

"No. Ohio sucks," confirmed the cabby.

When they pulled up to Delta's departure terminal, Ken tipped the cabby enough to make the guy happy but not enough to stand out. Ken went straight to the bathroom. He picked the last stall and dropped his backpack in front of the door. He squeezed into the toilet with the duffle bag and rested it on the ground. He urinated first and then unzipped the duffle bag. Julia was sleeping soundly.

From the thermal bag that was stuffed inside the duffle bag, Ken pulled out several bags of frozen breast milk and stuffed them into the pockets of his khaki hiking pants. He then lifted Julia from the bag and tucked her over his shoulder. Once he got out of the stall, he rested her on top of the bag while he washed his hands and threw on the backpack.

A middle-aged man who was urinating at the urinal asked, "How do women pee with three kids?"

"They remember strollers," Ken said and walked out of the door.

As he walked toward the security gate, Ken scanned the crowd. He spotted several females that appeared to be traveling alone, but they were either dressed in suits and carrying laptop bags or they were too old.

Then he spotted her. She was about ten people ahead of him, riding down the escalator. She had curly, brown hair tied back with a bandana. She was wearing cargo pants and a North Face fleece jacket. Her only bag was a small backpack, flung over her shoulder.

Ken stepped off the escalator and hurried to catch up with her before she entered the security queue. He slipped in right behind her as she approached the cordoned area. When the line slowed to a standstill, Ken bumped into her with his duffle bag. She turned around and smiled.

"Pardon me," he said. "I've got my hands full. First time dad, first time traveling." Ken glanced down at Julia who was still soundly asleep on his shoulder.

"It looks like she's cooperating, so far. Pray that she sleeps on the plane, too, for your sake."

"And everybody else's. I thought about waking her up, but she looks pretty cozy."

"What's her name?" the woman asked, peering down at Julia.

Ken pulled the blanket from her face. "This is Francesca Genevieve Brueggemann."

"That's a lovely name."

"It was her mother's name," he said with the words drifting off like dust.

"What do you mean was?" she asked quietly.

"She was killed in a car accident the week after Francie was born."

"God, I'm so sorry."

"It's been tough. Francesca went through in vitro fertilization to have her. Then boom, she dies. It's amazing how a split second can change your life forever. I'm Jake, by the way."

"Mary Beth. Mary Beth Conlan. It's nice to meet you."

"Could I ask a favor of you, Mary Beth?" Ken said, looking over her head at the bank of metal detectors.

"Sure."

"Could you help me with Francie as we go through the security check point? I don't think that I can hold her and manage everything else."

Mary Beth smiled. "Do you want me to take a bag or something?"

"No. Could you just hold Francie, while I go through?"

"I'd love to hold Francie."

As they approached the checkpoint, Ken handed Julia to Mary Beth and bent down to untie his hiking boots.

He looked up and smiled. "Flip-flops would have been more practical. Don't you think?"

"Depends on where you're headed."

"Texas. Francie's grandparents live there," Ken said as he stood up with his boots in hand. "They're going to watch her for a couple of weeks while I get my life back in order."

"Thank heaven for grandparents," Mary Beth said with a tight hold on his eyes. Finally, she asked, "Does Francie have your eyes or her mother's?"

"Mine. Her eyes are as green as the Emerald City."

"If her eyes are as green as yours, she'll be a knock-out in twenty years."

"She's already a beauty," Ken grinned. "If she'd wake up, you could see for yourself. Do you want me to wrestle her awake so you can take a peek at her eyes?" Ken dared to ask.

"No, you know the old saying, 'Never wake a sleeping baby.'"

"You're right. Well, it looks like it's my turn to be nuked by security."

Ken threw his boots and duffle bag into a plastic bin and pushed it onto the revolving table followed by his backpack. He padded through the metal detector without a problem, but once he was on the other side, the security guard asked him to step aside. A woman was digging through his duffle bag. She pulled out a pair of manicuring scissors and a baggy of milk that he had missed.

"Sir, what is this? You can't bring liquids like this onto the plane," the guard said.

"It's my wife's breast milk," Ken softly said, nodding his head toward Mary Beth who was carrying Julia through the metal detector. "It's liquid gold to her."

"It could also be a liquid bomb," the lady said and dumped the baggy into the garbage. "And scissors on a plane?"

"Sorry. My wife packed. She doesn't travel much. Is there anything else in there that's a problem?" Ken asked patiently.

"That'll be it. Have a good flight."

Ken grabbed his bags and boots and headed over to a chair. Mary Beth joined him with Julia nestled in her arms.

"Jake, I've got to catch my flight, but it's sure been a pleasure."

"Thanks for the help."

"Listen. If you're interested in a cup of coffee, give me a call sometime," she said, handing him her card. "I'm a sculptor. Unless I'm traveling, I'm rarely out of my studio."

"When will you be back in town?"

"Ten days," she said and handed Julia over. "Call me. I'd like to see Francie when she's awake."

"I'll call." Ken watched as the sculptor rushed into the crowd.

On his way to the departure gate, Ken bought two large cups of ice. He dumped them into the thermal bag and headed to the restroom. Again, he selected the most isolated stall. He pulled the baggies of milk from his pockets and stuffed them back into the cooler. He then drew a small vial from his windbreaker and sprinkled a droplet on his finger. He slid his finger into Julia's mouth and rubbed the liquid Valium on her tongue. Then, he returned her to the pile of clothes and zipped up the duffle bag.

Standing before the sink, Ken smiled at his reflection in the mirror. Even bald, women found him electrifying. Life was so easy.

Dicey's class ended at ten-twenty. She had plenty of time to get to Gale's house before Ken arrived. Dicey called Gale's cell phone to let her know that she was on the way, but no one answered. Gale's land line was also mute. Dicey tried to breathe slowly to control the panic that was rising in her throat. She dialed Hank's number, and he answered.

"Hank, Gale's not answering either of her phones. Something's wrong," she breathed.

"Maybe she's changing Julia or maybe she's in the bathroom or something. How many times did you call?"

"Many, trust me!"

"I'm just pulling out of the garage. I'll be there as soon as possible."

A few minutes later, Dicey was racing down Gale's street. She spotted her Volvo in the driveway and whispered a sigh of relief. "My God, why didn't you answer your fucking phone?" She pulled into the driveway, ran to the front door and pounded the knocker.

"Gale, open the door. It's Dicey," she yelled. Peering through the sidelight and into the foyer, she spotted the overturned table and Gale, who was motionless on the floor.

"My God!" she screamed. Dicey pushed over the heavy flower planter that stood next to the door, grabbed the clay drain plate and shattered the glass. She stuck her arm through the opening, but then realized the door knob was on the opposite side of the sidelight. She then dragged the planter in front of the bay window, climbed on top of the dead geraniums and shattered the window with the drain plate. Dicey lifted herself through the broken glass and ran to Gale's body. She bent down and listened to her chest. There was a faint heartbeat. She ran to the kitchen and dialed 911.

"She's unconscious, she's dying. Hurry, please!" Dicey begged.

The 911 dispatcher tried to calm her down with questions. The woman promised assistance within four to five minutes. "My god, my god, what have I done," Dicey cried. She ran to Julia's room who was nowhere to be found. Dicey ran back to the kitchen and called Hank on his cell phone. He picked-up on the first ring. "She's dying, Hank, and Julia's gone. He took her. He took her, Hank!"

"Did you call the police, Dicey?"

"Yes!" she screamed into the receiver.

"I'm on my way."

Hank arrived at Gale's house while the paramedics were trying to resuscitate her. Roger Becker arrived and issued an Amber Alert to the public for Julia Knightly along with a picture of Ken Tereus.

❧❧ ❧❧ ❧❧

Ken was sitting in the Dallas-Fort Worth airport watching *CNN* and feeding a bottle to Julia, when he saw his face appear on the television screen. An Amber Alert had been issued for infant Julia Knightly who was thought to have been taken by the famed plastic surgeon, Ken Tereus. Both child and father could be identified by their distinctive yellow eyes.

Scanning the departure terminal, Ken spotted a Hispanic woman with two small raven-haired girls. He gathered up Julia and his luggage and moved across the room to seat himself next to the woman. Ken smiled at the weary-eyed mother and continued to feed Julia. The little girls sat cross-legged on the floor, dressing and undressing their Barbie dolls. Ken studied the older one who looked to be about seven years old. She was very ugly. Her nose was flat against her face, and her narrow jaw line formed a pointed V at her chin.

Ken glanced down at Julia while she lapped down the milk. She would be the perfect female. Over the next five or six years, he would mold and manipulate her personality to his liking. By ten or twelve, a faultless intellect would be formed. Then, he would perfect her blossoming body, correcting any of her mother's blemishes that may have been inherited. His progeny, his peerless specimen, would be eternally indebted to him.

The Delta agent's voice booming over the load speaker interrupted Ken's reverie. His row had been called to board the plane, but he waited until the Hispanic family was ready to board. With Julia swaddled in a blanket, he shuffled behind the two girls as they bounced their way down the aisle of the plane.

The small family was seated in the row directly behind Ken. In his row, there was a businessman seated next to the window who was clamoring away at his laptop. The man paused at the keyboard only when he was forced to tell the rambunctious kids to stop kicking the back of his seat.

Ken was relieved that the flight to El Paso was less than an hour. Within two hours, if his plan continued without a glitch, Julia and he would be in Juarez, Mexico, the City of Death where admission was free but leaving was lethal.

He rested his head against the seat and smiled. Americans, especially young women, traveling to Mexico were warned about Ciudad Juarez. Over a ten year period, more than four hundred young girls had been brutally raped and murdered, and that many more had been reported missing by their families. Victims' bodies were found days and months later in deserted areas or vacant lots or abandoned buildings. Their beaten remains typically showed signs of sexual violence, torture and mutilation.

When tension boiled over, Juarez served as an easy alternative to Asia. Ken could slip into lethal anonymity in Juarez and return to the operating table in Crystal Springs, all within seventy-two, short hours. He had made this journey several times in the past. Once he completed the pernicious trip in just fifty hours. Thanks to Dicey Carmichael, he would be spending a lot more time in Juarez and Asia.

As the plane touched down in El Paso, Ken glanced at his watch. Julia and he would be walking across the Santa Fe Bridge to Ciudad Juarez in just forty-five minutes, three o'clock Mountain Standard Time. His planning was impeccable. The American children living in Juarez, who attended school in El Paso, would be walking back across the bridge to their homes. His groin started to pulsate with a rush of blood. He enjoyed following the Catholic girls dressed in their plaid uniform skirts.

Ken walked off the plane and headed straight to the men's room. From the duffle bag, he pulled out a baby carrier that Gale had packed for Julia. It was a body sling that rested against the stomach. Ken snapped it across his chest and tucked Julia inside. He pulled out the vial of Valium, laced her lips with the tranquil-izer, and then pulled on a baggy windbreaker that hid the sling.

Thirty-five minutes later, the cabby dropped him off at the Santa Fe Bridge. It was a balmy day in El Paso, sunny and sixty degrees. He looked across the river at Juarez. The stony mountain-side that sat behind the city held a painted message for the people of El Paso. Ken whispered the bold white words shining from the mountain, "'CD Juarez, La Biblia es la verdad. Leela,' *Ciudad Juarez, the Bible is the truth. Read it.*"

The same mountains that embraced the City of Feminicide held many of his own secrets.

Ken fell in line behind a group of school girls as he crossed the bridge. When he entered into Ciudad Juarez, he passed the pink monument dedicated to the women murdered in the city. A steel, pink partition held a wooden cross that was surrounded by hundreds of spikes, representing the girls murdered in the city. Ken grinned as he glanced at the structure.

He handed his passport to the border patrol office at the security checkpoint. The man looked at Ken's picture and then at Ken.

"No hair, Miguel Lopez?"

"No. Lice. I shaved it," Ken said quickly. He felt Julia begin to squirm in the sling, and he patted his stomach. The border patrol officer's eyes followed Ken's movements.

"Too much tequila last night. The worm bit me!"

"Si, si," the officer nodded. "Do you have anything to declare?"

"No, sir, I don't."

"How long do you intend to stay?"

"Three days at the Meson de Maruca." Ken rubbed the sling as if it was his belly.

The officer stamped the passport, waved Ken forward and greeted the next person in line.

Perfect planning. Admission is always free in Juarez.

The Meson de Maruca was a tiny hotel that was located within a ten minute cab drive from the Santa Fe Bridge. He had faded behind the hotel's nondescript walls on many occasions. No one ever bothered him there, but most people of Juarez were careful to never ask questions of anyone.

CHAPTER 35

Mutual Forgiveness of each Vice
Such are the Gates of Paradise
Against the Accusers of chief desire
Who walked among the Stones of Fire . . .

—William Blake,
"For the Sexes:
THE GATES of PARADISE"

The ICU nurse permitted Dicey into the unit for just a few minutes. She squeezed back tears before approaching the bed. Gale was lifeless and pale on the steel bed. She was covered with a single white sheet. This irritated Dicey.

"Nurse," she said turning to the woman who escorted her into the room, "Gale is always cold. Could you please bring a blanket for her? This sheet isn't enough."

When the woman walked away for a blanket, Dicey brushed the hair away from Gale's eyes. She whispered in her ear, "We'll find her, honey. I promise. Everything's going to be okay." A minute later she was ushered back to the private waiting room where Hank was talking with the police. Hank stood up from his seat and hugged her.

"Is there any word?"

Hank shook his head no.

❦ ❦ ❦

Hank and Dicey had called Dave's office on the way to the hospital, but he was not in. Hank asked for Tom Broadbeck, Dave's father. When he came on the line, Hank asked,

"Mr. Broadbeck?"

"Yes."

"Hello, this is Hank Daimon. I'm a lawyer in Crystal Springs. I work with Gale. My fiancé, Aster Carmichael, is her best friend."

"How are you, Hank? What can I do for you?"

"Well, sir. I have some emergent news for Dave, and I can't reach him."

"Tell me, young man," Tom Broadbeck demanded as he gripped the phone. "I'll find David."

Hank explained most details of the story to Tom, including the fact that Ken Tereus was probably Julia's father.

"We'll be there as soon as possible."

Hank promised to make arrangements for them to be picked-up from the airport and brought directly to the hospital.

"Young man," Mr. Broadbeck said, clearly shaken.

"Yes, sir," answered Hank.

"Is she going to live? She's like a daughter to me."

"I can't answer that, sir."

❦ ❦ ❦

When the police combed through Ken's house that afternoon, they discovered the small snuff bottles filled with locks of hair. Eight jars contained ebony hair. One contained blonde hair. There was a single empty bottle that was carved with an Asian panda and her cub. Roger Becker stopped at the hospital on his way back to the office to ask Dicey and Hank if they were familiar with the bottles and the contents.

"Ken went to Thailand, occasionally," said Hank. "Other than that, I don't know."

"The blonde hair is probably from Elle Pandion, our friend who allegedly committed suicide in July. She also dated Ken," Dicey said. "I've always thought that he had a hand in her death, and I told him as much last night when I confronted him at the hospital."

"What do you mean?" the detective asked. And with that question, Dicey began to unravel the evidence that she had discovered in Elle's paintings. Roger Becker was skeptical at first, but as she connected Pope Alexander VI with Pandion and Tereus with Philomela and the two physicians with Fuseli, Becker began to listen intently.

"Impressive research, Dicey. We will want take a look at your information and the paintings as part of the investigation."

Dicey smiled sadly. "Elle's story will finally be told for all to hear." She wiped a tear from her cheek. Hank put his arm around her and pulled her close.

"Roger, any other news from your end?" he asked.

"No, none, but how's she hanging in there?"

"Not well," said Dicey, running her hand through her hair.

☙☙ ☙☙ ☙☙

Talat Ashram lounged in his bed at the Oriental Bangkok Hotel watching *CNN*. He jumped from the sheets when Ken Tereus's picture flashed across the screen. There was a global search for the man who was wanted on charges of kidnapping and attempted murder. Talat gritted his teeth as he glared at Ken's picture.

"I was wrong. Never again, an American, never again! Attention mongers," he spat.

👁️ 👁️ 👁️

Four hours later, Dave and his father walked into the hospital. They were ashen. Dave's child, or who he thought was his child, was missing and his fiancé was on a ventilator.

Dicey was huddled next to Hank in the ICU waiting room when she spotted Dave and his father walk past the door. She jumped up from her seat to greet them as they headed down the hall. "Dave, Tom," she whispered forcefully. They turned and tried to smile as they saw her.

Dicey couldn't muster a smile in return. Instead, she waved them toward the waiting room. Gale's condition had deteriorated. Her oxygen saturation level had dropped dramatically, and the cardiologist and pulmonologist were working on her. The ICU nurse promised that the doctors would come out with an update whenever possible. As they waited for pieces of information, Dicey and Hank spent an hour with Dave and Tom, unraveling the tragedy that had begun with Ken Tereus's party one year earlier.

As she explained the sequence of events, Dicey noted the distinctly different reactions of Dave and his father. Dave's face grew stiff as stone as she spoke, while Tom's eyes welled up with tears.

👁️ 👁️ 👁️

The sun beamed through the sky lights at the Author's Lounge. Talat Ashram sipped tea and perused the *Bangkok Post*. An article about anti-government demonstrations in China by village farmers caught his eye. The flow of illicit antiquities from China had slowed because of the unrest, and it was hurting his business.

"Sheet," he grumbled. As he scanned through the business section, his phone vibrated.

"Hello," Talat answered quietly.

"Talat, Tereus."

"Ah, it is the infamous Ken Tereus. Hold one minute," he said. Talat stood and walked out to the veranda. He lit a cigarette and took a deep breath. "I thought that I might hear from you," he said letting the smoke plume from his lips.

"I need your help, Talat."

"Dr. Tereus, discretion is my business. You weren't discreet."

"Yeah, I know. Things got beyond my control."

"But you're a risk to me now, Dr. Tereus."

"Talat, I've made a lot of money for you over the years. You've got to help me. I'll make it worth it to you."

"I will listen."

"I need two passports to get out of Mexico, one for me and one for my daughter. Can you get them to me?" Ken asked.

"Dr. Tereus, I can't get involved now. Like I said, you have become too high profile for my taste."

"I'll pay you well, Talat. I've got an account at the Bangkok Bank. The name on the account is Arif Waseem."

"Pakistani? Who is he, is he one of our friends?"

"It's no one. It's me. I can wire you money today. I've got plenty to make you happy, very happy. You know people in Mexico, don't you?"

"Mr. Fox, himself," answered Talat.

"Good. Another question, who does favors— quietly in the States for you?"

"Ah, a good question. It depends on where you're talking."

"Chicago or Crystal Springs."

"Maybe the Giavianni family. The Giaviannis are very discreet, unlike you Dr. Tereus."

"Okay, I understand, but how much for two?"

"Four million plus my cut, maybe, I don't know. It could be more. I'd have to make a few calls."

"Four is steep." Ken said.

"What you're talking about is expensive, and I haven't agreed to anything, yet. Who, the mother and her boyfriend?"

"Yeah, Gale Knightly and David Broadbeck."

Talat took a puff on his cigarette and blew the smoke through his teeth. "I don't know about any of this. Like I said before, this is too much publicity. I don't like my clients to be in the spotlight. It's bad for business. You're on the front page of the *Bangkok Post*."

"Don't take the high road now. Some of your sins are sitting at the bottom of the Pacific Ocean, too, you know."

"Be careful, Dr. Tereus. I don't need you any longer."

"I'm sorry, Talat. I said that I would make it worth your time. I'll wire one million today to get things moving. Give me your bank account number and wire transfer number. I'll do it immediately."

The tone of Ken's voice was growing more desperate, and Talat sensed it. "Three million, today, Dr. Tereus."

"My God, Talat. Why do you want that much today?"

"Three or no passports. In eight hours."

Ken paused for a few seconds, scratching his hairless head. "Okay. I'll do it, if you can get the passports delivered to me within eight hours."

"No problema in Juarez," laughed Talat. He pulled his wallet from a thin satchel that he wore across his chest and gave Ken the tracking number on his bank account for the deposit.

Ken smiled with relief. "Have the passports delivered to the Meson de Maruca. It's at 3203 Hermanos Escabar, room seven."

"No problema, Dr. Tereus," Talat said, blowing a ringlet of smoke from his mouth.

"Thank you, Talat. I knew that I could count on you. Let me know more about the Giavianni family when you have information."

Talat clicked off the connection and smiled. He then dialed a telephone number whose owner was somewhere off the western coast of Mexico, on a luxury fishing boat.

"Pedro, Talat Ashram, here," he said into the receiver. "Yes, it has been a long time. How is your father?"

"Muy bueno," said Pedro Castellano. "My father is well."

"Pedro, tengo una problema. It is a doctor in the U.S. You heard about him, Tereus? You know, bueno. He is traveling under the name of Miguel Lopez."

"Ah, very high profile man, Talat. Not your style, not my father's," said Pedro.

"Yes, I know. He is an old client. He wants my help. Two passports. Si, I agree, it is risky."

"Where is the man?" asked Pedro.

"Ciudad Juarez. A little hotel called the Meson de Maruca."

"Si, we can find it," assured Pedro. "Your problem is my problem, Talat. We will take care of your problem. What about the kid?"

"Can you sell her on the market?" asked Talat.

"I don't know. A baby with yellow eyes is dangerous. Besides, her picture is all over the news."

"There's a million dollar reward for her. Do you want to dump her or collect the money?" Talat asked and then took a slow drag on his cigarette.

"We'll see, we'll see. I'll talk to my father."

Pedro disconnected the line and called Julio Sanchez, the Chief of Police in Juarez. It took Pedro's father a few years, but the Castellano family finally dominated the Juarez police force. A few months earlier, Juan Gomez Aruzza resigned as police chief for his own safety, after his assistant chief, Xavier Valdevisimo, was assassinated. The third officer in command was Julio Sanchez, a man owned by the Castellano family.

"Julio, Pedro Castellano."

"Pedro, how is that new wife of yours?"

"She's pregnant. My father's finally going to have a grandson."

"Congratulations, Pedro," he offered. "What can I do for you today?"

"Do you know about the American doctor who stole the baby?"

"Si, we're watching the borders for the man and the kid."

"I've got a tip for your FBI amigo, but I want the reward money for the baby first. You can take five percent."

"Si," he hesitated and then asked, "How much for my friend?"

"Give him part of your split, Julio."

"Pedro, you're a tough bargainer. Just like your father." Julio swallowed hard. There never was any bargaining with a Castellano, never.

ᴥ ᴥ ᴥ

Mary Beth Conlan was squeezing the lime into her Corona when she saw the Amber Alert roll across one of the sixteen televisions at the Blue Canyon Bar and Grill. She had arrived in Golden, Colorado an hour before and was still waiting on Joe, her climbing partner to show up. She took a gulp of beer, paying only half attention to the story until Crystal Springs, Ohio was mentioned. Then, the picture of Jake Brueggemann flashed on the screen. Even set with a thick head of hair and wearing a suit, she remembered him. The only real difference was the color of his eyes. Jake's were emerald green, "like the Emerald City," she whispered to herself. Ken Tereus' eyes, as well as the infant's, were yellow, so the reporter explained.

ᴥ ᴥ ᴥ

When the doctors walked into the waiting room, a grim draft followed them. Gale's oxygen saturation levels had improved, but her condition was still precarious. Dave asked if his father and he could see her. The doctors agreed but only allowed them a few moments.

Dave and Tom were startled by the machines that hummed to keep life pumping through Gale. Tom nudged Dave toward the bed. Steadying himself against the bed's guardrail, Dave bent down to kiss her forehead. He stood up and squeezed his eyes shut. Tom walked around to the other side of the bed. He took Gale's limp hand in his and brought it to his lips. Neither man spoke a word.

When they returned to the waiting room, Roger Becker was there, speaking with Hank and Dicey. The detective introduced himself to both men.

"I was just explaining to Hank and Dicey that we got a lead. At times like this, I have to remind my team that there are no perfect crimes because there are no perfect criminals, including this snake, Tereus."

"Detective, is it a lead that we can bet on?" asked Tom Broadbeck.

"I believe so. We got a call from the Golden, Colorado P.D. about an hour ago. A young woman went to them with a story about meeting a single dad who was traveling with an infant at the Crystal Springs Airport at around noon today. He was headed to Texas. She said his name was Jake Brueggemann. We checked it out. There was no Brueggemann listed on Delta's passenger schedule, but there was a Miguel Lopez who was connecting from Crystal Springs to Dallas to El Paso. The FBI ran a photo match on several thousand Miguel Lopez passport photos and bingo. One of them looked an awful lot like Ken Tereus. We've got people talking to the flight crew, and we've alerted Border Patrol. We've got to move fast, though. El Paso is a stone's throw from Juarez, Mexico, a cakewalk across a bridge."

"Have you contacted the Juarez police?" asked Dave.

"Yeah, but we probably won't get much out of them. Juarez is one of the most dangerous cities in the world, and much of the police force is corrupt."

"Roger, so what exactly are you doing?" asked Dicey who was gripping onto Hank for support.

"The FBI and the Border Patrol are questioning the border agents in Juarez, as we speak. They are also viewing security camera film from earlier today."

"How likely is it that Tereus crossed into Mexico?" asked Hank.

"I'd say about 99.9%. The passport activity shows six or seven trips to the city in the past few years," answered Roger.

"Don't you think that Tereus would be easy to spot, though? The guy's got yellow eyes and orange hair, and he's toting around an infant," said Dicey.

"Well, not if he shaved his head and threw in a set of green eye contacts. These guys know how to transform themselves," said Roger.

Dicey's face turned gray. "Please don't tell me that he disguised himself."

"He's a smart criminal. According to our eye-witness, 'Jake' aka Tereus had green eyes and was bald," affirmed Roger.

"Maybe it's just coincidental," said Dave.

"I don't think so. If Tereus is as dangerous as I think he is, then Juarez would be a great vacation destination for him. It is known as the city of Feminicide," Roger explained.

"Oh my God," cried Dicey.

"You've got to have faith. The Border Patrol Agents are on this. They're sick and tired of women and young girls being murdered, too. I understand that, if you want to get lost in a crowd, it's hasta luego in Mexico. But, we'll find him."

"Honestly, what's in your gut, Roger? Do you think that you'll find him?" asked Hank.

"Honestly, if we don't locate him in twenty-four hours, it will be tough. A lot bigger fish have been lost down there."

ଚଚ   ଚଚ   ଚଚ

Twelve hours later, Julia slept soundly in the center of the double bed in the Meson de Maruca Hotel. Ken Tereus was settled next to her, watching re-runs of *Miami Vice* dubbed in Spanish. He shoved corn chips in his mouth and watched Don Johnson track down drug runners. Somehow this Don, with a falsetto Spanish accent, seemed less cool. He switched the station to *CNN* and watched Wolf Blitzer in the *Situation Room*. He, himself, was no longer news. A bomb had exploded in the Green Zone, the only allegedly safe area in Baghdad, killing several Americans. Wolf Blitzer was explaining to the world that there were pieces of fifty-eight American diplomats and soldiers strewn across a cafeteria located in the compound. Ken was mesmerized as the camera focused in on a tattered military boot, standing in a pool of blood.

He was pulled from his trance by two sharp knocks that sounded from the door. Still sedated from the Valium, Julia didn't rouse from the noise. Ken quietly stood up from the bed.

"Un momento." He stepped into the pants and zipped up the fly. His pubic hair got caught in the zipper, and he winced.

Ken walked to the door and asked who was there.

"Open-up, we are friends of Talat," the voice reassured him in English. When Ken unbolted and cracked open the door, three Mexicans pushed their way into the room. The two bulky ones grabbed each of his arms. The thin elegant man pressed a revolver to his temple.

Ken was always intrigued by the fine line between life and death, but on this day, he was startled by the expediency with which he found his own life teetering on that thin line.

"You won't kill me," Ken said very calmly, trying to repress the fear that was rising in his throat.

"Why not?" asked the leader.

"Tengo mucho dinero. I will make it worth your time not to kill me."

"How much?"

"Four million American dollars, more than Talat can pay you," Ken answered.

Marco Castellano, Pedro's brother, slowly lowered the pistol from his temple. "Please talk, Dr. Tereus. You know what the Yankees say, 'When money talks, people listen.'"

"How much did Talat promise for my head?" Ken asked.

"I don't know. That's not my job," Marco said, pressing the tip of the pistol against Ken's cheek.

"Tell your boss . . . I paid Talat three million dollars today," Ken said, glancing down at the gun. "Who's hosing who? Ask your boss that!"

With his left hand, Marco punched Ken in the stomach. "My boss is my father. Remember that!" Marco screamed in his face.

Startled by the shouting, Julia let out wail. The three Mexicans turned to see her squirming on her belly, with her arms and legs flailing against the sheet.

"What are you going to do with the kid?" Marco asked, staring at Julia.

"I don't know. It was a mistake. Just get me a passport, and I'll get you four million."

Marco held his gaze on Julia. "Is it true that she has yellow eyes?"

"Golden," Ken said but then added, ". . . you can have her, along with the money. I just want a clean passport."

Marco pulled the pistol from Ken's cheek and walked to the bed. He rolled Julia onto her back and stared into her eyes.

"Golden," he whispered. He shook his and spat under his breath, "Dirty omen."

Turning back toward Ken, he said, "I'll talk to my father about the passport. Do not try to leave your hotel, until you are contacted by me, personally."

Marco walked back to Ken who was still held by the massive men. He punched Ken in the gut one last time. "Don't leave— you or the baby."

On Saturday morning at eight o'clock, FBI agents and the Juarez police converged on Meson de Maruca, room seven. Wearing a black bulletproof vest, Mike Rosilla knocked on Tereus's hotel room door. "Room Service," he yelled. His backup stood in silence behind him. He knocked twice more and then stepped aside so the owner could unlock the room. With his semi-automatic Glock in position, Mike entered the small room and slowly slid against the wall. He heard rustling beyond the partition that separated the toilet from the bed area. Scooting closer to the sound, he drew his gun to eye level. With his left arm, he motioned for two more officers to enter the cramped space. Slowly, Mike stuck his head around the partition and spotted the noise.

Like a field mouse, Julia's tiny fingernails were clawing at the sheet of the bed. Tereus was gone.

♋ ♋ ♋

Dave stared at Julia through a thick glass window of the pediatric intensive care unit. Tom put his arm around his son and pulled him close.

"Dave, she's a beautiful little girl, isn't she?"

Dave tugged away from his father and said, "Yeah, a million dollar baby."

"What in the hell do you mean by that!" Tom demanded.

"Dad, if she's not mine, she's not mine. She's Tereus's child." Dave's words were draped with pain.

Tom Broadbeck was disturbed by his son's response. "The hell she is."

"She isn't mine," Dave whispered. "I know that this is the wrong time to question it, but maybe Gale really knew that Julia wasn't mine. What woman wouldn't know?"

For the first time in his life, Tom Broadbeck was truly angry and disappointed with his son. "What in the hell are you talking about? That woman is stuck on a ventilator one floor above us right now because that fucker tried to annihilate her, and you are questioning her integrity."

The nurse in the ICU glanced up to warn them about their rising voices.

"Dad, please calm down. I'm just asking a few questions. My head is spinning. I would be nuts if I didn't wonder about a few things."

"She was raped you idiot. She never lied to you. She's a proud woman. I watched you jack her around for eight years. What did you want her to do, grovel? Who wants a husband who is going to jack you around? I thought that you'd finally grown up, finally learned how to think beyond the moment and beyond yourself. I guess I was wrong."

"Goddamn it, Dad! Calm down. Why don't you consider what I am going through?"

"What in the hell are you going through? You're not the one whose lungs don't work. Don't give me that bullshit!"

A baby started to cry. The ICU nurse jumped up from her desk. "I'm sorry, but you both have to leave! You can't behave like this in here. These are severely ill children!"

Tom Broadbeck apologized to the nurse. Dave and he were silent until they got onto the elevator. "Dad, listen to me. It's not what you're thinking. I'm scared as hell that Gale's going to die! I don't want anyone to die! I didn't want mom to die!"

"Dave, you can't use your mother's death as an excuse for your behavior anymore. I've given you a pass on a lot of things for twenty years because she died. Nobody wanted her to die, me most of all. You've got to grow up. What are you going to do for the rest of your life, never take a chance on loving someone, because they might die? Your mother would never have wanted that kind of legacy. You don't make a damn bit of sense. Is this all about your mom's death or about that Tereus maniac? Who are you going to blame when you abandon Gale?" The elevator doors reopened, and Tom Broadbeck walked his son out into the hospital parking lot.

"I'm not blaming anyone. I love Gale, but she just wasn't honest with me. I'm not that child's father. How do you want me to react?"

"I know one thing, young man. Gale has been honest with you for eight years, and she's loved you for as long as that. I love her like my own daughter. You've played games with her for a long time. Stop with the games. Either you walk back into the hospital willing to love the same woman you loved yesterday or head on back to Chicago. Other than that, I don't want to hear anymore of your excuses."

"She lied to me! Can't you get that through your head?"

"I don't know all of the circumstances to this mess just yet, but I'll tell you this much, that woman did not lie to you." With that, Tom Broadbeck turned around and walked back into the hospital.

 ☙☙ ☙☙ ☙☙

Hank took Tom back to his house to rest for the night. Dave and Dicey remained in the ICU waiting room. "She's got to make it," Dicey said half to herself and half to Dave. He didn't respond. He just stared at the television mounted to the wall. The sound was turned off, but he continued to stare at the rerun of *Hill Street Blues*. Dicey finally asked,

"Dave, how are you doing?" He ignored her, and she sharply said, "Dave, I asked, how are you doing?"

He slowly turned to her and said, "I'm a little rattled. It's a lot to take in."

Dicey paused and gave him a long look. "What do you mean that it's a lot to take in?"

"The whole story is a lot to absorb," he said, glancing down at his legs that were stretched out in front of him.

"Excuse me. What do you mean by a *story*?" Dicey asked with a tangle of exhaustion and irritation.

"This whole situation is the story. It's a lot to absorb."

"I'm sorry, but I sense something strange in your tone. Why are you calling this a story?"

"I don't know."

"Listen, Gale's had a lot to absorb for an entire year– and now this. And, it's not a story. It's a damn tragedy!" Dicey snapped.

"It is a tragedy that is a little tough to handle."

She burned a glare through his eyes. "Which part is hard for you to handle, that she has had a year from hell or that a psycho just tried to kill Julia and her?" Dicey asked.

"Dicey, please don't be so defensive. I'm just trying to think through everything."

Dicey moved to the edge of her seat. "Don't tell me not to be defensive. Gee, maybe I can help you 'think through everything.' Let's go over the year Gale has just experienced."

"Listen, I didn't mean to offend you. I'm just trying to work through this. I'm not trying to upset anyone," he said, turning back to *Hill Street Blues*.

Dicey moved a seat closer to him. "Is a show without sound really that interesting?" she asked.

"Sometimes you can find answers in silence."

"I agree with you, Dave. Look at Elle Pandion. She screamed without a sound."

Dave turned back to her. "I'm not here to argue with you. We're both under a lot of stress, and I'm just trying to get my mind straight."

"Well, maybe I can help you to understand what Gale's gone through in the past year," she sneered.

"Maybe, you know her better than I," Dave said, toying with anger.

"Okay, let me explain." Dicey unzipped her hoody sweatshirt, pulled it off and balled it up on her lap. Now, she was ready.

"It was a very long year, Dave. Gale finds out that she's pregnant. She calls you to tell you but finds out that you're in Europe. Then, she calls again and finds out that you're in a serious relationship. Bam! Just like that, you replaced her!"

Dave's olive skin turned a deep burgundy. "Wait a minute! I asked Gale to marry me. She declined. I tried to move on with my life. Why should I be blamed for that?"

"Nobody's blaming you for that. I'm blaming you for being such a jerk right now."

"Hold on there!" he said with gritted teeth.

"No, you hold on. Gale was tormented with guilt, pressured at work, and rejected by her mother, among other things. Nonetheless, she summoned the courage to call you and tell you about the pregnancy. You know what you did? You told her that she was a lying sack of shit. How's that for a nice guy?"

"Any man would have reacted the same way," he said with a steely glare.

Dicey stared right back into his hard eyes. "Not with a woman like Gale."

Dicey threw the sweatshirt on the ground and stood up. "That woman got on her hands and knees and groveled back to you, even after you called her a liar. Then, you finally did something right and asked her to marry you. Then, this monster raises his ugly head. In twenty-four hours, she finds out that she was drugged, date-raped and that Julia's father is not the man she thinks he is. Dave, that's one hell of a year, if you ask me."

"Can't you understand that I might be just a little confused?"

"Confused I understand, but being a self-centered prick is another thing. While you were out licking your wounds with other women, she suffered. She struggled like hell, trying to figure out what to do about telling you. A week never passed without pressure from me to call you. Finally, she met with her priest for direction. Doesn't sound like somebody caught in a quagmire of lies."

"But still, she could have found a way to tell me that she was pregnant. We've been together for eight years."

"That's the point, Dave. She did try to tell you. But she's proud and stubborn. The last thing she wanted to do was to force you into marrying her. Now, I'm the one who is feeling guilty for pressuring her to call you. If Gale hadn't called you, she would be dealing with only one asshole right now." Dicey said.

Dave sat up straight. "You're walking a fine line, Dicey."

Dicey smirked. "You don't get it, do you? Gale loves you. She's always loved you, but she wasn't going to set you up in a marriage that you didn't want. After a year of hell, why would she tell you that Julia was your baby, if she really thought it was someone else's. She wasn't asking you to marry her or asking you to take care of Julia. She finally told you out of duty. She told you because, at the bottom of her heart, that is what she believed to be true."

"Can you please slow down and give me a chance," Dave asked quietly. "To be honest, I'm confused about only one thing. Can I just ask you one question without you biting my ass off?"

"I don't know. It depends on the question. Try me," snipped Dicey.

Dave paused for a minute but finally asked, "How would a woman not know that she was raped? That's the only thing that confuses me."

"Are you serious?" She choked.

"Yes, serious as hell. It's tough for a man to comprehend that a woman wouldn't know that she was raped."

"Have you ever heard of date-rape drugs?"

"Yes."

"Do you know what they do?"

"I thought so, but maybe not." He leaned forward sincerely ready to hear what she had to say.

Dicey picked up her sweatshirt and sat back down. "Do a little research, Dave. The drugs can wipe out a woman's memory, and who in the hell knows what Ken Tereus put into Gale's body. He's a surgeon, for God's sake. He has access to anything. Gale had no clue. Trust me. She truly believed, up until yesterday, that you were the only man with whom she had sex. You are the only man whom she has ever loved. We've been best friends since the fifth grade. There aren't any secrets between us. I know what she thinks and feels."

Dave's chest deflated a little. "I'm sorry, Dicey. I'm sorry for questioning. This is tough. She's the only woman whom I have ever loved. And then, bang! All this is thrown in my face."

Dicey didn't know Dave well enough to trust him, and her patience was waning. She took a deep breath, trying to muster some understanding.

"I know this is difficult. I've been dealing with questions for the past six months. No one, including Gale, has believed what I've been trying to tell them about Elle, her father and Ken Tereus, for that matter." Dicey got up from her seat, sat next to Dave, and put her hand on his.

He looked at Dicey with softer eyes. "I know that I sound like a real shit, but I do love her, and you know the worst thing of all? It took me eight years to tell her," he conceded.

"I know that too . . . Think about what I told you. I'm going to go check on Julia, now. You need to think about her, as well."

෨ ෨ ෨

At five o'clock, Dicey was awakened by the cries of a baby. She jumped up from the recliner and looked through the glass partition of the ICU. Julia was flailing her arms and screaming.

A nurse walked up behind Dicey and said, "Hearty little thing, isn't she?"

"What's wrong with her?" Dicey asked in a panic.

"Nothing, come with me," she said, opening the door to enter the room. "It's probably a dirty diaper, or maybe she's hungry," the nurse suggested.

She bent over the bassinet. "Her vitals have been perfect through the night. Haven't they cutie-pie!" She picked-up Julia. "Yep, it's stinky pants. Do you want to change her while I get an order for formula?" the nurse asked, or rather told Dicey as she left the room.

Dicey cleaned Julia's bottom as she squealed and squirmed. "You can be as ornery as your mother, can't you?" Dicey caressed Julia's forehead and eyelids to soothe her, but nothing would stop the gnawing cry of hunger. She whispered into Julia's ear. The baby did calm down to listen, but within seconds, she cracked back into a hungry tirade. Dicey pressed the call button, and the nurse eventually came in with a warm bottle of formula.

"Whew, that's a relief. I'm not used to this. Do the babies ever start crying all at once around here?" Dicey asked the nurse.

"Sure, that's about the time when the residents skip out on you, then, or when a baby's got dirty pants."

The nurse returned to her station, and Dicey sat down in the rocker to feed Julia the bottle. Her tiny lips clung to the nipple, and she began to suck. She tasted the unfamiliar formula, pushed the nipple out of her mouth and began to wail all over again.

"Come on Julia, mommy can't nurse right now. You have to cooperate. Please, for me." Dicey tried to push the nipple back into her mouth, but Julia's tongue pushed it right back out. After ten minutes of a tug-a-war crying match, Dicey headed for the nurses' station.

"She's used to her mother's milk. Is there anything else we can give her," Dicey asked the nurse.

"When she gets hungry enough, she'll drink. Be patient. She's okay," the nurse offered.

Dicey went back into Julia's room. Screw patience! This little girl has been through hell and back, and she wants her mother's milk. She looked at her watch. It was five forty-five. She grabbed the house phone and dialed Hank's number. After two rings, he answered.

"Hank, honey,"

"Everything alright, Dice?" he asked in a sleepy haze.

"No. Julia's hungry, and she won't take the formula that they are trying to force feed."

Julia's crying made it hard to hear.

"What can I do about that, honey?"

"I need you to go over to Gale's. Get the breast milk out of the freezer. Gale always keeps a supply for the daycare."

"It's six o'clock in the morning, and her house is a crime scene. The police aren't going to let me in."

"Hank, please, for breast milk, they'll let you in. You're not asking for DNA, for God's sake."

An hour later, Hank walked into the hospital room with three bags of breast milk and Tom Broadbeck.

"It's about time," Dicey grumped. "She fell back to sleep from crying so much."

Tom Broadbeck walked over to the basinet to see Julia up close for the first time. He squatted down to look at her face. His breathing grew heavy.

"She looks a lot like Gale. She's got her mother's nose. She's got her mother's determination, too."

Tom Broadbeck patted her belly trying to resist the temptation to wake her, but it was too late. Julia let out a hungry yell.

"Since I woke her," he said happily, "I guess it's my job to feed her, isn't it?"

The breast milk was stored in a zip-lock bag. Dicey thawed it at the sink, poured the contents into a sterilized bottle and handed it to Mr. Broadbeck. He nestled Julia close to his chest and sat down in the rocker. Her lips latched onto the nipple and sucked down a third of the milk within a minute.

"Slow down there, cowgirl, it's time for you to burp like a real rancher," Tom laughed and propped Julia over his shoulder. She squirmed under his unfamiliar form but finally relented with a light release of air. "Good girl, now you can chug it."

Dicey scooted a stiff hospital chair closer to the rocker. She watched as Tom stared into Julia's amber eyes. His forehead scrunched into a pensive arch. Dicey couldn't ignore the gesture. "She's not like Gale in every way, Tom."

"No, you're right. She's got eyes the color of April honey. We can't deny that," he said.

"How is Dave doing," Hank asked.

Dicey took a deep breath and sighed. "We talked most of the night. I think that I helped him understand what Gale's been through for the past year."

"He's got to grow up. I thought he had," said Tom. "He's a good son. Reckless, though, since he was eleven. He's never dealt with his mother's death. It was a freak accident. She had horrible peanut allergies. Some kid at Dave's school gave out cookies for his birthday. Dave threw the cookie in his lunch bag. When Sandy was cleaning out the bag at home, she ingested peanut residue that came from cookie crumbs. Must've gotten on her hands, and she touched her mouth. Dave was outside playing with his buddies. When he went inside, he found his mother on the kitchen floor, barely breathing. The paramedics couldn't save her. He's felt guilty ever since. I don't know if he was punishing himself or just trying to escape from life all these years.

"I knew he'd never commit to a woman until he dealt with Sandy's death. Dave has loved Gale for a long time but wouldn't admit it. Afraid he'd lose her. I'm surprised that she hung on so long, but I could tell how much she loved him. It hurt to the core to see her hurt so much."

"I never knew the details about your wife's death. What a tragedy," said Dicey.

"It's been hard for a long time. I couldn't have been happier when this little angel came along, though. Forced Dave to take a good, long look at his reflection and make some tough decisions. Now, we'll just have to see if he can step up to the plate. Even for the strongest of men, this is a real test."

"Do you think he's strong enough to hang tough with Gale," asked Hank.

"That's a damn good question. I wish that I could give you a straight answer. If you were to ask the same question three days ago, I'd say yes. He's the one who has to look into these honey eyes and accept her, though, not you or me."

After Julia finished her bottle and fell back to sleep, Hank, Dicey and Tom returned to the ICU to check on Gale's progress. Dave was sitting in the waiting room when they walked in.

He stood up and smiled. "The docs just finished their rounds and are pleased with her progress. They're starting to reduce her sedative. They want to try to wean her off the ventilator today. They explained that if she's on it beyond three days her lungs will become too dependent on it," he said, stuffing his hands in his pockets.

"That's good news," said Tom. "When can we see her?"

"The nurse will come out and tell us when she's ready. It shouldn't be long. We have to take turns visiting her, though. The doctor said that patients can get agitated when they come off the drugs. They want to keep Gale as calm as possible."

Dave threw himself into a seat.

Tom saw that his son's hands were shaking. "Are you alright?" he asked.

Dave looked up at his dad. "I've been such a goddamn block-head, Dad. How could I question her?"

"What's important is that you finally recognized it. We don't need to rehash it now. Let's just focus our energies on Gale and Julia."

Tom sat down next to Dave and broke out into a smile. "Julia's a little piece of sunshine, Son. I just fed her a bottle, and she took the whole thing from me."

"That's wonderful. Is she doing okay?" Dave asked quietly.

"She's doing great. You know what else happened in that room?"

"What?" Dave asked guardedly.

"I heard her whisper 'Grandpa'!"

Hank and Dicey burst out laughing.

"Now, you've really lost it," Dave said, laughing for the first time in almost three days.

As the room rustled with a bit of mirth, the ICU nurse attending to Gale walked in. She gave the group a sour look. Dicey jumped up from her seat and tried to wipe away her smile.

"How is she?" Dicey asked.

"I believe she could handle her first visitor," she said with a frown. "But the room must remain calm."

Dicey turned to Dave. "Why don't you go in first," she offered.

Dave sat down next to the bed. Once again, he was taken aback by the narrow tube that was stuck down Gale's throat to keep her alive. As she slept, he listened to the steady sound of the ventilator. The unit reminded him of the bicycle pump he had as a kid. When his mom taught him how to ride a bike, she also taught him how to pump up the black rubber tires on his silver Schwinn. He remembered holding the pump between his legs and pushing down on the t-bar with all his might. As a seven year old, he felt so powerful, pumping air into the tires and watching them grow. He longed to pump the same life back into his mother and now Gale.

Dave took Gale's hand in his and squeezed her fingers. He was surprised when he felt a slight pressure in return. She opened her eyes. He saw panic in her face. She tried thrashing her arms but was prevented by the straps that tied her to the bed. Her heart rate jumped. The alarms on the monitors screamed in distress. The nurse came in. Gale must remain calm. Dave would have to keep her quiet or he would have to leave. He bent down close to her ear and whispered,

"Honey, please calm down! I'm here. I love you. It's okay," but she kept yanking on the straps and trying to talk. "I can't understand you. Everything will be okay."

The nurse returned and asked him to leave.

"I can't. I've got to talk to her."

Gale continued to grunt the same sound over and over, but Dave couldn't make it out.

"What's she trying to say?" he pleaded with the nurse.

The nurse walked over and caressed her head. She bent down and whispered, "She's fine. Julia is fine." Tears came to Gale's eyes.

"Oh God, of course! Why didn't I know what she was saying?" Dave gripped her hand again. "Babe, she's great. She's great. She's safe. She's on the floor right below us. It's okay. Honey, you've got to get off this thing so we can be together," Dave said desperately. She squeezed his hand and closed her eyes.

"Why don't we let her rest for a few minutes? She needs to wake from the sedatives slowly. She'll respond better, if she's not upset," the nurse told Dave. Reluctantly, he returned to the ICU waiting room.

When Dave saw his father, he broke down. "I just want everything to be okay, Dad. I love her. I'm such a damn idiot!"

Dicey walked over to Dave. She put her arms around him. "She's going to be okay. She's not going to give up now." He squeezed her tightly. His body shook with sobs. "Gale's a strong woman. She loves Julia and you too much to die. I know this much, at least," Dicey said. She gripped her lucky cubes in her palm. "I think it's our lucky day."

Later that evening, the doctors and respiratory therapist removed Gale from the ventilator, and she lived. It was that simple; she began breathing on her own.

😮 😮 😮

On Monday morning, Gale opened her eyes. She focused on Dicey who was sitting by her side. "How's Julia," she whispered.

"Just like her mom, a little trooper," Dicey said, grinning with relief.

"What did he do to her? Be honest with me."

"He may have drugged her a bit. He wasn't trying to kill her. He probably just wanted her to sleep."

"Why sleep?"

Dicey picked up Gale's hand and squeezed it. "We don't need to get into all of the details right now. You need to rest."

"Tell me," Gale said, with stiff lips.

"I'm not going into it."

Gale pulled her hand away from Dicey. She turned to Hank who was sound asleep in the recliner. "Hank! Wake up! Wake up!" she shouted as loud as her tired vocal cords permitted.

Hank's head popped up. "What! What's wrong?" he asked, scanning the room.

"What did he do to her?" Gale demanded.

"Calm down," Dicey said, pulling Gale's hand back into her grip.

Hank stood up and came around the other side of the bed.

"Dicey was right about him, Gale. He's a bad guy. The fact is he took Julia on a quick trip to Mexico."

Gale turned chalk white. "Where?"

"To Mexico. That's where he is right now, or that's what the police think."

"My God!" she cried. Gale tried to pull herself up from the bed. Hank grabbed her left arm, while Dicey held tightly to her right. "I've got to be with her. Let me go!"

"Stop," Hank said firmly. "You're not going anywhere. She's fine and she's safe. Dave and Tom Broadbeck are with her along with a guard. Now take a deep breath and calm yourself, or the nurses will sedate you."

Gale glared into his stern eyes. She turned to Dicey for help but was given an equally indignant look. A single tear drifted down her cheek and fell onto her pillow. She closed her eyes, and her arms relaxed.

"How did he get out of the country?" she asked, opening her eyes.

"A fake passport. He took a plane to El Paso with Julia and crossed into Ciudad Juarez. That's where Julia was discovered."

"Are they going to find him?" asked Gale.

"That's the plan. *CNN* and every other news network plastered his face across the globe. He'll be found. And the hospital is teeming with security. You're safe. Julia's safe."

Gale started to cry.

Hank patted her arm. "Gale, if you want to get out of here and be with Julia, you're going to have to keep it together, as hard as it is. Julia and you couldn't be safer than you are right now."

She tried to smile but couldn't. "How's Dave?" she asked hesitantly.

"He's hanging in there," Dicey said. She took a wet washcloth and wiped the tears from Gale's face. "His dad and he are feeding Julia right now. Tom gets a kick out of feeding his 'granddaughter'. It's precious."

"When you're feeling better, the police need to talk with you," Hank said. "Believe me, Julia's doing fine. She was in intensive care just for precautions. She was a little dehydrated but has no lasting effects. She could probably go home, but we've decided to keep her in the hospital for security reasons. After the ICU releases you, you'll be moved to the OB/GYN floor, so you can be with Julia."

As Dicey and Hank were explaining more details to Gale, Dave and his father came into the room. Tom Broadbeck rushed to Gale and lifted her with a thick hug. He kept his head tucked down, holding back tears. Dave went around to the opposite side of the bed, picked up her hand and kissed it. "Morning," he whispered.

"Morning to you," she whispered back.

Relieved that Gale had company, Dicey and Hank prepared to leave for much needed rest. "We'll be back before dinner," Dicey said, gathering her purse but then stopped in her tracks. "Oh, I forgot to tell you. Your parents and Amy are in still in Greece. I've talked to them way too many times, and being the nice friend that I am, I will continue to keep your mother up-to-date. But I must tell you— that woman still drives me crazy."

Gale finally laughed. "It's better that you talk to her than me!"

"She's rolling in the drama. Her voice goes up fourteen octaves every time I call. She's impossible!" Dicey said, shaking her head. She grabbed Hank's arm, and they headed out the door. Following them close behind was Tom who wanted to return to the nursery, but before he left, Gale asked what he thought of Julia.

Tom came close to the bed. "Now, I don't want you to be upset or jealous, but I think that she's fallen in love with her old grandpa. She won't take that bottle from anybody but me. She likes how I burp her." Gale laughed with doubt in her eyes.

"No, I'm serious. I prop her up in a special way on my shoulder, and bang, she burps like a frog."

After his dad left the room, Dave closed the hospital room door. He came around the bed, bent down and kissed Gale on the lips. "I love you," he said quietly.

She looked deep into his eyes. "I've always loved you."

Then, Dave turned all business. He grabbed a chair and pulled it close to the bed. He sat down and looked Gale straight in the face. "We've got a lot to talk about, honey." Gale was taken aback by the quick change in his demeanor. She peered at him with knitted brows.

"Dad and I talked about it," he said and paused for a second. "We would like Julia and you to move to Chicago, right now, rather than waiting until our wedding. It will be safer. We can get married right away, if you prefer. This week. Forget a big wedding, Gale. You need me. We'll work through all of this."

"Dave, slow down," Gale insisted. "I don't know about our plans now."

"What do you mean?"

"I mean getting married."

"What in the hell are you talking about?" Dave said with his neck turning beet red.

"Dave, she's not yours."

"I understand all that."

"But can you love her? Can you accept her? This is all coming too fast for me. I can't think straight."

"Gale, I've thought about nothing else for the past three days. I almost lost you, and I was afraid we were about to lose Julia. We can make it work."

She looked at him with a faint smile on her face. Dave touched her cheek with his fingers. "I promise you, things will be okay. I'm different."

"Are you sure about this?" she asked in a soft plea.

"Surer than I am about the sun rising tomorrow."

She smiled and closed hers eyes. Eventually, Gale dozed off. When she woke up, Tom Broadbeck was staring in her face.

"It's about time you woke up. Are you getting lazy on me?"

"No, sir," Gale whispered.

"I was just down in the nursery, taking care of little Juls. I hate to tell you this, Gale, but I think she might be prettier than her mother."

Gale laughed and said, "Dave tells me that you want a few visitors for a couple of weeks."

"No, not a couple of weeks, we want you forever. Somebody has to keep you out of trouble."

Dave walked over to the bed and stood next to his father.

"Dad and I spoke to the police. Until Tereus is apprehended, they agree that the move is best for Julia and you."

CHAPTER 36

In joy and sorrow they share each other's tears.

— Anonymous

New Year's Eve

Music hummed through the Peninsula Suite as the guests sipped their champagne. The glistening city lights of Chicago blended in with the white roses and evergreen that filled the room. The police security stationed at the Peninsula Hotel entrance and the suite's entrance didn't dampen the mood as each personalized wedding invitation and picture identifications were scrutinized.

Dave strode through the crowd with Julia, introducing her to small groups of guests.

"Dad's fallen in love. She's his little cowgirl. And he's already taught her to burp like a rancher," Dave laughed.

As Dicey helped Gale step into her wedding gown, she began to ramble through a list of babysitting directions for Julia.

"Gale, this is the fourth time you've gone through this. I think that the inch-thick folder on her care and safety will suffice. Remember, I'm her godmother and Hank has raised three children. We'll be fine."

"I know. But promise me that you won't take her out of the building."

"I have promised that, maybe eight times, now. Would you like my response notarized? Do you think that I'm going to risk a single hair on her head?"

"No. I'm sorry. I'm just a wreck. I was emptying a couple of moving boxes this week. I pulled out one of Elle's paintings. I must have forgotten to ask the movers to put it in storage. My anxiety has been bubbling over ever since." She hesitated but then continued, "Dice, I've got to get rid of all her pictures, but I feel so guilty. She was trying to save me, for God's sake, but I just can't stand to have them around any longer."

"Don't feel guilty, Gale. Her story was told, finally. That's all she ever really wanted, for someone to listen to her story. It's been told. For now, let's forget about it and have some fun. You're getting married in ten minutes."

Pachelbel's Cannon in D began to play prompting the start of the ceremony. Dicey led the way into the room filled with wedding guests. Dave was standing in front of the fireplace with Hank. Tom Broadbeck was holding Julia who had fallen asleep in his arms. Dicey took her place next to Hank, and Dave reached for Gale's arm. He pulled the veil away from her face and gently wiped a tear from her eye. He bent down and whispered, "I love you."

☯ ☯ ☯

Hank was changing Julia's diaper when his cell phone rang. "Dice, can you get that? My hands are full," he yelled into the kitchen.

"I'm sure it's Dave or Gale. And I'll tell them that Julia is still fine since their last call three hours ago," Dicey yelled back to Hank.

She put down the chopping knife and answered his phone. The caller was Roger Becker. Dicey grew cold.

"Roger, don't tell me anything that I don't want to hear."

Hank walked into the kitchen and saw Dicey's ashen face. He handed Julia to Dicey and took the phone.

"Roger, Hank. What's happened?"

"Hank, the FBI got a call from Puerto Vallarta authorities this morning. Apparently, it's fishing season in Mexico. An open sea fisherman caught a large cooler yesterday. There was a body in it along with Miguel Lopez's passport. They think that it's Tereus's body, but dental records will be required to confirm a positive identification."

Hank leaned against the counter. He ran his hands through his hair. "Thank God. I thought you were calling for an entirely different reason, Roger. Dave and Gale are on their honeymoon. On the Lake, but still, they're not in the building."

"Hank, somehow the guy was pretty connected. He pissed-off the wrong people down in Mexico, though. FBI says the drowning looks like the work of the Castellano family. They run Mexico. No one messes with them, including Vincente Fox or the new guy, Calderon. Gale's damn lucky. Listen, I got to answer another call, I'll talk to you in a couple of hours with some more information. Call Dave and Gale before the press finds them. I think that we can let them finish their honeymoon," Roger said and hung up.

Hank looked up with a slow grin. "Well, it looks like your golden-eyed Prometheus has been located, Dicey."

"Where, Hank?" she asked, still shaking.

"No need to chain him to the side of a mountain. He was locked in a cooler at the bottom of the sea." Hank wrapped his arms around the front of Dicey and rubbed her swollen belly.

"The nightmare is finally over, isn't it?" she asked.

"Let's hope so."

ACKNOWLEDGMENT

I would like to acknowledge my husband, Michael, for his enduring strength and support in this labor of love. I thank John Dreyer for his editorial direction and belief in the manuscript. Thanks to my mother, Norma Huber, and sisters, Vicki, Terri and Kelli, for they serve as sources of inspiration. I would like to thank my Aunt Sandra who taught me to love reading. I would also like to thank my friends, including Diane Grever who read the manuscript twice, just because she loved it! Last but most compelling, I would like to thank my daughters, Grace and Margo, my greatest cheerleaders of all. Also, I hope that a few of the true Romantics, Mary Shelley, Jane Austen and William Blake, find their spirits echoing through the pages of this book.

Reading Group Questions and Topics of Discussion

1. How does the role of silence drive the plot in the story? Is Elle Pandion's reaction and response to her world plausible? What words, if any, does Elle actually speak through dialogue? Does Elle ultimately discover her voice?

2. What were the forces that sought to silence Dicey throughout her life? How was she able to circumvent the power of these forces and prevail?

3. Gale seemed to be empowered with a voice at birth. What societal standards make this true? Were there any forces, internal or external, in her life that sought to quell her? Was she able to overcome their influences?

4. *The Marriage of Silence and Sin* explores the theme of parenting in each of the central characters' lives. How are the early influences of maternal and paternal parenting manifested in their adult lives? Ironically, whose parents provide the most

successful nurturing? Does the maternal or paternal force appear to be stronger than the other?

5. Ken Tereus collects rare antiquities primarily from Asia. His attitude and philosophy toward women are revealed through his art collections. What is his purpose in connecting women and art?

6. Considering that both Ken Tereus and Elle Pandion employ art as a tool, compare and contrast their use of art in achieving their different objectives. Who is most effective in achieving their ultimate goal?

7. In Mary Shelley's *Frankenstein, Or the Modern Prometheus*, the Monster, at first, appears to be the most deviant and destructive character in the book. However, once his creator's (Victor Frankenstein) rejection and abuse are unfolded, one may argue that Victor is the more deviant as his behavior is the origin of the Monster's sin. Discuss how Mary Shelley's themes of rejection and sin are alluded to in *The Marriage of Silence and Sin.* Who may be defined as the most tragic character in the book? Who is the most deviant? Identify the origins and motivations of their behavior that shape their human condition.

8. Beyond the shroud of silence and sin, this story explores struggles between the male and female psyche. In *Pride and Prejudice*, Miss Elizabeth Bennett struggles with her pride in relationships. Who best exemplifies this character? Is the person able to overcome his/her hubris? The story is laced with allusions to Jane Austen's other works. To her aficionados, can you identify other influences included in the pages?

9.   During a class lecture, Dicey discusses John Keats' "Ode to a Grecian Urn." How does the theme of this poem reverberate throughout the story? How is this theme echoed in the book cover artwork by William Blake entitled *The Visions of Daughters of Albion*?

10.   "Love at all costs" is a phrase associated with victims of abuse. Many people, especially women and children, cling to silence in the face of sin to keep the only love they know to be true. Is Elle's behavior consistent with this type of reality? Are there other characters that marry silence with sin? Why are some characters able to break free from these shackles? After reading the story, do you think that the silence can be as brutal as the sin, itself?

11.   The cover artwork for *The Marriage of Silence and Sin* is a William Blake plate entitled *Visions of the Daughters of Albion*. The image is also the cover plate for his poem bearing the same name which is an attack on the sexual repression and slavery of his time. The plate captures Oothoon who has picked the "flower" of sexuality with her lover, Theotormon, but she is soon raped by Bromion. Theotormon offers only silence and baseless philosophizing as comfort for Oothoon. After the violation, Oothoon challenges conventional morality by defending her inner purity. In an elegy, she calls on the "Daughters of Albion" to defend the many forms of self expression that are but should not be confined by social forces and norms (*William Blake Archive, blakearchive.org*). Do Blake's themes of sexual repression and slavery ring true today, almost two hundred years later? Compare and contrast the themes of sexual repression, enslavement, expression and silence as revealed in Blake's plate with the themes explored in *The Marriage of Silence and Sin*.

12. Mythological references are intertwined throughout the story. Identify some of the connections as with Thrace, Aster, Pandion, Dicey, Tereus and others that may have been discovered.

You are invited to contact Jacqueline M. Lyon at jacquelinemlyon@gmail.com for further discussion.

7156239R1

Made in the USA
Charleston, SC
28 January 2011